FALLING FOR YOU

After tossing and turning, Sabin switched on the hall light and cracked the bedroom door so that just a minimal amount of light entered. Then she sat on the floor with a comb and brush and proceeded to section off her hair.

The mindless activity allowed her to do the one thing she'd been avoiding, consider how she felt about Montgomery. After an hour, the same truth surfaced again and again.

She loved him.

BOOK YOUR PLACE ON OUR WEBSITE AND MAKE THE ARABESQUE ROMANCE CONNECTION!

We've created a customized website just for our very special Arabesque readers, where you can get the inside scoop on everything that's going on with Arabesque romance novels.

When you come online, you'll have the exciting opportunity to:

- View covers of upcoming books

- Learn about our future publishing schedule (listed by publication month and author)

- Find out when your favorite authors will be visiting a city near you

- Search for and order backlist books

- Check out author bios and background information

- Send e-mail to your favorite authors

- Join us in weekly chats with authors, readers and other guests

- Get writing guidelines

- AND MUCH MORE!

Visit our website at
http://www.arabesquebooks.com

FALLING FOR YOU

Kim Louise

BET Publications LLC
http://www.bet.com
http://www.arabesquebooks.com

ARABESQUE BOOKS are published by

BET Publications, LLC
c/o BET BOOKS
One BET Plaza
1900 W Place NE
Washington, D.C. 20018-1211

All Kensington Titles, Imprints, and Distributed Lines are available at special quantity discounts for bulk purchases for sales promotions, premiums, fund-raising, and educational or institutional use. Special book excerpts or customized printings can also be created to fit specific needs. For details, write or phone the office of the Kensington special sales manager: Kensington Publishing Corp., 850 Third Avenue, New York, NY 10022, attn: Special Sales Department, Phone: 1-800-221-2647.

First Printing: April 2002
10 9 8 7 6 5 4 3 2 1

Printed in the United States of America

For Lisa J

ACKNOWLEDGMENTS

A lot of people helped to make this novel possible: Lisa Jackson, who called me one night and said, "Have I got a story for you!"; Kanika Naylor; Dr. Mike; Shirley; Robert L. Humphrey, for "The Warrior's Creed"; Sgt. John Ewing; Daryl Johnson; ReTonya and Valencia, who are the wind beneath my wings; Capiz Green, my favorite body builder; Linda Knell, the first ninja I ever met; Jim Pearson, the hard rider with a heart of gold; and Cathy Richmond, for her wonderful insight and tireless red pen. Special thanks to Rochelle Alers for encouraging me to finish this story. You all have my eternal gratitude.

> The greatest deception comes not from the
> lies of others but our own imperfect vision.
>
> —Toda Kai

One

For the third time in a week, he was being followed. Montgomery Claiborne stared hard into the rearview mirror of his gray Jaguar and signaled a right turn. Whoever it was signaled too, and soon Montgomery and his pursuer were headed south down Giles Road.

He was beginning to think that his father could be right. Maybe he should have taken precautions. After all, it wasn't every day that you found yourself on someone's hit list. But two weeks ago, things started happening—strange things that made Montgomery more than a little cautious while he was out in public.

First, he was delivering office furniture to one of his warehouses when a stack of heavy boxes fell and nearly crushed him. Then, he was walking into the Federal Building, and a plank from the window washer's platform came crashing down and missed him by an owl's breath.

When the elevator in his loft office building went sailing uncontrollably to the top floor, he got suspicious. The only thing that kept his misgivings in check was the fact that he hadn't been injured in any of the incidents.

However, that truth was lost on his father. His old man had insisted that he was in danger and accused him of being too dismissive. When his father suggested that he take steps to protect himself, Montgomery was appalled. Reeves Claiborne had steered his automatic wheelchair to a faux air duct and retrieved a .45-caliber handgun and a horseload of ammunition.

"Are you crazy?" Montgomery had admonished, snatching the weapon away. "Someone could get hurt."

"Someone like who? There's no one in this house except Tilde and me."

"But, Father . . . a gun? What the hell are you doing with a gun in the house?"

For an ailing man in a wheelchair, Reeves was quite agile. He had taken back the weapon before Montgomery had a chance to close his hand around it.

"I'm doing what you should be doing—keeping the peace."

"Guns are a foolhardy way of resolving conflict," Montgomery said, stretching out his hand for the revolver.

His father did as he expected and placed the deadly weapon back where he had gotten it. "On the contrary, son. A bullet makes a mighty strong persuader. You put a gun in somebody's face, and suddenly people are eager to cooperate."

That dead-end conversation had been a week ago. Montgomery had left his father's house feeling frustrated, yet determined to go back and get that handgun before something terrible happened. But this person behind him almost made him wish he had taken his father's advice *and* the pistol he'd offered.

I need to be certain, he thought, pressing on the accelerator. Another glance in the rearview mirror told him that he was indeed being pursued. "I don't believe it," he said out loud, stepping harder on the gas. To his chagrin, his pursuer increased speed as well.

Tired of playing cat and mouse, Montgomery drove his Jag like the sports car it was. Giles Road was a long stretch of highway bent with turns and curves. But it was all familiar territory to Montgomery. He threw his car into fifth gear and went flying down the road and around a Z-bend. *That'll shake 'em,* he thought. But he was wrong. Not only was he still being followed, but the vehicle was gaining on him. And he realized, as he frowned into his side mirror, that a motorcycle had now taken the place of the car he saw earlier, and it was rapidly coming up on his left.

His evasive maneuvers had failed him. He briefly thought of calling the police, but fury drove him to handle matters himself.

Well, I may not be armed, but I'm definitely not defenseless. From a breakneck speed of ninety miles per hour, Montgomery slowed his car abruptly. He watched his side-view mirror as the motorcycle continued to propel forward. When it was almost even with his automobile, he wrenched his steering wheel sharply and sent his car lurching toward the bike.

The rider must have anticipated his move and swerved widely avoiding collision. Adrenaline quickened Montgomery's pulse as he tried to discourage the cyclist again. The vehicle made another approach and Montgomery veered once more, yanking the wheel forcefully. This time he came within inches of sideswiping the motorcycle.

"Who are you, the Terminator?" he asked, watching as the rider again avoided impact and maneuvered back into pursuit mode. This time, Montgomery didn't wait for the motorcycle to pull alongside him. Instead, he jerked the steering wheel to the extreme left, and his car whipped around into the path of the speeding machine.

He heard the wild screech of brakes, but it was too late, and the cycle crashed into the side of his car. The driver flipped over the handlebars, rolled across his car hood, and tumbled into a ravine.

Montgomery gnashed his teeth and stepped out of his nonmoving vehicle. He hadn't realized it until then, but his breathing was fast and ragged as if he'd been lifting something heavy. *I haven't been in a fight since I was a freshman in college,* he thought. *But I still remember how.* He marched deliberately toward the place where he'd watched the rider roll. Gravel from the road ground gritty beneath his steps. "If you aren't hurt now," he announced, "just wait. It's coming."

Montgomery walked to the edge of the furrow, just as a figure approached. He recognized it as the motorcycle driver, and his blood ran cold. His muscles tightened for battle, but something was amiss.

The person before him looked a little small for a hit man. The body in the black leather jacket and chaps was tall, slender, and sleek. Built more for running than killing. Montgomery was disappointed. Aside from a few grass stains and large smudges of dirt, the man looked unharmed.

"I'm not even going to let you explain yourself. I'm just going to beat you down," Montgomery promised, exasperated. The words sounded foreign coming from him. However, his recent brushes with death replaced his bias for nonviolence with pure and bitter aggression.

As he closed the distance between him and his assailant, the man removed his headgear. Montgomery stopped short as a cascade of long, thick hair tumbled out from beneath the large helmet, and a beautiful woman stood on the road with a hand on her hip and indignation on her face.

She stepped in front of him with one powerful stride. "What were you trying to do? Kill me?"

Anger produces rooms of hot breath and not
much else.

—Toda Kai

Two

Montgomery stood aghast as the smell of hot rub-
ber flared his nostrils. Adrenaline electrified the atmosphere. He could almost see the molecules colliding
in the warm evening air.

"Trying to kill *you*?" he bellowed. "You've been tailing me for miles! Why?"

"Tailing?" she fired back.

"What else would you call it?"

The woman shoved her black helmet under her arm
and yanked off matching leather gloves. "I tried to
pass you. *You* are the one who did a one-eighty in the
middle of the road!"

Montgomery felt his jaw muscles tense and con-
strict. "I don't know what you're trying to pull, but I
want a full and detailed explanation."

The woman stood her ground, unaffected. "Explanation of what? That I was trying to get home when
some loony decides to slam his car into my bike."

Montgomery didn't believe her. He watched in-
credulously as hot accusations pulled her features into

a stern frown. She looked as though she were tempering a firestorm.

Undaunted, he stepped closer. It took all his resolve not to grab her shoulders and shake the truth from her. "Look here . . . either you tell me what's going on or I call the police."

"Too late," she snapped, walking past him. She bent down and examined the mangled chrome of her front fender. "Somebody already called!"

"What?" he said, recoiling.

"I don't blame them. You have got to be the most careless, maniacal driver I've ever seen."

"I don't believe . . ." The approaching sound of a police siren cut him off. He turned as the blue-and-white vehicle stopped behind the debris of the cycle. The woman stood, casting Montgomery a sharp scowl.

"Well, I'll be damned," he said.

A rotund man in a dark blue uniform emerged from the police vehicle, pen and ticket pad in hand. Montgomery thought he looked like Jabba the Hut. "Is that your car, ma'am?"

"No," she snarled.

"I got a call from Dispatch regarding a possible drunk driver. A gray Jaguar with the license plate number matching that one."

Montgomery couldn't believe what he was hearing.

"Is it your car, sir?"

"Yes, but I . . ."

"May I see your driver's license and registration?"

"What about her?"

The policeman stepped to where shards of chrome and steel lay strewn and twisted in the street. "Was that your motorcycle, ma'am?"

"Yes."

"I'll need to see your operator's license and registration also."

"Certainly, Officer."

Montgomery stared in mocking disbelief. "Now you're cooperative. Just a few minutes ago, you were the Wicked Witch of the—"

"Sir, your driver's license and registration, please."

Montgomery stomped away. "I don't believe this is happening."

He retrieved a thin, brown leather case from the glove compartment and returned to what felt more like the scene of a crime than the scene of an accident. Was this the same woman who had just been screaming at him? Something must be up. She looked like a shy teenager right now. She was hiding something, his instincts told him.

He handed the information to the officer.

"It'll be just a moment."

The policeman returned to his cruiser, and the woman glared at Montgomery.

"I hope you have insurance," she said, pounding her boot heavily on the pavement. "Because my bike looks totaled."

"Don't worry," he said nonchalantly.

"I should sue," she spat.

"You don't look hurt to me." He took a sideways glance at her. She must have a guardian angel, because the kind of tumble she took could have easily caused broken bones or a concussion.

She paced, talking to the air, then the pavement, then the air again "He . . . rammed me. Tried to run me off the road. And then he stopped right in the middle of the street. What an idiot."

"Idiot!" he shot back. "I oughta—"

"What?" she asked, stepping into his path, hands locking firmly on her hips.

"Hold it!" the officer shouted, getting out of his cruiser. He returned each one's license and registration information. "Somebody want to explain what happened here?"

"I was driving home when—"

"Why don't you start, Miss Strong?" the officer said, interrupting Montgomery.

"Well . . ." she said, and drew in a breath. "I was on my way home from downtown and I saw him . . . or his car rather. It was weaving."

"You're crazy!"

"Mr. Claiborne, you'll get your chance."

Montgomery folded his arms and prepared to endure the offense of the woman's lie.

"At first I didn't think anything. Everyone weaves now and then. But he started making weird lane changes. Then he would speed up and slow down for no reason. I thought he was drunk. That must be why someone called the police."

"How did the accident happen?"

"The accident happened when I tried to go around this maniac. I wanted to get away from him before he crashed into something. Little did I know."

"That's not what happened!"

"Mr. Claiborne, if you don't wait your turn, I'll handcuff you and make you sit in the backseat of the cruiser until I'm finished with Miss Strong."

Montgomery clamped his teeth together and tried to strangle *Miss Strong* with his eyes.

She looked away and continued her story.

"As soon as I tried to pass, he tried to run me off the road. Then he really lost it and slammed on his brakes right in front of me. Now my bike is probably totaled, and I'm sure I'll be sore for a month."

The policeman licked the tip of his pencil and scribbled something on the pad.

"Okay, now you."

Montgomery didn't like the way the officer addressed him. Obviously, he had already made up his mind regarding who was at fault.

"Look, Officer, I was being followed."

"Miss Strong was following you?"

Montgomery glanced up into a starless sky. "No. A car was following me. I was trying to lose it."

"By driving erratically?"

Montgomery looked around. On this long stretch of country drive, there wasn't a car in sight. It was as if everyone on the planet had disappeared except for him, Jabba the Cop, and Lady Bizarre. "Not exactly," he responded.

The officer looked exasperated. "Then *what* exactly?"

"I thought someone was trying . . ." Montgomery wasn't sure if he wanted to admit all of his suspicions. At this point, they might support the silly woman's accusations. He resumed his account more thoughtfully.

"I was being followed. I don't know who it was. I tried to shake them. Then I noticed a motorcycle behind me. It seemed to be following me, too.

"When Miss Strong rode up beside me, I thought she was trying to cut me off. I—I guess I overreacted."

"Overreacted! Look at my bike. And look at me. I'm lucky to be in one piece!"

Montgomery glanced sideways and realized it was true. The bike was totaled. But somehow Miss Strong-Thing had gotten away with minor scratches. And for the first time, he allowed himself to take a good look at her. Almost mechanically, his mind had registered *beautiful woman* when she had removed her helmet. Then when she had gone on her tirade, his mind replaced that thought with *psycho woman*. But now, hearing her story, he returned to his original thought and added another—*sexy woman*.

"Miss Strong, both of your stories corroborate that you hit Mr. Claiborne. I'm going to have to issue you this citation for following too closely."

"Damn!" she said as her eyes flashed in anger.

"And, you. I'm issuing you a verbal warning, Mr. Claiborne. No more reckless driving."

Montgomery sighed, feeling somewhat vindicated.

The officer walked to his car, offering advice. "Next time you see a reckless driver on your way home, Miss Strong, you may want to hang back or choose another route."

"I can't. This is the only road to my house!" she called after him. But the officer was already in his cruiser and starting the engine.

She looked as exasperated as Montgomery felt. Maybe she was telling the truth after all. Besides, what would a strange woman on a motorcycle want with him anyway? *I'm just paranoid.*

All he wanted now was to get home, shower, and watch a good basketball game. He turned and headed toward his car.

"Shit," she said behind him. Against his better judgment he spun around and saw her standing dejectedly over her motorcycle. Somehow, a chivalrous Montgomery Claiborne emerged from the aggravated one.

"Can I . . . give you a ride somewhere?"

Her eyes shot razors across the road. He could almost feel them slicing his neck and chest. "If I had to choose between riding with you and walking fifteen miles in a blizzard, I'd be a snow-treadin' mama."

He retrieved his cell phone from its holder on his belt. "At least let me call someone for you."

"Look, Mr. Claiborne. You've done enough for one day. Go home—leave me alone."

Montgomery went to his car and copied his insurance information on the back of a business card. He came back to where the woman stood staring at him.

He handed the card to her. "Your bike is totaled. My insurance company will pay for it."

She took the card, never taking her eyes off him. She watched as he got into his Jag and slowly drove away. Sighing, she reached in her jacket pocket for her cell phone. It came out in pieces.

"Damn," she said as the gray sports car disappeared down the road.

The truth is always closer than you believe.
—Toda Kai

Three

"I can't calm down!" she screamed into the receiver. Sabin Strong paced in the bedroom of her new residence with fury charging her steps.

"No, no! My motorcycle is totaled!"

She held her breath while the person on the other end of the line droned on.

"All I know is, I nearly got myself killed today."

She shook her head as if she could be seen. "No. No! He said he thought I was trying to kill him. Can you believe that? That's when he decided to play demolition derby. The guy's got a screw loose."

She listened intently for a few moments.

"Yeah, well, all I know is, you owe me a new set of wheels."

Sabin nodded. "All right, I'll be in touch . . . I don't know when . . . good-bye!"

Exasperated, she slammed the phone down on her end table and focused on her breathing until it was deep and even. Anger slowly relenting, she removed her clothes, dropping them where she stood. *What a day,* she thought, heading for the bathroom.

She walked in and observed herself in the full-length mirror. Most of the cuts were minor. A few places near her right knee and forearm were sans skin. She took a bottle of peroxide and a cotton ball from the medicine cabinet and dabbed at her wounds.

A sure sign of age, she thought. Only a few short years ago, she would have taken her tumble without so much as a hairline scratch. But now . . .

"Ow," she winced, applying the antiseptic to the larger of her wounds. "Damn you, Claiborne. What in the hell were you thinking?"

"Nnuah, nnuah." Trails of sweat rolled down Montgomery's face and on to his chest. His muscles burned in protest. "Nnuahhh!" The sounds propelled fitfully from his lips as he used the last of his energy to hoist himself repeatedly above the chin bar.

How many pull-ups had he done? Seventy-five? One hundred? His legs bent behind him almost stiffened into place. His breathing, no longer deep and measured, came in huffs and gasps as he pushed his body beyond normal limits. His veins looked like tiny brown tributaries traveling the length of his arms. He could feel them protruding from his neck and shoulders, as well.

Ten more, he thought. *Just ten more and then I'll call it quits.*

He pulled hard.

Ten. He strained and released, his body dropping lower as the effort wore on his biceps. *Nine.* Again, and the motion shot bolts of searing pain where he imagined his muscles tearing and ripping. He grit his teeth and continued. *Eight . . . seven . . . six.*

Sweat came down like rain. He grimaced as salt from his forehead dripped and burned his eyes.

*Five . . . four . . . three. First the unexplained incidents.
Then I was followed. Two. And today. Almost there. Just . . .*
"Nnauhhh!" *One!*

Montgomery released the bar and dropped hag-
gardly to his feet. Wincing, he wiped the sweat from
above his brows. He grabbed his squeeze bottle and
drained the water in gulps.

He walked the length of his weight room, shaking
out his arms, rocking his head back and forth. Then
he cracked the knuckles in both hands and considered
working a while with the dumbbells.

As he reached for the thirty-pound weights, the
phone rang. Montgomery grabbed a towel and sat
down on his exercise bench.

He picked up the phone. "Yeah," he said, still
catching his breath.

A voice on the other end of the line said, "It's me."

Montgomery wiped the towel across his face and
down his bare chest. "What's up, Angie?"

"Unfortunately, the flu."

"Damn. It's only the beginning of May. I didn't even
know the flu virus was alive this time of year."

"Believe me," she said, coughing. "It's alive, and
I'm not well."

"Then stay home with that crap. I don't need any
further bad luck."

More coughs on the other end of the phone.
Montgomery pulled the receiver away from his ear as
if the germs could come through.

"Did something else happen?" she asked.

"Yeah. I had a car wreck."

"What! Are you all right?"

"I'm fine."

"How about the other driver?"

Montgomery's mind pulled the image of a woman
in black leather into clear focus.

"She's definitely fine."

"She?"

He smiled remembering how angry the woman had become. "Her motorcycle looks like a pretzel, though."

"Montgomery, you don't think your accident was related in any way to——"

"Right now, I don't know what to think. Let's just say I haven't ruled it out."

More coughs and then a sneeze.

"Woman, you sound awful. I don't ever remember you being sick like this before."

"I know. But when I get sick, I get *sick*."

He rolled his shoulders, easing out some of the tightening. "Is there anything you need? Progresso makes a great chicken soup. I could nuke some and leave it on your doorstep so the bacteria won't get me."

Angie huffed. "No, thanks. My mom said she would keep tabs on me."

"All right. I'll hold the fort down at the office until you're well. You just take it easy."

"Yes, sir, boss!"

Montgomery frowned. "Boss? We're partners, remember?"

There was silence on the other end. Then the sound of hacking.

"I'll call you tomorrow. Get some rest."

"Thanks. I'll do that."

Montgomery hung up, worried. He and Angela Miller had been partners for ten years. In that time, she had hardly missed a day of work. When she did, it was usually to take her mother to the doctor. Angie was the most health-conscious person he knew.

Strange things are happening all over, he mused, and reached for the dumbbells beside the bench.

* * *

Spring in Golden Creek, Maryland, turned out to be hotter than some summers he remembered. Montgomery tossed in his bed. His sheets were damp from perspiration. He finally sat up in disgust. There were six windows in his bedroom, all of them open, and still it must have been eighty-five degrees in the house. The large ceiling fan did little to cool the room. Frustrated, he headed for the thermostat to turn on the central air.

He closed all the windows and realized that although the humidity was a contributing factor, the primary cause of his restlessness had to do with the question that wouldn't let him sleep.

Was someone really trying to kill him?

Earlier, he had been so sure he was being followed. But was he really? After all, he *had* been driving erratically. If he had seen someone weaving the way he had been, he might have felt compelled to call the police himself. In the midst of his anger, he had freewheeled his vehicle like Avery Brooks in an episode of *A Man Called Hawk.* Then it hit him like a sharp blow to the stomach. His recklessness could have killed that woman!

Two A.M., yet he felt antsy. He had already lifted weights for hours. His muscles still ached and throbbed from the workout. *I don't care,* he thought, snatching his keys from his dresser.

A nighttime symphony was in full swing. Under the shine of a full moon, crickets and cicadas called out to their mates. Some of them sounded like bullfrogs, desperately seeking companionship. Montgomery walked barefoot around the side of his house and into the carport. It must have been ten degrees cooler outside than in. The night air felt good on his legs, chest, and arms.

He placed a bucket and a box of detergent on the concrete. Then he uncoiled the garden hose from its hanger and turned the water on. After sprinkling some detergent into the bucket, he filled it with water. Some of the crickets that had been near the house quieted down. Montgomery took a deep breath. Being outdoors always helped him relax. Living on the outskirts of D.C. gave him the advantage of both metropolitan amenities and country living. He wasn't fond of being around a lot of people. That's why he chose to live in "the boonies," as Angie called it. It was quiet, peaceful, and on hot nights like this, he could come outside in his boxers and wash his car without any—

"Awfully late to be pampering your toy, wouldn't you say?"

Montgomery turned in the direction of the voice. Unfortunately the garden hose turned with him, and the person talking to him was soaked within seconds. And he realized it was *her.*

"Eee-aah," she clamored, jumping back from the cold water spray.

"You!" he yelled. "What are you doing here?"

Sabin wiped water from her face and eyes. "I live here, you idiot!"

Montgomery's sore muscles tightened. "You've got one more time to call me an idiot."

The woman's eyebrows rose slightly. "Or what? You'll destroy something else that belongs to me?"

Her comment stung. He had acted like a crazy man. And he owed her an apology. "Miss . . . Strong . . . I regret what happened earlier."

She placed both hands on her hips.

"I was out of line and—"

"Out of line?"

"All right!" he relented. "It was a bonehead thing to do."

"Damn straight," she agreed. Her look was smug.

He smiled a little. The woman standing before him seemed as wild as a Kenyan leopard. And with her long, dark hair and sleek muscles, she almost looked like one. Did she say she *lived* here?

"Where . . . exactly . . . do you live?"

"There," she said, pointing to the house next door.

Montgomery gaffed. "Old Lady Greene lives there."

"She did until two weeks ago. Now she lives with her daughter in Michigan."

A droplet of water trickled from the woman's temple and down the side of her face. Montgomery watched as it meandered across the front of her neck and disappeared beneath a white, ribbed tank top. She was drenched. And through the thin fabric, he could see two perfectly symmetrical breasts. No bra. Just the top clinging snugly to nipples chilled and alert. In the starlight he could see white loose-fitting jogging pants. The black stripes down the side led his eye to the black-and-white Chuck Taylor tennis shoes.

"Mr. Clai-borne."

He jerked his head up and offered her a half smile. "Montgomery, please."

"Montgomery," she said, glancing down. "It seems you've managed to cause me more misfortune. I'm going to dry off. Good night."

He watched as she turned and walked toward the house she claimed was now hers.

"Good night, Miss Str—"

"Sabin," she called without looking back.

Montgomery stared curiously after her with a flow of cool water gushing from his garden hose.

* * *

Sabin took a thick, purple towel from the linen closet and dabbed her hair with it. *He's not too bright,* she thought, *but damn,* she'd never seen so many muscles on one person in her entire life. On television, yes, but not in the flesh. His perfection started with the sharp planes and angles of his face. Then a strong neck led to brawny pectoral muscles that Sabin had to fight an impulse not to reach out and touch. His stomach muscles were ribbed with strength, and the way his boxers hung from his narrow hips, gave the moonlight a place to hide in the shadows of his obliques.

Below the shorts, thigh muscles as big as barrels. And his calves! They looked as though he had spent the better part of his life running, on tiptoe. And as if he couldn't be any more tempting a specimen, his skin was a creamy toffee kind of hue. Like someone had mixed butter and a pinch of brown sugar with muscle and called it *man. And just what color* are *his eyes?*

Great! she thought. That's *all* I need. She sat down on her bed, where she had been before she had heard him stirring outside. Sabin picked up her journal to finish the entry she had started.

> *Kai,*
> *One hundred thousand dollars is a lot of money. But nothing is worth my life. On the other hand, I am the best money can buy. Maybe I'm crazy, but I think I'm going to give this more time. If it starts getting ugly, I'm out. Let the proper authorities handle it.*
> *PERSONAL NOTE: Speaking of proper . . . Mr. Montgomery Claiborne is definitely one proper brotha.*
> *S.*

Even angels have a past.

—Toda Kai

Four

The commercial district of Market City sat on the banks of the Potomac River. Hundred-year-old warehouses, storefronts, and other establishments refurbished by the city housed retail stores, corporate suites, and loft apartments. The business office of Secure Storage, Inc., owned by Montgomery Claiborne and Angela Miller, located in the basement of the Saunders Lofts building, was just one half block from the river. In the office, Montgomery made quick work of opening and sorting the daily mail.

He thought about Angie and how they had divided the workload at the onset of their partnership. He worked mainly in the warehouses, loading and unloading, designating space accommodations, and managing the repository staff. Angie was in charge of handling the paperwork—a task he despised. As he completed the simple chore of opening the mail, he reminded himself of how fortunate he was to have her as his partner.

"You are worth every penny you're paid," he said as if she could hear.

"Why, thank you" came a sultry response.

Arroya. He knew it was her without looking up. As a matter of fact, if he hadn't been so focused on dealing with the piles of correspondence on Angie's desk, he would have known she was in the room by sense of smell alone. He looked up.

"Hello, beautiful."

She smiled, showing a perfect set of brilliantly white teeth. "Good morning, handsome. Ready for coffee?"

Montgomery sat back in the navy, cloth-covered chair, glad for anything that would take him away from the endless paper chase. "I'm more than ready."

He stood, grabbing his suit jacket from the back of the chair, and followed her toward the door. He watched her full-figured body and smiled appreciatively. Arroya Lampier was a big, fine woman and he remembered a time when savoring her voluptuous body was a regular part of his daily routine. He had to admit, he had always been partial to women with *substance.*

The two exited his office and walked down the corridor into a small shopping area. There were various stores including a dry cleaner, a drugstore, and a snack shop. Every Monday morning, Montgomery and Arroya went to Café Noir to start their week over coffee and croissants.

The aroma of freshly ground Colombian beans surrounded them. Montgomery inhaled deeply, letting the fragrance lift his mood.

"The usual?" the clerk behind the counter asked.

"Yes." Montgomery nodded, reaching for his wallet.

Arroya placed her hand over his where it was still inside his back pocket. "My treat today."

Her fingers brushed lightly across his backside. Montgomery gave her a look of warning. Since their breakup, they had become good friends. And he didn't want anything to interfere with that.

Thinking back on it now, it wasn't a breakup per se, more like a mutual pulling apart. But her distinction still lived vibrantly in his mind. A voice as deep and resonate as the rolling ocean. It was captivating, mesmerizing, intentionally sensual, and unforgettable. She only wore Midnight Musk by Jiolí. And she wore it heavily, leaving a trail of full-bodied woman behind her as she walked. Her hair was often sculptured to perfection in something elegant and swept up. Her favorite color was red. And not the bright tomato red that seemed to be popular with some women, but a deep, crimson, almost burgundy type of red. Ah, Arroya. She would make some deserving man an extraordinary wife and a gratifying lover.

"Where's Angela?" she asked as they sat down in their usual corner booth.

"At home, sick."

"Sick?"

"Yeah. Can you believe it?"

"Well, at least we know she's human."

"Not a chance," Montgomery said, after tasting his coffee. "Anyone who can bring order to that tempest of paper of my office has got to be superhuman."

Arroya sat back in the vinyl seat. "I've told you before, I'm not that impressed with what Angela does."

Montgomery cocked his head to the side.

"Don't misunderstand. She's efficient and well organized. No doubt. But you rave as if she walks on water."

"For my money, she does," he responded.

Arroya took a long sip of her espresso and pinched off a piece of croissant. "Your opinion wouldn't have anything to do with the fact that you can't sit still for any longer than five minutes, would it?"

Montgomery said nothing—just sipped his coffee and then lifted his cup in salute. It felt good to have someone in his life that knew him and knew him well. For half a second, he considered inviting Arroya to his house for dinner. He knew they would forego the meal and take each other quickly in the confines of his bedroom. Then before it got too late, they would share their bodies one last time before Arroya left. Then sometime prior to week's end, she would call him and their cycle would begin again. *All too familiar.*

"So, how was your weekend?"

Montgomery felt his grip tighten on the paper cup. To avoid crushing it, he put it down on the table.

"Insane."

"Oh?" she said, eyes widening.

"I don't even know where to begin. Let's just say I had a car accident."

"Montgomery, no! Was anyone hurt?"

"No, although I'm still not sure why."

Arroya put down her tiny paper cup and frowned.

"It was some crazy woman on a motorcycle. I thought she was—I stopped my car suddenly, and she ran into it."

Arroya drummed her fingers on the tabletop. Her immaculately groomed nails glinted ruby red in the stark fluorescent light.

"Okay. I guess you want the whole story."

"That would be nice, M."

Montgomery licked his lips and sat back. The leather seat squeaked as if in protest. "I was on my way home from the Jones Street site, and I discovered I was being followed. Well . . . at first, I wasn't sure," he said, talking with his hands. "So, I changed lanes a few times. Then I sped up to see if I really had a tail. Sure enough, whatever I did, the car behind me did."

"How does a motorcycle fit into this?"

"I wish I knew. One minute a car was following me,

the next minute it was a motorcycle. And I did what any red-blooded American man would do."

Arroya snickered. "You went off, didn't you?"

"Ya damn skippy," he said, draining the last of his coffee. He summoned a server for a refill. A young man came over and filled his cup with the steaming black liquid.

"So I swerved to force the motorcycle to stop, and it slammed into me."

Arroya drew her hand to her chest. "Oh, my Lord."

"Yeah, and then Sabin Psycho accused me of trying to kill her."

His breakfast companion looked incredulous. "Well, I would, too!"

"All right, enough about my horrible weekend. Besides, women always stick together."

Arroya sipped her espresso and licked the excess from her sangria-colored mouth. "So how's life in *the vault?*"

A smile pulled back Montgomery's lips. The vault she referred to was his office. Saunders Lofts had once been First United Bank. The offices of the vintage structure had been turned into apartments, and the vaults in the basement had been turned into offices—all with their original shelving, steel-plated interiors, and three-foot-thick doors with crank wheel locks. Montgomery thought the décor gave his work environment a sort of eclectic ambiance not often present in an industry such as his.

"Just fine," he replied.

"Still the king of government contracts then?"

Keep talking, Arroya, he thought. *You are going to talk me right back into your bed, aren't you?* "Only those involving furniture and surplus, baby."

Montgomery saw the smoldering glow in her eyes. *It never fails,* he mused, taking a piece of her croissant.

His terms of endearment always generated a soft combustion within her. Most of the time he did it without thinking. Then other times, like now, he needed a serious refresher class on the power of a man over a woman. So, he would garnish his sentences with *baby*, or *beautiful*, or *luscious*.

"What are you thinking?" Arroya's ever-alluring voice pushed aside his introspection.

He watched as she licked croissant crumbs from a finger. "Have I told you how much I enjoy our Mondays together?"

"More or less," she said, implying that she knew, without him having to say it.

Montgomery felt a carnal yearning snake its way from his lower torso to his face. "Hmmm," he murmured. "Are you free tonight?"

"Yes," she answered, keeping his gaze.

"Want some company?"

Montgomery returned to his office trying to figure out what demon had possessed him.

"The loneliness demon," he said finally, sitting in front of Angie's computer. The sad fact was that he was lonely *with* Arroya and lonely *without* her. She was a good lover and an even better friend. But that was all really. And it left him feeling dull and unfinished. No matter how he tried to bury his unhappiness between her thighs, it never seemed to work.

He returned to separating the piles of mail. Anything that resembled junk he tossed in the trash. Despite his attempt at distraction, his mind lingered on his date. *I should just cancel,* he thought. *I can't keep doing this to her, to us.* Montgomery picked up the phone and dialed her home number. Arroya's familiar recorded greeting announced her absence.

"This is Arroya. You know what to do."

"Roya, it's M. Look, I've changed my mind about tonight. It's probably not such a good idea for me to see my best friend naked. I'll call you later. Maybe we can . . . Hey! What the——?"

Montgomery put the receiver on Angie's desk and walked to the door of his office. Someone had closed it, and strangely it sounded as if it locked.

That's ridiculous, he thought. The renovators disabled the inside locking mechanism. The only way to secure these massive vault doors was from the outside, and he and Angie had the only keys.

Montgomery gave the door a shove. It didn't move. He shoved again, harder this time. Still nothing. He slammed his shoulder against the door, planted his feet firmly, and heaved.

"Hey! Open this damned door!" he hollered, but he knew that was useless. His office was soundproof, bulletproof, and burglarproof. Disgusted, he went back to the desk and retrieved the phone. He pressed the talk button several times, but the phone was dead.

"I don't believe this!"

He glanced at the clock on the wall: eight-thirty P.M. How long before someone would miss him? He felt the first prickle of panic when he realized that it might be a while. He always kept irregular hours. Unless he was expecting a delivery, no one really knew what his schedule was.

He walked quickly back to the blocked entrance and hammered his fist heavily against it. Frustrated, he paced back and forth, then anger exploded in his veins, and he kicked the trash can over. Store coupons and seminar ads trundled onto the carpet.

"Okay, calm down. There is a way out of this. Think!"

And then he shook his head and laughed like an

embarrassed child. In his alarm at being locked in, he forgot about his cell phone. He removed it from its holder on his belt and coughed.

What's that smell? he wondered, dialing 911. Then the rancid fumes toppled him as he struggled for breath. When the emergency operator answered, all he could do was rasp into the receiver. Then the room tilted again and clouded over.

The lips pressed against his were soft, warm, and slightly moist. Dizzy. Was the kiss making him dizzy? Montgomery took a breath, and his lungs constricted. He gasped, coughed, and clutched his throat for air. His chest felt like it was filled with sand. *Oh, God! I can't br—*

"Montgomery, steady. Breathe shallow. Don't try to take it all in at once."

He heard the words, but could he obey? Panic-stricken, he forced himself to slow down, to inhale carefully. Even though every element in his body made him want to suck air until his chest exploded.

Gradually, his intake of oxygen slowed. With each breath, a fire raged in his lungs. The shallower he breathed, the calmer he became. Steadily, the room came into focus and Sabin Strong's queenlike features hovered obscurely above him.

Just then the atmosphere echoed with voices and footfalls. His thoughts jumbled and washed out as a wave of dizziness claimed him again.

"What happened?" a male voice asked.

A soft hand stroked his forehead. "I stopped by to talk to him, but I saw his door was closed. I was about to leave when I smelled something awful. When I opened the door, he was passed out on the floor.

That's when I dragged him out here and tried to re-suscitate him."

"Let's check his vitals," the man said.

Montgomery felt himself being poked and prodded. He was feeling better, but he was still disoriented.

"What's his name?" the paramedic asked softly.

"Montgomery Claiborne," Sabin answered.

"Sir," he said much louder. "Can you hear me?"

"Yes," Montgomery answered, voice gritty as if it were traveling through a gravel tube.

"What's your name?"

His brain felt thick, but he latched on to part of an answer. "Claiborne."

"Mr. Claiborne, do you know where you are?"

Montgomery tried to respond, but hacked instead.

"Let's get him outta here. I don't know what that smell is but it's making *me* feel light-headed."

"Where are you taking him?" Sabin asked.

"Charles Drew Hospital."

Two paramedics hoisted Montgomery's limp body onto a gurney and wheeled him out of the building.

"Get Mike down here," he heard one of them say. "See if he can find out what that smell is."

As the paramedics wheeled Montgomery into the emergency room, Sabin's heart still pounded a stac-cato alarm. When she had smelled the gas, she'd pan-icked and almost didn't get the door open. Then she drew hard on her breaking-and-entering skills. Like riding a bike, they came back in perfect balance, and she picked the lock with little difficulty.

The sight of him lying on the floor, eyes closed and face pale, chilled her like a Minnesota winter. She rushed to his side, praying he was alive. Her hopes fell when she saw his chest was stiff and still. Then her

fingers detected a weak pulse on his neck, and her
adrenaline surged. Slipping her arms beneath his, she
pulled him out of the office and into cleaner air.

She administered mouth-to-mouth—and gagged fitfully while fighting to inhale air for both of them.
Again and again, she forced air into Montgomery's
lungs until he took a ragged breath on his own. For
a split second, Sabin forgot the crisis and savored the
press of her lips against his. Though his face was pal-
lid, she could make out the golden tan of his skin and
the prominent contours of his cheeks and chin. If he
had pressed back, she knew it wouldn't have been the
gas that was making her slightly woozy, but something
quite different.

Walking into the emergency room, she watched as
a portly nurse worked over Montgomery's motionless
body. *This assignment is going to be even more difficult than
I imagined.* While the doctors ran tests to determine
what gas overcame him, Sabin already knew. As soon
as she had stepped into his office, she recognized the
odor as arsine. Extremely debilitating but not lethal
unless inhaled for perhaps hours instead of minutes.

"We'll have an orderly take you to X ray. We need
to make sure there was no damage to your lungs," the
nurse said, leaving Sabin alone with him.

His eyes were closed. An oxygen mask covered his
nose and mouth and glucose dripped from an I.V. into
his arm. Sabin felt helpless.

"Thank you," he said. His voice sounded hollow
and phlegmy.

She walked closer to where he lay partially covered
by a white sheet. His strong hands clenched into fists
at his side. Sabin could detect faint traces of the gas
seeping from his pores. The tart smell mixed with
strong astringent-style cleaners, and the faint aroma
of sickness reminded Sabin of every hospital she'd

ever been in. She shuddered and wondered why emergency rooms were always so cold.

"You're welcome," she responded, placing her hands on the cool metal of the bed railing. "How are you feeling?"

"Like there were paddles on my chest and someone in a white coat just yelled *clear.*"

Sabin smiled. "Well, you have to get better, because your insurance refused to repair my bike."

"What?" He rose slightly, then a coughing spasm forced him back down.

She said, "That's what I came to your office to tell you," but she thought, *I don't believe it. This man is handsome even at death's back door.* Sabin shut down her amorous thoughts. She had a job to do and she needed to keep focused on that.

"Montgomery, what happened?"

He opened his eyes and squinted.

"What's the last thing you remember?"

"Trying to get out. I was trying to get out of the office. And then I couldn't breathe."

Sabin realized that when she saw Montgomery lying on the floor, she hadn't checked to see if anyone else was in the room. His assailant could have been there. For some reason the sight of him unconscious usurped her training. Mistakes like that were costly. She'd be more careful in the future.

"Was there anyone in the office with you?"

Montgomery pulled aside the oxygen mask. "No."

The nurse returned. "Oh, you must be feeling much better." She reached over with a chubby hand and checked a reading on the oxygen machine. "Looks pretty good," she said, removing the monitor from his fingertip.

"You can keep the mask off. But if you feel short of breath at any time, you put it back on, you hear?"

Montgomery nodded as the nurse pulled the thin white blanket over his chest. Sabin sighed. She had rather liked the view.

"We're running a little behind, but it shouldn't be much longer before you're taken to X ray." The nurse looked at Sabin and patted her arm. "If you need anything, just touch the call button," she said, shuffling out of the room.

"Actually," Montgomery responded, adjusting his position, "I was going to ask her to help me sit up."

Sabin stepped to his bedside. "Here, let me."

He looked at her, hesitantly at first, and then as her arms wrapped around him and lifted, his expression changed to wonder as she easily hoisted him in the bed. Then she reached down and pulled the lever to raise the head of the mattress.

He donned an expression akin to wrestler Duane "The Rock" Johnson giving his devoted fans "The People's Eyebrow."

"I work out," Sabin responded, and tucked a strand of hair back into place behind her ear.

Montgomery managed to laugh without coughing. His smile reached all the way to deep gray eyes that caught hers and made her forget how cold the room was.

She stepped back to break free of his influence and reached into her pocket to retrieve her new cell phone. "Is there someone that I should call?"

The spark she'd seen in his eyes dimmed slightly, and he turned from her. "No," he said.

"If you have family, I'm sure they would want to know you're here."

"I don't want to worry them."

Sabin took a seat in the small chair next to the bed, still feeling a little too close. *There isn't much space in these rooms.*

"You're sure, then?"

He thought for a moment and then spoke. "There is someone."

A young woman in green scrubs entered the room, chart in hand. "Mr. Claiborne?"

"Yes?" he responded, looking up.

"I'm Sheila. I'm going to take you to X ray."

"I'm ready," he said as she attached the IV bag to a rod on his bed.

The bright-eyed orderly stepped behind the bed and released the brake. "Here we go," she said, pushing him toward the door.

"It'll be about fifteen minutes," she told Sabin.

Then they were gone, and Sabin was left to ponder who it was that Montgomery wanted to call if not his family.

> From the mouth of an enemy, your name is
> only noise.
>
> —Toda Kai

Five

They sent him here. To find . . . nothing, and keep him occupied. God knows, idle hands. . . .

Lucian Carvell knelt beside the plastic yellow bottle. Innocent looking and innocuous now, but three hours ago a horror story. One hundred and fifty people evacuated, one man hospitalized, and for what? Because someone on the maintenance crew put fertilizer too close to the furnace. Hardly a legitimate call for crime investigation. Still, they'd sent him and two of his assistants.

"You can never be too sure about these things," his lieutenant had said.

"Yeah, son," his father, Captain Henry Carvell, had agreed. "You'd better go check it out."

So he'd grabbed a notebook and rode over with officers Gina Vendetti and Stanford Morrison to investigate a crime that didn't exist.

He stood and peeled off latex gloves. He may have a jackleg assignment, but he wanted to present some semblance of professionalism.

Turning, he saw Morrison headed toward him. The man always made Lucian want to offer him a cigar. With his long trench coat, dark hair, and fedora, it was the only thing missing from his detective-guy persona. He also found it impossible not indulge the young man's fantasy. After all, this was Golden Creek, Maryland. Not much to do for excitement otherwise.

"Whatcha got for me, Morrie?"

Seriousness stiffened the junior detective's dark face. "I talked with ten people. Most are residents. A couple were patrons at the coffee shop. They all say the same thing. By the time they smelled the fumes, the paramedics were already arriving. Shortly after that, they were evacuated until Mike from Toxicology gave them the all-clear."

"Good work, Morrie. What else?" With Morrison there was always something else.

"One of the residents says he saw a woman fiddling with the lock on one of the offices. He didn't think much of it. He says people seeing the vaults for the first time are often fascinated. But it just so happens that the office is leased by one Montgomery Claiborne."

"The man who was hospitalized?"

"The same."

"I got a description of the woman. Turns out she's probably the one who saved him. I got a half-dozen witness that say a woman matching her description gave Claiborne CPR until the guys in yellow jackets showed up."

Lucian didn't think that information was relevant, but he wanted to encourage his protégé. "Excellent. Now, what's next on the protocol?"

Morrison almost smiled, but Lucian knew he wouldn't. He simply said, "Examine the scene for evidence."

Lucian nodded and motioned toward the bottle of fertilizer. Morrison nodded back and handed Lucian his notebook. He snapped the latex gloves onto his hands, then called Vendetti downstairs. She joined the two men, camera ready.

Lucian stepped back in the dark of the cellar. With all the recreation of the upper portions of the building, you'd think some attention would have been paid to upgrading the basement, as well. He noted the thick gray cobwebs dangling and swaying from the ceiling and the damp places where the concrete floor was cracked, and imagined that someone may have pocketed the money slated for renovations. Morrison and Vendetti went to work. They were good at their jobs, such as they were. Lucian knew that they had aspirations of joining the D.C. force. He wished them well, but realized that filing reports on accidental chemical spills would do little to prepare them for the arson, homicide, and heinousness of the big city.

Vendetti took photographs while Morrison made notes and drew diagrams. Lucian figured a rat or stray cat probably ran past the bottle and tipped it against the furnace. A trail of the now dry-liquid led from the spill to the ventilation system. Some custodian was going to receive a severe talking-to for not screwing the cap on tighter. Such was life in the small town.

When Vendetti finished her roll of film and loaded another, Morrison used tongs to pick up the bottle and cap and place it in a plastic bag.

"What else?" Lucian asked.

"How about pictures of Claiborne's office? Seems funny that he was the only one who took a nap."

Lucian wanted to point out that the place where they were standing was directly under the guy's work area and that it seemed perfectly logical that he would be the first to succumb, but sometimes it was better to let the kids learn their own lessons. "Let's do it," he said.

A few minutes later, an older woman from building management let them into the office of Secure Storage. It was a small room. Neat and organized. If it hadn't been for the trash strewn on the floor, you wouldn't have suspected that anything was amiss.

The light bulb flashed. "He must have knocked it over when he fell," Vendetti said.

Lucian liked her. She was smart—too smart to be a cop. She was dead set on following in her brother Gino's footsteps all the same. She enjoyed things like the symphony and intellectual discourse. He'd seen her with a book on quantum mathematics once. She told him she was reading it for pleasure. And he'd also been privy to her crime photography. Some of it looked hangable. For the past two years, he'd wanted to tell her to save herself. That she should enroll in some Ivy League school where she'd be surrounded by people her own brain size. Most of the cops he knew were big cowboys and cowgirls who drank beer and spit a lot. They not only fit the stereotype, they substantiated it. And he didn't want to see their caricatures, or his own for that matter, convert her into another tin flasher.

Under Morrison's methodical direction, Vendetti snapped away. Lucian listened as Mr. Gumshoe obtained an update on Claiborne's condition at the hospital. His prognosis was excellent and he would probably be released tomorrow.

"We'll want copies of the doctor's findings," Morrison said.

Lucian fought a yawn. "Agreed. What else, Officers?"

Morrison spoke first. "Make sure that our documentation is thorough."

"Why, Vendetti?"

"Because without proper documentation, you are unable to prove your interpretation of the scene," she answered.

Lucian clapped his hands. "Okay, lady and gentleman, get to it."

While they made final remarks in notebooks, he shoved his hands into his pockets. He wanted this to be over so he could go back to his desk where there was filing, and phone calls, and stale coffee.

Montgomery's chest hurt. So far the medication to help him breathe wasn't doing much good. Each time he inhaled, an inferno raged in his lungs. And every time he thought about what happened, that rage spread throughout his entire body.

An unfortunate mishap—that's what the investigators called it. They actually tried to convince him the whole thing happened accidentally. The detective on the case had calmly explained how a bottle of fertilizer *somehow* spilled into the furnace. The chemicals then leaked into the duct system and the resulting fumes spread to his office. Montgomery was about as sold on that as he was that ostriches could tap dance.

And now, for the first time in ten years, the administrative office of Secure Storage was closed. Angie was still out with the flu and there was no way Montgomery could have made it in to work. So he stayed home and tried not to go crazy with boredom. Unless taking his yearly vacation, he hated being away from the office. Twice, he almost dialed into the company voice mail system to transfer calls to his home. But the doctor at the hospital made him promise that he would rest over the next few days and return to work the following week. He only hoped Angie got better so someone would be in the office at least by Wednesday.

Montgomery did the channel sprint through all the cable stations. He rarely watched television. He was more of a newspaper man. But having read every newspaper in the house, he was reduced to talk shows, soap operas, and music videos.

"This will never do," he said, and got up from a brown leather love seat. He decided to go for a walk. Moving slowly, he managed to shower and change into something loose and comfortable. As he finished dressing, the phone rang.

"Yeah," he said.

"I just called to check on you."

Montgomery smiled. "Thanks, Arroya. I'm all right. Up and around at least. I was just about to head outdoors for some fresh air."

"Well, don't overdo."

"I won't." He thought about mentioning their missed date. He could ask for a rain check or something.

"Arroya . . ."

"Yes?"

He wavered. "Thanks for coming to get me from the hospital this morning."

"You're welcome, M."

"Well, I had better go."

"Sure," she said. "Call if you need . . . anything."

"I will," he responded, and hung up.

Whew, he thought, hanging his head. *There's got to be a way to conquer this loneliness. There's—*

The doorbell startled him. He walked to the window wondering who knew he was home. The silhouette on the porch made him groan. Tall, slender, feline, *her.* If she thought that he would grovel at her feet for saving him, she was in for a swift enlightenment. He swung open the door and donned a smile.

"Sabin! Hello."

She smiled back, but only slightly. "Good afternoon. How are you feeling?"

"So good, I was just leaving."

"Really? Then I won't keep you. I just wanted to drop this off." She held up a small pot. Montgomery could smell garlic and celery from where he stood.

"What is it?" he asked, taking the container and the warmer beneath it.

"Chicken soup."

Montgomery smiled earnestly this time. She wasn't here to gloat at all. "It smells wonderful," he said. And then the loneliness he'd been fighting took over. "Care to come in and have a bowl with me?"

"I thought you were leaving."

He inhaled the aroma of the soup with a grin. "My walk can wait." He stepped aside and let her enter.

"Hmm . . ." she said looking around.

Montgomery closed the door behind her. "What's 'hmm' for?"

"Just checking out your décor. Classy and sophisticated. Not at all what I expected."

He gave a look down. He was tempted to make a similar comment about the purple sweats she wore, but decided against it.

"I'll take that as a compliment," he responded. "Come on into the dining room and have a seat while I serve this up."

He went into the kitchen and retrieved two ceramic bowls from the cupboard. *What's the purpose of making money if you can't buy yourself nice things?* he wondered, dismissing her comments. When he returned with the piping bowls of soup, he discovered that she wasn't sitting at all, but hovering over a pile of papers on his living room table.

"What are you doing?" he asked.

Sabin turned slowly. "Leafing through your newspapers. You don't actually read all of these, do you?"

A vein at Montgomery's temple throbbed rhythmically. He carefully placed the bowls on his wooden table. "Look, do you want some soup, or not?"

Sabin offered a half smile. "I'm sorry. I just thought I could speak my mind since we"—she gave him a long and thorough once-over—"know each other so well now."

Montgomery remembered the other night when he'd been standing before her in his underwear and felt like a raw steak.

"Sabin, I appreciate you bringing the soup, and I will be eternally grateful to you for saving me, but let's get something straight. It's obvious that we don't care for each other. We're just being civil neighbors here. But you will respect me in my own home, or you'll leave."

He saw her eyes squint to slits and expected a loud and intense retaliation like the one he'd received when they first met. But the storm on her face lasted only a moment, then her eyes softened and a smile peeked out from beneath the anger.

"I apologize. Some people don't know how to take me. I tend to speak my mind, then think about it later. It saves time, but occasionally gets me into trouble."

"Apology accepted. Now, can we eat, or are we going to get on each other's nerves some more?"

"Let's eat," she said, taking a seat.

"Can I get you something to drink?"

Sabin tucked a strand of hair behind her ear. "Sure. Whadaya got?"

Montgomery placed soup spoons beside each bowl.

"Well, I've got skim milk, tomato juice, carrot juice, and water of course."

"Yuck," Sabin said, scrunching her face. "Brother-man, you are way too healthy for me. I'll just skip the beverage."

Montgomery hesitated for a moment wondering if he should reveal his weakness. Then he looked into eyes as turbulent as a wild river.

"I also have some A&W root beer, if you'd like that."

She sat up straighter in the high-back chair. "Now you're talking." Then she smiled the kind of smile that makes men want to conquer nations. "I'd like that in a tall glass with lots of ice."

"Yes, ma'am," he responded with a nod and re-treated into the kitchen.

"I'm being too nice," he mumbled. He hoped she didn't turn out to be like that stray cat he once fed. After the food, he couldn't get rid of her for weeks.

When he returned with the root beer, she was already digging in.

"Hungry?" he asked, sitting across from her.

She looked up, eyes dark and sexy. "You could say that."

Montgomery stirred the soup still piping in the bowl. Carrots, celery, potatoes, peas, with generous chunks of chicken, simmered in a thick stewlike broth. He hadn't eaten much that day, so the aroma generated chaos in his stomach. He hefted a spoonful into his mouth.

"Delicious," he said, surprised. She didn't look like the type of woman who could cook.

"Thank you," Sabin responded, scooping another spoonful for herself.

Montgomery watched her quietly. She wasn't wearing any make-up. She didn't need it. Prominent forehead. Eyes dark and catlike. Nose long and sloping. Lips soft and rose colored. Her hair was combed back and hung loosely about her shoulders. Her skin was a warm golden brown that glowed regally like a lioness.

She seemed to thoroughly enjoy her own cooking. He soon discovered that he liked watching her eat. He found the manner in which her mouth wrapped around the spoon and the careful way she licked off any excess stock hypnotic. *The lips that saved me.* He imagined those same lips on his again, parting this time to welcome the invasion of his ready tongue.

I don't believe it. I'm turned on by a woman I can't stand. And what's that sound? He looked around and realized that it was her fingers. She was tapping short unpolished nails against the table. *I'll bet she's a raker,* he thought. He could almost feel the tips of her fingers curling into his back and down . . .

"I asked you a question!"

"What?" He looked up and smiled.

"Do you have any crackers?"

In his current state of arousal, he didn't dare get up. "No. Sorry."

The aroma combined with the spices and seasonings made Montgomery's mouth water for more. At least that's what he convinced himself. Of course it had nothing to do with the woman sitting across from him. His insides warmed. *It's the soup. It's just the soup.*

"What's in this? It's pretty good."

"Just your everyday vegetables, salt, pepper, garlic, onions, parsley, oregano, pinch of cayenne, and loads of chicken. Guaranteed to cure all respiratory ailments. I'll write down the recipe if you'd like."

Montgomery thought of his culinary skills, or lack thereof, and decided to decline. "No, thanks. I don't cook much."

He was almost finished. And even though she annoyed the hell out of him, he wondered, despite his earlier reservations, what he could do to get her to stay.

"Do you have more opulence or is this the extent of it?" Sabin asked, looking around.

He laughed in spite of her insinuation. "I'm quite proud of my humble surroundings. Would you like to see the rest?"

"Don't mind if I do."

When they finished eating, Montgomery felt recovered enough to take their bowls and glasses into the kitchen.

Then he started the tour with the basement that ran the length of the ranch-style home, and showed her his weight room. He gazed at the smooth cut of her arm muscles. "You work out?"

She shrugged. "I keep in shape."

"Well, if you ever want to come over and use the equipment, it's no problem."

Then he took her upstairs and led her to the den, then worked his way toward the living room. He explained along the way how he wanted a home that had lodgelike qualities: vaulted ceilings, wood interior, fireplace. Each room featured sturdy and oversize furniture that he thought spoke to his taste for things rustic and natural.

The air was moist with the aroma of fresh soap. *Must have just gotten out of the shower,* Sabin thought. Montgomery's quick tour included the hardwood floors of the common areas, through the archway, into a guest room with bay windows and a mammoth ceiling fan. There were hints of the pueblo in the dark brown and peach patterns in the wall painting and throw rugs throughout the guest bath and into the interior hall.

She expected the master bedroom to be as formidable and overbearing as Montgomery. She was not disappointed. The all-wood furniture was a deep mahogany and massive. Thick and polished, she imagined that it must have taken two men and a dolly to move the dresser alone.

"So," Sabin began as they came back to the dining area, "are you rich, or do you have some great job that provides you this kind of kickback?"

"No, I'm not rich. I'm a government contractor. I run a company called Secure Storage."

"Is that a warehouse-type facility?"

"Yeah. When the government needs a place to store things like furniture, nonclassified documents, equipment, and even uniforms, they bid it out just like other procurements."

"No kidding?"

"I've had a steady relationship with Uncle Sam for eight years. Two weeks ago I underbid Worldwide Storage for a key contract—office furniture from the Pentagon."

Sabin lifted a suspicious eyebrow. "Sure you did."

"Look, I don't have to prove anything to you. But I will say this. The government has been trying to renovate the Pentagon for over fifteen years. Since the tragedy of September 11, the government has gotten serious about renovating the entire facility. That means a lot of things that were just taking up space there have to be moved and stored until the construction is complete. Some of the shipments we're getting probably haven't seen daylight in over twenty years."

The two sat down in the living room.

"So, what do *you* do, Sabin?"

"Just call me the people's contractor."

"Really? Why?"

"I'm a personal safety consultant."

"And what does a personal safety consultant do?"

"I help prevent people from becoming crime victims."

"Really? How's that?"

"I conduct seminars and workshops on how to make your home safer, what to do if you are walking alone, traveling alone, driving in unfamiliar areas, and how to reduce theft and robbery in neighborhoods."

Montgomery smiled. "I'm impressed."

"Thanks." Sabin crossed one leg over the other. "I even facilitate workshops on handgun safety."

His smile dissolved. "Hand-gun safe-ty. Now there's a cold contradiction."

"Not if you know how to use a firearm correctly."

"Well, that's the problem, isn't it? Using it *correctly* means shooting someone. There's nothing safe about that."

"There is if you are using the gun to protect yourself."

"So, you're one of those *right-to-bear-arms* types." His tone heavy with sarcasm.

"I'm a realist. And when it comes right down to it, I'd much rather be judged by twelve than carried by six."

"We aren't God, Sabin."

"No, but sometimes He chooses us to carry out His will."

"There's absolutely no justification for murder."

"Sometimes"—Sabin's voice faltered—"you have no other choice."

Montgomery leaned forward. "That's where you're wrong. There's always a back door."

He noted that every curve of her body spoke defiance. "You'd better wake up and smell the gunpowder. This new millennium comes complete with helicopters flying over neighborhoods as if it were Vietnam, schoolchildren who are armed and dangerous, and civilians that have more firepower than the SWAT!"

He stiffened at her challenge. "All the more reason to get handguns off the street!"

Sabin looked as though her mother had just been insulted. Montgomery thought for sure that she would blow one of those veins popping out of her forehead. "What are you, a member of the gun control society?" she asked.

"Actually, I'm president of the local chapter."

"Oh, man! So while you guys lobby for bills and legislation that takes years to pass, let alone enact, innocent people will be killed *today.*"

His eyes narrowed darkly. "I think you had better leave."

"Well . . . you've finally said something I agree with." She got up and walked toward his front door with unhurried purpose.

Montgomery followed behind her, unrelenting. "What you're advocating would turn the clock back to the Wild West."

Sabin waved him off as if dismissing a child. "That whole Wild West mystique is mostly American mythology. The West was actually pretty tame. Why? Everybody had a gun. So riffraff thought twice about doing wrong. 'Cause they knew there was a good chance they'd get shot."

She walked down the stairs and onto the sidewalk. Montgomery stood in the entryway absolutely certain that not only did he dislike Sabin, but he believed she needed immediate counseling.

"I can't believe I shared my root beer with her," he said, closing the door.

> In the battle for your life, everyone is
> an enemy.
>
> —Toda Kai

Six

"I just left his house . . . yeah. He's all right . . . unless you want him to find out, you can't expect me to be around him 24/7."

Sabin stopped pacing. "There's not enough money in the universe for that. Because my body is not for sale!"

She slammed down the phone. Fury streaked through her as she realized that her one-hundred-thousand-dollar arrangement meant that her body was indeed for sale.

Kai,

I keep wondering if I'm doing the right thing. I mean, after all these years, maybe it's better if I don't find her. And who knows if the information I have is even correct? Why did you have to die, Kai, when I still have so many questions?

S.

* * *

Montgomery returned from his walk wearied. He'd assumed spending time in the woods would invigorate him. He'd been wrong. Soon after he'd started on the trail, he was halted by a coughing spasm. He rested for a moment against a large spruce. When his breath returned, he continued. Determined to prove that he was recovered enough, he pushed on, toward his favorite place.

The trail plunged into a thicket. The promise of luxuriant greenery was heavy on the budding branches. Trees lined the sanctuary like sentries, keeping watch over nature's domain. He knew each one by size, bark pattern, and leaf shape. The area just a mile behind his home was as close to paradise as he had ever come.

The only thing that could make his walk more enjoyable would be his mother. If only she could join him one last time up to the overlook. Before his sister was born, this had been the place he and Ma, as he called her, would go walking. Sometimes just to spend time together, but more often it was to get away from his father, whose favorite pastime seemed to be arguing.

Once when Montgomery had had enough of his father's bickering and unsound moods, he had stormed out of the house. He was twelve then and had every intention of running away. But his mother caught up with him and had brought him to the overlook. They talked for hours and she told him that his father hadn't always been mean-spirited. She said that when they had first met, he was an officer in the army stationed at Schofield/Shafter in Hawaii. She had just taken over her father's bar, which was two miles outside of the base. One night when everything was going wrong, beer tap busted, cook sick with the flu, and a brawl that had broken two chairs and a table, the most handsome man she had ever seen pitched in and helped her get through the night from hell. He kept her laughing with his corny jokes and bad impressions. Despite the disaster at the bar, he had made her feel happier than she had ever been.

She told him how scared she was to tell her father that she was not only in love with, but wanted to marry a black man. Her father took his Hawaiian ancestry very seriously. But he was neither angry nor disappointed. He seemed glad to see his daughter so happy, and so she and Reeves Claiborne got married on July 15, 1950. With Reeves granting her wishes, she had a traditional Hawaiian wedding. Mei Young, now Mei Claiborne, and her husband were blissfully happy.

But a bullet in Reeve's back during the Korean War changed all that. His mother told Montgomery that his father wasn't really mad at him; he was mad at his paralysis.

Reeves Claiborne was mad because he believed that his disability made him less of a man. His tough love was a way to make sure that Montgomery grew up to be a full man. Unfortunately, nothing Montgomery did seemed to convince his father that either one of them was indeed a full man.

The snap of a twig halted him. He turned to the right following the sound and scanned the area. Sassafras, black haw, and angry red burning bushes as far as the eye could see, but nothing else. Not even a bramble twisting in the wind. He replayed the sound in his head. It was too heavy for a raccoon or a fox. Perhaps it was a deer, but at this range they usually made a lot more noise than the simple one he'd heard. No, someone was tracking him. That sound was made by a foot stepping, inadvertently he suspected, on a fallen branch.

Another coughing spasm convinced him it was time to return home. He trudged defiantly out in the open.

Come on, he thought, *this is getting old.* But there were no more snapping twigs or unusual noises—just the sound of birds calling into the sky and the wind moving over light branches.

When he got back to his house, he found a note posted on the front door.

> Mr. Claiborne,
> *I stopped by to discuss the accident at your office.*
> *Give me a call.*
> Detective Lucian Carvell, GCPD

Montgomery removed the business card inserted into the door frame, unlocked the door, and went inside. He headed for the medicine cabinet where he kept a recently purchased bottle of extra-strength pain relievers. Arroya had taken him to the drugstore when he was released from the hospital. In addition to his prescription, the doctors recommended an over-the-counter acetaminophen for pain. And right now, there was a brushfire spreading in his chest. He wanted to snuff it out before it became a firestorm. He threw three tablets to the back of his throat and washed them down with tap water.

The only thing he wanted to do now was lie down and let the medicine take effect. Instead, he sat on the couch next to the end table and picked up the phone. He dialed the cell number on the business card and waited.

"Carvell."

"Detective Carvell? This is Montgomery Claiborne. You wanted to talk to me about the incident in my office."

"Yes. Hold on a moment while I pull over."

Montgomery waited.

"You still there?"

"Yeah."

"Officer Morrison told me you had some questions about the accident."

"I just want to make sure there was no evidence that the spill happened deliberately."

"No, Mr. Claiborne, there was not."

"Really . . . ?"

"Why do you sound surprised?"

"Because for the past two weeks, I've had mishaps like that all too often. Just a few minutes ago, I was being followed in the woods."

"Mr. Claiborne, our chemical expert is one of the best in the region. He's assured me that what happened to you was—"

"I know, an unfortunate accident."

Montgomery rubbed his hand across his chest. It felt swollen. *No more lifting for a while.* "Isn't there any chance that someone manufactured this chemical reaction?"

"If there was, my people would have found it."

"I see. Well, tell me, Detective, who else was hurt?"

"No one."

"No one?"

"That's correct."

"And that doesn't seem just a little odd to you?"

"Considering the circumstances, no."

"Humph. Well, Detective, thank you."

"Look, Mr. Claiborne . . . I don't normally do this, but if you'd like, we could get together and talk about those other incidents you mentioned. Maybe there is something to what you're saying."

"Now you're talking."

"Mornings are typically bad for me. Unless anything unexpected comes up, I'm available Thursday and Friday afternoons this week."

"That works for me. How about we meet at three on Thursday? I'll be at 3355 Elins Boulevard."

"I think I can find it."

"Good. Thursday then."

"Goodbye, Mr. Claiborne."

For Montgomery, two days felt more like two weeks. The problem was his life as a model patient. He had taken his doctor's orders and kept his activities to a bare minimum. As a result, boredom was taking a mighty toll. He was tempted once to knock on Sabin's door to see if she was home and wanted to argue.

The nights weren't as bad as the days. Arroya had come over every evening around six P.M. and stayed until ten. She brought him a plate of food each visit and even tidied up the living room where he'd spent more time than he ever had in any one place. They talked, watched movies, and even listened to a book on tape. He was grateful for her companionship and her compassion.

The days, on the other hand, were a different story. The only thing that kept him from tearing his hair out was the regular contact with Angie. She called from the office at nine and three-thirty just to reassure him that everything was going smoothly and that he needn't worry. Fat chance. As a matter of fact, a couple of times he'd called Randy at the warehouse to see how things were running.

"Not much shaking over here, big guy. Same ol' routine," Randy assured him. His comments and Angie's helped him to feel better about being away from work, but come Monday, he would be glad to be back on the job.

"Oh, would you stop moping."

His father's admonishment jarred him and set him on edge. "I'm not moping, Father."

"Sure you are. You're sitting over there wondering about your precious job and what's going on at the office. Well, let me tell you, if you're any kind of boss, they'll get along just fine without you for a couple of days."

Montgomery ground his teeth for a moment. "Isn't it time for your nap, old man?"

"You're not over here to give Tilde a break. You just come to harass me."

Every Thursday, Tilde, his father's primary caregiver and not so secret love interest, went to the beauty salon. While she was gone, Montgomery would come and see to his father's needs, which most often were few.

"So, when's this detective coming?"

"We said three o'clock."

Reeves glanced at the watch on his arm. "Then he's late."

"Who's late?" came a female voice.

Montgomery turned to see his kid sister walking into the kitchen. Cherlyn took after his mother. She was sharp-eyed, petite, and had a memory like an elephant. He smiled, watching her almost-five-foot frame walk over and kiss their father's forehead.

"Ah, Cher. You're just in time to save me from your brother's insults."

Montgomery gave an exasperated breath. "He lies."

"You see!" Reeves proclaimed, victorious.

Cherlyn frowned. "Keep it up. I'll lock you in a room together and leave you there until you say nice things about each other."

"Like hell."

"Not in this lifetime."

The ends of Cherlyn's bone-straight hair swished

against her ear as she put her hand on her hip. "Then play nice."

The two men scoffed.

"Now I'd love to stay and referee, but I've got a date."

"A date!" the men said in unison.

"Yes, with Huntsville Hospital. It's time for C.C. to make an appearance."

Cherlyn was a medical student at Howard University. In her spare time at home, she volunteered at various hospitals' children's wards as C.C. the Clown.

She ran upstairs. "I'm going to get ready."

Montgomery recognized the expression on his father's face. Pride as big as ten mountains. He couldn't remember the old man ever looking at him that way.

As usual, he shrugged it off. "Well, can we call a truce long enough to have a late lunch or an early dinner? I'm starving."

Reeves rolled his wheelchair toward the dining room. "You're not starving. Children in Africa are starving. You're just hungry. And to answer your question, yes."

Montgomery prayed for Tilde's rapid return and set about the task of making a couple of turkey sandwiches and nuking some soup.

The sandwich was good. The soup wasn't Sabin's, but it was filling. Sabin. Now why had he thought of her? Before he could explore the notion further, someone knocked on the front door. Two bicycle horn honks from the living room meant his sister would answer it.

Lucian wiped his hands again, but it didn't do any good. They were filthy. And his suit looked as though he'd been rolling on the ground. Of all the times for him to have a flat tire. Unfortunately, he only had an address for Mr. Claiborne. So, he couldn't call to let him know what had happened. Oh, well. He would just have to make . . . his . . . apologies. . . .

He blinked, but it was still there. A clown. He'd never seen a clown up close. "I'm sorry," Lucian said. "I'm looking for Montgomery Claiborne?"

The little clown smiled, and he could see that *she* was motioning him into the house.

He stepped inside and a tall man filled the entryway. "Detective Carvell?"

"Mr. Claiborne." He reached out and shook the man's hand, but his gaze went back to the clown.

"This is my sister, Cherlyn."

The little clown scrunched up her face and put her hands on her hips. A cherry-red tie flapped beneath her chin. Its white polka dots were the size of quarters.

"I'm sorry. What I meant to say is, this is C.C. the Clown."

She smiled, did a little curtsy, then she gave the horn on her belt two quick squeezes.

"Pleased to meet you, too," Lucian said. Those eyes, he thought. In the midst of the paint and make-up, they were shining like beacons.

C.C. the Clown skipped out of the house toward a blue Volkswagen Bug. Lucian wondered how she could manage with the flipper-size shoes she wore.

"As you can probably tell, I had some car trouble. Is there someplace I can clean up?"

"Sure."

Claiborne led him to the bathroom where Lucian scrubbed away most of the grime from his hands. After a few minutes, he came out to where the foyer spilled into a generous intersection of living space.

Lucian liked what he saw. Expansive rooms, minimal furniture, and functional in a feng shui kinda manner.

Nothing extraneous like clusters of photos or still-life paintings as meaningless as their label implies. "Nice place."

Claiborne motioned for him to take a seat in the living room. "It's my father's. He'll be lurking in the background while we talk."

Lucian smiled. "That's fine."

"I appreciate you taking the time to talk with me. I hope you don't think I'm some kind of paranoid kook."

Lucian had met some paranoid kooks in his time. The man in front of him didn't appear to fit that category. "No, Mr. Claiborne, I don't." He took out a small notepad and pen. "So, what's been going on?"

"Well, first of all, call me Montgomery. Secondly, I've experienced enough life-and-death situations recently to star in my own television show."

"How's that?"

"I think *The World's Most Unlucky Man* might generate interesting Nielson Ratings."

Lucian laughed.

"Problem is, I don't think it has anything to do with luck. Someone is out to do me serious harm."

For the next twenty minutes, Lucian listened and took a few notes as Montgomery recounted recent events. From what he could tell, luck may have truly played a part in keeping Montgomery from severe injury.

"Do you have any enemies?"

"No."

"Have you had an argument with someone recently?"

"No."

"These next questions may sound strange, but with the information age, I have to ask them. Have you had an encounter with someone you didn't know?

Maybe you cut someone off in traffic or typed a harsh remark in a chat room. Anything like that?"

"Nothing."

Lucian doodled a big *no* in the middle of the notepad.

"Are you married?"

"No, I'm not."

"Have you recently broken up with someone?"

He waited while Montgomery thought for a minute.

"Yes, but she would never . . ."

Lucian sat forward. "What's her name?"

"Arroya Lampier."

"And her address?"

"3017 South Minor, but she—"

"And, Arroya, is that a-r-o—"

"Look, Detective. Roya would never do anything to hurt me."

"I understand how unsettling it must be to imagine that someone you were once intimate with could hurt you. But the reality is most people in this country are injured by, robbed by, and unfortunately killed by people they know. And surprisingly, people they care about."

Lucian felt his stomach twist a little.

"How is your relationship with your family?"

Did the expression on Montgomery's face change?

"Fine."

"Not fine!"

He turned to see an inky, grunt of a man in a wheelchair enter the room.

"Detective Carvell, this is my father, Reeves Claiborne."

"Don't get up," the elder Claiborne said, trundling over. He extended his hand and Lucian took it. His grip was surprisingly firm.

"Is there something you'd like to add, Mr. Claiborne?"

"Yeah. He and I don't get along worth shit."

"I see, and are you responsible for the mishaps your son has experienced of late?"

"Certainly not. Ever since this stuff started happening, I've been trying to get the boy to protect himself. But, he won't listen to me."

"That's because you're not saying anything I want to hear. And just so we get this straight, I am a grown man. Don't you ever call me *boy* again."

Great, Lucian thought. The way these two were going at it, it was quite possible that the father was responsible in some way. He'd seen enough. While the Claibornes traded potshots, he made a note to probe for family information during another meeting.

"Ahem. Sorry to interrupt, but I'm due for another appointment." He rose.

Montgomery rose with him. "I apologize for the drama."

The gruff old man furrowed his unibrow. "You should. You caused it."

"Good night, Mr. Claiborne," Lucian said, before they could start up again.

"So, what now?" Montgomery asked as they reached the front door.

"Now I look into the incidents. See if there's anything out of the ordinary. Or if there are any similarities." Montgomery opened the door and Lucian stepped into the threshold. "It shouldn't take more than a week. In the meantime, read this." He handed Montgomery a small pamphlet. "This is a list of safety tips. If someone *is* after you, the information in the booklet will help."

They shook hands.

"Thanks again, Detective."

Lucian walked toward his car, trench coat swaying behind him. "I'll be in touch."

"Thirty-four, thirty-five, thirty-s—" Montgomery barely heard the phone over his own breathing. He released the chin bar and marched over to where it was ringing on the small table. He grabbed the receiver.

"Yeah?" he said.

"Big Boss Man! Wasuuuuuuuuuup!"

Montgomery chuckled as Randy Ford, his resident manager, used a greeting from an old television commercial.

"You tell me," he responded.

"Ah, you know. I'm holdin' it down. Colonel Maxwell sent some soldiers to get the uniforms in Unit 35. Guess they didn't need them, after all. They're going to army surplus now."

Montgomery took a seat. "Good, what does that free up? A ten-by-twenty-five?"

"Ten-by-thirty. But that's not why I called."

"Oh?"

"This might be my only time to gloat that Dolomite got knocked on his boo-tay."

Montgomery fought off a laugh. "You don't like your job, do you?"

"Are you kiddin'? I love my job, especially now that the boss is away."

"You just make sure everything runs like a thief from five-oh until I get back."

"No probs, Big Boss Man. No probs. Just do me one favor."

"What's that?"

"Call off Angie, man. She's is gettin' on ma *last* nerve."

"Look, Angie is good people. And she's also your boss. Besides, I'll be back on Monday."

"Dang. Forget what I said about Angie. You ain't gotta rush back here."

"I'm coming back on Monday. So enjoy your freedom while you can."

"Ah-ite, man. Later."

"Later."

Montgomery hung up the phone remembering the first time he saw Randy. He and Ted Johnson had been unloading office furniture. One of the desks was solid oak and fit for a king. At first, he and Ted thought they could carry it themselves. Montgomery had just gotten started in the business and dollies were next on his list of equipment to purchase.

At the moment when he thought he and Ted were going to drop the desk, Randy dashed in between them. The three of them carried the desk off the truck and safely into the storage area.

After talking for a few moments, he discovered that the kid was looking for a job. Montgomery wasn't in a position to hire anyone else right away, but the kid was persistent. He agreed to work for free until Montgomery could afford to pay him.

Turned out the boy was a runaway. Over the years, Montgomery assumed the role of mentor as best he could, attempting to guide him in the right direction. And Randy had stayed with the company when others had come and gone. Now he was second in command at the warehouse with Ted as his assistant. And just like his boss, he ran a tight ship. Montgomery trusted him implicitly.

Although the call had disturbed his workout, he wasn't too disappointed. Feeling almost one hundred percent now, he trotted up the stairs and headed for the shower. He had a gift to buy and now was as good a time as any.

When Montgomery approached Sabin in the backyard, she was trying to slow her breathing, and it was hard. In addition to running through the house and dashing outside, she had a sneaking suspicion about what he was up to, and it made her jittery.

For a large man, he walks quite softly, she thought, keeping her head down. Before charging outside, she had grabbed some garden tools and gloves from the back porch. She hoped she looked convincing.

He cleared his throat. She kept working—displacing weeds that had grown close to the house.

"How about a truce?"

She looked up.

He smiled. "We could agree to disagree."

Sabin stopped pruning. "You kicked me out of your house, Montgomery."

"We were talking about something that I've committed part of my life to. Sometimes I—"

"Apology accepted," she responded. "Now, what do you want?" She thought she saw him bristle but wasn't sure.

"I have a peace offering."

"Really?" she asked, swatting at a fly.

"I'll be right back."

I knew it! she thought. When she had followed him this morning, she was surprised when he drove into Motorcycle Plaza. When he hooked the bike trailer up to his car, she had dared to hope. And now . . .

"I can't express in words how awful I feel about the accident. But maybe I can show you."

Sabin rose and wavered a bit. Her heart beat a bass rhythm in her chest as she stared at the shiny, new motorcycle. It was a Harley, but not just any Harley. This was a *Fat Boy*.

"I wasn't sure what kind you rode, but the guy at the shop said that this was one of the best."

One of the best? she thought. This machine was every rider's dream. She had plans to buy one day. But now . . .

She moved toward it, stunned. No one had ever given her a gift like this. She was about to speak, when something unfamiliar happened. She felt her eyes forming tears. She hadn't cried since she was ten. And she wasn't about to do it now.

She strode up to the bright chrome-and-maroon machine, her fingers slow dragging across the smooth cool surface of the metal. Her stomach tightened.

"I can't accept this."

Montgomery frowned. "W-what?"

"I appreciate the gesture," she said, stepping back, "but I couldn't possibly . . ."

She looked up from the Harley. The light in Montgomery's eyes had dimmed, and his smile flattened into a tight line.

"This is more than a *gesture*. This is a motorcycle. And it's the least I can do since I'm responsible for totaling your other one."

Revulsion replaced Sabin's initial excitement. *A bike! A Fat Boy! How could she accept something like that?* The notion centered her thoughts on the real reason she couldn't accept the bike. Earlier, she had been ready to go loping into his arms to thank him. She wasn't often on the receiving end of gifts or, for that matter, the giving end. When she watched him leaving the motorcycle shop, her smile was as broad as Michael Clark Duncan's shoulders. But just like the incident in his office, developing feelings of appreciation for Montgomery's actions might compromise her mission.

"Thank you for being considerate—really, really considerate—but the answer is still no."

"Did I get the wrong model?"

"No, the model's fine."

He rubbed his chin. "So, what are you going to do for transportation?"

Sabin's head throbbed. She wasn't sure if it was from the conversation, or the fact that his nearness always made some part of her body pulse. "I'll probably rent a car for a while." She didn't dare tell him that she had already rented a car and it was parked on the dirt road behind his house.

"You're sure?"

"I'm positive."

Montgomery wheeled the vehicle back to his garage. Sabin returned to where she had actually started making progress ridding the side of her house of weeds.

"Hey, Sabin!"

She turned to where he stood, hand on the garage door. "You know anyone that wants to *buy* a bike?"

With the money she was being paid, maybe she could . . . splurge.

"Whoa! Wh-oa!" Montgomery held tightly to Sabin's waist as a line of trees whizzed by on his right and oncoming traffic streaked past on his left.

"Hang on!" she insisted, twisting the throttle. The motorcycle sailed into third gear and the two vroomed down the expressway on Sabin's newest purchase.

Big mistake, he thought, gripping close. When she invited him for a ride, he hadn't wanted to admit that he'd never been on a motorcycle. He'd imagined that it couldn't be much different from riding a big bicycle. He was wrong.

As they took a corner, his heartbeat increased with their speed. Sabin's thrill-heightened voice blared through the speakers in his helmet.

"Lean!" she insisted.

He did as he was told. When he'd purchased the high-tech accessories, he hadn't envisioned himself using them. He wanted to talk, to tell her to stop, or at least slow down. But to use the built-in microphone, he would have to press a button on the side of his headgear. And right now, neither several million dollars nor industrial vice grips could pry his hands from Sabin's midsection.

"You okay?"

Montgomery hoped she could feel him nodding.

"You haven't been this quiet since we met."

He shrugged.

"Woo!" she hollered as they took a hill like she'd created it. "As soon as we get to the top, I'm going to punch it and she what he can really do!"

Montgomery's stomach flopped like Marmaduke on a couch.

At least he could breathe regularly now. At first, the air came rushing into his nostrils so quickly, he thought he would choke on it.

They were probably going sixty or so miles per hour, only it felt more like one hundred. The two whirred by cars, people, and trees with such velocity, he wondered how Sabin discerned the road ahead of them.

They reached the top of the hill, and Montgomery's apprehension solidified into a golf-ball-size lump in his throat.

"Here we go!" his thrill-seeking chauffeur called.

And there was a moment. Fleeting at best. But there was a moment when he could have sworn that they left the ground. And not just left the ground but hovered silently above it. *I believe I can fly,* he thought, and something he didn't understand made him hold on to Sabin tighter. Not because he was concerned he might fall, but because he wanted her near him—this daredevil, this modern-day Bessie Coleman. He wanted her near.

And then the notion was gone, and the revving sounds of the cycle's motor muffled his thoughts. He smiled. Maybe he would go motorcycle riding again one day. Just not anytime soon.

> *Kai,*
> *I hate this assignment. I can't maintain my distance. And when I get close, it's always too close. Like today, we went riding. I could tell he'd never been on a motorcycle before, but he put up a bold façade. I told myself that going riding was a means of keeping an eye on him. And in a way, that's true. But the greater truth is that in this business, intimacies are dangerous. And I was as thrilled by his nearness and the press of his inner thighs against my backside as we went flying down that hill. I can't deny that along with practicing shito, a move that can break a man's leg in three places, I'm anticipating smiles, touches, and the next time I'm within smelling distance of the man for whom I become a dark angel.*
> *S.*

Sabin closed her journal and knew that what she was feeling was wrong. Connections to others were not just risky, but messy liabilities that caused confusion and great pain. Not even her years of mental and emotional training could stop the opening she sensed. Gently, quietly, Montgomery Claiborne had unlatched an area of her heart that she thought long irrecoverable.

The den of the house contained several small teak-wood tables. Candles stood at attention on each like lonely soldiers from a forgotten war. One by one Sabin lit the wax watchmen then approached the center of the room. Her headache from earlier that day hadn't gone away. She hoped a slow meditation would work its healing on her aching temples.

She stood loose and limber, ridding her body muscle by muscle of all tension. Then focusing on the largest candle in the room, she opened herself for a mantra that would order her thoughts and clarify her direction. Begrudgingly, she relented to the only thought that would enter—Montgomery, Montgomery.

When the world changes, become the world.

—Toda Kai

Seven

Montgomery wasn't having much luck. He had been to Web site after Web site and was still unable to find the kind of suit that he liked. As the CycleCity homepage downloaded to his hard drive, he knew that he had again surfed onto the wrong site.

Just like the others, the models on this page looked more like superheroes than bikers. The bold, multicolored outfits were far beyond his tastes. *Do people actually wear these?* he wondered as the last of the image materialized and Montgomery stared at a couple in a pose just shy of a romance cover clinch. The models looked like something out of *Lost in Space* with leather body suits dyed red and white with black lightning bolts striking down the sides of skin-snug pants.

Sometimes it was a trade-off. The loud colors were replaced by one-color leathers with numerous teethlike zippers in strategic and sometimes unique places. When he saw the fifteen-hundred-dollar Bad Ass Bones Suit, his jaw nearly unhinged. The leather unigear was white with a black full-body skeleton painted on the front.

The matching anatomical gloves were two-hundred dollars extra.

He clicked back to the search engine determined to find something. The ride he had shared with Sabin would probably not become a regular occurrence. That might turn his stomach into Silly Putty. But he resolved to do it again, and perhaps again. And he would not be made out a wimp or an inexperienced geek. Maybe if he looked the part, he'd feel the part.

He selected ChopperShoppers and hoped that this time he wasn't treated to generous helpings of jackets and pants that looked as if they had been dipped in five colors of paint. The page did its slow dissolve onto the screen, and so far so good. There were no pictures on the opening page. Just the name ChopperShoppers in big, bold letters. In the left panel, navy blue letters arranged to look like tire tracks detailed the web's contents. Tops. Bottoms. Suits. Gloves. Boots. Leather Cleaners. Accessories. He chose Tops.

It took a few moments and then five pictures displayed showcasing ChopperShoppers' finest. The first jacket was a brown, rawhide-looking leather. It might have been passable if not for the long fringe hanging from the sleeves. The one beside it wasn't much better with silver studs shot into the fabric like bolts in a girder. *Too riveting,* he laughed. *Let's try the suits,* he mused, clicking on another of the tire-tread selections. The page touted new colors. Montgomery knew he was in trouble. The first three suits that appeared were in Harley orange, magenta, and neon green respectively. *I give up,* he thought, scrolling to the bottom of the page. And then he saw it. He drew closer to the screen to make sure that he was seeing it clearly. He clicked on the picture to enlarge the image. *Yes,* he thought, getting his credit card ready, *this is more my style.*

The set was all black—a jacket and pants that looked more like a pilot's outfit than something off of the World Wrestling Federation. He scrutinized the details. He wanted to make sure there weren't any dragons or tigers emblazoned on the back like so many others he'd seen. The only detailing came in the form of two large pockets on the front with thin silver zippers across the top. The description boasted one hundred percent waterproof and quilt-lined. He ordered an extra-large.

The phone rang as Montgomery shut down his computer. Wanting to go for a long walk, he was tempted to let the answering machine get it. After the third ring, he picked up.

"Yeah."

"Monty!"

"Henry," he said. He hadn't heard from Henry Bijan in weeks. "To what do I owe—"

"The honor of my call!"

"Yes."

"I heard you were beneath the weather!"

Henry was Nigerian, effervescently happy, and notorious for ruining American colloquialisms. He was most known for Triage, a new moving company. Recently, he had been trying to convince Montgomery that they should become partners.

"I'm feeling much better, thanks."

"That is good! Do you need something? I could bring you something. Aspirin or Vicks Rub?"

"No, thank you. I'll manage."

"Yes. You always do. Well! I won't hold you then! I just wonder if you've changed your mind."

"No, Henry. I haven't, and I won't."

"Oh-ho-ho-ho-ho." Henry laughed like Santa Claus.

And it seemed to Montgomery that he always laughed at the wrong time.

"Mr. Secure Storage, I think you will change your mind. Ho, ho, ho."

"What I told you before still stands, man. We might be able to do business if my guys get overbooked. But I don't really see that happening too often."

"So, you are saying you are that good."

Montgomery thought about it. He had conducted benchmarking for best practices in his area, but quite often, it was his company that was benchmarked. They had won several industry awards and he was even presenting one at this year's conference. He didn't think there was a better staff in the business. "Yes, that's what I'm saying."

"Ho, ho, *ho!* Then I will leave you with your superiority!"

"If that's how you want it—"

It was too late. Henry had hung up.

Montgomery had heard of persistence, but that man was hound city. They both had thriving businesses. He didn't understand why it was so important to Henry that their companies merge. It was true; their lines of work were compatible. Maybe in the future it would be profitable to build an alliance such as the one he proposed. But right now, Montgomery was comfortable with the way things were. He stuffed his feet into a pair of hiking boots thinking that he was going to have a serious talk with Angie or Randy or whoever it was that gave Henry his home phone number.

Stretching, he rose from the dining room table where the product of his *rest* lay strewn across the cherry wood surface. Since he couldn't go to the office, he brought the office to him. Earlier that day he had called Angie and had her fax three months of

pending files to him. The records were filled with the
names, phone numbers, and referral information of
people who had called to get quotes. They kept detailed information on individuals who contacted Secure Storage. The tracking system showed that people
who called became customers twenty percent of the
time; however, people who called and came in to see
the facility became customers eighty-five percent of the
time. Roxanne Scales, the sales assistant, typically
made the callbacks to all those who had not come in
to see the facility. But since he was laid up, Montgomery decided to take on that task. It gave him something to do besides watch the idiot box.

He grabbed his walking stick from its holder near
the front door, thinking he was getting too involved
with work again. It always happened when he was
forced to deal with himself. The cold reality was that
he didn't much care for being alone, but he wasn't
one for jumping in and out of relationships, either.
And the times when he wasn't in a relationship, he
threw himself into his work. Unfortunately that always
worked to his detriment, because by immersing himself, he closed himself off from the real world and any
potential companionship that might be waiting there.

Recently his only solace had come in the form of
periodic excursions to the Blue Ridge Mountains in
western Maryland. Five years ago he had visited there,
and on a whim had gone cliff diving with a group of
vacationers at a resort. The effect was so profound
that he had taken up the activity as a way to detox
from the stress and demands of running a business.
He had planned to go diving a month ago, but he'd
won the Pentagon contract. *Maybe it's time to dust off
those plans,* he thought, stepping outside.

Sometimes Montgomery would walk and let the
sounds of nature guide him. The caw of a blue jay

would usher him leisurely down a brambled path. The rustling of leaves would escort him to the edge of an embankment. The babble of a brook would lure him toward a clearing. Or silence would summon him onward or stop him to shallow breath. But not today. Today he wanted the blood-surging sound of the blues to be his walking companion. He clipped the portable CD player to his belt, set the headphones on his head, and started out.

His footsteps matched the tempo of Kenny Neal's Louisiana playing, beat for beat. Yep, "Blues Fallin' Down Like Rain!"

Montgomery had always fancied himself a blues man. He couldn't write music or play an instrument, but he could carry a fairly decent tune. And if he hadn't gone into the storage business, he would have loved to be in a band—traveling the States, playing small, smoke-filled juke joints. Too many times to count, he had imagined himself on a ramshackle tour bus, eating at greasy spoons, sleeping with loose women or whatever groupies refused to go home, and changing the alternator or busted motor part du jour.

But then he would take a look at his home. He had all the creature comforts anyone could imagine—designer furniture, satellite TV, and a big screen to watch it on, not to mention his Jag. And when he got tired of that, there was a Chevy pickup in his garage. He wondered if he could really forgo what he had for life on the road—not to mention what his father would say.

Montgomery wandered down a familiar path thinking the trees in Maryland were wondrous in early summer. Strong, sturdy maples, oaks, and hickories stood as straight as soldiers, their thick branches held out like arms demanding attention or maybe just respect. These trees had been here longer than most people on earth had been alive. He touched a few of them in awe of their antiquity.

He widened his strides to accommodate a change in song rhythm. "Shadow on the Moon" was a full-textured, bayou ballad that featured the vocalist's dexterity in raw earthy growls and smooth changes.

Sunlight, seeping through tree leaves like misty golden planks, surrounded him. Its warmth created prisms in the sky and a whisper of sweat on his arms and neck.

He huffed in tune. At the instrumental bridge, he made up his own words.

"Too late ta be sad now, woman.
I ain't comin' back no time soon.
Think whatcha had now woman.
Just a shadow on the moon."

He was no B.B. King, but he could probably pass for a green Robert Cray.

Although the song called for a softer pace, Montgomery walked briskly through the wooded area. He was eager to get to the overlook. It was a place on the edge of the forest where he could see all the way to D.C. Since most of his neighbors were working today, he hoped to have the scenic view to himself. If he had been interested in photography, he could have taken panoramic pictures each time he came. The juxtaposition of nature and concrete jungle might have made for a unique subject. But his interests lay more in the mental and emotional pictures his mind could take—the immediacy of being there, and the pure and simple beauty of nature.

Montgomery could smell the hickory, almost as if it were roasting in his fireplace. It was a broad energetic aroma that reminded him that he hadn't eaten breakfast and made him yearn for fresh ground sausage and thick country pancakes.

He pushed repeat on the CD player. *One more time, my man,* he thought, heading toward the overlook. He was eager now to shift his perspective. For too many days he had been introspective, brooding even. He refused to let paranoia take over.

Charging uphill, arms pumping, he moved toward what he needed. A stark reminder that he was part of a larger reality of nature's expanse of hills and valleys, and that perhaps he was just a shadow on the moon. In the grand scheme of things, the recent events of his life were like shadows on the moon.

"Big girl, be changin' her tune
Like a shadow on the mo-on
Big girl be—"

He came to the summit and saw the distant horizon rise to meet him. The view thrilled him. Then the earth moved.

At first, he thought he had merely lost his footing—tripped up by swift guitar licks and backwoods drums. Then he realized that it wasn't his feet but the ground that had given way. An avalanche of soil crumbled beneath him and fell down the cliffside like so much dust. Like an amusement park ride he had once been on as a teenager, the bottom dropped from under him and he knew his number was up.

Unlike in the movies, when they say your whole life passes in front of you, Montgomery's life drifted by in a slothful fox-trot. But it was the life he *wouldn't* have. No reconciliation with his father. No whistling from the audience as his little sister walked across the graduation stage. No more exhilarating thuds as linebackers collided on Monday-night football. No more delirious sinking into the space between Arroya's thighs. And no more arguments with psycho Sabin.

His back smacked into the ground and slid downward. His legs dangled for a moment then plunged off the edge of the embankment. He grabbed at shrubs and nearby bushes. Instead of slowing his descent, they ripped from the ground in clumps of dirt-packed roots.

The Fates have won, he thought as his body slid forward like a Jamaican bobsled toward the boulders below. He closed his eyes and hoped that his next sight would be his mother's childlike face.

If someone had asked Sabin to describe her actions while saving Montgomery Claiborne's life for yet a third time, she wouldn't have been able to do it. She would remember tracking him. And almost giving herself away by snickering at his singing. She might even remember liking the way his thick legs carried him to the top of the overlook. But when the earth collapsed beneath him, fear drew icy lines down the center of her veins and white-hot instinct took her over.

The possibility of Montgomery dying would obscure the memory of her running to where long tracks made by his fingers stopped at the edge of the cliff. Her need to get to him would block out her hands grabbing his wrists. And fear that she was too late would prevent her from ever recalling the way she dug her heels deep into the shifting edge of the embankment and pulled like a Mack truck.

Her body surged with adrenaline. Her breaths came in ragged gulps. She leaned against a tree, hands trembling. Montgomery lay expended beside her, heaving for air, as well. His clothes were smeared brown with loose dirt.

"W-where did you come f-from?" he asked, sitting slowly.

"I was taking—taking a walk." Her words echoed loudly in her head. It took several minutes for her body's state of red alert to power down.

She has to believe I'm some kind of mollycoddle. Rescuing me like I'm a damsel in distress. And what had she seen, he wondered. Him giving in? Hell, he'd been ready to meet his Maker. Not good, not good.

"Are you all right?" she asked, taking his arm.

He pulled away. "I'm fine."

She watched him stand. Her mouth cocked with displeasure. "Are you sure you're fine? 'Cause just a few minutes ago your ass was hanging over a cliff." Sabin stood.

Here we go again. "Yes, well," he said, brushing soil and grass from his clothes, "I'm grateful f—"

"Grateful!" She crossed her arms and looked him up and down. "You outa be kissing my feet right about now."

He looked down. Her *feet* were in those Chuck Taylor tennis shoes again. *What kind of woman wears Chuck Taylors?* "Not even if you saved me three more times."

"All I expect is a simple thank-you."

"For swooping in like you're some superhero?"

"That's supershe-ro to you, ya biscuit."

"You're right." He smiled. "You'd make a great Hell Spawn."

Her gaze was rank. He could all but see angry smoke rising from the top of her beautiful head.

"I'd better go," she said, "before I put you back where I found you."

Montgomery watched as she headed down the trail. The tight black leather suit she wore reminded him of Eartha Kitt on *Batman*. Despite himself, his eyes settled on the turbulent roll of her backside as she marched away. *Did she call me biscuit?*

Montgomery tossed the remains of his CD and player into the trash. Then he picked up the can and flung it at the wall. He knew no amount of iron pumping would ease his frustration. He was being attacked from all sides. Now even the environment acted against him. He had walked that trail for years. He knew it was tricky, the way bushes and low branches obscured the path. The edge of the hill almost popped out of nowhere. But he'd never known anything to cause the ground to give way like that. Even after torrential rains.

Something wasn't right.

Hurrying, he grabbed a tape measure from his toolbox and rushed back to the overlook.

This time he took the path carefully. He stopped two feet short of where he had fallen. Grabbing on to a large oak, he stamped a foot on the ground. After a few hearty stomps, he jumped up and down, careful not to lose contact with the tree. Nothing. No crumbling. No falling away. Just clouds of dirt that settled mostly on his boots. Taking hold of one of the tree's thick branches, he inched to the edge, stamping and stomping as he went. Still nothing shook loose except a beetle that crawled out from under a fallen leaf.

"I'll be damned."

He used his tape measure to gauge how much of the cliff was missing. Just about four feet from what he could tell. Stepping back to look fully, he saw that the end of the embankment cut fairly straight across. Not jagged or ripped as is customary of Mother Nature's handiwork. Someone, he reasoned, took on a lot of trouble to shorten his favorite trail. *If it weren't for Sabin,* he mused, taking a dizzying look down, *my sorry carcass would have crashed into those rocks.*

> *Kai,*
> *As if he hadn't had enough the first time, the idiot went back again. I think he was trying to see how strong the edge is now. At first I merely disliked this job. Now I hate it. But a new life in Ghana. That's well worth a few cardio workouts.*
> *S.*

When Montgomery returned home, he flipped through his Rolodex for Detective Carvell's number. Here was something else for Carvell to add to his list, he thought, dialing the number. And oh, by the way, would he send some plainclothes guys over here for 'round-the-clock surveillance? This was getting ridiculous. He groaned when the officer's voice mail answered.

"Hello. You've reached Detective Carvell of the Golden Creek Police Department. I'm sorry I'm un—"

"I'm sorry, too," Montgomery said, hanging up the phone. He refused to come across like an impotent clod. Besides, he didn't actually expect the police to be much help. He knew it had only been a few days, but he'd hoped that by now he would have heard something regarding his suspicions. But as usual, the only person he could really count on was himself. And if the lunatic plotting against him was going to be stopped, then Montgomery was going to have to do the stopping. As he picked up the strewn trash on the floor, he decided that he would turn over every rock and hiding place until he found the person or persons responsible for these attempts on his life. Then he would make sure they were brought to justice or maybe . . . just to their knees.

Every man has an answer.

—Toda Kai

Eight

Montgomery walked out of the bookstore, tearing the cellophane from his newest purchase. Discarding the plastic in a trash receptacle, he made his way to his Jag and slid into the driver's seat. He turned on the engine and placed the CD into the player on the dash. He briefly considered Sabin, then chased the thought away. No way was he going to wus out and ask her for help.

While on the way to his first appointment at Loft Building Maintenance in his office building, he listened raptly to L. Pike's audiobook *P.I. 101—A Do-It-Yourself Guide*. The reference manual, read by the author, provided instructions to anyone interested in conducting private investigations. As per a list in chapter one, Montgomery stopped at an office supply store and purchased a notebook, a digital camera, a tape recorder, ten floppy disks, and ten blank cassettes. At Burman's Executive Hides he picked up a medium-size leather duffel bag to keep everything in.

From what he could tell, quite a bit of the text focused on ways to dig up personal information on people. There were some gems of discovery provided, as well.

"Get comfortable with the concepts of objectivity, detachment, and impartiality. These are an investigator's greatest tools. Even if you are on the trail of a loved one, such as a spouse or a child, emotions will taint your judgment and possibly prevent you from seeing the most obvious piece of evidence simply because feelings often make people distort what they see."

Montgomery couldn't imagine being more emotionally involved in what he was doing. It was, after all, his life. As the author gave tips on how to obtain government, financial, and criminal records on family and friends, Montgomery focused on the road and tried to come up with ways he could divorce himself from his pathos and render an unbiased examination of the facts as he uncovered them. Not sure he could do it, but nonetheless determined to try, he pulled his car into his parking space.

Instead of tracking to the left as he usually did upon entering the building, Montgomery took the long hall all the way to the back to the building office.

The glass front of the office displayed LBM in large gold letters. Through the see through front, Montgomery could see a receptionist's desk, printer table, small printer, white walls, and a large round clock. The brass trim gave it the character of a giant's pocket watch.

He stepped inside and walked past the place where he made his monthly lease payments.

"Morning, Mr. Claiborne," the receptionist said mechanically.

"Morning, Sue."

The last room in the back belonged to Hershall Meyer, the commercial property manager. He was in charge of the retail and office properties. He made sure that the tenants were happy as beavers, and they in turn paid some of the most expensive lease rates in Market City. But it was worth it. The amenities were outstanding. Those willing to pay the higher prices tended to make for better clientele, and you couldn't beat the location.

When he entered the office, Hershall was in his usual position at his desk, bent over a stack of papers.

"You sure you want to do this?" he asked without looking up.

"Yes," Montgomery responded.

"All right, let's go."

Before walking through the massive glass doors, Meyer leaned over Sue's desk. "Sue, page Ronnie. Have him meet us on the tenth floor."

"Yes, sir," she responded, as they walked out into the corridor.

Montgomery frowned. "I thought there were only nine floors in this building."

"The tenth floor only runs half the length of the building. We use it primarily for storage and elevator maintenance."

As they rounded a corner, Hershall walked through the lobby and down the hall to one of the two service elevators. He used a key to gain access and up they went.

The doors opened on the tenth floor and Montgomery was surprised. He expected dark and gloomy shadows. What he found was a well-lit open area with a door at one end and three elevators directly across from it. He opened his portfolio and took out the camera, notebook, and a pencil.

The ceiling hung low and Montgomery's head was only about a foot from the top. He resisted an urge to bend slightly. The whole area looked relatively clean.

A ding sounded the arrival of the other freight car. A man Montgomery only knew as Ronnie stepped out of the opening doors and joined them in the corridor. Montgomery shook hands with him, noting that he already looked grimy with work. Dirt beneath his fingernails, dust smeared on blue work pants, and what could easily pass for oil spots on a navy-and-white shirt told Montgomery that whatever Ronnie had been doing, grime and filth had played a prominent role.

"So what's on your mind?" the building manager asked. "I feel like my building has suddenly decided that it doesn't like you."

Montgomery adjusted his portfolio. "Well, I'm just here to see if I can get a better handle on what happened. I'd like to take a few pictures, visit with the equipment up close and personal, and then review your maintenance records."

"No problem . . . Ronnie."

The grungy-looking man took a tool that Montgomery was unfamiliar with and opened the doors to one of the elevator shafts. "This is the one that went haywire when you were on it." He leaned in. "You can see the gears and motors from here."

Montgomery gritted his teeth. Besides the machine that almost killed him, he had no idea what he was looking at. "What keeps the elevators from flying up or down out of control?"

"Counterweights. A long time ago, cars were balanced by a series of gears, pulleys, and levers. Now most of that's computerized. So there's a signal sent to the weights telling them to engage so that the elevator can go up smoothly."

"Where are they?"

"There," Ronnie said.

Montgomery leaned in and saw where the young man pointed to large black objects suspended above them. He turned on the camera's flash and snapped several pictures.

"What would cause the signal to fail?"

"Any run-of-the-mill computer glitch."

"So other than that, the weights should work fine."

"That's right. The only other time they don't work is when we're testing."

Montgomery remembered the memos he received every other year from the building office notifying him that the elevators were being tested. Even with the memos, the sound of the elevators crashing would always catch him off guard. He switched from the camera to the pad and pencil. "Tell me about that."

"The tests?"

"Yes."

Hershall chimed in this time. "We do regular tests to make sure the brakes work in case of emergency. So we'll drop the elevators or let them rise to the top without the counterbalance."

"When was the last time you did that?"

"About six months ago."

"And how often do computer glitches like the one I experienced happen?"

The two men looked at each other. "Never," they said.

"Never?"

"This is the first time I've ever heard of anything like this happening. So right after we found out that you were okay, we took the elevator down for maintenance. We decided it had to be a ghost."

"A what?" he asked, and stopped writing. He looked at the two men to see if they were pulling his leg.

"A ghost. Elevators do strange things that sometimes can't be explained. They stop on floors when there's no call. They pass by floors they should stop on. They go up when the light says they're supposed to go down."

"Stuff like this is pretty standard. So, a lot of maintenance guys chalk this stuff up to the ghost in the machine."

Montgomery listened. Whoever caused his incident was no ghost.

They went to the basement next. Montgomery wanted to see for himself what landed him in the hospital. Ronnie escorted him to a locked utility room.

"Here's where we keep the maintenance chemicals now." He opened the door and they stepped in. "We really didn't have a special protocol for locking things up until after what happened to you."

Shelves of cleaners, mops, buckets, and gardening tools lined the narrow room. "Is this it?" Montgomery asked, picking up a large plastic bottle labeled Green Grow.

"Yes."

Montgomery replaced the bottle and took pictures of it. He took a close-up of the ingredients and wrote down the name of the product in his notebook.

"Where did it spill?"

"Right over here," Hershall said.

The dry thick heat of the cellar pressed against Montgomery as he joined the stocky man at a large furnace. He could tell they were standing directly under his office.

"This is only the top of the furnace. The rest of it extends to a maintenance level one floor down."

Montgomery walked around the furnace, examining, taking notes.

"From what we can tell, the bottle was tipped over, probably by a varmint, and then seeped into the internal part of the heater. After that, it's fume city and lights out Mr. Claiborne."

After taking several pictures, Montgomery grabbed his notebook again. "You said 'we,' Ronnie. Who's we?"

"Well, myself and Chandi Stewart. He works nights and is pretty much in charge of the world down here."

"I'd like to talk to him also."

"Sure. If you stop by anytime around ten, he should be here."

"Will do."

The two were wrapping up the tour of the Saunders Lofts basement when a twinge of curiosity hit Montgomery. "Hershall, did the police talk to Mr. Stewart?"

Hershall frowned and paused. "No. I don't think they did."

He wrote a few more notes, snapped a few more pictures, then headed back with the men to the building office.

Once there, he sat down with Hershall and poured through the report of the malfunction, as well as documents on file certifying the condition of the elevators. Whoever it was covered his tracks thoroughly. Montgomery was satisfied with the information he'd collected.

He rose and shook the older man's hand. "Thanks, Hershall. I appreciate you letting me check out everything."

"I'm just glad you're all in one piece to do it."

Montgomery walked to the office door and paused. "Hershall, how many people have keys to the service elevator?"

"Just me, Ronnie, and Tyler, the other maintenance guy."

"And if someone had programmed the computer

for a test without your knowledge, is there any way to trace that?"

"Every test we do creates an automatic diagnostic report. If someone was savvy enough to program an unscheduled test, I suppose they'd be able to prevent any record of it in the logs."

"Thanks," Montgomery said, and headed out.

His next stop was the Federal Building, where the incident with the scaffolding occurred. The audiobook's information about grounders, shake cards, and freelance enforcers kept him company until he arrived.

After what seemed like much confusion and incompetence, the man at the information desk finally located someone for Montgomery to talk to. The person was Albert Wingate. He'd worked as a custodial engineer for the government for over thirty years, or so the information officer told Montgomery three times before they reached his work area.

Montgomery took a seat opposite the man that looked like a black Yosemite Sam—short, bow-legged, and hairy. The man's office was a disaster of paper. There were more stacks of files, letters, and reports than Montgomery had ever seen in one place. Obviously this man hated paperwork as much as he did.

"They call me ToolBelt."

"Nice to meet you." Montgomery guesstimated the man's age at about seventy.

"When they call me special for somebody, it means they didn't know what to do with you."

Montgomery laughed. What he was asking was a bit out of the ordinary.

"Well whoever *they* are, I'm sure they didn't. You see . . ."

"You're the one what dang near got his noggin' lanked off."

Smiling, Montgomery took out his notepad and pencil. "How do you know that?"

"Oh, I never forget a face. Especially one as full of shock as yours when that plank busted beside ya."

He remembered a feeling of paranoia and dread that day, right before he'd gone inside the building. And when the board fell, it was like a dark premonition made real. "That's what I'd like to talk about, actually. I remember being told that it was an accident. I'm not so sure that's true."

Yosemite leaned back in his chair, whiskers twitching. "You think somebody tried to punch your clock on purpose?"

"Yeah."

Every woman is a question.

—Toda Kai

Nine

Sabin wrapped her peace offering in gold-and-white paper. She even stuck an ivory bow on it to make it look like a real present. Though she hadn't been planning to give him the jacket so early, she told herself she was doing it because things had changed. The stakes were higher, and the more time she could spend with him, the better. It also occurred to her that since she was being paid for her services, Montgomery didn't owe her a thank you at all.

And she reminded herself that it had nothing to do with the woman at his house for the seventh time in eight days. When he was recovering from the gas inhalation, she could understand having a friend help out. But he was probably one hundred percent now, and the thought of that woman over there again needled her like pins in a cushion. *And besides,* she thought, locking her door behind her, *the woman just looks too intentional.*

Sabin rang Montgomery's doorbell and waited. *It's taking too long. What could they be doing?*

When Montgomery opened the door, he was smiling. When he saw that it was her, his smile faded.

"So, if it isn't *Storm*. Sorry, I'm fresh out of life-threatening situations."

Sabin was proud of herself. She didn't body-slam him. And she didn't tell him how grateful he should be that he wasn't on *her* hit list. If he had been, his funeral would have taken place three weeks ago. Instead, she smiled tentatively and held out the package. "Truce?"

He stared at the box in her hands. *Damn, Montgomery. For once in your life, give.*

Finally he grunted and stepped aside. "Come in," he said.

He closed the door behind her and she walked determinedly into the living room. The smell of fresh popcorn made her stomach grumble. Then the sight of the woman on the couch made it flop. Most of her hair stood up on top of her head like an elaborate pinwheel, shiny sections gelled and hair sprayed into place like ornaments. Her make-up seemed painstakingly overapplied for that *natural* look.

Sabin thought the woman's bloodred dress was way too tight, and the matching high-heel pumps looked like something out of Frederick's of Hollywood. Sabin's first thought, considering her own sleeveless T-shirt and Capri pants, was *Thank God for Old Navy.*

"Arroya, this is my neighbor Sabin," Montgomery said, taking the gift.

The all-woman spoke first. "Nice to meet you, Sabin."

"Same here."

"Are you the one from the accident?"

Sabin served up a half smile. "Yes, unfortunately."

Arroya's left eyebrow went up. "M, you didn't tell me she lived around here."

Sabin plopped down in the love seat. "M?"

He shrugged his shoulders. "Must have slipped my

mind." He took a seat beside Arroya on the couch and Sabin watched with eagerness.

"I suppose you want me to open this now?"

"That would be nice. Unless I'm interrupting."

"Not really," Arroya said, sounding disappointed. "We're just having a movie marathon."

He ripped the paper off the carefully wrapped box, then looked up. "You're welcome to stay, if you'd like."

Sabin looked at the stack of Blockbuster movies on the floor. There must have been ten or eleven. "What did you rent?"

"The Fugitive, The Pelican Brief, Silence of the Lambs, The Bone Collector, Blow Out, Passenger 57. He even rented *The Maltese Falcon."*

"For some reason, I got the mystery bug, and I—" Montgomery lifted the leather jacket from the box. Sabin watched as his face reflected his approval. She thought the jacket suited him. It was hard leather, and refined. She'd hoped that he would understand her invitation to ride with her again. The nod he gave her told her that he did.

"Sabin, I don't know what to say. I've seen jackets like this before. This must have cost—"

"I'm not worried about that. And you shouldn't be, either. Just promise me you'll put it to good use."

The light in Montgomery's eyes darkened with possibilities. "I promise," he said.

Two hours later, the el grande bowl of buttered popcorn in the middle of the coffee table was nearly empty. After watching *Enemy of the State,* they were debating which movie to put in next.

Arroya pointed a manicured finger in the air. "I say *U.S. Marshals.* It's got action *and* Wesley Snipes. You can't go wrong with that."

"This marathon was my idea. I'm going for the *Maltese Falcon*."

Sabin grimaced. "Don't put in *The Maltese Falcon*, yet. Save the best for last. Your best bet at this point is *Fargo*. We've already had some action. Why not go for the more poignant drama?"

Sabin watched Montgomery size her up. "And what do you know about poignancy, Ms. Hat to the Back?"

Arroya laughed but he didn't. He gave her a warm smile that suggested he might just like her casual ways. "You didn't seem to mind what I was wearing when you were screaming down that hill."

"You have never heard me scream."

She sat forward. "Are you kidding? Ah! Ah! Ahhhhhhh!" She exaggerated. He hadn't been that bad. But he hadn't been silent, either.

"If you *ever* hear me making those kinds of noises," he said retrieving a videotape from the pile, "something else is goin' on."

Sabin smiled as he put *Fargo* into the VCR.

When Montgomery sat down on the couch, Arroya smacked him on the arm. She looked as though she were going to comment and then thought better of it. "I won't even go there," she said.

I would, Sabin thought.

William Macy's face was a tight mixture of panic and awe. He'd just found out that the jig was up. Forty-five minutes into *Fargo*, and Sabin and Montgomery hadn't stopped talking yet. "That's how your face looked when you got off the Big Boy."

"I'm trying to watch the movie. Will you check yourself?"

"That's what I wanted to ask you when the ride was

over. Check yourself. Because I thought maybe you had . . . had . . ."

Laughter consumed them both, and Sabin all but kicked up her feet. Her stomach hurt from laughing so hard. She hadn't had this much fun in a long, long time.

"So I haven't ridden in a while."

"A *while?*" She grabbed her stomach. "I can't take it," she said through her laughter. "Shut up, Montgomery, okay? Just don't say any more."

He reached into the bowl and threw some popcorn at her. She batted away most of it and snickered. "Stop playing. Besides," she said, turning her attention to the movie, "this is the best part. Steve Buscemi gets his jaw shot off."

"Gee, thanks! Just tell us what happens," he snapped with a smile.

"Okay. The part where that one guy puts the wife's body in the wood chipper is really great!"

He threw more popcorn, and Arroya stood.

"I gotta go, M. Walk me to the door."

He frowned at Sabin. "See what you've done," he quipped, following the lady in red. "We'll be good. You don't have to go."

Sabin careened her head so that she could hear them in the vestibule.

"Yes, I do."

"If it's Sabin, I'll ask her to—"

"As a matter of fact, it is Sabin. I don't like her. But obviously you do."

Sabin heard the door open.

"I'll talk to you later."

"Roy-a . . ."

A few seconds later Sabin heard the roar of a car starting and then the creak of the front door closing.

When Montgomery entered the living room, she did her best Steve Urkel impression. "Did I do that?"

His expression was firm. "Yes, you did."

"Well, it takes two to tango, mister."

"I know," he said, returning to the couch.

"I'm sorry," she said. And she was. Her intention was to scope out the woman, not to cause a rift between her and Montgomery.

"I'll call her tomorrow. Roya and I are old friends. We'll work it out."

There was silence as they both settled back into the movie. Then he asked, "Do they really put the wife through a wood chipper?"

Montgomery hadn't seen *Fargo* before. Surprisingly, he liked it. He took the tape out of the VCR. "Good choice," he said. "What's next?"

"Food!" Sabin exclaimed. "What do you have to eat?"

"Just snack stuff. Some soy nuts, pretzels, trail mix, blue corn chips, and some wings."

"Wings?"

"Yeah. I was going to try to talk Arroya into making some hot wings, but—"

"I'll make 'em," Sabin said, getting up.

"That's not necessary."

"Oh, yes, it is. I'm starving!" She put her hands on her hips. *Her favorite pose,* he thought. *Or is it mine?*

"Just give me the nickel orientation to the kitchen then get out of my way."

Montgomery stood. "Even in a domestic capacity, you are still wild. Come on."

He did as she asked and showed her around the kitchen. Then he went back into the living room. "You want me to wait?" he called back.

"No, go ahead. Put in *Silence of the Lambs*. I've seen it already."

He stuck in the tape and settled back on the couch. Before long, Sabin joined him with a tray of delicious-smelling hot wings and a fresh bowl of popcorn.

"I'll get some plates," he said.

"Plates! Here, grab some of these napkins. I'll show you how to eat chicken wings."

"Where did you grow up? Brooklyn? The Bronx?"

"Never mind that," she said, shifting next to him. "Taste."

He took one of the wings from the tray and bit into it. It was juicy, flavorful, and hot! "Mmm," he said, smacking his lips. "Two points!"

"Three," she responded, and bit into one of her own.

"Hold up," Montgomery said. He wiped his hands on a napkin and headed downstairs to the basement. Once there, he retrieved two Michelobs from his bar fridge. Arroya wasn't a beer drinker, but he'd bet the farm that her royal badness was. When he returned, Sabin's eyes grew bright.

"Now, you're talkin'," she said.

He twisted off the caps and handed her a bottle. Just then, he got a good look at the popcorn in the bowl. It was pink.

"What's wrong with the popcorn?" he asked, taking a seat.

"You put too much butter on yours."

Actually, he thought, Roya was the one who always insisted on extra butter. "What do you put on yours?"

"Tabasco."

"Oh, God."

She reached for the bowl. "Don't knock it 'til you've tried it."

Now why did that phrase make him think improper thoughts?

She nuzzled into the seat beside him. "Okay, what have I missed so far?"

Montgomery caught Sabin up on the events of the film. While he talked, she kept her eyes on the television and he kept his eyes on her. He remembered the last time she had been in his house and how he couldn't pry his eyes away from her lips. He was having the same trouble now. And when she sucked on a chicken bone and drew it slowly out of her mouth, he thought he might explode. But nothing prepared him for what she did with her fingers. One by one she licked them until there wasn't a speck of hot wing sauce left. He forced himself to look away and concentrate on the movie.

Sabin reached for the bowl of popcorn and put it in her lap. "You don't know what you're missing."

"Yes I do," he responded.

She nudged him with her elbow. "Just try it."

So far, everything she'd made had been wonderful. But pink popcorn? He reached into the bowl and grabbed a few kernels. He tossed them into his mouth prepared to rebuff a bad taste. He smiled instead.

"Not bad," he said, surprised that it honestly tasted good. The corn absorbed the flavor of the Tabasco in a way that made it taste spicy without being too hot.

Her expression was smug. "Next time you'll trust me."

They turned their attention back to the movie and watched in silence.

Montgomery reached for more popcorn. The back of his hand brushed like a whisper against Sabin's. She withdrew her hand quickly.

"This is the part where he kidnaps a senator's daughter," she said, kicking her shoes off. And then before he could blink, she propped her narrow feet on his coffee table—his one-thousand-dollar coffee table. Hell, he didn't care. She had the loveliest toes he'd ever seen.

His original intent was to create an investigative mind-set. He thought by watching mystery-type movies, he would absorb, perhaps even by osmosis, some of the skills he would need to find out who was behind the attempts on his life. But more importantly, the movies would put him in the mind-set to end the chaos his world had become. What he hadn't planned on was Sabin. Being with her tonight was like being on a date. And he liked that.

As he scooped up more popcorn, he felt Sabin's hand moving against his. She was getting popcorn, too. Or was she? It felt more like a kiss or a dance. Skin to skin. He wanted so badly to hold her hand. But instead, he moved his away.

They watched quietly for a while. Then Sabin announced, "Check this out."

He could tell by the sound of her voice that something important was about to happen. They both sat up a little. Then, in anticipation of a pivotal moment, he went for more popcorn. Sabin did, too. Just then Hannibal Lecter reached between the bars of his cell and stroked Clarice Starling's finger. Montgomery turned to Sabin, who was already looking at him, and smiled. She smiled back. After that, neither of them seemed to be in too big a hurry to remove their hand from the popcorn bowl.

"I wish I could have rented some of the episodes of Peroit. Talk about a top-notch detective," Montgomery announced.

"Peroit! That wet sock? Be for real."

"No, I wouldn't suppose that you would agree with me. Let me guess. You're a feminist, and as a feminist, you'd pick someone like Angela Lansbury."

"Don't make me choke on this popcorn. Of course I'm a feminist."

"I knew it!"

"I don't understand men. You'd think you guys would be grateful that women no longer have you doing things for us that we are capable of doing for ourselves."

"The problem is you women don't know what you want."

"Bull."

"Oh, yeah? Well, from now on, open your own damn doors."

"I've never asked a man to open a door for me."

"No, but I'll bet it snags your nose hairs when we don't."

He considered her silence a victory. "Humph. Thought so. So, tell me . . . who could possibly be a better sleuth than Peroit?"

"Columbo, of course!"

"Columbo? That—that—wrinkled suit? He couldn't detect snow in Antarctica."

Eight hours and four movies later they were still going strong. Debris from various snacking and drinking surges cluttered the coffee table. Sabin searched among the empty beer bottles, chicken bones, and corn kernels for the remote.

Montgomery leaned back against the couch, arms outstretched. Sabin sat forward, watching the screen almost unblinkingly while crunching her second cup of ice. Montgomery watched her lips move. He felt something inside him beginning to unthaw.

"You've heard what they say about women who eat ice?"

"What?" she asked, eyes still on the television.

"That they're sexually frustrated."

Sabin's hand stopped inches from her mouth. Her head turned slowly to him as she resisted the urge to dump the rest of the ice down his shorts.

He could see the ice chips between her fingers beginning to melt. Her eyes hardened as if he had just entered dangerous territory.

"What do you know about it?" she asked, resuming her ice munch.

"I know if you were my woman, you wouldn't need that ice." *Damn.* It came out before he realized he'd said it.

"Why don't you make yourself useful and clear this stuff away while I put in another movie."

"I don't think so," he said, relieved his remark didn't set off another argument. "I have *yet* to pick a flick. And this was my idea."

"And a great one it is," Sabin said, getting up. She strolled over to the VCR and removed *The Fugitive.* After replacing it in its case she picked up *The Pelican Brief.*

"There's not much gore in this one, but the suspense is five-star."

"I say *The Maltese Falcon* is next."

"I told you, *M*, you should save the best for last." She already had the video out of the case and in her hand.

"And I told *you*, the next video is my pick."

Montgomery saw the grimace on her face and huffed. "You are rotten. Everything can't be your way, Sabin. Sometimes you have to—"

When she dropped the movie and doubled over, he

moved without thinking. He was at her side within seconds and holding her in his arms.

"What is it?"

At first, all he heard was the thin moan of distress and the jackhammer of his heart as a result. Then her words came, whisper thin. "My legs, they feel—oh, God!"

The pain in her voice sliced though him. Impulsively he picked her up and laid her on the couch.

Sabin thrashed forward, grabbing her calves. "Cramps!" She shot out, then pounded her fists against the seat cushions.

The anguish on her face twisted his stomach into knots. "I know this is going to sound absurd, but relax." For once, there was no snide comment, no rhetorical remark.

"The more you fight against it, the tighter your muscles coil." Montgomery took two cold Michelob bottles from the table and placed them, one each, behind Sabin's legs. She cried out; he gritted his teeth.

"Hold these in place, and breathe slowly. I'll be right back."

Sabin nodded and replaced Montgomery's large hands with her trembling ones.

When he returned, he saw tiny pearls of sweat resting atop her upper lip. He set a tall glass on the table and filled it with water from a large pitcher.

"I'm going to stretch out your legs and you're going to drink this water," he said, handing her the glass.

"I hate water," she said, eyes murky with pain.

"I'm going to stretch out your legs and you're going to drink this water," he repeated. "All of this water."

Montgomery stood at the end of the couch and slid his palm beneath Sabin's left heel. She drank the water, eyes large and liquid, as he stabilized the ball of her foot and pushed her toes back toward her knee. Then he pulled her ankle toward him.

"Resist, and keep drinking."

Barely blinking, her eyes rested where his hands worked, pulling and pushing with equal force.

"Better?" he asked.

"Yes," she responded, handing him an empty glass.

He filled the glass with more water and handed it back. "Other side," he said, repeating the same treatment on her right leg. He watched as the scowl that had become Sabin's face slowly dissolved into the beautiful features he'd become so fond of.

"Better?" he asked again.

"Much," she said, sitting up.

He thrust up his hand. "No, don't move or the cramps might come back. You have to give your muscles time to reset. Finish that water and I'll be right back."

He returned with a bottle of PowerAde. He took the empty glass and handed her the squeeze bottle.

"I can't stand jock juice."

"Too bad. Your body needs potassium. Drink."

Sabin screwed her face around.

"It's either this or I'll make you eat a banana."

"Give me that," she responded, snatching the drink from his hand.

Montgomery cleared away some of their earlier mess. "Be still for the next fifteen minutes. The water goes to your muscles instantaneously, but the potassium takes a while before it takes effect. In the meantime, I'll get some ice to keep your calves cold instead of those bottles."

Sabin relaxed against the pain and felt it subside. She wondered why life always dealt her a bad hand, just when things started to go well. She needed this job, and now her own body had betrayed her. She couldn't protect Montgomery if her muscles cramped up at the wrong time. And something told her that her handsome neighbor was in more trouble than she had first imagined.

Heal your enemy . . . heal yourself.
                                    —Toda Kai

Ten

Montgomery parked his Jag on the street and plugged the meter with three quarters. It wouldn't take him long to gather a few files and turn over the projects he'd left unattended.

Walking into his office, he felt like he had been gone for months instead of days. Everything was in its place: filing cabinets, photocopier, fax machine, bookshelves. But it was as if someone else worked here and not him.

"Thank God you're here," Angie said.

He walked to her desk and dropped his briefcase in an empty seat. "Gosh, not even a 'Welcome back,' or a 'Get outa my face.' "

"Nope," she said, pushing back from her desk. "Take a look."

A look, he thought. One good blink and you would miss her, even if she were sitting right in front of you. Only if she smiled, would you get a hint of her presence. She had the largest teeth Montgomery had ever seen. But that was the only thing about her that was large. Aside from her bicuspids, Angie

Miller looked like a prime candidate for the school of anorexia.

He came around to where she sat staring into her computer screen. A small dialogue box displayed on the desktop. It read: "Unrecognized Function Click OK to Continue."

"So," he said, amused. "Just click OK."

A dark smirk took shape on Angie's face. "I did. I've been clicking OK for the past half hour."

"Silly." Montgomery shook his head and cut the power to the computer from the grounding strip on the floor. "When all else fails, shut her down."

Angie took a deep breath but remained silent as they waited for the computer to reboot. When it did, the same dialogue box sat mockingly in the middle of the screen. Montgomery's jaw went slack.

"I tried that, too," Angie offered.

"What caused this?" Montgomery asked, now seated beside her at the desk. He turned the keyboard toward him and tried various key combinations. ALT+F4. CTRL+ESC. CTRL+ALT+DEL.

"I was reading my E-mail. I had just opened a letter from my mom and then that message popped up."

"How long ago was that?"

"Probably about forty-five minutes ago. You think I should call Victor?"

It never ceased to amaze Montgomery how Angie thought her new boyfriend was the answer to every problem she had. He wished she would think more for herself.

"I think we should call Trey."

"Trey's on vacation."

"Great!" he said, frowning.

"I think the system is shot," Angie said.

"Can't be. There's always a back door." He slid the

keyboard back into place in front of the monitor. "Move over."

Angie did as she was told. Montgomery took out a book and two CD-ROMs from the bottom desk drawer. They read: "Genie Disk Recovery System—Works Like Magic!"

For the next thirty minutes, he booted and re-booted the computer. He tried to jump-start the CPU from a disk and then from the operating system CD-ROMs. He also accessed the system's DOS environment and tried to reset the hard drive from there. Nothing worked. Even in the operating system, he kept getting the response: "Unsupported Function— Please press ENTER."

After Angie had brought him a second cup of coffee, he conceded. "Looks like we'll have to wait for Trey."

"What do we do in the meantime?" Angie asked.

"Telecommute," Montgomery said without hesitation. "I was going to put in an indefinite leave of absence anyway."

"What do you mean?" she asked, leaning against the desk.

"I mean that I will be working from home for at least a couple of weeks. I guess you'll be doing the same." He took a short sip from the steaming black liquid.

"You still have that old clunker?"

"My computer is only four years old!"

"Yeah, but in computer years, that's what, forty?"

Montgomery chuckled. "Stop insulting me. I can work at home for a while just fine." Angie walked across the room to the locked file cabinet. "I'll take the backups with me and install them tonight. They won't have last week's work on them, but that's all right. I can reenter the contracts from the paper files."

"Good. But before you do that, I'm going to back up the backups. We can't have anything happening to these puppies now."

Angie closed the file drawer with a metal clash. "I can do that if you want."

"No. That's okay. I'd feel better doing it myself. When I'm finished, I'll drop them off at your house."

"All right, whatever."

Another scorcher, Montgomery thought, squinting against the sunlight. He glanced up into a cloudless sky. It was as if the gods were angry and their entire wrath had come cascading down upon him—hot, angry, and full of vengeance. He just wished he knew what he had done to cause their searing attention.

As part of the natural rhythm that came from years of parking his car in the owner's space at the warehouse, his hands pulled a twenty spot out of his wallet. He slid the bill inside a ratty paper sack. "Thanks, Clyde."

The man in the green trenchcoat stirred groggily on the sidewalk. His coat was a disaster, caked with muck and grime, and torn or perhaps eaten away in spots. The clothing beneath was no better. But Clyde seemed to like it that way. Once, Montgomery bought Clyde a decent change of clothes. Clyde smiled toothlessly and promptly sold the new threads for a small bottle of whiskey.

However, he did look like he had shaven or been shaved since the last time Montgomery sweetened his pot. He was always careful not to get too close. One good whiff of Clyde would probably send him careening toward the nearest john.

Before he entered the building, he initiated their time-old dialogue.

"Everything okay, Sarge?"

"Yep," the craggy gentleman said, hoisting himself from where he always lay about twenty or so feet from the loading bay. Clyde's voice sounded like it was twisting itself through phlegm to get out. "T'ain't been no prowlers, er notin'. You're all clear."

"Good job, Clyde," Montgomery responded, opening the door. "You gonna get cleaned up today, buddy?"

Clyde coughed and growled. "Yep."

Montgomery entered the warehouse, eyes quickly adjusting to the fluorescents overhead. Sometimes Clyde actually did clean himself up. But mostly, he just bought more liquid anesthesia.

He pushed the thick, walnut door of the storage facility wide. It collided against the concrete wall with a clunk. Montgomery announced his presence. "Ay! What's goin' on in here?"

Randy came down from the upstairs apartment. "Big Boss Man!" What's up?"

The two shook hands and swung their arms around each other for a quick soul brother embrace.

Randy smiled. "Wassup, mister?"

"Just tryin' ta get back on top, that's all."

The only time Montgomery had been away from his work for any substantial span of time was when he was on vacation, skydiving off the lower Appalachian Mountains and his recent recovery from the gassing incident. If he thought about it long enough, he would probably talk himself out of taking off from work. There were marketing projects to finish, strategic plans to create, administrative details to oversee, and personnel to monitor. But no matter how many of his business responsibilities loomed like unpacifiable obstacles, there was another matter much more serious. His life.

"Randy, I need you and the team to run the show without me for a while."

The force of Randy's laughter shook his chest like mammoth-size hands were tickling him. "Sure you do."

Montgomery's lips curved up slightly. "I'm serious."

Silence. Randy stopped laughing, seemingly waiting for the "I gotcha!" There wasn't one.

"Are you going on vacation or are you still under the weather?"

He fought the ridiculous urge to blurt out, "Neither. I just want to find out who's trying to kill me, so I'm going to pretend to be Easy Rawlins for as long as it takes for me to solve this freakin' mystery." Instead, he said, "As a matter of fact, that gas leak made me want to take some time to get my body back to the shape it was in before the accident. I don't think I could do that if I had to work eight to ten hours per day."

"Any idea how long you're going to be gone?"

"No. But you'll be in charge until then."

He could see the younger man's chest inflate just a bit.

"All right," Randy said, nodding his head.

"I just stopped by to do a once-over before I take this time off."

"Be my guest. It's about time for one of your inspections anyway." Randy headed back upstairs. "You know where I'll be."

Montgomery had a tough reputation when it came to the quality of his facilities. But he liked it that way. When current and potential customers came to Secure Storage, he wanted the warehouses to be impeccable. So he checked for smells. Sometimes customers would inadvertently pack food among their belongings. He checked for pests. He ran a high-end storage facility.

Most of his customers could afford exterminators whenever they were needed. But sometimes he would come upon a unit that would be the source of mice, or insects. If his exterminators couldn't eradicate the problem, the property owners were promptly asked to remove their belongings.

Montgomery grabbed the visitor's log from the file room and went walking. The storage area was basically a long procession of what looked like elongated barns. He walked down the center aisle with rows of storage units on either side of him. They looked like small tin interconnecting garages. As he went, he randomly checked the locks to the units making sure they were secure. Customers had the option of purchasing a combination lock from the facility or using one of their own. Most chose the latter.

The place was surprisingly quiet, even for a Monday. There was almost always someone either moving in, moving out, adding to, or taking away. Montgomery kept himself on top of the warehouse traffic. He was sensitive to any change, and worked continually to ensure that business always stayed healthy and active by marketing to potential customers, pitching sales and special offers to current customers. Funny he thought, coming to the end of one row, he had gotten into the business because he loved doing things that involved physical labor. And now he was more of a salesman than anything.

So far so good, he thought checking another lock. Everything was neat, clean, and secure. He would walk across the street to Building B and give it the same spot inspection. He remembered when he bought Building A. First American Bank had just reviewed his business plan and approved his loan of five hundred thousand dollars. He had had his eye on a downtown property farther away from the river and had even been in contact with the Realtor. Unfortunately, the property was sold before his loan was approved.

A few days later, the Realtor called him and said that he had a tip on another property that was about to be listed and asked if Montgomery wanted to take a look at it. He agreed and the following week he got a tour of the facility. It was only half the size of the one he'd wanted before. The catch was that it was split into two separate buildings across the street from each other. Montgomery smiled, remembering that the Realtor built a substantial part of his sales pitch on the fact the buildings, which used to be department stores, were connected by an underground walkway. At one time, shoppers had used the walkway to travel from Woolworth's to JC Penny. The walkway was a novelty when he'd first started. But since it wasn't large enough to move boxes, furniture, and other storage items through, it soon outlived its usefulness. That part of his property hadn't been inspected in years.

Montgomery headed outside and over to Building B, almost exclusively devoted to his new contract with the Pentagon. He knew it would be in order just like Building A. So his goal was to gather the examples of just how well in order everything was so his praise to Randy would be specific.

Montgomery pulled aside the hunter-green drapes to get a good look at Sabin's house. He wondered if she had recovered from her muscle spasms. At one point, he thought he would have to take her to the hospital instead of next door. Then she seemed to recover a bit, and he wasn't quite as worried. He argued with himself about whether he should check on her now or later. One glance at the smokestack of books on his dining table told him it would have to be later.

He sat down, notebook in hand, and removed the first book from the pile. *Private Detection For Dummies*. Although Montgomery fancied himself quite an intellect, the book was the cheapest of all those he purchased and it seemed to be the most comprehensive.

He scanned the chapters. "What is a Private Eye and What Does One Do? Beyond the Magnifier—Tools of the Detective. Searching for and Identifying Evidence. Cataloging Evidence. Deductive vs. Inductive Reasoning. At the Crime Scene. When to Involve the Police. Nothing is Elementary, My Dear Detective." Montgomery started reading. It was lunchtime before he looked up again.

He stood, stretched, went to the bathroom, and came back to his stack of books. Having read nearly all of the *For Dummies* text, he chose another, more technical, selection. This one was *Simply Murder—A Layperson's Guide to Crime Investigation*.

This book was a step-by-step guide of police procedure for ordinary citizens. Montgomery highlighted passages, made notes in the margins, and folded down the pages of important parts. He was surprised at how much he enjoyed reading about investigations.

The Amateur Sleuth's Guide to Crime Solving took Montgomery into the early-morning hours. At three A.M., he finally decided to go to bed. He had read through most of the books he'd purchased and was beginning to see a pattern to their approaches. With some variation, the formula was: Reconstruct the last twenty-four hours before the crime. Identify all those who might in any way be implicated, connected, or somehow linked to the occurrence. Collect and catalog anything that might be evidence. And draw inferences and conclusions based upon the assemblage of the documentation. Like putting a jigsaw puzzle together, the perimeter of the crime establishes a boundary within which to concentrate the investigation. Once established, work to the solution piece by piece until all that is left is a clear image of the truth.

A great deal of the work sounded like something a journalist would do. Interviewing people, assembling facts, writing descriptive accounts. But it would be by no means easy. Unlike a jigsaw puzzle, there was no ready-made picture on the box cover. In fact, there was no box cover at all. The whole point was to paint your own. To use the brush strokes of the investigative process to create a picture—the picture of the person responsible for the strange and threatening overcast that had followed him of late.

Montgomery postponed his shower until the morning. He undressed groggily, leaving his clothes in a heap on the floor and climbed into bed his favorite way—naked.

Thank God! Sabin thought as the lights in Montgomery's house finally went off. She had been keeping an eye out for several hours, wondering what he was doing up so late. Last week, she had purchased binoculars and a telescope just as a precaution but hadn't yet found a reason to use them. However her concern increased as the hours progressed and she reluctantly took out the pair of binoculars.

At first, she couldn't see much. Then her eyes adjusted to peering through Montgomery's miniblinds and she could see him seated at a table reading. She watched as he inexhaustibly devoured book after book. He looked as though he were cramming for an exam, highlighting and taking notes. She wasn't aware that he was taking a class. But he was definitely studying something.

When he finally got up at around three, Sabin was

beat. She could barely keep her eyelids open. The only thing that kept her marginally coherent was the police scanner blaring loudly on an end table. When the light came on in Montgomery's bedroom, she was ready to call it a night. She was packing her surveillance equipment into boxes when curiosity cajoled her into taking one last look.

From her bedroom window she raised the binoculars once more and the spectacle in the viewfinders prompted a low cougarlike growl.

She only caught a glimpse of his backside before he flicked off the light, but that was enough. *Round like a Spaulding basketball and probably just as firm.* "Uh, uh, uh. Ain't nothin' on this earth made like a black man," she said, and flopped into bed.

Sabin awoke the following morning to urgent pounding on her front door. Startled, she checked the clock: 10:00 A.M. Oh, great Christ, she thought. *I overslept!* As soon as she got rid of whoever it was at her door, she would hurry into town to check on Montgomery.

She grabbed her oversize T-shirt from where it hung on the back of a chair and pulled it over her head. She walked quickly to the door and looked out of the peephole. "Well I'll be," she mumbled and cracked the door.

"Mr. Claiborne," she said, voice muffled with sleep.

"Hey," he said, "I just wanted to see how you were doing. Any more cramps?"

"No," she said. "I feel about as stiff as an English butler, but other than that, I'm in decent shape."

"Make sure you drink plenty of water."

"I will," she responded.

"And eat some bananas."

"I hate bananas."

"Then drink some sports ade. The potassium will help bolster elasticity in your muscles."

"Anything else, Doctor?"

He hesitated, then smiled broadly. "Yeah. Come watch movies again with me sometime." He gave her a nod. "It was fun the other night."

"I had fun, too," she said, thoughts whirring from his invitation. Sabin realized she wasn't thinking clearly around Mr. Bronze Body.

Sabin's mind slowly wrapped itself around the idea that she'd overslept. She made a mental note to discreetly install a motion detector on Montgomery's property. She couldn't afford mistakes.

The sun was out in force and making a good impression on Montgomery's body. His arms and legs glowed golden bronze in the light, and memories of his well-toned torso made themselves comfortable in Sabin's mind. She smiled despite the crick in her neck.

"Well, I won't keep you."

"Thanks for checking on me."

He reached into his shorts pocket and pulled out a small slip of paper. "Here's my number. Call me if you need anything."

Now the sunlight was dancing in Montgomery's eyes. "I will," she said.

She watched him cut across her yard and head back to his house. Shutting the door carefully, she scolded herself for sleeping so late. *There's no way I'm staying up that late ever again.*

She grabbed fresh towels from the linen closet and headed toward the bathroom for a quick shower. She was lathered from head to toe with lavender silk body gel when a question popped into her head: *What is Montgomery doing home today?*

* * *

Montgomery decided to treat each incident indi-
vidually. He would reconstruct each attempt separately
and then see what correlations he could make. His
task would be easier if he chunked it into manageable
pieces.

From midmorning to late afternoon, he recorded
the details surrounding the last four weeks. With each
accident he wrote a detailed chronology of the events
of his life for the twenty-four hours prior. Some oc-
currences were so far back that the details were
sketchy. He filled them in with the help of his day
planner.

He created files for each piece of the puzzle and
put them in order. Now and then he would reference
one of the books he purchased, but mostly he worked
from memory to get it all down and workable. In doing so, he went through three glasses of water, two
bottles of root beer, and four power bars. By four P.M.,
his stomach ached. He couldn't tell if it was because
of what he had eaten or what he hadn't. One thing
was for sure, he had had enough research writing for
one day.

Stretching, he walked over to the window. The
neighborhood was still and serene. *So this is what goes
on when I'm not around,* he thought. Then a black van
pulled into Sabin's driveway. Montgomery watched as
a young man stepped out with a bounce. The guy
looked to be in his early twenties. He pulled a large
flat suitcase from the back of the van and walked up
the front steps.

He stared transfixed as Sabin opened the door wearing a tiny, terry-cloth robe.

"What the . . . ?" Then Montgomery's jaw disen-
gaged as Mr. Spring In His Step walked right in.

Who's this guy? he wondered. *He's got to be half her
age.* Disconcerted, he walked into the living room

where he could almost see what was going on inside the house. Squinting, he could make out a blur of white. That must be Sabin. Then the blur of white dropped, taking Montgomery's heart with it, as he realized that had to have been her robe falling to the floor. Then the hazy brown figure near the window moved away.

"Why am I geeked out about this? She ain't *my* woman."

But sometimes she felt like his. When she stood before him, soaked by his water hose, she felt like his. When they had gone riding and the rise of her breasts rested against his arms around her waist, she felt like his. When her lips shared her breath and saved him, she felt like his. Even when they argued over the world's greatest detective, *she felt like his*.

Montgomery decided that the gas had affected his brain as well as his lungs. He reminded himself that he really didn't like Sabin Strong. One well-placed thought about her philosophy on gun control was enough to turn his attentions away from whatever was going on next door and place them on something more important, like eating.

Montgomery headed to the refrigerator where he used lettuce, tomatoes, pickles, cheese, turkey and ham slices, mustard, mayonnaise, and Texas toast, to erect a Dagwood-style sandwich. Assorted combinations of luncheon meat and bread were the extent of his culinary skills. That suited him just fine until he got a taste for a real meal. Whenever that happened, he would chuck aside his disdain for his father's company and have dinner with him and Tilde.

When he returned to his work, he selected another book: *How To Solve a Mystery*. He liked this one because it simplified the investigation process. It narrowed it down to five W's. The first one was: Who is the victim? The goal was to construct a profile not unlike the way a writer constructs a character. He spent the next hour and a half writing down information regarding himself. The kind of person he was. His family background. His job and his financial situation. He described each in detail and tried as objectively as possible to come up with things that might best assist his research.

He skimmed the pages wondering who would want him dead.

After several minutes, his notes blurred. Frustrated, Montgomery pushed away from the table and walked to the window. The van was still there. He stomped away, got another glass of water, and returned to his work.

He wrote a little more about himself, and the urge to go to the window tugged him again. Snapped him up out of his seat actually.

What the hell's going on over there? he wondered, staring at the van. It might be a service call. Maybe an appliance had gone out. But there was no sign on the van. *Must be a relative,* he mused. Just then Sabin's front door opened and his phone rang.

Damn, he thought. He considered letting the answering machine pick up so he could watch the exit of Hopalong Heartthrob. But it could be the warehouse or Tilde calling about his dad. So he dashed over to the phone, grabbed the receiver, and trucked back to the window.

"Yeah," he said as he watched as the two stood on Sabin's stairs talking.

"Mr. Claiborne. It's Detective Carvell. Is now a good time to talk?"

His hand is on her shoulder. He's rubbing it. "No!"

"Well, all right. What would be a better time?"

She's got that skimpy robe on again. And she looks like . . .

like . . . like she's just had the best sex of her life. I'll be damned if she isn't glowing. Plus she's got that dopey look women sometimes get when it's really good.

Montgomery glanced at the clock. "Three hours."

"I'll be off duty then, but I can call you from home if you like. I just want to set up another meeting time."

She smacked him on the butt! "That's just great."

"All right, Montgomery. I'll talk to you then."

Montgomery stared after the truck as it backed out of the driveway and then watched as Sabin moved in slow motion. She rolled her shoulders and then yawned like a kitten being scratched behind the ears. It wasn't until he heard a blaring pulse coming from the receiver that he remembered he had the phone in his hand.

Must have been a wrong number, he thought, and hung up.

War is contagious.

—Toda Kai

Eleven

Next on the sleuth's supersolver list was: Where.
Where did the crimes take place? Montgomery spent
the next day describing the location of each occurrence. He jotted down notes of why he was at each
place, how long he spent there, and the time of day.
The more he wrote the more he discovered just how
much a creature of habit he really was.

He had always thought of himself as a spontaneous,
no-boundaries kind of person. But his notes showed
a distinct pattern to his life (one which anyone intent
on interfering could easily pick up on. Up at five A.M.
Out by six. In the office by seven. Paperwork and callbacks until lunch. Errands, deposits, inspections, sup-
plies after lunch. Home by five. Work out until six.
Dinner at eight. Bed by nine. On paper, his life
seemed monotonous and boring.

Needing a break, and something to remind himself
that he could change his regular routine, he grabbed
the *Baltimore Sun* from a bin beside the table. Maybe
he'd call Arroya, see if she'd like to take in a movie.
Or if there was nothing interesting at the theater, he'd

call Randy. Randy was always in the mood to go club-bing. Montgomery usually didn't go. But the logical-thinking detective was in need of some spicing up.

Speaking of spice, he thought as the doorbell rang. He knew it was Sabin. The red alert going off in his gut told him so.

He swung open the door. She wore a baggy gray sweat suit like someone going to boxing camp. Her hair was pulled back into a ponytail. A white towel hung loosely around her neck.

"Yes," he said, curious about her getup.

"You said if I ever wanted to use your weight room . . ."

"Yes, I did," he said, and glanced at the books and papers taking over his dining room table. "But now isn't a good time."

"Really? Why not?" she asked, walking past him and heading downstairs.

Montgomery followed her. "You certainly came pre-pared," he said, glancing at her gym bag. She dropped it gently on the basement floor and looked around. Montgomery looked around, too, seeing his workout area with new eyes. Squat rack, dip station, leg-press machine, bench press, rowing machine, chin bar, ex-ercise mats. He had more equipment than some gyms he'd seen.

"Do I need to explain how to use anything?"

"No, I'm pretty familiar."

Montgomery thought, *In more ways than one.* "Well, I've got a project I need to work on, so if you need something, just yell."

The disappointment on her face made him pause and reconsider.

"I was hoping that you could spot me. But I under-stand if you're busy. I did barge over unannounced."

"I do need a break actually. Let me go get changed."

Montgomery jogged up the stairs, into his bedroom, and removed his slacks and shirt. He replaced them with shorts, the black Lycra ones he hardly ever wore, and a muscle shirt. He returned to the basement to see Sabin sitting Hindu-style on the floor. She was warming up and meditating at the same time, her movements fluid and extending and contracting her body like a soft dance. He leaned against the wall and watched, fascinated.

It wasn't yoga, and it wasn't tai chi, either. It was just . . . Sabin. And while he waited for her warm-up to end, he fought off visions of other ways she could probably move her body and what she was hiding under all those clothes.

After three deep breaths, he figured she had finished her routine. "Ready?"

"Yes," she said.

He watched the reflection on a mirrored wall as Sabin slipped off the sweats she'd used as a cover-up and stood before him in a white tank and matching shorts.

He allowed himself a grin. "Now, those guns I like," he said admiring her upper arms along with several other body parts.

Her eyes sparkled and surveyed. "Back at cha."

"So," he said, closing the distance between them, "what do you have a taste for?" As soon as he said it, he realized the innuendo. What surprised him was that he didn't mind. Their eyes caught, and Montgomery knew exactly what he had a taste for. Long and sinuous legs wrapped around his waist. He was beginning to perspire and the workout hadn't even started.

Sabin stepped closer. "How about the bench?"

Just watching her move in the tank top and shorts told him that it was about to get awfully warm in his basement. Montgomery pulled the chain on the ceiling fan.

"Considering your muscle cramps, do you need a longer warm-up?" he asked, trying to come up with an excuse to touch her.

"Maybe?" she responded.

"All right," he said, motioning to the floor mat. "Lie down."

"What?"

"Don't worry. I won't hurt you."

"That's what they all say."

"That may be true, but *I* mean it."

"Humph," she retorted and lay on the mat as she had been instructed.

He knelt beside her. "On your stomach."

"I don't think so. Whatever you're going to do, I want to see it coming first."

"Suit yourself," he said, taking her right arm and placing it across his lap. Then he used his knuckles to work out the tension in her upper arm. With a steady rotating motion, he visited each pressure point and worked it until the tightness had loosened. Inch by inch he repeated the same movement until there was nothing but raw muscle left.

"Mmm," Sabin purred. "This feels more like a cooldown. I'm going to be too relaxed to lift anything."

"On the contrary. I'm stripping your muscle of everything prohibitive to a good lift. What you'll have when I'm done is pure muscle. No knots. No kinks. No cramps. No pins and needles. No tension."

"Really?" she said, her voice lowered an octave by his deft attentions.

Montgomery switched sides and started the same motions with her left arm. "I guarantee it."

This time, he paid as much attention to her face as he did to her arm. He watched as she closed her eyes.

He watched as she let the tension slide out of her body completely. He watched as she gave herself over to the sensations of his hands across her skin.

"Did you know that regular muscle stimulation helps to—"

"Rid toxins from the body," she finished. "Yes, I know."

The expression on her face was so incredibly content and satisfied, he wondered what it would look like in the throes of good hard lovemaking.

"How's that?" he asked, standing. A few more seconds in the direction his thoughts were taking him and his arousal would become abundantly clear.

Now a smile creased the veil of serenity on her face. "That was magnificent."

"Okay, then show me what you can do."

He helped her up and walked her to his workbench. She took a seat and he took off some of the weight on the bar. "What do you usually do?"

"That's fine," she said, smiling at the fifty pounds he'd left on the bar.

As she situated herself on the seat and prepared to lift, he took position above her, ready to spot.

"Ready?"

"Always," she said, removing the bar from its cradle. She lowered the weight to just an inch above her chest, then pushed up.

"Let's do five of five," he suggested.

"Five of five? What do you think I am? A Wet Nap?"

"All right, Carla Dunlap. I do ten of ten. Can you hang with that?"

"We'll see," she responded, and proceed to lift and lower the bar in sets of ten repetitions.

After a few minutes, Montgomery grabbed the bar. "Hold it."

"Why?"

He placed the bar back on the pedestal. "You've got skills, but your technique is a little sloppy."

She rolled her eyes.

"Try it again, but focus on slow control."

He watched as she repeated her routine with more concentration this time.

"That's right," he said. "Nice and easy."

Sabin drew in a breath as she lowered the iron rod to her chest once more. She focused on making her movements slow and deliberate. Using an even momentum, she lifted the weight and watched the spark of approval dance in Montgomery's eyes.

Why was it so important to her to please him? She wasn't sure. She'd never needed anyone's sanction before. Heck, that was one of the things she was most proud of. But something in her, something strong and extremely feminine, longed to satisfy him. Her entire body warmed at the thought.

After a few minutes of high-intensity training, Sabin noticed that the weight felt more like eighty pounds instead of fifty. And it wasn't as easy to get through her repetitions as she had imagined.

"Don't slow down. You've got just the right pace."

Montgomery's words helped focus her concentration as she ended the eighth set of ten. Beads of moisture collected on her upper lip and around the base of her neck. *Maybe I should have chosen five of five,* she thought, feeling her biceps strain against the pressure.

"Seven more, Sabin. Come on."

She would like nothing more than to finish the last seven, but the relentless force of gravity had other plans. *I had to be a show-off,* she chastised herself as the trembling started in her arms. She looked up into Montgomery's eyes feeling embarrassed and vanquished. But the confidence she saw there renewed her strength.

"Breathe, and lift!"

She took a deep breath a pushed the bar away from her chest.

"Only six more. Just like that."

"Montgomery . . ."

"Don't talk. Concentrate."

The air around her filled with the aroma of sweat and exertion. She could see bright overhead lights hanging from low ceilings, and the sound of the fan blades shoop-shooped through the air. Threatening to drown out all her senses was the groan of her own breathing coming in long labored strains.

"Don't quit on me now."

She wouldn't. Pushing up the iron rod, she realized that the first time she laid eyes on Montgomery Claiborne she was in for the long haul.

"You said you wanted ten of ten. So go get it. Come on five!"

"Aah!" she said, and grit her teeth.

"That's it. Four."

She was going to strangle him as soon as she got the strength back in her arms. "Aah!"

"Beautiful! Three."

Did he call me beautiful? she wondered, pushing up again. This time she almost smiled.

"You are so baad! Two more."

Sweat was dripping now. She could feel it sliding off of her temples. She'd had enough.

"Mo—"

"No! You can do this, Sabin."

Was he right? She pushed off from her chest again. Oh, God, it hurt. Her arms felt like twigs about to snap. She couldn't hold on. She gave in to the law of gravity and her arms came down too fast. But before the bar slammed into her chest, Montgomery caught it.

"Just one more. All you have to—"

"Take it, Montgomery. I've had enough."

He exhaled forcefully and lifted the bar back into its cradle. She let her arms fall down at her sides and dangle to the floor.

"Ow!"

He knelt beside her. "You all right?"

"Don't talk to me, Mr. Seven More."

"You could have finished the set. You only had one more to go."

"You and your high-intensity training. Why didn't you warn me?"

Montgomery walked over and retrieved a white towel from a cabinet. Then he took a plastic bottle of water from a small refrigerator. By the time he handed them both to Sabin, she had calmed somewhat from her fury and was grateful for the offerings.

"What happened?"

She tensed at his question. "I ran out of juice."

"I don't think so," he replied, sitting on the floor beside her. "I know what it's like to hit the wall, and you hadn't even seen yours on the horizon yet."

Sabin swallowed hard. How could she tell him his encouragement sounded foreign to her ears? So much so that it caused her to doubt herself.

Sabin discovered that she much preferred her style of workout. Exercise and meditation provided just the right combination of mind/body training. But this, this was an all-out assault. Already her arms were sore and aching. She wanted to tell Montgomery "Never mind," but she didn't want to appear like some whimpish little girl. So she continued. Even when he stopped her and told her that her technique left something to be desired, she stuck it out instead of telling him where he could put his darned dumbbells.

"Where do you feel it?" he asked, watching her. The scowl forming on his face was already familiar to her.

She smiled slyly. *Where, indeed.* Should she tell him she felt it in her toes when they tingled the first time she saw him? Should she tell him she felt it in her hands on the day of the accident when she wanted to reach out and smack him and at the same time grab his face and kiss him? Should she tell him that she felt it in her bed each time she turned over and wished he was there with her?

I feel it, Sabin thought at last, wondering if working out with Montgomery was a good idea. The scent of their sweat mingling in the air was catapulting her to places in her libido she'd deemed off-limits. If this continued, she would have to make a choice. Either she would remain on the payroll as Montgomery's bodyguard—in which case she would back off substantially to keep her feelings in check—or she would resign as his protector and do what her body wanted so desperately to do.

"Underneath," she said, answering his question and straining to keep her pace.

"That's what I thought."

Now what? she wondered. "Where am I supposed to feel it?"

"Let me show you," he said, standing.

"Form and technique are the keys to just about everything," he remarked, centering his stance on the mat. She watched with piqued interest as he lifted the weights into place. The change in the contours of his arm made her agree that form is key.

"Now, when you lift, you want to concentrate on specific muscle groups. You can't work them all at once."

A large bicep nearly erupted from his upper arm. "Put your hand here."

She stood and did so gladly. He began to lift. Slow and controlled movements. "Now, where do you feel it?"

Truth be told, she felt it all over her body, with a special pooling of warmth radiating near her lower abdomen. However, she gave him the answer he wanted.

"I feel it in the top part of your arm."

"That's because that's where my focus is." He continued his measured routine, concentration cutting deep lines on his face. Sabin was getting used to the rhythmic tightening of muscles beneath her hands.

"Okay. Now try again."

She sighed, remembering that the primary reason she came over was her job, not her interest in his ripped muscles. "You are really serious about this stuff, aren't you?"

"I take my body very seriously. After all, it's the only one I've got."

You can have mine at any time, she thought. "Can we do some lower-body stuff?"

"Sounds good."

They walked over to the leg press. It looked like a new age dentist's chair. Sabin took her place in the seat.

"How much weight do you work?"

"Let's see what one hundred feels like."

Montgomery removed two of the large weights from the machine and settled in beside her. With the weights secure, he nodded for her to push.

Sabin extended her legs then let them come slowly back. He moved in closer with her first push and counted as she bore out the weights in slow, controlled movements.

"You've done this before."

"A few times," she said through deep breaths.

"How many reps?"

"Five of ten," she said, huffing a bit now.

"Where do you go?"

"The Y usually."

"The Y?"

"Yeah. What's wrong with the Y?"

"Nothing. I just pictured you more of a Gold's person."

"I think you're projecting. Now stop asking me questions and let me work."

Together they moved through his exercise equipment like a circuit course. They spent time with each machine. By the time they worked their way to the rowing machine, a generous sweat had broken out on Sabin. Her skin glistened with moisture and Montgomery thought it made her look alluring and sultry.

"What are you looking at?"

"You," he answered honestly.

"Why are you staring like that?"

"I like a woman who's not afraid to sweat."

She smiled then and said, "I like a man who likes a woman who's not afraid to sweat."

This is getting interesting, he thought.

Lucian checked his watch as he strode toward the door: 1:50 P.M. This time he was ten minutes early. He knocked, preparing himself just in case C.C. made another appearance. She did not, and as the door swung open, he felt a twinge of disappointment.

"Detective," the large man said, stepping aside.

"Mr. Claiborne."

The two shook hands and went into the living room.

"Can I get you something?"

"No. Thanks."

They sat.

"So what have you got for me?"

This time he noted that Claiborne had a legal pad and pen, poised to write. Too bad he didn't have much to report.

"I checked out your story. I took a couple of assistants with me and visited each scene. I spoke with quite a few people."

"And?"

"And I'm not sure if this is good news or bad news, but we've turned up nothing."

The man sat back and tapped the end of the pen against the paper in his lap. "Nothing."

"That's right. They were all explainable accidents. Unfortunate, but explainable."

Lucian wondered what Claiborne was writing on the pad. "I did discover something that concerns me."

"What's that?"

"You weren't quite truthful when you said that you hadn't had any altercations with anyone recently."

"What do you mean?"

"I mean, I have a report from traffic that says you had an accident approximately one month ago."

The man frowned. "That's right."

Lucian scanned the paper in his hand. "Says here a motorcycle was totaled and you and the driver were less than amiable."

He thought he saw Claiborne smile. "So?"

"So how many of these incidents have you experienced since that accident?"

"Just one, but Sabin's the one who resuscitated me." Then he looked distant for a moment. "It couldn't be her."

A commotion in the entryway diverted their attention.

"Heavenly God! What happened to you!" Montgomery sprang from the seat and headed toward the front door. Lucian's instincts kept him on Claiborne's heels.

Reeves Claiborne wheeled his chair back and forth next to a woman slumped onto the floor of the entryway. Her body shook fitfully.

"Cher!" Claiborne shouted, dashing beside her. He grabbed her up into his arms. "Are you hurt? What's wrong?"

Mascara tracked tears down the woman's face. A rip in her blouse exposed part of a blue-laced bra. From the tears on other places on her shirt and skirt, Lucian guessed he had either been in a fight or perhaps attacked by a dog. From the dazed look on her face, she appeared to be going into shock.

"Set her down on the couch and get her some water," Lucian ordered.

The two Claiborne men did as he instructed. When Reeves returned with the water, he tried to get the woman to take a sip. The water dribbled onto the remains of her blouse instead.

"Never mind that," Lucian said. "Bring me a towel."

The younger Claiborne took off then and returned in record time with a medium-size cloth. Lucian took the water, poured it onto the towel, and then placed the towel against her head. She closed her eyes then, and her tears stuttered in her throat.

"Cher, I'm Detective Lucian Carvell. I need to know what happened so I can help you."

When she opened her eyes, Lucian felt something in his chest go warm. *Those eyes,* he thought. *They're C.C.'s.* He smiled.

"He—somebody . . . tried to . . . hurt me."

He noticed her rapid breathing and realized that she was about to hyperventilate.

"Cher. Cher! Look at me. Or should I call you C.C.? Are you C.C. the Clown?"

Her eyes widened and her breathing quickened. "Somebody tried . . ." Now she was gasping.

Lucian's heartbeats nearly matched her breaths.

"Call an ambulance!" Reeves shouted.

"I need a paper bag!" Lucian said.

While Montgomery ran off toward the kitchen, he worked to calm Cherlyn.

"Cher, I want you to look at my face. Can you do that?"

Her eyes were wide with panic, but she did as he instructed. "Everything's going to be okay. We won't let anything happen to you. Do you believe me?"

Her gasps grew more insistent.

"I'm calling the paramedics!" Reeves shouted, and rolled his chair to the phone. Montgomery returned, bag in hand.

Lucian took the bag, blew it open, then scrunched the top together. "Cher, I'm going to put this bag over your nose and mouth. It will help you breathe better. It will calm you down. Okay?"

She sobbed and struggled to catch her breath. Lucian did as he had told her. Her eyes never left his as he held the paper sack against her face.

"I want you to try to relax. The more you try the better you'll feel." Absentmindedly, he stroked her hair and lowered his voice. He could tell the carbon dioxide was working to regulate her breaths.

"Well, I think you're feeling better already. What do you think? Yes, I do believe you're calming down. Listen to your breathing, Cher. It sounds hard now, but see if you can make it softer. See if you can make it softer. That's right. Keep it up. Softer. Wow. You're doing great."

Montgomery, who had knelt beside them, held his

sister's tiny hand in his large one. Reeves's gruff voice bellowed into the receiver.

"Aw, never mind!" He turned around. "Is she gonna be okay?"

"Of course she is. Right Cher?" Lucian continued to stroke her hair.

Montgomery patted her hand and swallowed hard. Lucian was right. She was calming down. She was breathing better. Her eyes were still full of fright and tear filled. He took the bag from her and smiled. "I think the best thing now is for you to lie here. Later we can talk about what happened."

Cherlyn nodded and started shaking.

Lucian knew he should follow proper procedure by asking for a description, finding out whether she knew the person, and asking where it happened. But she was too distraught for that.

"I'll get a blanket," Montgomery said, and dashed upstairs. When he returned, his sister was stretched out on the couch. Lucian had removed her shoes.

Montgomery covered her with the blanket and she closed her eyes. All three men went into the dining room to give her some quiet.

"When she wakes up, she'll probably feel like she's been hit by a train. Give her a pain reliever and plenty of water. As soon as she feels up to it, give me a call and I'll come over and take a statement," said Lucian.

> The best way to hold a lover is with an
> open hand.
>
> —Toda Kai

Twelve

Montgomery jogged downstairs to get a full view of himself in the mirror. Jake, his tailor, had to find four more inches of jacket width. It looked good when he tried the suit top on in the shop. But now with a shirt, tie, slacks, and shoes, he wanted to make sure what he saw in the store wasn't just wishful thinking.

He stood at attention, hands at his sides. No, it wasn't wishful thinking. The jacket fit well. He barely recognized himself as a man who spent most of his time in Dockers and Polo. *Well at least one of us will look good,* he thought.

He doubted whether Sabin owned anything that didn't say Old Navy, Eddie Bauer, or Bum. But she was his date anyway. One minute he was spotting her on the one-hundred-pound bar weights, and the next he was talking about the storage conference and inviting her to accompany him. As well as they got along, he expected her to say no. But her stern concentration broke and he thought he saw a smile lurking beneath the surface.

He and Arroya had attended the Annual Storage Conference for the last five years. She wasn't too thrilled when she'd found out he'd asked someone else.

"Remember the midnight-blue chiffon number I wore to the convention last year?"

"Yes."

"I just bought a maroon one just like it. You know what red does to my skin."

"Yes I do. Look, Roya . . ."

"Hmm?" She'd sat in the coffee shop absentmindedly twirling the corner of her napkin.

Montgomery took a slow sip from his black coffee and glanced around the café. *This is going to be hard.* "Roya, I already have a date for the convention this year."

She stiffened, but her smile remained intact. "Oh. Well, I just assumed that you and I would . . ."

"I know. I'm sorry. We were lifting, and it just tumbled out of my mouth before I realized it."

"Lifting? You invited someone to lift with you?"

"The other day, Sabin came over to—"

"Sabin?"

"Yeah."

Arroya crossed one well-proportioned leg over the other. Her stockings were so sheer that if it weren't for the sound of thigh brushing against thigh, he wouldn't have known she was wearing any. Funny how they seemed like regular ol' legs and not triggers for his libido like usual.

"That woman is definitely strutting in my yard."

"Roya," he'd said, taking her hand. "You and I go back too far. We've got much history. Nothing can change that."

"It's not our history I'm thinking about."

Montgomery had smiled. It truly was a blessing to

have someone in his life that cared about him so deeply. God knows his father didn't. "You and I will be friends forever."

He now took one last look in the mirror before bounding up the stairs. He stuffed his remarks sheet into his inside pocket, grabbed his keys, and charged outside.

He couldn't believe summer was approaching. And just when the weather should have been getting warmer, the breeze in the air felt like early spring. And the birds sang as if thankful for the reprieve in the heat.

He slipped into his Jag. A few seconds later, he was in Sabin's driveway. He sent up a prayer as he turned off the ignition. "Please let her be presentable. Please let her be—"

He didn't even have a chance to get out of the car. Her front door opened, and Cinderella stepped out. The hair that typically hung down her back was swept up and sculpted into something resembling a crown. The moonlight danced on her face. *Is that make-up?* he wondered. She descended the stairs slowly. "Well, would you look at that?" The black gown she wore closely followed the contours of her body all the way to her ankles. *High heels! She's wearing heels!* He'd never seen so much woman coming at him at one time in his entire life. He sprang from the driver's seat and met her at the passenger's side. And to top it all off, she was smiling.

"Allow me," he said, opening the door for her. When she got in, part of her dress fell away at the split and a long brown leg seemed to have his name on it. Sabin adjusted her gown.

"Montgomery, close your mouth and close the door."

"Right," he said, forcing himself to breathe regularly.

He got back in and tried to convince himself this was the same woman who had cussed like a Black Jack when she stubbed her toe on a dumbbell in his exercise room. He backed out of the driveway and headed toward the expressway.

"Who are you?"

"What do you mean?"

"I mean, did I kiss a frog or something? You look great!"

More sailor talk. "All I know is I shaved my legs, so this *better* be worth it."

"I'm just trying to pay you a compliment."

"Yeah, well . . . the last guy to pay me that kind of compliment got a right cross."

Montgomery laughed.

"What's so funny?"

"You. How much do you weigh?"

"What kind of question is that to ask a woman?"

He laughed again. "You talk a good game. But look at you. You're so . . . what's the word I want . . . lithe?"

She sized him up. "You don't have to be gargantuan to have strength."

"No, but it helps."

"Really? What about ants?"

"Ants are an exception."

"No, they're not. They're the rule that we should all follow. It's about leverage, Montgomery. How you leverage the earth, gravity, the wind, your mind, even your own breath. It's about using all that and more to your advantage. Not about brute strength."

Damned if she didn't have a point. But he wasn't about to concede. "Maybe," he said.

* * *

Sabin wasn't sure how it happened. Throughout the reception—meeting and greeting, mixing and mingling, looking for anyone who fit in just a little too well, being introduced, and trying to remember as many names as possible—Montgomery's arm had settled comfortably around her waist. At first, it was just a slight press at her elbow during introductions, or a gentle steering at her back as they wove through the crowd of attendees. But eventually that touch lingered and now the thrill of Montgomery's intimate contact warmed her to her toes. The conference facility at the downtown Embassy Suites reminded Sabin of a domesticated jungle. High ceilings, warm brown wood polished to a shine, seafoam green accents, and a babbling indoor brook added to the outdoor feel.

"Would you like a fresh one?"

Sabin looked down at the champagne flute in her hand. "I'm fine."

"You've been sipping that drink since we got here. Would you prefer a beer?"

"No, thanks, Montgomery."

Sabin's reflexes were on red alert. She didn't want anything to compromise that. Montgomery was a perfect target at this banquet and she would make sure no one had the opportunity to finish what they'd started.

Contrary to what some folks believe, Sabin knew that most crimes occurred in broad daylight and often when there were a bunch of people around. The distraction of a noisy crowd made for just the cover a good assassin needed to accomplish a job successfully.

"You seem keyed-up."

"No. Just enjoying the evening, so far. Thank you for inviting me."

The hum of the champagne reception kicked up a notch as attendees filed out of the foyer and into the

dining area. Row upon row of tables, set in rounds of
eight, took over the room. Each table was draped with
a salmon-colored cloth. The place settings sat simply
and practically with trios of votive candles serving as
centerpieces.

Montgomery and Sabin threaded their way to the
front of the room where several tables were marked
RESERVED. He helped her with her chair then sat beside her.

She completed a quick survey of the room, getting
her bearings on the layout. High ceiling, no balcony.
That meant no bad guys up top. Two kitchen en-
trances. She watched them both. A large podium and
lectern concerned her. Someone could be hiding inside one or both. She would have to think of something. Luckily the tablecloths didn't come down to the
floor or Sabin would have had to come up with a way
to evacuate the entire dining room. To their immediate left was an emergency exit. She hoped it wouldn't
be necessary to use it, but she embedded its location
in her mind just in case. Nonchalantly she adjusted
her hair and palmed one of the air-claw stars she had
tucked between the thick twists. Then she discreetly
knocked her napkin off her lap.

"I'll get it," Montgomery offered.

"No," she said, bending down. "I've got it."

Before retrieving her napkin, Sabin placed the star
between her first and second finger, stabilized it with
her thumb, hurled it spinning into the dark beneath
the podium, and waited for the yell. When there was
no outcry, she scooped up her napkin and replaced
it jauntily on her lap. *One down,* she thought.

Salads and desserts were already on the tables, so
as soon their table was full, they dug in.

They were into the third course when Montgomery

touched Sabin's wrist. The sensation was electric and the jolt of it curled her toes.

"I don't ever remember you being this quiet. Is everything okay?"

"Yes," she said, feeling her cheeks warm with a smile.

Sabin was having a good time. And it surprised her. She had imagined that going to some banquet, especially one part of a storage industry conference, would be the ultimate in boring. But the people she met were interesting and lively. She even anticipated the awards presentations, especially the one Montgomery was scheduled to make. The night's experience made her forget at times that the reason she came was for business and not pleasure.

As the group finished their desserts, a woman from the reserved table on their right went up to the lectern. The after-dinner talk quieted down.

"Good evening, ladies and gentlemen. I hope you all enjoyed your meals tonight. I know I certainly did. Please continue eating as we move into the awards portion of our banquet."

Sabin leaned over. "Who is she?"

Montgomery leaned, too. "That's Jessica Scott. She owns StorUSA. She's also president of the Regional American Storage Association."

"Oh," she said. "How come you're not the president?"

Montgomery smiled with a black man's confidence. "I was president two years ago."

A woman sitting across from them frowned at their conversation. Sabin didn't care. She and Montgomery lowered their voices, but kept right on talking.

As Ms. Scott presented business owners with awards for community service, environmental safety, and customer care, Montgomery explained a little bit about each award and each recipient. Sabin listened closely yet maintained her surveillance of the attendees and servers.

Montgomery and Sabin moved closer together and lowered their voices even more, but continued talking. His lips moved dangerously near to her ear. She imagined them pressing closer and his tongue plucking gently at her lobe. She purred at the thought, then embarrassed, turned to him. A fire smoldered in his eyes, and Sabin turned her attention to the thank you speech being made by this year's outstanding political advocate.

When Montgomery placed his arm around the back of Sabin's chair, she thought she would melt. If it hadn't been for the introduction of the next presenter, she knew she would have.

A generous applause rose from the audience. She could tell by the crowd's reaction, Montgomery was well respected. He stood, but not before whispering in her ear, "I'll be right back." She joined in the applause as he shook hands with Ms. Scott and took his place behind the lectern. *Well, here goes,* she thought. *If someone is going to make an attempt, this will be their best shot.*

Her eyes skimmed the area for anything amiss, out of place, unusual, or a little too usual. She checked for strange movement of wall hangings, people suddenly reaching for things, or anyone running.

Montgomery looked very comfortable standing there, like he belonged in charge or at the center of attention. Even if he hadn't been standing at the head of the room, there was an aura about him—the confidence in his stance, the breadth of his shoulders, the focus in his eye. Sabin had watched amused and more than a little pleased as the heads of several women had turned to Montgomery many times that evening.

Gorgeous could not describe him properly, but it sure came close. And the fact that the temperature in the room seemed to jump significantly whenever he touched her told her how much she was affected by that fact.

"Industry professionals, friends, and honored guests, it is my honor and privilege to stand before you this evening to present the award for Storage Facility of the Year. Those who have been so bestowed in past years represent the finest that the service industry has to offer, especially last year when my company received the award." The audience met Montgomery's mischievous smile with laughter.

"In continuing a long tradition of honoring distinguished service, outstanding quality, and leadership in the industry, I am proud to present this award to David Bernard, chief operating manager of B & B Storage."

There was an uproar of applause and the award recipient joined Montgomery on the podium. Then, one by one, the audience stood until everyone was up in ovation.

Sabin had no clue that there was such depth to the self-storage field. And she would never have guessed a conference, let alone an awards banquet. She was quite surprised and enjoyed it all, especially being with Montgomery.

It was the movie marathon, she told herself. Ever since then she'd had this unshakable sense of longing and desire, and heaven help her attraction. When she'd gotten those awful cramps, he'd been right there and taken care of her. She couldn't put her finger on how it happened or what exactly he had done to her, but whatever it was she was determined to undo it. She wouldn't allow strong desire to jump his bones to jeopardize her chance of finding her mother.

The dollar in Montgomery's hand brought her back

to the present. He was handing it to her as he took his seat.

"What's that for?" she asked, relieved that there had been no bad guys to ruin the evening.

"Your thoughts. Knowing you, I figured it would take more than a penny."

Sabin's bright laughter sounded like music.

Montgomery's eyes and lips spread wide as if he were both shocked and pleased at her reaction. Smiling, Sabin snatched the dollar from his hand. Then she, not so discreetly, tucked it below the crest of her cleavage. "I'll tell you later," she said, turning her attention to the speaker.

Montgomery wrenched his eyes away from the spot where he saw his dollar disappear. *Down, boy,* he thought.

After the ceremony, the couple said the appropriate congratulations, good-byes and nice to have met you's. Montgomery's arm slid around her waist as if it had been created for just that purpose. Sabin felt like silk. *This is nuts,* she thought, feeling her femininity taking over. She knew she was putting just a little more sway in her hips. She knew she was standing just a bit straighter, pulling in her stomach, and sticking out her breasts. She knew her eyes were probably dilated from her arousal and that her lips were slightly more pursed as if expecting a kiss. And there was something else. . . . She couldn't help herself.

She wanted to be more womanly for this man of all men. Wanted him to feel the curve of her hips brushing in rhythm against his own. And she wanted him, darn it, to want her.

"Care for a nightcap?" he asked.

Sabin, who felt like she had just been injected with the best drugs in the world, wanted a chance to regain her composure. "I could really go for some coffee."

"I know a great place. And besides," he said, taking a quick glance at her bosom, "it will give you a chance to earn that dollar. It's just a few blocks from here, if you don't mind walking."

"No, I don't mind."

The two exited the hotel and entered into the D.C. night. Large billowy clouds rode low in the sky. Their deep blue hues made a rich background for the downtown buildings and monuments.

"And they say New York never sleeps." Sabin took a sweeping glance around her at all the people. They seemed so sophisticated with their intentional walks and swift pace. Where were they all going? she wondered.

"There's a lot to do in D.C. at night," he said, smiling at her.

Sabin detected a quick dart of mischief in his eyes. "Where are we going?"

"Someplace special. I promise. It's just around the corner."

To their right, taxis raced up and down the street. A lonely siren cried out in the distance adding to the night clamor. As they walked, Sabin watched for anything or anyone threatening.

"Look at that."

Sabin stopped beside Montgomery and followed his gaze.

"The architecture in this city is just phenomenal."

They stood across from a building that looked to be the size of an entire city block. The structure testified to the influence of Greek and Roman architecture so prevalent throughout the city. Its hard and majestic lines stood stoically Byzantine with granite columns reminiscent of the forum.

They entered a small hotel with marble stairs, plush maroon carpet, and gold trim on the ceiling.

"Wow," Sabin said, taking inventory.

Montgomery guided her to the elevators and pushed the up button. She admired the gold trim on the call button. "I wonder if that's—"

"It is," he said.

When the elevator came, they got on and he pushed the button for the top floor. "I can't imagine staying here," she said, considering that the rooms could easily be one thousand dollars per night.

"Oh, I don't know," he responded. "It might be fun to do once."

The elevator doors opened and they stepped into the hallway.

"It's just down here," he said, smiling wistfully.

They passed several doors and Sabin hoped that Montgomery hadn't been so presumptuous as to get a room. Then he stopped at two large French doors that opened into an outdoor restaurant on the roof of the hotel. Sabin gasped at the view.

"Two?" a small East Indian man asked.

Montgomery took her arm. "Yes."

The host led them to a table near the edge of the balcony. She sat down, quite pleased with his choice.

"Your server will be with you in a moment."

Sabin crossed one leg over the other. The gesture revealed a generous portion of her thigh and calf. She didn't care. "This is fabulous. How did you discover this place?" She looked over at the Washington Monument illuminated so brightly. She thought she could feel the warmth of the light on her skin.

They could see for miles. And in the shadow of the night and the focal point of their vision, the White House stood out intensely luminous, making a bright and bold statement in the darkness.

Montgomery's eyes followed the long line of her leg and then met hers. "A couple of years ago, I attended a Mad Dads convention and one of the wives suggested it. I've wanted to come back since then. I just never made the time."

"What's Mad Dads?"

A beautiful olive-skinned woman stepped to their table. "Would you like something to drink?"

"Two coffees, please," he said.

The server slid the order pad and pencil into her apron pocket. "I'll be right back."

"Mad Dads is the organization I mentioned during one of our many arguments. We sponsor and organize projects that get handguns off the street."

Sabin listened to Montgomery and swayed her head gently to the music she heard coming from across the hall. "I see."

"But I'm having such a good time with you tonight, I don't want to spoil it, so let's change the subject."

"Okay. What should we talk about?"

"How about your motorcycle? How's it handling?"

Sabin didn't want to admit that she hadn't ridden it much. Since Montgomery spent so much time at home these past few days, she hadn't had the opportunities she would have liked. Although once, when he had gone to his father's house, she had decided it was okay to go for a spin, especially since there was a cop with Montgomery. After twenty minutes, she had turned and headed back. She knew that twenty minutes could easily turn into two hours of riding.

"Fat Boy rides like the king he is."

"Good. Maybe I can go with you again sometime."

"Only if you promise not to scream."

"Do you need cream or sugar?" The server placed two white china cups on saucers in front of them. She poured coffee from a sterling-silver pitcher.

"Black," they both said in unison.

"All right. Can I get you anything else?"

They both shook their heads no, and the server left.

"Well, imagine that," Sabin said, picking up her cup. "Something we actually agree on."

"Yeah," Montgomery responded, watching her. "It almost makes me want go for the sugar and cream."

Sabin gave him a quick but soft kick on the shin.

"Hey!" he protested.

She took a sip of the dark hot contents of her cup. "Sorry. It was a reflex."

Montgomery took a sip of his coffee as well, eyes focused and hot on hers. She lost the stare down and lowered her eyes to his hands, his big working man's hands. *How come I never noticed that before?* she wondered. *They say a man with big hands has—*

"I'm going to have to put that thought on my American Express Gold."

"What?" she said, slightly embarrassed. Why was she acting like this? She had never lost focus with a man before. What was it about Montgomery that made her feel like a seventeen-year-old with a crush?

"Where do you go when your eyes smolder like that? And what are you thinking?"

"I was just . . . speculating."

"About?"

"About things . . . you."

"What about me?"

She told herself she was asking because of her job as his protector. "Are you seeing anyone, Montgomery?"

"Right now," he said, leaning forward, "all I can see is you."

Sabin stiffened. "Cut the BS. And don't treat me like any other woman you've known. I'm not like them." She let her anger diminish. "To tell you the truth, I think you're handsome and interesting. You and I have been fighting like rappers at the Source

Awards because of the simple fact that we've been honest with each other. And I like that. So, don't start throwing me lines now. Not when I'm already fascinated by the bait."

Montgomery nodded in assent. "True to your name, and point taken. So, to answer your question, no. I'm not seeing anyone."

A stampede of relief ran free inside her. She kept it from showing on her face. "What about Arroya?"

Montgomery drew in a breath and released it slowly. "Arroya is my best friend."

"And occasional lover, I'd suspect."

"And you'd be right. At least, that was true in the past. Our relationship has grown in a different direction lately."

"Does *she* know that?" Sabin asked, and took a sip of coffee.

"Look, if we're going to play Twenty Questions here, who's that guy I've seen making booty calls at your place?"

Sabin smiled sweetly. "What guy?"

Montgomery folded his arms. "Now who's shoveling BS? The guy with the big-ass suitcase. You know, comes over every other day at six."

"Oh, *him.*" *He's jealous,* she thought, laughing.

Their server returned. "More coffee here?"

"Yes," Montgomery responded sharply.

Sabin was still laughing. And it felt good. "You look cute when you're jealous."

"Jealous? I barely *know* you," he said lightheartedly. Then seriousness stole his smile. "Now who is he?"

Sabin's smile broadened. "He's my masseuse."

"You have a private masseuse?"

She considered the amount of money she was being paid and the muscle spasms that occasionally knotted in her legs. "Doesn't everybody?"

"No!"

"Well they should. Larry's great!"

Montgomery sipped his coffee. "I'll bet."

"He is. His back rubs are the best in town."

"And all he rubs is your back?"

"Well not exactly. He rubs my legs, arms, hands, shoulders, and neck, too. He keeps the cramps away."

The idea of another man's hands on Sabin's body cut through Montgomery like a hot poker. He sat quietly knowing that if he opened his mouth, he would say something inappropriate like, "Don't you know I'm the only man that's supposed touch you?"

"You want your dollar back?" Sabin asked.

The fire in Montgomery's eyes ignited. "Later."

Their server returned once again. "Is there anything you would like before we close?"

Montgomery sat up straight. "What time is it?"

"Almost eleven-thirty, sir."

"Sabin?"

"No, thank you. I don't want anything."

"Leave us the bill, please."

The woman smiled and placed the check on the table. "You two have a good night."

Montgomery pulled a ten out of his wallet and left it next to the bill. Music from the party across the hall came over loud and clear now. Most of the restaurant patrons were gone and the sounds from the party across the way wafted in smooth and resonate. Peabo Bryson sang, "I'm So Into You," like a tattletale blabbing Montgomery's thoughts.

"Would you like to dance?" he asked.

"Here?"

"Why not?"

"This is a restaurant. Not a ballroom. There's no dance floor here."

"We'll make one."

Sabin relented at the earnestness in his voice and took his hand. He guided her toward the entrance and they stopped just short of the French doors. The music was louder here. Sabin could feel it moving over her body and when Montgomery pulled her into his arms, she went swiftly as though she had become magnetized.

She followed his every movement and sway, not because she was such a good dancer, but because she had no will of her own. The heat surged between them like a direct current. Sabin was overcome. Their eyes caught and she was desperate for an irreverent remark to cool the inferno raging on her skin, through her soul.

She looked up. "Just how tall are you?"

"Six-five," he said in a voice deeper than Sabin remembered. "How tall are you?"

"Five-ten," she swallowed—"and three fourths."

It's not working, she realized, wanting to slide her tongue into his mouth that was oh so close. "How much do you weigh?"

"Two-sixty-three, or thereabouts. How much do you weigh?"

Sabin couldn't answer. His arms had closed tighter around her and he had pulled her closer. Besides, she was too busy fondling the back of his neck and rolling her fingers across the fine hairs there.

"Mm," he moaned and kissed her softly on the forehead. "Let's go."

> A full heart bursts easily.
>
> —Toda Kai

Thirteen

In the entryway of her house, Sabin braced herself for his kiss. Instead, he lowered his head to the crook of her neck and inhaled like a lion imprinting the scent of his mate. "You smell . . . forbidden," he murmured.

His chin nuzzled feather light against the side of her face. Sabin's skin tingled then ignited with the sensation of Montgomery's stubble on her jaw and across her cheek. His breath came out hot and moist. It stoked embers of desire she only vaguely admitted to having. Although she was fully clothed, she felt naked and laid open by the shock wave detonated by his almost-kiss.

The lips that had fascinated her for so long lightly touched hers. Then with exquisite slowness they pressed deeper. His warm tongue slid forward and took a smooth survey of the outer part of her mouth, studying, learning, devouring. The sensation was maddening as Sabin prayed he'd probe further. Their breath mingled in gasps and surprised inhalations. The dampness left by his tongue was just enough to create a light seal between their lips, and then, like an answer to her deepest craving they parted.

She opened her mouth wide, inviting him in. Her body temperature skyrocketed at the flick of his tongue at the corners of her mouth. She moaned, and as she did his fleshy tongue slid between her lips to meet its twin. Lavishly they danced as Montgomery's hands slid up past her wrists, below her elbows, over her shoulders, across her chest to finally curve up and around her aching bosom. As his tongue mingled in a circular motion with hers, his thumbs followed a similar lazy pattern on the hardened nipples of her breasts.

An explosion of sensations overwhelmed her—the moist sweet aroma of his breath, the hot manly smell of his neck and shoulders. Her desire for him came down like a driving rain. Their kiss deepened and he kept time as his lips pulsed over hers. She closed her eyes as a thin shiver streaked down her spine and settled between her thighs where it began a strong warm throb. He pressed himself closer and evidence of his arousal hardened against her.

Sabin couldn't catch her breath. The feelings rushing within her filled her with both fear and desire. She'd been with men before, but in this brief interlude, Montgomery had made love to her mouth in more ways than most men had ever made love to her body. When he swept her into his arms, she felt powerless and vulnerable, and unstrung.

"Which way?"

"Montgomery, let's . . ."

"Where's your bedroom?"

She relented. "Upstairs."

He carried her easily up the staircase and down the hall.

"In there," Sabin said.

He walked into her room and laid her on the queen-size bed. She willed herself not to tremble as he undressed her.

With each button unbuttoned, with each article of clothing removed, he kissed the area of her skin uncovered by his action. When she was completely naked, he paused to look at her. "So, this is what you've been hiding under all those clothes," he said, taking off his shirt.

As he removed the rest of his clothing, Sabin watched, transfixed. His body was exquisite. All sinew, tight, rolling, chiseled. When he removed his last article of clothing, she wondered if any manufacturer made condoms big enough and how she was ever going to accommodate him.

His hands mapped slow paths over her skin—from head to toe like a tropical storm rolling in from all directions. And then he stopped.

"Did I do this?" he asked.

Sabin opened her eyes and saw he was looking at the places on her right leg scarred from the accident. She said nothing.

"Baby, I'm sorry."

"Montg—"

"No . . . I am sorry." His lips tended every place on her leg that had been bruised. "I," *Kiss.* "will," *Kiss.* "never," *Kiss.* "hurt," *Kiss.* "you," *Kiss.* "again." He opened his mouth and the inside was moist and warm on her leg. From her ankle, he began a slow, sucking, licking ascent. Sabin felt as though he had pulled a thread and was unraveling her like a handmade sweater. She wanted to stop it, but she couldn't. It felt too good.

And then she saw it. The black-and-golden packet said Trojan Magnum. Montgomery had already ripped it open and was rolling the condom to the base of his swollen manhood. Just watching him made her throb.

He moved on top of her, all two hundred and sixty three pounds, and kissed her. His mouth was searing and hungry on hers. His hard weight felt good. Oh, so damned good. She didn't know her skin could catch fire so quickly or that her reason could be whisked away in an instant. She could feel his fingers probing and spreading her. If she opened her legs just a bit more, he would slide so easily inside.

"No," she whispered.

"Sabin," he moaned, inserting a finger. She was sopping, and eager, and . . . coming apart.

"Montgomery, stop."

His finger slid in and out of her wet essence. His thick legs nudged hers apart. "Baby, don't stop me."

She felt like she was being driven down an unfamiliar street in the dark. She couldn't be sure of what would happen if she kept going. Her body went rigid. "Montgomery, please . . ."

He groaned and rolled over. "What!"

"This isn't right."

"Really? And you wait until we're both buck naked and I'm hard as Kevlar to make this pronouncement."

"I'm sorry."

"I don't believe you."

"Why would I lie?"

Montgomery rose and collected his clothes. "Hell, I don't know. But then again, I don't know why you do anything." He blew hot breath between his lips. "This was almost a good night."

"Almost?" she asked, sitting up. "So it would have been a good night if you had gotten some, huh? Then everything would have been perfect, right?"

Sabin planted her hands on her hips. Montgomery's eyes grazed over her naked, puma-brown skin. An acute need to immerse himself in the ocean of her woman-space propelled him forward.

"Damn, Sabin," he said, reaching for her.

"Back off and get out."

Montgomery grabbed his shirt from the floor and shook his head. "You don't understand me at all, do you?"

"No, and after tonight, I don't want to."

He yanked on the rest of his clothes and, enraged, left her dressing in the dark. A thin sliver of light led him from the bedroom down to the dining room. When he rounded the corner into the living room, he stumbled into a sofa table. Cursing, he bent down to pick up the notebook he'd knocked onto the carpet. He froze when moonlight streaking through a window illuminated his name written in cursive on the page.

Montgomery's on the warpath now. I guess he thinks by playing amateur detective, he'll find out who's been trying to kill him. I've got to be more careful than ever.

The entry was dated today. Anger tightened his jaw. Before he could rip the book to shreds or hurl it against the wall, he heard Sabin's determined steps approaching. He quickly replaced the book on the table and left the house.

Kai,
What you said about the heart and feelings sometimes being a liability is true. Tonight, I almost let my heart get in the way of everything. I can't let that happen again. I won't. Not when I'm so close to finding her.
S.

When the motion detector went off, Sabin dropped her journal and rushed outside. Within seconds she vaulted from her yard and into Montgomery's, then folded into the night like a whisper. His back door was ajar. She slipped inside the opening, letting the darkness conceal her.

When she first learned how to soft-walk, she passed out from the sheer concentration of training her muscles to work in opposite patterns. Now it was like breathing, and she did both imperceptibly.

Her quarry on the other hand, lumbered through the dining room like a Sleestack. Sabin worked quickly before the commotion woke up Montgomery.

She crept behind the intruder, and before he could take his next breath, put him in a sleeper hold. With her left arm covering strategic places on his body and her right hand over his mouth, she issued her order.

"If you so much as move or moan, I'll snap your neck." To make sure he understood the sincerity of her threat, she tightened her arm muscles across an artery in his throat. He didn't groan, but his eyes bulged in agony.

"Now, here's what we're gonna do. We're gonna leave Mr. Claiborne's house right now. I'll guide us out, and *you* will never, ever come back here again. Got me?"

One more tighten for good measure. She could smell the pungent odor of fear rising like ether from his pores. Then she realized she hadn't caught a hit man. *This guy must be a vandal or more likely a thief.* As she backed him gently out of Montgomery's kitchen, she wondered what her prisoner had come to filch.

Once out of the house, she maneuvered him into her yard. "I'm going to uncover your mouth. When I do, you're going to tell me what you came for. Understand?"

His pulse jackhammered against her arms. "One, two . . . three." She took her hand away and the ex-

pletives that spewed out of the man's mouth prompted
a *shito* to his stomach. When he doubled over, Sabin
knelt beside him.

"Bad idea, Jack-o. Now listen, that was a love pat
compared to what I would *like* to do, but I want information."

More expletives. This time they sounded strained,
as if he was sitting on the toilet trying to push out a
brick.

Sabin stood and stepped back. "Since I'm not into
torture, here's what we'll do. Go back to whoever sent
you and tell 'em that *Monty* has a guardian angel with
a *serious* attitude. And the next person she catches
even *thinking* about harming him gets sent to the hospital. Ya feel me?"

But the man was already gone, scurrying away like
a cockroach in bright light. She tiptoed back to
Montgomery's open door and closed it. As she headed
for home, his bedroom light blinked on. Sabin slipped
easily into stealth mode and eclipsed herself beside a
bushy shrub. When the blinds in the bedroom
cranked open, she stood motionless and on the qui
vive. When they closed, she obscured herself against
the darkness and silently entered her house.

The next morning, Montgomery parked his Jag in
the vacant lot across from Mary Rose Apartments. This
small gray building sat on the cusp of one of D.C.'s
many 'hoods. Trey Williams, a self-proclaimed black
geek, was the closest Montgomery had ever come to
knowing a genius.

Montgomery carried a Zip cartridge and his office
hard drive with him and ascended the three flights of
stairs to Trey's apartment.

When he reached the door, it opened before he could knock and out came a beautiful Cuban woman.

"*Hola*, Carmen."

"What's up, Monty? *¿Es su computer, otra vez?*"

"I don't know what you just said, but it sounded as pretty as you are."

"*Gracias*, Papi."

Carmen bounced down the stairs smiling. Montgomery entered the apartment and closed the door behind him.

"What's with her?" he asked, knowingly.

A thin black man in a bathrobe and biker shorts smiled with big white teeth. "Computers aren't the only things I do well."

Montgomery placed his hard drive on a long table. The two men embraced and Montgomery detected the faint aroma of whatever was going on just moments before he arrived. He considered mentioning it, but Trey had quite a few quirks. It seemed his intellect came at the expense of normalcy.

"How was your vacation?"

Trey perched himself on the edge of the table. His thick hair was in need of a large comb. "It's was cool, man. But you know Rio."

"Ah, actually, I don't."

"Oh. Well you should go one day, man," he said, scratching at his head. "So, what's up with Sarah?"

Trey named all the computers he worked on after women he'd slept with. Sarah was a girl he'd met in reform school. She was easygoing and didn't need much tending to. "Virus. Didn't Angela tell you?"

He hopped off the desk. "Naw. She just said I should call you as soon as I got back in town."

He picked up the tower CPU and headed into what should have been a dining room. Instead it looked more like Dr. Techenstein's laboratory. In no time, he had Sarah hooked up to a monitor and plugged into an outlet. Then he pushed the button on the front panel and waited.

When he saw the message "Unrecognized Function Click OK to Continue," he shrank back. "Uh."

"What?"

"Nothing. It's just that this bug is in your operating system. This is going to take a while, *if* I can restore it."

Montgomery sat down. "What do you mean 'if'?"

"If, as in if I can do it. I'm a geek, not a miracle worker."

Trey sifted through the disarray on the desk: floppy disks, CDs, CD cases, circuit boards.

"In other words, I can't wait for this one."

"Not unless you don't have anything to do for the next twelve to fifteen hours."

"How much is this going to cost me?"

The young man finally found what he was looking for. He inserted a yellow diskette into the hard drive. "I'm sure we can work something out."

Montgomery tried to imagine just what that might entail. Knowing Trey, there would be referrals to his storage clients involved. But he didn't mind. Trey loved computers the way some people loved chocolate. More probably. And aside from an occasional weird trait, he was the best at what he did.

"Can I wait for this?" Montgomery asked, handing him the Zip drive.

"You just need a copy?"

"Yeah."

Trey's house-shoe-clad feet carried him to computer equipment stacked like poker chips on the other side of the room. He slid the disk into a drive, turned a few knobs, slid another disk into another drive, and typed a series of quick commands on a keyboard.

"That will take about five minutes."

Montgomery's survey of the room reminded him of just how far Trey had come. When they first met, Trey was a thirteen-year-old kid in trouble for breaking into a Radio Shack. In addition to community service, an understanding judge also sentenced the youngster to participation in the Mad Dads Sankofa Rites of Passage program.

Montgomery soon discovered that Trey was the brightest kid he'd ever encountered. He was being raised by an elderly aunt and had acquired more computer equipment than most electronics stores. Trey was a genius when it came to technology. By ten, he had hacked into his aunt's state Social Services file, increasing her monthly disbursement and food stamp allotment by two hundred percent.

But Montgomery didn't find out about that until much later. What he learned early on was that Trey was a kid too smart for his own good. He was easily bored, and despite his involvement with the Mad Dads, he dropped out of high school at fifteen. The upside was that he kept working with computers.

It was a while before he could get Trey to commit to following a straight and narrow path to his inevitable fortune. But after he explained the government's interest in his misappropriation of funds and the anguish his aunt would experience as a result, Trey acquiesced and with Montgomery's help had been operating a legitimate business ever since.

Trey opened a drawer and took out a clear plastic case full of small tools. He placed them near Sarah.

Montgomery grew concerned. "What are those for?"

"In case I have to perform surgery."

* * *

Kai,

I checked with the Corps again. They wouldn't tell me anything. I can't imagine what she's doing over there. Maybe she feels guilty for giving me up and so she wants to absolve herself by helping others. I guess we're alike in that way.

S.

"What? Did you get your days mixed up?" Reeves Claiborne asked as Montgomery entered the house.

"Morning, Tilde," Montgomery offered, ignoring his father's remark. In recent years, the only time Montgomery had come to visit other than his regular Thursdays was the other day to check on Cherlyn. Since filing the police report, there had been no new leads on the case. His sister was still a bit shaken.

Tilde smiled, nodded, and made herself busy in the kitchen. Montgomery remained with his father in the living room.

"I need a favor," he said.

Before he could finish his sentence, his father was already shaking his head. "It's my gun, and I'm keeping it."

Years-old tension staked a familiar claim in Montgomery's neck and shoulders. "It's not that." He held up the case of Zip cartridges. "I need to keep these in a safe place." Then before he could stop himself, he retorted, "And I thought I'd store them here until I can find one."

Reeves rolled backward just slightly, the wheels of his chair squeaking as he did so. "Humph. Now tell me the real story." He crossed two muscular arms against each other and waited.

Not one decent conversation, Montgomery thought. *Not one. Why can't I just sit down with you, without you always thinking you know better than I do?* "Look, my computer crashed. Until I can get it fixed or buy a new one, I want to keep the backups off-site. Would it put you out terribly if you kept them here?"

Tilde came in quietly, leaving a tray of tea and homemade bread before returning to the kitchen.

"Did your computer crash on its own or did it have help?"

"Okay, would you quit with the doomsday lectures! This is not some thriller, chiller movie where an innocent bystander gets chased by some bad guys!" Montgomery knew it was only a matter of seconds before his father would whip out his all-too-familiar lecture on self-preservation. This time, instead of letting him go on and on, he would stop him, tell him to shut up, and mind his own business.

"All right. It's your life," his father said, wheeling toward him. "Give me those things. I'll put them in my safe."

"What?" he said, as his father took the plastic case from him.

"I'm going to put them up for safekeeping. Isn't that what you wanted?"

Montgomery was stunned. He expected a battle and got accommodation. "What's going on?"

Reeves placed the case in his lap, turned his chair toward the dining area, and wheeled away from his son. "You asked me for a favor. I'm doing you a favor. Can't a father do a favor for his son?"

Montgomery followed close behind. "Some can. But you? Never without a fight. What gives?"

The old chair creaked in rhythm as the wheels, lap-lapped across the hardwood floor.

Reeves spun abruptly, facing his son. "What gives! You hear that, Tilde! He wants to know what gives!" He moved in closer. "*I'm* giving, I think, son. I'm giving us a chance to get along, without fighting, or bunkering in against each other, or turning my living room into a combat zone. But can you accept that? No! You have to go and ruin it by assuming something's wrong.

"Well, I guess maybe you're right. Something is wrong, son. I'm old, and I'm tired, and I want peace. And if we can't coexist in complete peace, I'll settle for a cease-fire."

Montgomery was not the least bit swayed by his father's proclamation of innocence or his sudden concern for their peacekeeping. Something was up, and he knew it. "Old habits are hard to break, Father. Wouldn't you say?"

"I'd say you'd better stop riding me like some pony in a horse show."

"Or what? You'll turn me across your knee?"

Reeves rolled into the den with his son following close behind. He took a set of keys from his pocket and opened a desk drawer. Dropping the drive case into the drawer, he signed heavily. "If that would put some sense into your head, then, yes, I'd do it in a heartbeat." He locked up the desk and wheeled around to face his son.

"I'm sure you would," Montgomery responded, turning away. On the way out, he nodded to Tilde, still keeping her distance in the kitchen. "I'll be back this evening."

"Are you sure you don't mind doing this?" Montgomery thought of how his anger had cooled and hoped that Sabin's had, as well. Since their argument in her bedroom, Montgomery decided he had been rushing things and told her as much. She had accepted his apology and his request to help his sister.

Sabin fastened the seat belt. "Of course I'm sure. I do this for a living." Then she glanced at a concerned Montgomery behind the wheel. "Are *you* sure?"

"I just want to make sure my sister is safe. Anything I can do to ensure her safety, I'll do."

"Including putting up with me?"

A shrewd grin slid across Montgomery's face. It made him look sexy and alluring.

"There must be something wrong with me, but I think I'm getting used to you."

"Stop the presses."

"No, really. I . . ." He took his eyes off the road for a moment. "I'm actually beginning to enjoy your company."

At his words, something warm and exciting shifted inside Sabin. "Same here," she said, noticing that her voice sounded different, kinda whispery and far away.

"So," Montgomery said, maneuvering the car toward the city, "I noticed you don't have any books or pamphlets. How does a session like this work?"

"A little differently than when I conduct a workshop. Since this will be one-on-one, I'll try to get a sense of Cherlyn's habits." Sabin adjusted the seat to allow more room for her legs. "Then I can tailor our discussion to her specific routine."

The Maryland foothills whizzed by on either side of the car, their greenery growing dark in the coming evening.

"It really is beautiful."

"Yes, it is," Montgomery agreed, smiling at her.

She watched as his expression grew more serious. "We also never talked about how much this will cost. I'm familiar with the price of consultants these days. Feel free to send me a bill."

"I couldn't do that, Montgomery."

"Of course you can."

Sabin thought about the ramifications of that. No, she would simply add the cost of her consultant fee to her other services rendered, which were late this month for some reason. "I understand the benefits of occasional pro bono work. Just give me a good referral, and we'll call it even."

"Hmmm" was his only reply. "How do you feel about dinner? I'm sure Tilde, my father's companion, will prepare a feast and insist we all partake."

"Lovely," she said, imagining a home-cooked meal. "I haven't eaten since breakfast."

The rest of the drive was filled with talk of the weather, sports, and music. They both thought it was way too hot for the time of year. They both were eager for football season. However, neither of them could agree on what constituted good music.

"You mean you've never heard of Aerosmith!"

"Never. What do they sing?"

Montgomery's question rendered Sabin nearly speechless. "Only the best rock music on the planet—aside from The Stones that is. You have heard of The Stones, right?"

"Now them I've heard of."

"But you've never heard the song 'Crying' or 'Don't Want to Miss a Thing'?"

"Nope."

"Certainly you've heard of 'Walk This Way'!"

Montgomery frowned. "Don't jump out of the car, but no, I haven't."

"Man, what boulder do you live under?"

He laughed. "One that plays real music."

"And that would be . . . ?"

"The blues. What else?"

Sabin made a gagging sound.

"What? Etta James, B.B. King, Bobby Blue Bland."

"Yuck!"

"I'll trade ten rock stars for one blues man anyday. Half the rock stars out there wouldn't know how to pick their noses if it hadn't been for John Lee Hooker."

"Who?"

"Oh, now who's out of touch?"

Montgomery turned on his CD player. "Now tell me this doesn't soothe your soul."

Sabin didn't know who was singing, but her voice was strong, guttural even. The woman sang a story about her life and growing up. She could hear hard times in the woman's full-bodied tones.

Sabin turned to Montgomery, who was rocking his head to the slow drag of the song.

"It's the honesty I go for," he said. "Blues people tell it like it is. Just like jazz people . . . straight, no chaser. Only, jazz is so often fixed up and made pretty these days. But blues . . . the blues are raw and rough around the edges. What you see is what you get. And what you get is the truth, whether or not it sounds nice or feels good."

A twinge of guilt closed Sabin's eyes. She wondered how it would affect Montgomery to know the truth about her. She'd never considered the fact that he might find out. She had just imagined that she would keep him safe until whomever was after him went away, got tired, or was arrested by the police. But what if he discovered her lie? *So what?* she told herself. *I won't be the one he'll turn his anger to.*

"Well?" he asked as they came into the city.

"She's no Stevie Nicks," Sabin replied.

Montgomery snorted. "I give up!"

Within twenty minutes, they pulled into a short driveway. The ranch-style house was nestled in the middle of an older, middle-class neighborhood.

"Before we go inside," Montgomery said, escorting her to the door, "I have to warn you about my father."

Sabin turned to see a strange strain in his eyes.

"There's no love lost between us. I mean, he can do and say some mean-spirited things, especially when it comes to me. And being that you are someone I'm bringing to help his one and only daughter, you may encounter some of the fallout." Montgomery drew in a long breath. "I apologize in advance if that happens."

"No need," Sabin said. "I think I can hold my own."

Montgomery nodded and they went in.

Sabin liked the simple elegance of the home. Plenty of room. Not too much of anything, but what was there was of exquisite quality and well taken care of.

"Cher," Montgomery called.

"She's working at the hospital," Reeves said, coming into the entryway.

"Father, this is Sabin Strong."

"Mr. Claiborne," she said, extending her hand.

His eyes flashed briefly as they touched. Then a smile flickered across his lips and was gone. "A pleasure," he said, then turned to his son.

"Tilde's just about done with dinner. You two care for a drink?" Reeves steered himself into the dining area and Montgomery stared after him in disbelief. Sabin smiled and followed behind him.

"What'll ya have, Miss Strong?"

"Sabin, please. And I'll have ginger ale if you have it."

"Coming right up! How 'bout you, son?"

"I want to know what you've done with my father."

Reeves smiled sweetly. "He's so funny! Just a riot." He chuckled a little too loudly. "Why don't I make it two ginger ales, huh?" he asked, and set about making their drinks.

"What's gotten into you?"

Reeves presented the two with their drinks. "Maybe I'm just not used to having such a beautiful young woman in my presence."

Montgomery took a sip from his cup. "Uh-huh."

"Give your dad a break. He's obviously trying to be nice."

Sabin and Montgomery took their drinks into the living room and sat on the sofa. Reeves settled in near them. "That's right. And nice is a hard thing to be if you're a war vet like me and you've seen what I've seen."

"Aw, jeez." Montgomery groaned and ran a hand down his face.

"What war, Mr. Claiborne?"

"Reeves, please. And the Korean War." He leaned back in his chair and glanced upward. "See, the Korean War was the first time U.S. military units were integrated. It was also the first time we had the opportunity to be platoon leaders in the Army."

Montgomery helped his father say, "I was one such leader. Pulled me as an officer right out of Tuskegee."

The elder Claiborne frowned his son into silence and continued. "All right. I'll spare you my usual spiel and just say that I never knew there were so many ways to die, and my experience was so influential on my life, I wrote a book about it."

"Really?" Sabin asked.

"Sure did. Of course, I never had it published, but Tilde typed up all my stories and took them to a copy center. I had copies made for some family members and a few of the fellas from the Vet's Club." Then he smiled. "Would you like to see it?"

"Father, I don't think . . ."

"I'd love to."

"Great. Son, go down to the basement and look in my cedar chest."

"Oh, for heaven's sake, Father. Sabin didn't come over here to listen to your overblown war stories."

"Overblown!" Reeves pulled back the blanket covering the lower half of his body to expose two atrophied legs in what looked like children's sweatpants. "Does this look overblown to you?"

"Please, Montgomery," Sabin said, rising. "I'd like to read your father's story."

Montgomery took one look at his father and then at Sabin. "Whatever," he mumbled, and left the room.

As soon as Sabin heard his footsteps on the stairs, she walked quickly to where Reeves was sitting and grabbed the front of his wheelchair.

"Where's my money, old man!"

The truth strikes hard, like an iron palm.
—Toda Kai

Fourteen

"Keep your voice down," he insisted.

"You either give me my money, or I tell Montgomery about our nice arrangement."

"I'll pay you when you do what you're supposed to do."

"He's alive, isn't he?"

"Just barely. Cher told me about the incident at the lookout point. You're supposed stop that from happening. Not rush in when it's already in progress."

"Your son could have been dead many times over if it wasn't for me. Now pay up or the next time someone tries to take him out, you'll be paying funeral expenses instead of a bodyguard fee. But I warn you . . . someone—"

"Are you sure it's in the cedar chest?" Montgomery called up from the basement.

Reeves kept his eyes on Sabin. "Yeah, I'm sure. Keep looking."

Sabin squatted down to eye level with the elder Claiborne. "Someone has a severe interest in doing your son harm. And I'm damn good at what I do. Now, if you love Montgomery, you'll pay me what you promised and let me do my job."

Reeves frowned and reached into his pocket. He peeled several thousand-dollar bills from a wad. "You better be worth it."

"Don't worry," she said, rising. "I am."

Montgomery's voice bellowed up from the basement. "It's not down here!"

Reeves wheeled his chair over to an end table. He opened the drawer and removed a spiral-bound book. "Never mind. I found it!"

When Montgomery got back upstairs, Sabin and Reeves were deep in conversation over a picture in his book.

"This is right after we had come through an ambush."

Sabin watched out of the corner of her eye as Montgomery added a shot of vodka to his glass of ginger ale. He sat in the chair across from them and looked on in silence.

Three drinks and ten chapters later, he still sat quietly, while Sabin laughed at Reeves's military jokes and listened intently to his near-death experiences.

Sabin was enthralled. Now that they understood each other, she and Reeves were getting along tremendously. Montgomery, on the other hand, looked as though he were in a great deal of pain. She was about to comment on his grimace, when a five-foot clown startled her.

"Cher!" Reeves said brightly.

"Sorry I'm late. One of the kids had surgery yesterday and was in a lot of pain. I spent some extra time with him to try to cheer him up."

"Did it help?" Sabin asked.

"I think so," she replied, crossing the room. "You must be Sabin."

Sabin stood, extended a hand. "Yes. Nice to meet you."

"Thanks for coming to talk to me. I'm still kinda jittery, ya know."

"I know," Sabin said. "We can talk about that after dinner."

"That sounds great. I'll just go and get changed," she said, bouncing past Montgomery. She slapped him playfully on the shin. "Stop brooding, big brother."

"Humph," he said, eyeing everyone in the room suspiciously.

By the time Cherlyn came back, the dining table was set and Tilde was bringing food in from the kitchen. Sabin was ready. Her stomach had begun to react to the hunger-inducing aromas a good twenty minutes ago.

It didn't take long for her to pick up on the dynamics of the Claiborne family. Reeves, though wrinkled and frail looking on the outside, had the intestinal fortitude of a raging bull. His love and affection came in bittersweet jibes into his son's side. His daughter, however, received the rain of whatever affection he had left in his terrible soul. His respect he gave to Tilde. Now she was easy to figure out. Unnervingly quiet, she kept to herself most of the time. Sabin imagined that in private she was quite the opposite and brought a steadying hand to Reeves's angry disposition. Cherlyn, the apple of her father's eye, was all hope and dedication. Her plans to become a pediatrician were definite and specific. She took her seat between her father and her brother. The way she deflected potshots from the both of them was practiced and effective. She was the neutral zone that kept father and son from truly despising each other.

And then there was Montgomery, the great enigma.

Not even guilt could make him as dedicated to his father as he pretended not to be. Despite his many groans, exasperated sighs, and wisecracks, Montgomery's eyes betrayed him. The love he had for Reeves forced its way to the surface and shone on his face like a distant star.

"Don't you agree, Sabin?"

"I'm sorry," she said, joining the conversation.

"It's a good thing Montgomery didn't go into the service."

Cherlyn elbowed her father lightly. "Dad, stop."

Sabin saw a shadow of anger move across Montgomery's face. "I don't think so," she said.

"Well, that's because you haven't known him as long as we have."

"I disagree. In my business I have to be able to size people up fairly quickly and determine within a split second what they're capable of. My gut tells me that Montgomery is not to be underestimated."

Montgomery's eyes caught Sabin's and the anger she saw faded.

Tilde cleared away the dishes and Reeves went to bed, although he called it an early-evening nap. That left Montgomery alone with his sister and a woman whose life events had become a series of successful rescues. He just hoped that she would be as successful at helping his sister overcome the fear created by her recent assault. If she could do that, he would do whatever it took to repay her.

Sabin walked over to where he stood leaning against the wall. "Montgomery, I'm going to need your help."

"Anything."

"I need you to give us some privacy."

"Anything but that."

"Don't you trust me?"

"It's not that," he said, peering down at her. "I think it's pretty obvious that I can trust you with my life. But my sister's life on the other hand . . . I'd feel much better sticking around."

"Well, all right. But keep quiet. I'm a professional. I don't appreciate being interrupted or disrupted in my work."

Montgomery held up his hands innocently. "I'll be on my best behavior."

"That should be interesting," she said, walking back to where Cher sat patiently on the couch.

He watched as Sabin sat beside his sister. She was the epitome of self-possession. Cher, on the other hand, had had a fearful expression in her eyes since the incident. It was as if she was on the brink of tears, tears caused by terror. He wanted that gone. If he ever got his hands on the person responsible, well, he wouldn't be responsible for his actions.

"Cherlyn, I'm going to give you a condensed version of a workshop I do on personal safety. I thought if we could just talk about what happened, I could share some things with you that will help you through all the emotions you must be feeling."

The young woman sat still for a moment, then nodded.

Sabin sent a quick glance and a reassuring smile in Montgomery's direction before beginning. "All right. What's been going on since the attack?"

"Don't you want to know about the attack itself?"

"Montgomery, I thought we had an agreement."

"Sorry," he said, crossing his arms.

"Go ahead, Cherlyn."

"Well, it's been pretty much business as usual."

Montgomery groaned.

"Ignore him," Sabin responded. "You said 'business as usual.' "

"Well, yes, except that I don't go out at night anymore."

Sabin nodded. "What else?"

"I, uh, look over my shoulder a lot. And I'm easily startled."

"Those are your self-preservation instincts taking over. Anything else?"

"I've been thinking about taking up karate or something. You know, so I'll be better prepared next time."

"The best way you can be prepared is with this." Sabin pointed to her brain. "Not with this." Sabin took her hand and made a fist. "At the beginning of every workshop, I tell people that the key to personal safety lies in your thinking, not your kicking or punching."

Intrigued, Montgomery took a seat across from Sabin.

"I teach a four-step safety method. I call it AIMS. AIMS stands for Awareness, Intuition, Movement, and Sound. If you can remember what to do in each of these steps, you can prevent most incidents from occurring in the first place."

Cherlyn smiled. "That sounds good."

"Awareness is when you really pay attention to what's going on around you."

"Like me looking over my shoulder."

"No. That's paranoia. When I say Awareness, I mean observing and processing what is actually happening as opposed to worrying about what might happen."

Tilde came into the living room with a tray of oatmeal cookies and cider. She placed the tray on the coffee table and sat in the chair next to Montgomery's.

Sabin took a cup of cider and continued. "What were you doing right before you were attacked?"

"I was trying to change my flat tire. I couldn't get the lug nuts off, and I was mad about that."

"So, were you aware of what was going on or were you distracted?"

Cherlyn frowned. "I guess I was distracted."

"Then what happened?"

"Then I heard footsteps. When I looked up, I saw a man coming toward me."

"How did you feel when you saw him?"

"At first relieved that someone was coming to help me. And then . . ."

"Yes?"

"And then I felt uncomfortable. Like something was wrong."

Montgomery, Tilde, and Cherlyn took cookies from the tray.

"That's the Intuition part of the process," Sabin said. "We almost always know when someone is up to no good. Something makes us feel creepy or like you said, 'uncomfortable.' We've got great built-in radar, if we'd only listen to it."

"How does Motion fit in?"

"Motion is displaying confidence. Appearing in control, even if you're not. Showing no fear. The fact that you had a flat tire, plus the fact that you were frustrated because you couldn't fix it, put you in a very vulnerable position."

Montgomery reflected on the events of his life recently, noting the vulnerable positions he'd put himself into lately.

"And Sound?"

"Sound can be the most powerful prevention tool. Let me ask you a question. What did you say when the man came toward you . . . when you felt uncomfortable?"

"Nothing. I was going to say something, but I starting thinking that he must be coming to help me."

"I'll bet that if you would have firmly, confidently, asked him what he was doing or what his problem was, he would have thought twice about harming you."

"I don't think so," Montgomery said. She'd had him until that point.

"Well, I know so. Assailants want a mark, an easy target. Someone who's not going to give them any trouble. If they think for a moment that you might be trouble, they usually back down and find someone else."

Cherlyn took a sip of cider. "Suppose AIMS doesn't work? What then?"

"Then you have to fight."

Montgomery sat up straight in the chair. Tilde cleared her throat.

"What about pepper spray?" Cherlyn asked, the apprehension returning to her face.

"Pepper spray is great if you have it ready at all times, if your attacker comes at you straight on, if the wind isn't blowing, if the dispenser doesn't malfunction, if you're not accosted by the percentage of the population unaffected by pepper spray."

Cherlyn's shoulders sank. Sabin touched her hand reassuringly.

"I can show you some basic self-defense techniques."

"That's out," Montgomery said. "Fighting back would just make an attacker angry. No telling what might happen then."

"If she's being attacked, fighting back may be the only chance she has. Now, Cherlyn, I can show you some techniques that you don't have to take up martial arts for. Are you interested?"

"Yes."

"Good. The first thing you need to know is that there are two important blows for you to strike—opening and finishing. An opening move makes it possible for you to get loose if someone has grabbed you. A finishing move allows you to incapacitate an attacker long enough for you to get away. Montgomery . . ."

Sabin stood and motioned for Montgomery to stand, too.

"Sabin, look, I don't think . . ."

She smiled. "Don't worry. I won't hurt you."

"You won't hurt me?" he replied, standing to the challenge.

Sabin stood facing Cherlyn. Tilde sat forward in her seat and took another cookie from the tray.

"Come up behind me, Montgomery," Sabin said, shaking out her shoulders. "And do it in slow motion so I can demonstrate."

This ought to be fun, he thought. Sure, she'd swooped in like a caped crusader in the past, but she was probably acting on adrenaline. He walked up slowly and wrapped his left arm around her throat while grabbing her right arm with his right hand. When he pulled her back into him, he hadn't prepared for the soft impact of her rear end against his groin. *Yes, this is going to be fun.*

"Cherlyn, do you wear heels?" Sabin asked.

"Sometimes," she said.

"Then an opening move in this position would be to raise your foot and drive your high heel down as hard as you can into your attacker's foot. If you have to leave a pair of two hundred-dollar stiletto pumps behind, by all means do so. Otherwise, if you're wearing flats, a hard backward kick to the knee is a good idea.

"After your opening move, you can finish him off.

And when I say finish, I mean *finish*. You've got to fight with everything you've got. So this time you want to kick the person in the head as hard as you can. Montgomery?"

"Yeah?"

"You can let go of me now."

"Oh," he said, stepping away.

"Okay. Let's try it again in real time."

Montgomery nodded. "You want me to come from the back again?"

"It doesn't matter."

Cocky, he thought. *I ought to do something that shuts her up and proves that sometimes fighting back can make things worse.* And with that thought, he went after her. Unfortunately, all he heard was Sabin shouting "Open!" and "Finish!" Then he was looking up at her from the ground.

He was going to ask what happened, but his force of his father's approaching laughter explained it all.

"Now," Reeves said, steering himself next to where Montgomery lay dazed on the floor, "I've seen everything!"

Montgomery took off the helmet and put his hand on his chest. Yes, his heart was still there, but it felt like it was tap dancing instead of beating.

"Let me," Sabin said, climbing off her chrome monster. She turned to where he was still seated on the bike and placed her hand where his had been.

Her touch jolted him like a tiny electric current shocking his body.

"Wow," she said, smiling. "I feel it."

"Me, too," he said, placing his hand over hers.

"Don't worry," she said, pinching the side of his face. "You'll get used to it."

Never, he thought, watching her walk toward her house. She looked good in a pair of hip-hugging jeans and denim vest. She removed her helmet and waves of sleek black hair cascaded down her back. "You wanna grab a bite to eat later?"

He stepped off the bike that now sported the vanity license plate of SABIKER. "Are you kidding? I think I left my stomach at the top of the first hill we took."

She laughed. It was a summery kind of laugh that made him smile and want to touch her face. "Actually, I've got an errand to run, but after that I'm free."

He headed off toward his house then turned, conjuring up another way to keep her close. "Sabin?"

"Yes?" she said, opening her door.

"Why don't you come with me?"

Kai,
Once, when I was by myself, three guys came up on me. I guess they thought they were going to pull a train on me or something. I put all three of those guys in the hospital. So why does Montgomery make me so weak, I can't defend myself?
S.

"You really believe in this peace-on-earth thing?" she asked as they walked to his driveway.

Montgomery believed in a lot of things, but the notion of a peaceful world was number one. "Yes, I do."

"Despite the fact that most people are butt heads?"

"Most people are good, honest, hardworking folk who sometimes need a hand to keep them on the right track."

Sabin thought about the people she'd known in her lifetime. The nuns at the orphanage, the kids there, her first boyfriend, all the people who were willing to pay her to harm others. No, most people were in dire need of an attitude and/or behavior adjustment and were to be avoided at all costs.

"Sounds like rose-colored glasses to me."

"That's exactly why I invited you," he said, opening the car door for her.

She slid in. "Oh, it's not my personality and my good looks?"

He got in beside her and started the engine. "Well, it's definitely not your personality."

"Oh, this from a man who owns a storage facility. How much more boring can you be!"

"Boring? Boring! I'll have you know that running a storage facility is an exciting line of work. Shoot. I can . . . well, I . . ."

They both laughed freely.

"See, you can't even lie about it."

Montgomery grinned. He shifted gears and headed the Jag toward the interstate. "Well on a serious note, I have had some interesting things happen in my time."

Sabin turned to him, arms crossed. "Like?"

"Like the time a family stored ten roach-infested boxes of clothing in a unit."

"That's nasty."

"After I pinpointed where the roaches were coming from, I called pest control services every week for a month. They made a small dent, but those suckers were still hanging on. Now you know I couldn't have that."

"How did you get rid of them?"

"I had to go back to the old school. When my family first moved here, we rented a house that had its share of critters. My mom bought some boric acid from the drugstore and put it down. Those things were gone in no time.

"For a whole month, it looked like winter in Building A. But after that, no more roaches."

"Anything else?"

"Once, I discovered that a woman who was renting three fairly large units was growing marijuana in them."

That got a big chuckle from Sabin. *I guess she likes my stories,* Montgomery thought.

"Hmm. What else?"

"Well, there was the time I found a bomb in one of the units."

She uncrossed her arms then. "You're kidding! Was that recently?"

"No. That was about six years ago. It was a new contract. The guy had paid for one month and then just stopped paying. Well, we have a grace period before we get rid of someone's belongings, but the grace period came and went and there was no payment and no pickup.

"So Randy and I were loading these boxes into a Dumpster, when we discovered this radio that had been rewired. I was just going to toss it into the trash, but Ted told me to hold on."

"And it was a *real* bomb?"

"Yeah. It wasn't armed, though. Just waiting for someone to come and turn it on."

"I guess you *do* live an interesting life."

"Well, by far the most interesting discovery in a unit so far was the time that Randy was making his rounds. We do walk-throughs on a regular basis just to make sure everything is copacetic. So he was walking through and he heard a sneeze."

"No . . ."

"Yep. He said that at first he assumed he was hearing things. And then it happened again. He called out to see if it was me or the trainee. But of course it wasn't. So when he heard it again, he opened the unit where he heard the sound and sure enough, there was a man living in there with his stuff. He claimed that our facility was cheaper than renting a house or apartment and cleaner than a boarding room."

"Wow. What happened?"

"Randy kicked him out, of course. But ol' Clyde still haunts the warehouse. Sleeps right outside the loading area most of the time."

"You should call the police."

"Nah. He's harmless. Besides, he thinks he's protecting the place. And I pay him for his security guard services."

Montgomery maneuvered the car to avoid a chuckhole in the road. "Enough about me. What interesting adventures have *you* had?"

Sabin sat back against the black leather. "There was the time I rode to Canada."

"Canada? What for?"

"Just because. Riding a motorcycle makes you do things like that."

He noticed that her voice sounded like it was coming from someplace distant.

"You get on and the next thing you know, you've been riding for hours. I was living in Texas at the time, angry at the world, and needing to get away from it all. My intention was to spend the morning riding. But by the time I really realized what I was doing, I was almost to Nebraska.

"So then I thought, why not? Why not just keep going? So I did. When I finally stopped for good, I was in Winnipeg."

"Jeez. That's a long ride."

"Who are you telling? My legs felt like someone had

chopped them off, performed terrible experiments on my thighs, and then reattached them. My butt felt like it had just disintegrated. I stayed in a hotel for a month and did nothing except lie on my stomach."

As much *back* as Sabin had, he could not imagine it disintegrating. He couldn't imagine a month in a hotel. That must have been nice . . . and expensive. *I'm definitely in the wrong business.*

He glanced sideways to check her reaction, but she was staring out the window. There was something unpleasant about the silence.

"Sounds like a great adventure. Have you had others?"

"No," she said, still looking out. "Just the usual motorcycle stuff."

"Like . . ."

"Bugs in the teeth."

"Ugh. Disgusting."

"It's not so bad," she said, turning back. "Like today when I told you you were choking my waist, I got a moth in my mouth."

He stomach twinged. "Guess I won't be kissing *you* anymore."

Sabin laughed. "I don't blame you. Moths are the worst. Kind of bitter. And they leave an aftertaste. But the rest, you just scrape 'em off and spit 'em out."

"No, thanks."

"Well, there are the JSTs."

"What are JSTs?"

"I was in a motorcycle club once and JST is what we used to call stuff on the road that's just sitting there."

"I don't get it."

"One time, a bunch of us were riding to Oklahoma, and we saw a king-size mattress just sitting in the middle of the road."

Montgomery laughed. "I see."

"You wouldn't believe the all the JSTs I've seen. Shoes. Sometimes both, sometimes just one. A radio. A loaf of bread. Once there was a spray of lace panties that dotted the highway like pink freckles."

He laughed even harder.

"But by far, the strangest JST I've ever seen was a rocking chair. It was smack-dab in the middle of the road, straddling the highway yellow lines as if some little old lady had just gotten up to go see about her tea."

They were both laughing now. And it felt good. Montgomery realized that he didn't laugh nearly as much as he used to. And he'd missed it.

He was going to tell Sabin as much, but his ringing cell phone interrupted his thought. He placed the phone in the hands-free cradle in the dash.

"Claiborne."

"Mr. C. You got a minute, man?"

"Sure. What's up, Trey? How's Sarah?"

"Sarah's in ICU, man. I don't think she's going to make it. Can you come now?"

Montgomery glanced at Sabin, who was looking strangely solemn in the seat next to him. "Do you mind if we take a detour?"

"Of course not. This sounds serious."

"I'll be right there."

"Cool."

Twenty minutes later, they were pulling into a vacant lot. They exited and Sabin followed Montgomery across the street and into the apartment building.

"Your computer tech lives *here?*"

"Yeah, and he actually likes it."

They ascended the stairs. "Be careful. I'm not sure what holds this place together. But I am sure of one thing—anything could fall, shake loose, or crash in at any moment."

"Thanks for the warning."

He knocked on the door and they waited. After a few seconds, Trey opened the door. He looked tired and a bit sad.

"You're too late," he said. "She's dead."

> Death is a brilliant monster that comes
> for us all.
>
> —Toda Kai

Fifteen

They entered Trey's apartment.

"Trey, this is my neighbor Sabin Strong."

Trey bowed like a prince. "Nice to meet you, Miss Strong."

"Sabin, please. I don't think I've ever been a miss in my life."

"Okay, then. Sabin. Can I get you all something to drink?"

"Nothing for me."

"No, thanks," Sabin said, looking around. "Nice place you've got here."

"Thanks. Why don't you guys have a seat?"

Montgomery took a seat next to Sabin. "All right. Lay it on me."

Trey propped himself against a ramshackle maple desk. His expression was grim. "If Sarah had been human, I would say that she died of complications due to internal injuries."

Something at the back of Montgomery's neck was scratchy and agitated. "Sounds serious."

"Man, you don't know about serious."

"What do you mean?"

"It's like she bled to death. Memory, operating system, software, all gone, sucked out, siphoned away."

"Did you recognize the virus?"

"Yes, and no. I recognized the fact that it was a virus. But it's not any virus I've seen. And I've seen my share."

"Maybe it's something new."

"Yeah, I'd say it's pretty new. I'd also say that it's probably the only one of its kind."

"I don't get you."

"This virus was made, manufactured, in a high-tech lab. Somebody spent some time and some money to create it. And I think it was specifically made for your computer or something on it."

"What?" Montgomery and Sabin said in unison.

"That error message you received was like a smoke screen. But in actuality, a program, called a Carnivore, worked its way through your hard drive. It was slow and methodical. I tracked the last phase of it. Looked like a damned search-and-destroy mission."

"Why would that kind of virus be on my computer? I don't keep anything on it except company records." He looked at Sabin. "And those are boring."

Sabin frowned. "That's very weird, Montgomery."

"Oh, that's not the weird part. The weird part is that while I was trying to restore your hard drive, I found an Easter egg."

"You what?"

"I found a miniprogram installed on your computer. Sometimes programmers, in their infinite boredom, hide programs within programs to do cool, unique, or strange things on your computer. They're amusing but harmless. The one in Photoshop displays about sixty secret messages. But there are all kinds of

Easter eggs," he said, talking with his hands. "Not just those on computers. People hide stuff in movies, art objects, books, songs." Trey pointed to Sabin's wrist. "Some have been found in watches. There's even an Easter egg in the Bible that spells out Shakespeare."

"What has that got to do with Montgomery's computer?"

"Yes, right. Well, there's an Easter egg on his OS that displays these fragmented messages. When Sarah was taking her last breaths, it was like dueling programs. The more the virus tried to erase the egg, the more it struggled to keep itself running. Must have had a fail safe just in case."

"In case what?"

"In case it was discovered before it was activated."

The creepy feeling at the back of Montgomery's neck rolled down into his stomach and took up residence. "I'll be damned. What did it say?"

"Take a look for yourself. I turned on my screen capture when it started happening."

Trey went to a table in the corner of the room and double-clicked on an icon on the desktop. The screen flickered, dimmed, and flashed sporadically. Between flashes, "Unrecognized Function Click OK to Continue" appeared then dissolved into a series of phrases:

RIE DOCS

C. BRUMMEND

THIRD DRAWER

Montgomery felt his jaw go slack. He noted a similar reaction in Sabin as they both walked closer to where his computer appeared to be having a nervous breakdown.

"It looks like something off of the SciFi channel."

"I know," Trey said, rubbing his palms together. "It's one of the coolest things I've ever seen."

Sabin frowned. "You sure this isn't just a virus?"

"No, it's both. You see, the virus is trying to *eat* the Easter egg."

"Damn."

"I don't believe it."

"The only time I've ever seen anything like this was when June Bug was doing research for his novel. He was on the Internet and just surfed into this restricted government site. At least it was supposed to be restricted. Juney writes mysteries and was looking for information on anthrax.

"Well, Big Brother wasn't too happy. A couple days later, Agent Silva shows up at Juney's job. He takes Juney to lunch, checks him out. I guess he decided June was harmless, but the very next day, Juney gets a virus on his computer. It left a slow trail of destruction on his hard drive. Luckily, I managed to isolate it and delete it, but not before it cut a path of destruction through Juney's fiction files like a F5 tornado." Trey waxed childlike. "Looks like the same kinda thing took out Sarah."

"Jeez."

Trey rubbed the CPU case as if he were stroking a cat. "How did you get this virus?"

"I didn't. Angie did. She said she opened a letter from her mother and the next thing she knew, she got an error message."

"Well, talk to her. She must have done something else to execute it. These things have to be activated. Maybe she thought she was opening a picture or something."

Montgomery felt as though he'd been snatched up and toppled by a mammoth wind. *This can't be a coincidence.* "You have a pencil and some paper I can borrow?"

Trey rifled through the mosaic of items strewn

across his desk and finally came up with a pad and pencil. Montgomery wrote down Sarah's last words and handed the pad and pencil back to Trey.

"Sabin and I are late for a Sankofa session," he said, reaching down to pick up his lifeless computer.

Trey stepped quickly between Montgomery and the computer. "Actually, I was hoping I could keep her. I wanted to study the virus some more if I could. But I don't want to get your hopes up. This computer will never work again."

"Well, I appreciate everything you did. Just send me a bill like always."

"No way. This one's on me."

Sabin and Montgomery walked to the door. Trey followed behind them. "Give Leon some dap for me."

Montgomery turned before heading out. "I will."

"Nice to meet you, Sabin."

"You, too, Trey."

"I'm sorry about your computer, Montgomery."

"Thanks."

Sabin felt him drifting away. *It's that thing that men do,* she thought. *When they have a problem or a concern, they just close down.*

She wanted to tell him that he could talk to her about it. That she understood. And not only that, but that she knew what was bothering him, and that she was here to help. Doing that, however, would forfeit any chance she had of getting to Africa. She'd had it with America. No place she'd gone—not Texas, not South Carolina, not Nevada, not Oregon, and not Maryland—had allowed her to escape the demons that followed her everywhere. Every place she went she wondered if her parents were there. Could she find them?

But since she'd discovered that her mother was working as a Peace Corps volunteer in Ghana, she had made plans to go. Maybe once there, her demons would be silent and stop driving her mad.

They arrived at the Gold Lion Center just after six-thirty. Montgomery seemed to regain some of his buoyancy. "We'll go in through the back."

They got out of the car and walked together down a cobblestone path to a rear entrance. Once inside, Sabin was drawn to the lively colors and the open space of the building.

"Hey, Mr. C. I didn't know you was comin' tonight."

"That makes two of us. This was kind of a spur-of-the-moment thing."

The young man was seated behind a small table. With his big shirt, and big jeans, he looked very much the product of Hip Hop culture. He smiled warmly at Sabin, and she smiled back.

"Tony Parker, this is Sabin Strong."

Tony extended his hand. "What's up, Miss Strong?"

"Not a lot, Mr. Parker. How about you?"

His smile broadened and a dark hand covered his numerous teeth. "You can call me Tony." Tony smiled even more broadly. "She's a hottie, Mr. C."

Montgomery cocked his head and frowned. "A what?"

"Oh, no disrespect!"

Sabin spoke up in her own defense. "None taken, Tony."

"I'm going to show her around. See ya later, T."

Montgomery and Sabin strode off together, but Tony had piqued her curiosity. "Do all young men call you Mr. C.?"

"All the ones that go through the Mad Dads programs."

"Is that how you met Trey?"

"Pretty much. He had just stolen a truckload of electronics from Radio Shack, and the judge sentenced him to enroll in the Sankofa program." Montgomery stopped in front of three wall plaques. They were shiny and black with gold lettering engraved into each. Montgomery read from the first one.

"The Mission of Mad Dads is to attract, challenge, and prepare men to be vocal, visible, and vigilant in restoring safe communities and healthy families." He nodded and smiled. "Hopefully that's what I've done for Trey. I spent a lot of time with him, and I think he's going to be okay."

Sabin had no doubt. That young man knew more about computers than she cared to know in a lifetime. "I believe you," she said.

"This used to be a school," Montgomery said. He took her hand quite naturally and said, "Let me give you a quick once-through."

Their palms felt good together, Sabin thought. *A matched fit,* a voice in her mind whispered. He took her first to the administrative office side of the building, then led her through to a small computer lab, a one-room library, and an indoor basketball court.

"It's like a rec center," she remarked.

"Actually, it's more than that. We have a lot of these things in order to attract the kids. But once we have their attention, we provide counseling, tutoring, and manhood training. That's what's going on tonight. It's called Sankofa. It's run by a guy named Leon Harris."

Montgomery stopped at the computer lab. His expression suddenly turned sour. She knew he was thinking of how his computer was sabotaged. *I hope he doesn't feel overwhelmed,* she thought.

On impulse, Sabin leaned forward and kissed his chin.

"What was that for?"

"You looked like you needed it."

"Hmmm," he said, moving closer. "My computer may be on the fritz but my lips work just fine."

And they did, better than Sabin remembered. All at once they took possession of hers like a claim staked and renewed with heat. When he stepped back, he took her breath with him and left her tingling. "We're going to have to do that more often," she said breathlessly.

"No doubt," he said, eyes on fire.

Now his hold on her hand was possessive and commanding. The idea of belonging to someone that way had never appealed to Sabin in the past. She had belonged to the two most important people in the world and they had abandoned her. But now, the idea intrigued her. And it wasn't just the belonging, but the being taken—taken and consumed by a man like Montgomery. Could she really open herself that way?

They walked down a long corridor and into a common area. "Where is everyone?"

"In the assembly hall. Tonight the kids are focusing on respecting differences." The two walked past mahogany plaques lined the walls, the Mad Dads vision, Essence Award, and community proclamations. "Do you mind if we pop in for a minute?"

"No."

They made their way across the common area and into a combination auditorium and conference room. As soon as they stepped inside, several of the young boys offered up happy greetings. "Hi, Mr. C!"

Montgomery waved to the group of about ten and called several by name.

"They're glad to see you."

"Nah. They just act that way because they all think I look like The Rock."

"The who?"

Montgomery frowned.

"Just kidding."

A short, stocky, and boyishly handsome man approached them. "Montgomery, just in time."

"Oh, no. We're just visiting. Leon Harris, this is Sabin Strong."

The two shook hands.

"Nice to meet you, Sabin." Then Leon turned to Montgomery. "Didn't you get my message?"

"Sorry. We've been hanging out almost all day. What's up?"

"Well, as you can see, I'm the only one here. Rod sprained his ankle and Larry's wife went into labor this morning."

Montgomery drew in a breath. "Sabin, I'm sorry about this, especially since I don't have time to take you home."

"No problem," she said, looking at the young boys. They were seated in groups of four and were all writing. They looked to be between the ages of fifteen and twenty. Sabin remembered being their age. The people who had tried to intervene in her life then hadn't succeeded. She'd ended up floundering for another ten years before the impact of Kai's teachings changed her life. She blamed it on the fact that the nuns really weren't interested in working with her to change—only to be adopted. And when that didn't happen, they had given up on her and others like her all together.

"Can I help?"

The two men eyed each other. Then Leon answered. "I don't see why not."

For the next two hours, Sabin helped the men facilitate discussions, games and activities on values, perceptions, and open-mindedness. She even threw in a minitalk about the difference between defense and aggression. But most of all, she paid attention to Montgomery. She noted his easy way with the young men, and how they respected him. Some of them had trouble at school, some of them had trouble at home, a few were even ex-gang members. But they all had one thing in common: their respect for Montgomery. It was more than obvious. When he talked, you could hear a fly snore. When he gave them a task, they went to it with fervor and shone like beacons when Montgomery approved of their progress.

"What do you think?" he asked during a break.

"I think you're marvelous," she'd wanted to say. Instead she said, "I think the program is wonderful."

"Here ya go, Mr. C." A young man, who looked to be about seventeen or eighteen, handed Montgomery the papers he'd collected from the others. He wore a Falcons jersey and black parachute pants. There was a terrible scar on the right side of his face. It looked as though a chunk of his flesh had been cut out and resewn. Other than that, he was a nice-looking kid.

"Thanks, Les."

Les nodded and then swung himself on crutches back over to where some others were gathered and talking.

A hard lump rose in Sabin's throat. "Bullet?" she asked.

"Yeah. A .22 lodged inside his head. I don't know exactly what it struck, but I do know that before he got shot, he could walk just fine."

Sabin waited for the lecture or the didactic comment about gun control. It never came.

Montgomery spent the next day trying to keep tabs on Sabin. She's only left the house once. He'd followed in his car. It seemed she just wanted to go for a quick ride. When Angie showed up with her boyfriend, Victor Willis, he hoped that he wouldn't miss her if she left again.

After Angie went over all the work that she'd completed for the past few days, Victor wanted to talk. Something about Victor always made Montgomery want to clear his throat. Mostly because Victor always sounded like he needed to clear his.

"Who do ya pick for the game tonight?" Victor's phlegm-choked voice asked.

"Nobody," Montgomery replied. "I'm waiting for the regular season."

"Yeah, but those international exhibitions can be good, too."

That was another thing. Victor was always talking sports. He was caught up by them all, constantly touting who the winners would be.

"I've got Germany," he garbled.

After a closing remark on the merits of football during the off-season, Angie and Mr. Gravel Voice left. Montgomery went back to work, keeping a look out for Sabin, and occasionally jotting down notes in his notebook.

The day settled down into night. Small birds flitted about in the last rays of sun and the sky began its familiar descent into colors on the lower spectrum of light. Montgomery stepped outside in tan shorts and bare feet with a bucket and a product labeled Car Wash in a Can. He walked over to the carport and stopped short. That damned green van was in Sabin's driveway again.

Methodically he unwrapped the water hose, turned it on and doused his car with water. *What does she see in that guy?* he wondered. *He's just a kid.* He resolved to take his mind off of what Sabin could want with a young buck when the door to her house opened and out stepped Mr. Young Thing himself.

Montgomery opened the can of soap and attached it to the hose. All the while, he pretended not to notice Sabin standing on her top step in a short, very short, terry-cloth robe. As she talked with her guest, he continued applying soap and pretending not to eavesdrop.

"You are so good. How soon can you come back?"

"How soon do you need me?"

"The way I feel now, I'd say tomorrow."

Laughter.

"I mean it. You have the most marvelous hands, Larry."

"Thanks. Well . . . how about this time next week? If you can't wait that long, page me, or call me on my cell."

He kissed the back of her hands and headed off toward his van. As the van backed out of the driveway, curiosity got the best of Montgomery.

"Are you sure that ain't your boyfriend?"

Sabin turned, arms crossed. "I've never been with a *boy* in my life."

Before he could respond, she had gone back into the house.

Kai,

I went riding today. You should see my face. It's wind-burned, just the way I like it. Not even the meditation you taught me can match what I feel being out on the road. Pure bliss. I think I'm turning into a hard rider. The pipes on my Hog are so loud, people turn to watch me pass by. I rode my leathers today. I looked good.

The man next door watches me sometimes. He did today and I could tell he liked what he saw. I like him, Kai. I'll keep him safe.

S.

* * *

After trying his hand at rump roast, Montgomery gave in. The beef came out resembling charred Play-Doh, and Montgomery's kitchen looked as though imps had been in a food fight all afternoon. Relenting, he had called Tilde, who'd agreed to whip up something special and rescue him from the disaster in his kitchen.

Two hours later, she'd shown up with a spinach salad, baked cod fillets, and asparagus tips. Montgomery thanked her profusely and agreed to relieve her on Wednesday and Thursday of next week. She'd smiled and left him with the piping hot dishes.

He did, however, know how to set a table. That had been his job as a kid. He remembered when there was just the three of them—him, his dad, and his mom. Whenever his father was in town or not on duty, they would all sit at a tall sika wood dining room table and eat together.

My first job, he thought, placing dinner plates on intricately woven cinnamon-and-tan place mats. Montgomery chided himself for going to all this trouble. *When Randy or Trey come by, we just sit on the couch and use paper plates.* But he knew he had to uncover the truth about Sabin. Either she was the one trying to kill him or she was involved in it somehow.

For a moment, he considered confronting her, getting it all out in the open. But if she had been this deceptive already, she'd just deny his accusation, and it would be little more than his word against hers. No, he had to have proof, evidence.

He'd start by investigating her background. Then he'd keep a close eye on her. He positioned crystal flutes into place, thinking, *What's done in the dark always come into the light.*

Sabin was ten minutes early. Montgomery had just transferred dinner from Tilde's baking containers into serving dishes when he heard her knock. He knew his mission was to get information, but he couldn't stop thinking of their evening as a date. As he approached the door, he felt a jolt of adrenaline under his skin, and a heightened sense of awareness. When he opened the door, he understood why.

Sabin's milk-chocolate frame looked delectable in a pastel flowered sarong skirt and matching bra top. Her beauty reminded him in no uncertain terms why he had wanted, and still wanted, to make love to her.

"We were having dinner tonight, right?"

"Dinner. Nothing else."

Sabin waltzed past him and he closed the door. "I know that, silly."

His eyes locked on to her backside that hung like an upside-down heart. *Straight bootylicious,* he thought. "Woman, you've got more curves than a capital *S.*"

She turned. "Montgomery, I need to say something about the other night."

"No, you don't," he said, remembering himself and why he'd asked her to dinner. "Let's just eat, drink, and be merry."

She smiled in a way that was becoming more familiar to him each day. "I can handle that."

"Have a seat," he said, heading into the kitchen. "I'll go get dinner."

"From where? KFC? Because I know you didn't cook."

He balanced the serving dishes in his arms. Perturbed, he returned to the dining room. "How do you know that?"

"A woman knows these things."

"Really?" he said, placing the items on the table. "And just what else do you think you know?"

"Well," she began, sliding a finger across her knife, "I know that you are practical and conservative but have an appreciation for the finer things in life. I can tell that you are loyal, despite your own best judgment sometimes, and that sentiment runs a deep tread in you. If I had to guess, I'd say you're probably a Taurus."

Montgomery took a seat across from Sabin, astonished by her accuracy. "We better eat before this gets cold."

He picked up the heaping salad bowl. "Here."

She didn't move. "Am I right?"

He recognized it, the arch of the left eyebrow, jaw clamped and set. There wouldn't be peace until he answered her question.

"Yes. It's uncanny how right you are."

She took the salad and helped herself to a generous portion. "Now do me."

Montgomery placed a cod fillet on his plate. "I was trying to the other night. You wouldn't let me."

They exchanged serving dishes. "You know what I mean."

Unfortunately, he did. And something about that knowledge caused a sick feeling in the pit of his stomach.

He passed the asparagus. "Well, uh . . . I think that once something gets under your skin it stays there for a while. I think that you are feisty and full of grit. I think that you like to be in control because deep down inside you wonder if you really are. I think that under the right circumstances, you can be extremely passionate, but have a tendency to be wildly jealous."

"Jealous!" Sabin said with a mouth full of spinach. "No way."

Montgomery poured them each a glass of wine. "Yes. I'm absolutely certain that it was you who sat right there in my living room, giving Arroya the kind of looks that could melt steel."

"Well, what about you and your 'Is that your boyfriend' interrogation?"

"I never said I wasn't the jealous type."

The room fell to silence. They eyed each other for a moment then went back to eating.

"Were you really jealous of that kid?"

"I'm still jealous. He's put his hands on places that I can only fantasize about."

"Look, Montgomery . . ."

"No. Stop. We said we weren't going to talk about it."

"But I want to."

Another Sabin trademark. Her up-front, cards-on-the-table attitude told Montgomery they were going to talk about the other night no matter what. He stopped eating.

Why isn't this working? Why can't I get down to business? For all I know, she may be a contract killer, or worse, just a crazy woman who murders for fun.

"I'm so attracted to you, Montgomery, that sometimes it's all I can do to keep from stripping naked every time I see you."

But then again . . .

"But I just can't be with someone right now. I've just moved here. I'm trying to get my bearings. I'm trying to establish my presence here as a consultant. And for all I know, this may not be the place for me, either. I mean . . . I may leave Golden Creek."

Sabin's last statement caused Montgomery's temples to throb.

"So until I get some of my issues smoothed out, I don't want to add anything—or anyone—to my unsettled life." Sabin cocked her head to the side and her eyes softened. "Do you understand?"

He understood one thing. He wanted her now more than ever. And at the core of his heart was the belief that she wouldn't—*couldn't*—be out to hurt him.

Montgomery buttered a roll and placed it on his plate. "Where do you hail from, Sabin?"

She stopped chewing and took a sip of wine. "That's hard to say, really. I've lived so many places, you might say I'm from all over."

"You must have been born somewhere," he said, trying to sound casual.

Her eyes surveyed his face. "I was born in North Dakota. Bismarck."

"Hmm. What's that like?"

"I don't know. I didn't live there long enough to find out."

"I see." He lifted the bottle. "More wine?"

"No, thanks," Her words were flat, almost accusatory.

"I was born in Hawaii, but like you, my folks moved when I was very young."

Sabin helped herself to more salad. "Oh."

"Were you an army brat like me, or did your parents just like moving around?"

Her silverware clinked and scraped against the plate. "I never knew my parents."

"I'm sorry," Montgomery said, now regretting his line of questioning.

"I'm sorry, too, 'cause they could have had one terrific daughter."

Sabin kept her head down and her eyes on her plate. Montgomery's heart sank.

"Are they . . . ?"

"They abandoned me when I was six months old."

"Have you ever thought about . . . ?"

"No." She sat her fork on the place mat and looked up. Her eyes glistened. "Every day."

"You know, I could help you. . . ."

"That's all right," she said, and drained her wineglass. "What about you? Your dad seems cool."

"I have a father who bleeds American red. A patriot who believes in defending self and self-interest at all costs."

Sabin finished off the last of her bread. "Sounds like my kind of guy."

"I'll bet. You and he would probably—"

The ringing phone cut off Montgomery's well-timed insult. He excused himself and went over to pick up the phone from where it rested on an end table.

"Yeah?" It was Randy.

"Whoa," he said into the receiver. "That's twice in a week . . . Aw, man. Can't we all just get along? Okay, look. After this leave of absence, I'm going to sit you two down in a room together and we're not leaving until we're one, small, happy family. Got it? Peace—and I do mean peace!"

He returned to the table.

"Trouble in paradise?"

"No. Just Secure Storage. My partner and my facilities manager do not get along. I try to keep them separated but even when they talk on the phone, it's a war."

Sabin cracked a wiry smile. "Sounds familiar."

"We're not that bad." And for the first time, Montgomery realized that that was true. They *weren't* that bad. They had their differences. Sabin had the worst taste in music and TV detectives, but for the most part, he liked her. And they had a flow. And if he could just persuade her to let him, he could . . .

"So what about your mom, Montgomery? You've never mentioned her."

"My mother is dead."

"Wow. I'm sorry."

"I don't know why. If my father isn't, I don't see why you should be."

Montgomery pushed the remaining food around on his plate. Asparagus into spinach into cod. "That was wrong. I shouldn't have said that."

"Has she been gone long?" Her voice sounded almost hopeful, as if she was wishing that he had experienced the loss of a parent at a young age.

"It's been fifteen years." Staring into Sabin's eyes, he added, "She was murdered."

"Oh, God. Wh . . . how?"

It took him a while to let go of the breath he was holding. When he did, it didn't calm him at all. He felt the same old rage. The same old pain. The same old everything.

"I was twenty and in love with a Nissan 280Z. I was working at a gas station at the time, trying to save enough money to buy it. When I finally had a down payment, I went to the dealership. Well, the guy wouldn't let me drive the thing off the lot without insurance."

Sabin smiled. "Uh-oh."

"Uh-oh is right. When I found out how much the insurance cost, I pounded my fist on a desk so hard, I shattered a bone in my small finger and broke a desk leg.

"After I came to my senses, I did what any desperate twenty-year-old would do. I begged my parents for the money. I promised never to ask for any more money as long as I lived. I promised to cut their grass for the rest of my life. I even promised to hang out with my little sister who was only ten at the time."

Sabin chuckled.

"Finally my mother gave in and that very day she went to the bank to withdraw the money. Turns out there were some other people at the bank withdrawing money, only they were doing it at gunpoint."

"Oh, no."

"Yeah. My mother walks into the middle of a bank robbery and the guy panics and starts shooting folks. She and two other people never knew what hit them . . ."

Montgomery stopped, wondering why he hadn't gotten over his mother's death. Why it still hurt to talk about it. And why, when he never discussed it with anyone, he had told Sabin about it.

He stood, frustrated by the wound that refused to heal, and walked to the window. How many times had he stood here, watching as if any moment Mei Claiborne would come walking over the hill?

All at once, his emotions overwhelmed him. His father, his sister, the attempts on his life, even employees that were constantly bumping heads. He needed to forget about all of that for a few days. He needed . . .

Sabin's arms felt good and they circled around his waist. He stood still as she pressed in closer. He felt her head cradle in against his back and his blood surge. Turning slightly, he spun her around to him and took possession of her beautiful mouth. Montgomery watched through his lashes as her eyes flitted closed and passion consumed her face. Delicately, he probed the soft inside of her mouth then drew back.

"Go away with me," he said.

To have it all, you must let go of everything.
                                              —Toda Kai

Sixteen

Montgomery looked her up and down, a warm smile taking over his face. "Now you're going to experience *my* kind of fun."

Sabin couldn't believe she was actually going through with this. She looked around at all the other people wearing jumper gear and parachutes. They all seemed like normal everyday folks. Sabin would bet her next payment that the man with the combed-back hair was an executive at some large firm. And the young guy in the corner looked like Joe P. College, maybe even Howard University. And the woman standing across from him was a B. Smith type, probably crocheted doilies in her spare time. So why in God's blessed name would anyone with good sense jump off the side of a cliff?

"Look at you. Your eyes are as big as Frisbees. Trust me. This beats riding a motorcycle."

She could tell Montgomery was trying not to laugh.

"Nothing beats riding a motorcycle." Then she remembered how close they'd come to making love and thought *Well, almost nothing.*

The diving instructor droned on about last-minute safety tips, but Sabin's mind focused on discerning Montgomery's change in behavior. For the past week, it was as if their roles had reversed. The way he kept tabs on her, made her job as protector easy. She almost couldn't walk without tripping over him. First, he helped her in the yard. Then, he had taken her out to dinner. But what curled up the hairs at the base of her neck was when Montgomery asked to go bike riding. At first, she thought he'd been joking, standing there in all leather. When she realized he was serious, she became suspicious.

The thought occurred to her that he may just be like a lot of men who, having been turned down once, try that much harder to get a woman into bed. But so much about him was uncommon and fascinating, she couldn't imagine that his increased attention was the result of his need for conquest.

No. It was something else, something . . .

"Ready?"

With her heart beating double time in her chest, she nodded.

Because it was built on the plateau of a hillside, guests at the Wingren Lodge could opt to drive to the top or walk the mile to the summit. Like many others, Montgomery and Sabin trekked the embankment on foot. Conversation buzzed around them as eager daredevils headed off to seek their thrills.

"Tell me again why we're here."

Montgomery trudged beside her, a grin on his face as big as Texas. "I do this every year. Believe it or not, jumping off a cliff helps keep me grounded. Reminds me of the magnificence of life, and pulls important things back into perspective."

"Like?"

"Like the fact that there's so much to be thankful for."

Lush trees and forest-green vegetation fell away on her right. The higher they went, the more the clouds looked like they had been hung in the atmosphere like pictures on a wall. A large bird soared overhead, its wings spread out proudly against azure sky.

"See that? In just a short time, that's going to be you."

Sabin's chest muscles tightened. "How can you think that skydiving is easier than riding a motorcycle?"

"Simple. Because it is."

"You're crazy."

"Look, when you're on a bike, it's not like being in a car. You are exposed. Out in the open. Unprotected."

"I don't see any protection around here!"

"That's because you don't need any. You are your own protection."

She could see some of the others nearing the top of the hill. Her mind was made up. There was no way she was jumping off any cliff. It was just . . . just too risky.

At the top of the incline, people garbed up in their free-falling best, lined up like lemmings that commit mass suicide by following each other into the ocean. The wind whipped around them in short blasts that echoed in Sabin's ears. She stopped walking.

"Montgomery, I'm not jumping. I'm sorry."

His shoulders sank and the look on his face ventured far beyond disappointed. "I'd ask if you were afraid, but you probably wouldn't admit it. If you want, I can use my clips and harness us together and . . ."

"It's not that." She fidgeted with the nylon straps of her pack, anxiety making her nerve endings tingle.

"It's not natural. What if something happens? I mean, you can't control gravity."

She looked at him silhouetted against the mountain. Why was it that no matter what Montgomery wore, he always looked like something she wanted to put in her mouth? Even now, with the squeaky nylon of the jumpsuit, the fabric made a snug curve around his glutes and led her eyes straight to his thighs and the muscles there she longed to stroke.

So now, the real reason she came was surfacing. Anything to keep his company. In all honesty, their intimacy had rocked her. The other night her rational mind had slipped quietly away, replaced by gripping rapture and dizzying need. Since then her secret wish had come true and she and Montgomery had occupied nearly the same space and time like twin souls, thirsty for each other's nearness.

To prove it, she was going to jump off a cliff with a man she'd been hired to safeguard.

"I don't believe it!" she blurted.

"What's the matter?"

It had happened. Despite her plans, her focus, and her concentration, she had forsaken her duty.

"We can't do this."

She realized that if Montgomery jumped off that cliff, he would be an easy target for someone to pick off, or heaven forbid, sabotage his parachute. She had surrendered her head for her heart, and now *she* had jeopardized his life. Thank God it wasn't too late.

Her earlier words echoed in his mind. *You can't control gravity. You can't control gravity.*

"That's it, isn't it? You have to be in control. I don't freakin' believe this! All this time I kept wondering what *I* did. Did she want to be on top? Did she want to do it at my house? Was it too soon? Was I too late? Am I a terrible lover? Ha! Turns out I'm not such a bad lover after all."

He laughed as the full realization hit him like a cold slap on the face. "All that energy you have on hold. You couldn't keep it in check, could ya? Man, you were soup in my hand. Fresh, hot, and delicious, I'll give you that. But you were soup! And that bites your ass, doesn't it? You can't stand it. *Why*, Sabin? Don't you trust me?"

"No!" she screamed. "I don't trust you! I don't trust anyone!"

Montgomery hiked his parachute on his shoulder and replaced his goggles. "That must be why you find it so easy to substantiate killing. If people aren't worthy of something as vast and important as trust, then they're easy to dispose of. I hate that about you, Sabin. It's the only thing I've ever wanted to destroy."

Then he retreated down the slope and left her alone in the howling mountain wind.

She turned toward the cliffside. Was it true, she wondered? Was her need for control really that deep-seated? By the time Sabin realized that the sound she heard was Montgomery's footsteps thudding up behind her, his flying tackle had propelled her off the side of the cliff. And if it weren't for the wind blaring into her ears, she might have heard herself screaming as a result.

For the longest seconds in Sabin's life, she plummeted toward the ground with such maddening speed, she expected her heart to burst from her chest in order to save itself from the impending impact. She could feel the sides of her face folding and flapping as the wind created impact ripples against her skin. She was only vaguely aware of Montgomery's arms crossed against her chest holding her.

They fell for what seemed an eternity. Sabin remembered that she wasn't going to hit the ground immediately and that by opening her chute, she might just survive. Her clear thoughts could mean only one thing; they must have reached terminal velocity. According to Montgomery, terminal velocity is the point at which acceleration stops and you simply fall at the same rate of speed until you open your chute. And then she stopped screaming.

She didn't care if this was the point where she was supposed to pull the rip cord or not. She was ready to put the brakes on this fall. For the first time she became fully aware of the man pressed against her back and how tightly he held on to her. Montgomery's grip prevented her from reaching her cord. She struggled against him, but he wouldn't let go.

"How does it feel to be out of control?"

He shouted directly into her ear. But his words sounded like they had traveled miles through a tunnel to get to her.

"Idiot!" she screamed back. "Let go!"

The wind sounded like a convoy of Mack diesel trucks rumbling past her ears.

The rushing air muffled his voice, even though she knew he was shouting. "Stop struggling!" he said. Then he held her with his left hand and latched them together with his right.

The skyscape moved up so quickly, she couldn't tell if they were in danger, and that frightened her. *What does your training tell you about this?* she wondered. "That nature is always your first master," she heard her sensei say in her mind. "And you have no other choice but to learn and obey."

"Kai," she said, but couldn't hear herself.

"What would a bird do?" Kai's image asked her. She grunted. *A bird wouldn't be strapped to a maniac.*

Montgomery's counting brought her out of her thoughts. "Four, three, two . . ."

"Oh, God. He's going to—"

The opening parasol yanked them up and unfolded above them. And then, a loud silence surrounded her and she felt like she had been sucked deep into a black hole or maybe someone just turned down the volume on the world.

Although they continued to fall, it looked as though they were suspended in the sky. A mile or so up from the ground and they floated so far away from everything that nothing seemed to get any closer. She smiled and allowed herself to relax, as Montgomery held them above the earth while the wind blew fiercely from below.

How beautiful the world looked from up here. The green and lush tops of trees, the gradient colors of grass and flora, the contour of the land as it bent against the horizon, the absolute absence of sound. So peaceful.

If only life on the ground was as serene as flight among the clouds. If only . . .

"Are you still angry?"

"Yes!" she said. The only protection she could offer him now was her body in front of his. But that was all. She scanned the landscape for any signs of threat. She didn't see any, but from this altitude, a threat would be difficult to perceive. She prayed that they made it to the ground safely. And then she would tell him exactly how she felt about his actions.

They soared above the Potomac River. The water raged south on its way to the Atlantic. They flew over two deer hopping over foliage in a dense thicket. Right before landing, they sailed past a couple kissing beneath a tree.

Montgomery guided them into a smooth glide to

the landing point. They came down at an angle, hit the ground roughly, and rolled a few feet before stopping. Montgomery's bulky body pressed down upon hers. He didn't seem to be in any hurry to move.

"Get off me!" she insisted, and rolled. Unfortunately, they were still hooked together and where she went, he went.

"Unhook me! You crazy, irrational . . . ooooh!"

"Calm down," he said, releasing his harness. "You're all right."

She stood like a panther ready to pounce. "We could have been killed!"

"I told you," he said, moving closer, dragging the parachute behind him. "I won't let anything happen to you."

He won't let anything happen to me, she thought. Sabin had had enough. She would have to find another way to finance her search. This secret bodyguard role was impossible to maintain. She had to tell Montgomery that his life was in danger. She had to confess that she was hired as his bodyguard. Then she could do some real protection work instead of this haphazard attempt at security.

"Montgomery, I have something to say and it's—"

He moved closer. "Me, too. But not here."

"We could have been killed!"

"Sabin, I've been doing this for years."

"That's not the point!"

"Well what is the point?"

Tell him, she thought. *Just tell him and be done with it.*

Montgomery stomped around in the grass. He looked almost comical with the multipanels of blue and gold nylon and long shroud lines of the parachute trailing behind him. "I think the point is that I'm right. For whatever reason, you lose control when you're around me, and you can't stand it.

"Where are you going?" he called after her.

"Home." By the direction of her marching, she would have thought that was obvious.

"Wait, Sabin, I'll . . ." He jogged up beside her. "I'll take you."

"I know you will," she said, still seething.

Montgomery rolled up the parachute and walked with her to the lodge where they changed, and then they headed back to the car.

Once on the road, Sabin settled back against the seat and closed her eyes thinking men were just too frustrating a species. *Why are they so knuckleheaded?*

"Is that a smile I see?" Montgomery asked, getting onto the interstate.

She turned away from him and faced the window. "I'm tired, Montgomery. I don't want to argue anymore." Truth was, his argument made her uncomfortable.

She sighed. The engine of the car was so much more quiet than on her Big Boy. It made it easy for her to relax. Out the window she saw the sun hanging in the sky like a bold hitchhiker among the clouds. She closed her eyes, remembering the silence of the skies, and wondered why anyone in their right mind would trade paradise for the stress-inducing clamor of the city . . .

The smell of leather told Sabin she was not in her own bed. She stretched and opened her eyes. Montgomery was just entering the Golden Creek suburb.

"You called my name in your sleep."

Sabin's mouth dropped open. "I did not."

"Why would I lie?"

"Why would you force me off a cliff?"

"Okay, look, I'm sorry. I shouldn't have done that.

I wanted to show you that I could be there for you, too. I mean, you step to my rescue any more and I'll have to paint a big red S on your chest.

"I wasn't trying to put you in danger. In fact, you weren't ever in danger, really. But I had to do something drastic to get you to trust me, to trust us."

"Us? What us?"

"Now who's treading dangerously? Us, Sabin. There's an us. Unconsummated, yes. But there's an us."

Sabin's stomach fluttered. Of course he was right. But when had it happened? When had she fallen? She looked at him sitting behind the wheel and as she expected, her temperature rose.

"What do we do now?"

"We take it to the next level."

"Dang! Why does everything revolve around sex for men?"

Montgomery smiled. "Not everything. Just the important stuff."

"Stop the car!" Sabin insisted, grabbing the door handle.

The Jag screeched to a halt on the shoulder and Montgomery's hands grabbed tightly onto her wrists. She yanked free and rushed out of the car.

"Are you crazy!" he shouted, coming around to where she stood fuming.

"No, Montgomery. I'm not crazy. I'm not easy. And I don't sell my feelings cheap." She slammed her hands down on her hips.

"So you admit you have feelings for me."

"I never said I didn't!"

"Then make me know it."

Sabin recoiled, in awe of how nonchalant he sounded. "Just like that, right?"

"No." He stepped in front of her. "Just like this."

His large arms encircled her, pulled her close. She fought, but only slightly as his kiss siphoned her strength and her resistance died an exquisite death. How long since the last time? she wondered. Weeks since they'd held each other like this. Since she had made him leave her bed.

He stepped back, walked to the passenger side of the car and opened the door. Sabin's insides twinkled like stars in the sky. She took a deep breath and got in.

For the next ten minutes, as they drove, they remained silent. When Montgomery turned the car onto their street, he glanced in her direction.

"I won't force you ever again, but I will say this. I want you, Sabin. I have for a long time. And I believe you want me."

He maneuvered the Jaguar into her driveway. "When you're ready, my door is open."

She stepped out quietly and closed the door. She stood watching as he backed up, turned into his own driveway, and parked. She kept on watching as he went into his house and closed the door behind him.

Montgomery threw his car keys on the living room table and waited. A few seconds later, there was a knock on his door.

He yanked it open. "What took you so long?"

He pulled her against him and his lips crashed down upon hers. Their tongues mated, sliding over and around each other while Sabin leaned closer. At the intensity of his kiss, she lost her breath and her will. She knew she couldn't pull back or stop.

He broke away long enough to guide her inside and close the door; then their bodies slammed together like magnetized steel.

If she could have pulled him into her right then and there, she would have. Instead, Sabin let her head fall back as Montgomery's lips ignited a firestorm across her neck and shoulders. She closed her eyes and he unbuttoned her blouse. Sabin realized with each movement, it was she who was coming undone.

He slid off the silken garment, and as his hands kneaded her breasts through her lace bra, she gave in to the wondrous torture wrought by his touch.

She could smell him—his breath, his urgency, his manliness—a quilt of aromas weaving its way into her soul. Her thighs trembled. "Montgomery," she whispered, and before her legs betrayed her and gave way, he scooped her up and carried her to his bed.

The sheet cooled her arms and back but only for a moment. Watching Montgomery undress was a delightful agony as she waited for him to join her. She watched each piece fall—shirt, boxers, and pants—to reveal the man she had wanted inside her like breath.

He stood naked before her, massive and cut to perfection. He was all sinew and determination. Her eyes feasted on inch after inch of skin that was flawless, smooth, confident, and aroused.

"You look . . ." she said, but could not find words to describe the magnificence of his form.

He bent over her, kissed her forehead, and set to work removing her jeans.

"So do you." he murmured.

His eyebrow went up when he caught sight of her black thong. Yes, she admitted, she'd hoped they would end up like this. No, hoped was wrong. Wanted. Needed. Would have perished if they hadn't.

Sabin reached for her bra.

"No," he said, crawling onto the bed. "Let me."

She relented as he slid a strap off of one arm and then the other. Afterward, he gently rotated the fabric until the fasteners emerged. Sabin looked down at his fingers then up into his eyes. They were serious, exotic, and darkened with desire when he freed her breasts and she lay nearly naked beneath him.

"I was wrong, Sabin. You don't look good."

She blinked back the hurt rising from his comment. "You are exquisite and divine."

Nothing could be more perfect, she thought, opening her arms. He came to her, like a jungle cat—strong, powerful, staking a claim and moving in his territory. She welcomed his weight. His heart beat hard and pounded coarsely against her chest. The contours of his body undulated like a throbbing landscape of bold black man.

This time his kiss came softer and sweeter, like she had dipped her tongue in warm honey.

His lips kissed. His hands caressed. His hips rotated. He was touching her everywhere at once. The sensations radiated throughout her body like a brilliant fever.

His tongue lightly lapped against the side of her face, then across to her ear and down to her neck where he suckled gently. She drew her arms up around his shoulders and responded in kind.

"No," he whispered. "It's not your turn."

Moving ever downward, he paused at the juncture of her bosom. Then taking each mammary into his hand, he paid lavish tribute to the tight peaks that formed there. Sabin closed her eyes and whimpered as his subtle loving washed over her like slow rain.

His mouth resumed its slow languid journey down the center of her body. She arched and moaned.

"I want to make you crazy," he said, and flicked his tongue across her navel.

Sliding off her thong, he paid delicious attention to her hips. His mouth stirred up a tropical storm at the spread of her thighs while his hands scorched finger patterns across the backs of her knees and calves.

"I want to make you delirious."

She sighed. Wasn't she already? She was so close now. He hadn't even been inside her but, oh, oh, God!

When he put his mouth on the apex of her thighs and dipped his tongue into her woman-space, she shattered as if she'd been kissed by lightning.

As she shuddered with release, Montgomery soft-kissed his way back up her body. He reached underneath the pillow and retrieved a condom. "You weren't the only one who wanted this."

Sabin watched with anticipation and interest as Montgomery tore open the packet with his teeth, tossed the wrapper to the floor, and unrolled the latex sheath to the base of his engorged member.

He lowered himself to her then. She sighed, relishing the press of his hard weight. His fingers fondled then opened her. Sabin inhaled sharply when the head of Montgomery's manhood replaced his fingers. Inch by inch he moved into her until they were fully joined.

Their pleasure was audible as each surrendered to the sensation of becoming one.

Slowly, Montgomery slid himself in and out of her sopping center. Sabin was too overcome by ravishment to move. She simply wrapped her arms around his neck and held on.

"Make me a promise," he whispered.

"Anything," she said, feeling herself open completely.

"Don't ever make me stop again," he said in hushed tones, and then kissed her forehead, her temple, her cheek, her lips.

Sabin's body reacted before she could speak. Her hips swung upward as if a mighty ocean rolled beneath her. Catching his rhythm, she whispered, "I promise."

His enormous maleness filled her. It was as if their bodies had been fastened together by fate.

"You're . . . so . . . big," she said, sliding her hands across the ripples in his back.

"I know," he responded, slowing his movements.

"No," she said in a small breath. "I like it."

"Hmm," was his response as his lips took hers. She pulled him close, angry that they could get no closer. As his lips and tongue seared a path down the side of her neck and on to her shoulders, Sabin realized that Montgomery was slowly, steadily, claiming her. Possessing her. Taking over her soul. And heaven help her, she wanted him to.

Closing her eyes, she allowed the intensity of his lovemaking to flow through her. Sounds she didn't know she was capable of making emanated from her mouth.

They cried out together as passion swept them closer to the brink. The air around them was humid with their sweat and pungent with the aroma of sex.

And then, as if their fit was not tight enough, she drew up her muscles around him.

"Ah . . . um," he moaned.

Again, she drew herself in, squeezing as he descended into the depths of her womanhood. This time, Montgomery growled like a leopard after conquest.

"Yes," he groaned.

She continued. Firming herself around him and then letting go. She kept time with his plunges into her core, which came harder and faster.

"Yes," he said again.

She was spinning out of control. Montgomery was right. Being in control was all she ever had and now he was taking it away from her.

"Oh, God, Montgomery, please . . ."

"Hold on," he whispered, lifting her leg and wrapping it around his waist. He deepened his syncopated movements inside her. "Hold on, baby."

"Ah, oh, Montgomery . . ."

"Let go, baby. Let go."

She thrashed beneath him, overwhelmed and flying apart. She felt tears sliding down her cheeks. *Oh, God, was she crying?*

Sabin held on as Montgomery took her over once more. This time, he followed her over the edge. With one final thrust, they catapulted like shooting stars into ecstasy's sublime abandon.

Sleep was a foreign concept to the new lovers. They united again and again, reaching for each other in the night, the side effects of a marvelous addiction. When sleep finally claimed them, it was early morning and they slept contentedly, spooned in each other's arms.

"Ow!" Montgomery exclaimed, releasing the skillet handle. He took one of the oven mitts hanging from the kitchen wall, shook the dust off, and placed his left hand into it. Then with his right, he scrambled the eggs that were bubbling in the pan.

The spring of the toaster caught him off guard, and he spun around to see two slices of light brown toast sticking up out of the holes. "Not dark enough," he said, pressing down on the lever once more.

He turned back to the eggs, which were now the color he wanted the toast to be. He finished scrambling them and turned off the electric burner.

In the next skillet, a giant pancake was about ready to be flipped. He had wanted to make six pancakes, but when he poured the batter into the skillet, it had spread and covered the bottom of the pan, so he had left it.

In yet another skillet, he was frying bacon. It had started as long strips, but had now cooked into small brown circles. Hopefully it would taste as good as it smelled.

The last item on his agenda was to squeeze some oranges for juice. He had a bag full of the ripe fruit in the refrigerator. As soon as that was ready, he would go and wake the beautiful woman sleeping in his bed.

"What's going on?"

He turned to see Sabin standing in the doorway wearing only a T-shirt. He saw all the wondrous curves of her body as if he had X-ray vision. His body reacted instantly, with memories of their night still fresh on his skin and in his soul.

"What have you done to the kitchen?" she asked, walking past him.

He ambled up behind her and snuggled against her. The scent of fresh soap rose from her skin to meet him. "Um," he said, giving in to all that was her. "Something about last night made me want to make breakfast."

"But, Montgomery, you can't cook."

He held her close and rubbed her arms. "Hmmm?" he moaned, feeling whole and complete and content.

Sabin laughed. "This is a disaster."

He glanced around. Yes, Bisquick mix clumped in several mounds on the table. Eggshells lay cracked and broken on the countertop. And a trail of maple syrup led from the cabinet to the microwave. But he didn't care. It was all for Sabin. He wanted to please her.

He turned her around. "This is anything but a disaster." He kissed her for a long time. *Could he make her feel what he felt?* Rolling his tongue against hers, he would try. Caressing her breasts, he would try. Grinding gently against her, he would try.

Moaning, he lifted her onto a clean edge of the counter, and pushed up the shirt. The thighs he had worshiped last night opened eagerly to receive him. He teased her, first with one finger then two, amazed at how quickly her body prepared itself for his entrance.

"Montgomery. Please, don't make me wait."

He rubbed the tips of his fingers against her succulent opening. "They say waiting is half the fun."

"I want you now," she said.

"You can have me . . . under one condition."

"Anything!" she said, going crazy with need.

He knelt and placed a kiss on her ankle. Then he worked upward with his lips and tongue. "No more masseuse," he whispered. "Promise, me."

The temperature of her skin warmed and he could all but taste her arousal on his mouth. Her thighs quivered at his approach and her moans grew deep and more urgent. "I promise, Montgomery," she moaned.

As he moved closer to her core, he watched pleasure wash over her face. Her closed eyes, her head back against the cupboard drove him on. Reaching up slowly, he caressed her stomach and then found the nipples of her firm breasts. They hardened at his touch.

"Mmm," he said, nuzzling his head into the place he longed to be. *Can I make her feel what I feel?* he wondered again, touching his tongue to the space between her legs where it was damp and warm.

Sabin cried out and slammed both hands onto the counter space. Montgomery slid his tongue along the soft and wet textures inside Sabin and marveled at the rapturous taste of her. He wanted more and moved his mouth in and out, then back and forth.

Her legs opened even wider as he felt her give herself over to him like a delicious surrender on his lips. Finally, when her breathing came in rapid gulps and her hips ground rhythmically against his face, he descended upon the orb of her pleasure and flicked his tongue gently across it.

"Montgomery," she whispered. "Um, Montgomery," she said louder.

"Yes, baby," he thought, feeling a steady tightening just below his abdomen. He flicked faster.

"Mont . . . gom . . . oh . . ."

Her thighs vibrated against his cheeks. He sighed, while she rode out her quiet storm.

"That was marvelous," he said, standing and licking his lips.

"Just hold me," she said, and leaned into his arms.

After holding her for a few moments, he helped her off the counter and they both stared at the debacle that had become Montgomery's kitchen.

He scratched his head. "I guess you're right about my cooking."

Sabin sucked her teeth. "Ya think?"

"What should we do?" he asked, lifting an eggshell that dripped clear ooze onto his kitchen table.

"You are going to clean up this mess, starting with the table. Since I'm starving, I'll run home and get us something quick to eat."

"Deal," he said, slapping her behind. He watched her walk. Her hips rolled gently beneath his shirt like a fond memory. "Hurry back," he called, then grabbed a towel from the sink.

Kai,
I never thought there was anything better than riding a motorcycle. I was wrong.
S.

* * *

When Sabin returned, Montgomery blinked in amazement. "You can't be serious."

She placed the cereal box and milk on the freshly cleaned kitchen counter and searched the cupboards for bowls.

"When you said something quick, I was thinking bagels or more fruit."

"What's wrong with cold cereal?" she asked, taking two spoons from a drawer.

"Nothing. But Cap'n Crunch?"

She poured generous potions of the small toasted corn squares into each bowl. "Don't you know about black women and Cap'n Crunch?"

"No," he said, plopping down into a chair. "But I'm sure you'll tell me."

Sabin turned her chair backward and straddled it. "We like our cereal the way we like our men. Crisp, but not too hard. Sweet, but not syrupy. Brown like us. And with the right amount of coaxing," she said while pouring the milk, "melt-in-your-mouth good."

Montgomery stirred his cereal. "You just made that up."

Sabin smiled in response and crunched her breakfast.

"Speaking of melt-in-your-mouth good," he said between spoonfuls, "how was I?"

Sabin looked up in shock. "Don't tell me you're one of those guys who has to be told how good he is."

"Actually, I haven't been, until now."

"Hmmm. Couldn't you tell?"

He didn't speak. He'd never asked a woman anything like this before. He always assumed the women he'd been with enjoyed themselves. But with Sabin, he had to be sure.

Sabin looked soft. The expression on her face became sensual and sleek. Suddenly he wanted to be inside her once more.

"Montgomery," she said, sounding like the passion he felt, "your love is king."

"Mmm," he said, smiling and scooped a spoonful of cereal into his mouth.

They finished one bowl of cereal and then another. Montgomery made fun of the way Sabin unabashedly turned up her bowl and slurped down the milk.

"Since you cooked, I'll clean," he said, taking their bowls to the sink. He hummed a little while he rinsed away the cereal remnants.

"Quid pro quo, Montgomery."

He knew what she was asking and stopped humming. "You are . . ." And then the words wouldn't come. He knew he felt something for her. What was it? Certainly it was more than lust. He enjoyed her company, her discussions, her *wild hair,* their disagreements. Did he love her? Of course not. Who could fall in love in this world knowing that at any moment, the one you love could be taken from you?

"You are . . ." he began again. When the phone rang, he was grateful.

"Excuse me," he said, then trotted off into the living room.

"Yeah? . . . Yes, I am . . . I'll be right there!"

Sabin had followed him into the living room. "What's wrong?"

His heart thumped like a bass drum in his chest. "The warehouse is on fire."

Objects in the mirror are closer than they appear.

—Anonymous

Seventeen

By the time they arrived, Building B was engulfed in a tornado of smoke. Lights from two fire trucks whirred like giant yellow strobes. Montgomery zigzagged through a crowd of onlookers, stepped over cables, and splashed through pools of standing water to get to the front of the building.

Ted Johnson, his associate manager, paced in front of a fire truck. A harsh scowl turned his forehead into a mass of wrinkles. Not far away, Angie stood next to Victor, staring at the flames and chewing on a fingernail.

"Ted, what happened?"

The man looked up, eyes murky. "All I know is, I heard the smoke alarm and got the hell out. Then I realized . . ."

An ambulance siren drowned out the rest of his sentence. The rescue vehicle screeched to a halt between the yellow trucks.

Alarm twisted Montgomery's stomach into a hard knot. "Where's Randy?"

Paramedics raced from the ambulance and up to the front of the building with a long stretcher. Montgomery watched with trepidation as a firefighter emerged with Randy's limp body in his arms.

"Randy!" Montgomery shouted, running past other firefighters on the way to his friend's side.

The emerging firefighter laid Randy on the ground and the paramedic went to work. Montgomery rushed up and was blocked by two large men in thick lemon-colored raincoats. "Please, he's like a son to me."

They let him through and he knelt beside the man he'd known from boyhood.

Black soot caked Randy's skin and clothes. The paramedic pounded the young man's chest and administered CPR.

Montgomery scooped up Randy's hand. "Hold on, Chief," he muttered. "Hold on."

After a few frantic moments, Randy coughed and gasped. His head lolled over to where Montgomery knelt by his side.

"Big Boss Man," he whispered. "I tried to—"

Then he closed his eyes.

The attending paramedics went into overdrive, but Montgomery only saw a blur of movement. His own life twisted slowly out of him while one medical technician shouted commands to the other and both worked feverishly—and unsuccessfully—to resuscitate his friend.

Grief and despair tore at his heart. One of the paramedics looked up at him in sorrow. Montgomery sighed heavily and turned to Sabin.

"I'm going to the morgue," Montgomery said to Sabin.

She nodded. "Give me your keys. I'll follow you."

"No," he said.

"Claiborne!"

Montgomery recognized the voice calling him and gritted his teeth. Henry Bijan strode up. He could swear the man was almost grinning.

"This is a terrible thing to happen to you. I hope no one was hurt."

Montgomery grabbed him by the collar, lifting him off the ground. "Did you do this?"

Henry's eyes grew large and fearful. "Let me go! Someone help! I am being assaulted!"

Montgomery threw the man to the ground. "If you had anything to do with this, I'll . . ." Disturbed by his own reaction, he shook away his anger and stepped back.

Henry's thick accent trailed behind him. "Something bad is going to happen to you, Mr. Claiborne. Something very bad."

As the coroner's van approached the still-burning warehouse, Montgomery stared at Randy's tarp-covered body wondering what could be worse than this.

"I'll get it, Tilde!"

Cherlyn got up from the couch, where she had been studying medical textbooks all evening, to answer the ringing bell.

"Detective Carvell," she said upon opening the door.

"Sorry to bother you. Is this a bad time?"

"It is if you're looking for my brother. He's not here."

"Well, that's all right, because I came to see you."

She smiled. "Come in, Detective."

"Lucian," he said, stepping inside the house.

Since her anxiety attack, he'd called her twice to see how she was doing. The first time they talked, she provided him with a description of her attacker, ex-

plained that the man had stolen her purse, and re-
capped the entire incident for him. During the second
of those conversations, she had told him how thankful
she was that he had calmed her down and talked her
through her ordeal. She hoped he was stopping by
now with good news of an arrest.

They sat down in the parlor adjacent to the living
room.

"Any word?" she asked.

"No, I'm afraid. That's what I came by to tell you.
That, and to see how you are feeling."

"I meant about the fire."

"Not yet. I've got two of my best detectives on it
though."

"You'll tell us as soon as you hear anything, right?"

"Yes."

"Well, in that case, I'm fine. Haven't missed a beat,
actually. And I've been taking self-defense classes.
They help me feel more in control and less paranoid."

"An experience like the one you had could ad-
versely impact a woman's life. I'm glad you aren't letting that happen."

Lucian seemed slightly nervous. She wondered if he
knew he was pulling up the nap on the arm of the
couch. She also wondered why she thought that was
so . . . cute. "So, have you decided?"

His eyes flickered brightly. "Miss Claiborne, there's
no need to feel obligated. The city pays me to assist
and protect people."

"I don't care what you say, *Mr.* Carvell. I would like
to do something for you. Unlike my brother and my
father, I *can* cook. Or maybe I could buy you some
flowers or a plant or something." Suddenly Cherlyn
realized that she had no idea how to really thank him
for what he'd done.

He stood then. "I'd better be going."

She joined him at the door. He remained there a moment. Hesitant and thoughtful. *Like a lone ranger,* she thought. *Probably not used to people doing things for him.*

"Thanks for the offer."

"You're welcome," she said.

He was almost to his car when he pivoted and said, "Take me to dinner."

"When?"

"Tomorrow."

"Where? What time?"

"Grisantis. Seven o'clock."

"Deal!"

He smiled, waved once, then got into his car and drove away.

It had been this way for five generations. Carvell men, so the story goes, fall in love at first sight. No ifs, ands, or buts. Lucian knew the recollections of his father, grandfather, and great-grandfather by heart. According to Carvell legend, when they saw the women they were meant to spend the rest of their lives with, they just *knew.*

Lucian, of course, never believed all the hooey and dismissed their fantastical tales. But here he was in a restaurant waiting for the woman he knew without a shadow of a doubt would bear his children.

Even though the events and circumstances were all different, his father and grandfather explained how they *fell* in the same way.

"It's like being run over by a truck," his father would say.

"No. Not a truck. A train," his grandfather would correct.

"But it's a good running over."

"The best feeling in the world."

"Like you've just seen the answers to all of life's questions."

"And they're all packaged up inside a woman."

And then they would laugh and say in unison, *"The* woman."

To prove them wrong, Lucian had indulged himself as a playboy throughout college. Strangely enough all that activity just left him tired and empty. Once, when he had been dating the local beauty queen, he'd decided he wanted to get married. Corina was as close as one in a small town could come to a supermodel. She did a lot of work in D.C. on local commercials, department store ads, and the like. Lucian thought he had hit the jackpot when they'd ended up in bed together.

They were engaged six months later. When his father and grandfather asked him what it felt like, he had exploded. He'd told them that they were just two silly old coots who had suffered the misfortune of believing their own lies. He realized later that the anger he'd unleashed on them was his frustration at the fact that he really wasn't in love with Corina. He only wanted her because she was gorgeous. She had never forgiven him for calling off their engagement.

Two weeks ago, the Carvell men had gone fishing. They had been talking about plastic lures versus live bait, and Lucian just blurted it out. "It was like being flattened by the giant ball from *Indiana Jones and the Temple of Doom,* and it was glorious."

He'd expected, a duet of "I told you so's." What he got was a nod and then his grandfather asking, "What's her name?"

He told him her name was Cherlyn Claiborne and explained how they met.

"Well, now comes the challenge," his father had said.

"Yep," his grandfather agreed, scratching his stomach.

"Even though we'rc as sure as a Jordan jump shot about them, they're never too sure about us."

Lucian set down his fishing pole. "What are you saying?"

"I'm saying that your mother still thinks I'm crazy."

He'd laughed at that. But glancing at his watch now, it was 6:55 P.M., seeing his bride-to-be was no laughing matter. He patted his jacket pocket where a two-carat diamond ring inside a black velvet box waited for Cherlyn's beautiful left hand.

She arrived just as the waitress brought him a glass of water. He was going to need it because Cherlyn looked as hot as a July noon in a short sleeveless dress. It clung to her as if she'd been made in it.

She slid into the seat opposite him, her straight hair bouncing against her face. "Sorry I'm late. C.C. made a surprise visit this evening at the children's home and lost track of time."

"That's all right."

"I told Montgomery I was meeting you tonight. Any word on the investigation?"

"Not much more than when I spoke with him yesterday. We know it was arson. That's about it."

Sadness settled into her eyes, and what he couldn't see, he could feel. She loved Montgomery very much.

"Something's going on with my brother, Lucian. But he won't tell me what it is. Do you know?"

"Yes."

"But you won't tell me."

"That's right."

She slumped back into her chair. "I guess if you did, I wouldn't have much respect for you."

"And I wouldn't have any for myself."

The waitress joined them then, depositing another glass of water on the table. "Good evening. I'm Glenda. May I bring you something from the bar?"

Cherlyn deferred. "Lucian?"

Lucian smiled. "I'm being wined and dined this evening."

Cherlyn's laughter caught the air like a beautiful wind chime twisting in a summer breeze. *Oh, he was going to have a wonderful life with her.* "Are we on a budget here?"

"Not at all."

"In that case, a bottle of wine please. Badia a Passignano Chianti, '96."

"That's one of my favorites," the waitress said. "I'll be right back."

Cherlyn folded her hands in front of her. Because of her petite size, she looked like a young girl trying to be good in class.

"Just remember that I'm a college student splurging."

Now it was his turn to laugh. "You can't possibly think that I'm going to let you pay for dinner."

"Oh, yes, you will. And if you don't, I'll tell my brother. And he's bigger than you."

That he is. "Enough said."

They skimmed their menus. It was going to be a long dinner. But at the end of it, he was going to pop the question. "What looks good?"

"I think the pasta with seafood is calling me. How about you?"

He took a sip of his water before answering. "I'm going to have the fettuccine with ham sauce."

The waitress came back with the wine, and they ordered their meals. In no time they were talking as if they'd been born friends. She told him about medical school, wanting to become pediatrician, and what it took to be C.C. the clown. He told her about life on the force and what it was like being part of a cop family.

They continued talking over dinner. Cherlyn shared stories about Montgomery and the work he did with Mad Dads. Lucian soaked it all up like a sponge, wanting to know everything about her and her life. Then one bottle of wine turned into two and they were laughing like children in a city park. Lucian felt giddy and realized the truth of his grandfather's words. It did feel more like a train—a long freight train going ninety miles per hour.

"Are you up for dessert?" she asked.

"If you are," he responded.

They ordered chocolate royale and two forks.

"I have to warn you," Cherlyn said, eyes dancing, "I'm a chocoholic."

"Really? I've heard about you people."

"Well, be prepared. You may not get very much of that dessert. There's still time to order one of your own."

"No, that's all right. I don't want much."

Their sweet treat came in the middle of a large glass plate. The texture and color changed from dark chocolate on the bottom layer to white chocolate on the top. Chocolate syrup zigzagged across the top and sides of the plate along with powdered sugar and milk chocolate shavings. Cherlyn's smile at the luxurious confection warmed him in strange places.

And then what happened next excited him beyond anything he could have ever imagined. She purred— low at first, and then with each successive forkful of dessert, it became louder and more sensual.

"Mmm, mmm. Oh. This . . . is . . . *so* . . . good."

When she licked her lips, she purred. When she

chewed, she purred. When she swallowed, she purred. It was the most erotic thing he had ever experienced.

Something inside him felt under pressure and about to explode.

"You don't know what you're missing," she said, reaching for a chocolate shaving and dropping it into her mouth.

He had waited long enough. Without another thought, he reached into his jacket pocket and pulled out a small black box. He snapped it open just as Cherlyn licked sauce from the corner of her mouth.

"You did what!"

"Well, what else was I supposed to do?"

"Ya dern fool."

"Knucklehead."

Lucian pushed scrambled eggs and link sausage from one side of his plate to the other. "I don't understand what happened."

"Well, what did you expect?" his father asked. "She don't know you from a hole in the ground."

"Yes, but she's the one."

The eldest Carvell drained his glass of orange juice and stared at his son. "Didn't you explain how it works?"

"You know he don't listen. He never has. Especially when it comes to falling."

Falling. That's what they called it. The wondrous and frightening truth that comes over the Carvell men. And his father was right. Whenever they tried to include him in those ridiculous conversations, Lucian would tune out or make excuses to leave.

"Look, she and I are meant to be together. So, what's the problem?"

"Did you tell her that?"

"Of course!"

"And what was her reaction?"

"She told me to stay away from her and stormed out of the restaurant. When I followed her, she threatened to body slam me."

The other men's laughter roared up in the air like a great blast of wind.

Lucian pushed his half-eaten plate away. "It's not funny. I mean, what good does it do to have this . . . this fall, if the woman doesn't fall with you?"

"That's why you should have paid more attention to your grandfather and me when you were growing up. Because then you would have learned the fine art of wooing."

"That's right!" his grandfather said, slapping a knee.

"Wooing? What do you mean wooing? All I want to know is when does Cherlyn fall?"

His grandfather stepped to his side and cast a thin arthritic arm around his shoulders. "As soon as you woo her."

Montgomery had talked to Randy's parents only once, and that was years ago. After Randy's refusal do it himself, Montgomery had contacted Mr. and Mrs. Ford to let them know that their son was turning into a fine and responsible young man. Their reaction was not what he expected.

After assuring them that he wasn't calling for money on Randy's behalf, they proceeded to ask Montgomery for money. Or rather, insisted that their son let them *hold* one hundred dollars.

It was the most bizarre conversation Montgomery had ever had. Mrs. Ford talked, while her husband yelled out commentary in the background.

So it didn't surprise him that upon being told of their son's death, their primary concern was whether he had an insurance policy and if so, how much the proceeds were.

As fate would have it, Randy did have an insurance policy. His parents were dumbfounded to discover he'd named Montgomery beneficiary. Ten thousand of the forty-thousand-dollar policy paid for Randy's funeral. Montgomery was at a loss as to what to do with the rest.

"Don't think about it now," Sabin said. She was lying beside him in bed as she had been for the past week. Although they hadn't made love recently, she'd been a comfort. Just to be near her kept him from sinking into a deep and dangerous sadness.

She let him nuzzle into her softness. "The answers will come."

Right now, the only answer that would come was that he was responsible for Randy's death. Whoever set that fire, set it for Montgomery. He was certain of it. But certainly whoever it was knew that he wasn't at the warehouse then.

Was it a warning? Was it retaliation? And *who did it*? He couldn't figure it out. One thing he vowed was that Randy's death would not be in vain. Montgomery would hunt down the murderers and . . .

Sabin's fingers caressed the side of his face. He closed his eyes at the pass over his temple and cheek. Her hands slid smoothly down to his neck and shoulders.

"You are holding a lot of tension, Montgomery. That's not good."

He sighed. "I know." Then he looked down into the seduction in her eyes. "Can you help me?"

"I thought you would never ask," she said, and straddled him. Emotions and desires pent up by mourning uncoiled slowly in the lower part of his body.

Her lips were on his throat relaxing him, moving him away from the anger and sadness that had become his companions of late.

"I missed you," she said, grazing his lips.

He pushed back her silky hair from the sides of her face. "I missed you, too."

They kissed tentatively, as if exploring new territory. Then a small taste wasn't nearly enough, and Montgomery rolled Sabin onto her back and sucked on her lower lip first before covering her mouth with his.

His blood boiled slowly in his veins and he wasted no time getting them naked. Sabin removed a condom from his nightstand and Montgomery sucked in air as her hands rolled their protection onto him—the sensation firing his nerve endings like Morse code.

Eager and impatient to have her, he slid himself down the length of her body. Kissing her neck and shoulders, he quickly coaxed her left nipple to bloom for him. Then he slid his fingers inside her. She moistened and moaned. With the skill of a practiced lover, he found her love bud and made circular movements around it. With each rotation Sabin opened her legs wider and his maleness grew harder.

He kissed her deeply and circled faster and faster with his fingers until they quivered deftly inside the place that grew warmer and wetter by the second.

Her eyes closed and she clung to him, her hips swinging wildly to match the quick reverberations of his hand. She looked beautiful and he was mesmerized by how fully she'd given herself over to his pleasuring. He felt ready to burst apart.

He covered her face, neck, and shoulders with delicate kisses. She in turn screamed out as her internal walls contracted against his hand.

"You look so beautiful when you do that," he said. Then before he burst into pieces, he entered her. Steadily he pushed into her until he felt swallowed whole.

Before he could get a good rhythm going, she rolled him over and situated herself on top.

"I want to see you now," she said, rotating her hips.

Her hips lowered to his, a gentle press of ambrosia. His eyes traveled up to where two orange-size mounds set out from her chest ripe for his picking. Brushing his hands back and forth against her nipples, he teased them until they were pebble hard.

Sabin rocked herself above him. He lifted his hips to meet hers knowing that if he had been standing he would have surely fallen. Her movements staggered him, and made him think of honey, scotch whiskey, and down-home blues.

She leaned over him. His mouth was ready and took each luscious mammary. He worked each one, inhaling the sweet scent of violets, tasting salt, sex, and Sabin. She moaned her pleasure. The sound heightened his own.

The swirling of her hips spun him like a cyclone. He wanted to tell her how good it felt. "Sabin . . . baby . . ." was all he could manage. She was riding him fully now, taking in so much. He yearned to keep pace, but the tightness of her rendered him still, dazed, and in sweet pain.

"Don't stop, baby. Suck me."

Her words brought him out of his stupor and his mouth returned to capture her breasts. Pushing them together, he flicked his tongue from side to side. Then he tugged each one with his lips until she cried out.

"Mmm," she moaned, urging his attentions further.

He suckled lavishly. She rode furiously. Then the sounds of her impending eruption escaped her lips.

"Ah," she screamed in what Montgomery knew had to be high C. Seconds later, he felt her muscles contract strongly against him.

"Oh, oh, Montgomery," she said, slowing down. She leaned forward, and he kissed her sweat-misted forehead. Her eyes looked sleepy, drunk with sated passion.

"That was so good," she whispered.

He smiled. "I guess so. You look like you've had a six-pack of beer."

"Mmm," she said, giving him several loud smacks on the mouth. "It was much better than that."

"And how would I know?"

"Let me show you," she said, moving again. This time he closed his eyes and let her ride.

She took him slowly at first. Strength drained out of him replaced by the power of her lovemaking. He reached up to touch her, but she pushed his hands away.

"Lie still," she said. "If you can."

Bouncing steadily she coaxed him closer to the edge. In a movement that made him gasp and moan, she ground herself lower then reached back to fondle him. He moved then, joining in her rhythm. His loins quivered with a sensation he never thought possible.

Moving faster now she jounced and bobbed. The ocean in her hips tossed him like a boat in a sea storm—and he loved it!

"Faster, baby," he said, and she obliged.

Her quick and full slides up and down his manhood shot through him like a blast of hot adrenaline. Both of them bucked wildly, crazed with the need to reach completion.

Montgomery felt himself tighten more with each thrust inside her. "Ah," he cried, hurtling closer. "Damn!"

"I'm cumming again," she moaned. "Montgomery . . . please . . . cum . . ."

At the urgency of her plea, he exploded.

> *Kai,*
> *I haven't felt the emptiness in so long, I'd forgotten it was there. I've been looking for my mother for so long. But now I wonder, is it her, or just a sense of belonging I need? I always thought that if I found her, I'd finally belong to someone. I wouldn't be alone. Because of Montgomery, I haven't felt alone in a long time.*
> *S.*

Ninjas don't fall.

—Sabin Strong

Eighteen

"Two hundred dollars! They're worth three times that." Angela Miller stared in disgust at the man behind the counter.

"If you don't like my offer, Payday Jewelry and Loan is right across the street."

She winced and almost took the man's advice. Then she realized that the two businesses were probably working together to scam customers. If she had more time, she would find another pawnshop, but for now . . .

"I'll take the two hundred."

"Harrumph," the man said. He reached beneath the counter, retrieved a sales receipt, and began to write. His big ruddy hand swallowed the pen. "Name?"

"Angela Miller."

"Address?"

"624 West Broad Street."

"Phone?"

"555-7563."

"Sign here," he said, handing her the receipt. She took the paper and scanned the man's jerky handwriting. The description read, "Gold diamond earrings," but it was incorrect. They were going to be heirlooms—something she could pass on to her a daughter when she had one. And she *would* pass them on—eventually. Just as soon as Victor got things straightened out. *If only Grego had won the fight.*

She signed the receipt, right below the fine print that asked if she came upon the merchandise by legal means. *Of course!* she thought.

Angela left, reminding herself that she hated pawn-shops. But even more than her disdain for pawnshops was her love for Victor. She would do anything for him. *Anything.*

Sabin hesitated. The dress she had chosen made it almost impossible to bow. The jade-green silk wrap hugged her fiercely. She'd gained a few pounds since she wore it last. But she made an effort to honor the restaurant host as she and Montgomery entered the Japanese steak house.

The restaurant was divided into sections, each par-titioned by thin wooden walls that didn't quite reach the ceiling. There were six tables in each section and customers watched in various stages of awe and appre-ciation as master chefs prepared their food in dazzling and humorous ways.

"Careful," Montgomery said as they walked to their seats. "That dragon on the front of your dress is about to roar."

Sabin smacked him on the forearm with the back of her hand.

His eyes flashed like lightning. "I'm not complain-ing now. I like the way he ripples when you walk."

Although she could listen to Montgomery's compli-ments all day, she rolled her eyes at him anyway.

The steak house was murky with ambient light and the smoke from grilling food. The host escorted them to a table for eight. In the center of the table was a large grill where their meals would be prepared before them.

A young Japanese woman brought menus and took their drink order. When she returned with their sodas, Montgomery and Sabin were deep in conversation. Six others shared their table, but to Montgomery and Sabin, it was as if they were the only two in the room.

By the time the cook arrived at their table, Sabin and Montgomery had talked through three sodas. She hated to miss the opening protocol of their meal preparation, but her bladder was full after all that liquid. She excused herself and walked toward the ladies' room, catching the cook's appreciative glance in the corner of her eye.

When she returned, zucchini, onions and bean sprouts warmed on the perimeter of the grill. She took her seat and the cook spoke to her in Japanese.

Montgomery frowned. "In English, please."

The cook, whose name tag read Eddie, smiled politely. "I said she moves like smoke."

Sabin returned his smile. "Thank you," she said.

Montgomery gave her a sideways glance. "Was that a compliment?"

"I think so," she said, raising her glass for another sip of Sprite.

On the one hand, she was grateful for any proof that her training was a natural part of who she was. On the other hand, there were times, like now, when she didn't want to be recognized, or be reminded of her background. More than anything, she just wanted to have a quiet dinner with the man she . . . Oh God. Did she love him? Impossible!

Instead of crazy notions, she focused on Eddie.

From the very start of his grilling, nothing was ordinary. From mincing vegetables, to seasoning meat, to filling bowls with rice. Eddie performed intricate feats of culinary magic and legerdemain that could surpass any magician's sleight of hand. Every step of the preparation came as part of one artistic event in a series, providing Montgomery and Sabin with an eclectic dining experience.

Montgomery watched nearly transfixed as Eddie placed a stack of fresh raw onion rings in the center of the grill, poured on wine, and lit it. The result was a volcano with flames shooting up toward the smoke vent. Eddie feigned difficulty extinguishing the blaze.

"I'll bet you were a handful when you were a kid," Montgomery remarked.

"You can say that again." Sabin smiled. She could almost laugh about it now. "I didn't have the best of childhoods. So I took out my frustration on everyone around me.

"I was the stereotypical abandoned child. I lived in an orphanage run by nuns until I was sixteen. That was before the state took over the placement of children without parents."

"What about other members of your family? Aunts, uncles, cousins, brothers, and sisters?"

"I wish I knew. From what I could get the sisters to tell me, I was left at the door like you see in movies. And believe me, I grew up committing every act associated with that cliché."

Montgomery watched as Sabin's eyes traveled up and to the left.

"I was unruly. I ran away several times. I even started stealing. That's what landed me, at the ripe old age of thirteen, in a diversion program."

All Montgomery could think about was how effective a Mad Dads program might have been for her back then. "What happened with the diversion program?"

"The usual. They subjected me to extensive counseling, and community service work. At the time, it didn't help to reform me much, but it did give me a way to channel my frustration."

"What's that?"

"As part of my anger management treatment, I had to take a martial arts class. My sensei, Toda Kai, was a master teacher and became my best friend. He chose an art form that suited me and helped me gain perspective on defense, harmony, and balance."

"And it didn't help you?"

"Not right away. When I was sixteen, my boyfriend, who was almost ten years older than me, convinced me to leave the orphanage. He was a thief and we were going to spend the rest of our lives paying for things with other people's money. We were going to be the black Bonnie and Clyde."

"What happened?"

"Things have a way of escalating. First, we just shoplifted stuff. Then, we would break into small grocery stores and department stores. But most thieves take things because they are trying to fill a void within themselves. For me that void was my parents. Only, I didn't know it then. So no matter what we took, it was never enough.

"One day, Mark decided that we needed to up the stakes and rob a convenience store. He pulled out these guns. I didn't even know he had them.

"At first, I hesitated. But that hole in my heart was as empty as ever, and Mark's plan sounded like something that would fill it.

"So we picked out a convenience store. Checked it out to determine the slow times, and rehearsed our plan. When it came time to do it, I was ready and I'm sorry to say, a little excited about the whole thing.

"Everything went smoothly. We got the money from the register and were on the way out, when Mark got greedy. He asked the cashier for his wallet. I kept trying to get him to leave, but he wouldn't. We might have gotten away if the man had cooperated. But he refused to give up his wallet.

"Well, Mark went ballistic and threatened to kill him. Then I got really scared. I didn't want to be a part of a senseless killing. I have no idea what came over me, but I turned my gun on him and ordered him to come out with me. He called me a traitor and told me that for my treachery, he would shoot him." Sabin took a deep breath. "God help me, but I shot Mark before he could shoot the cashier."

Montgomery's shocked expression didn't surprise her. What did surprise her was the fact that she shared that story with him. She had never shared that story with anyone except her sensei.

"Did Mark live?"

Sabin shook her head.

"The orphanage got me a good lawyer—a guy who had once been an orphan there. I was a minor and he was able to get me back into the diversion program with five years' probation. The nuns took care of me for two more years and I threw myself into martial arts. When I was eighteen, I left officially and I haven't looked back since."

Montgomery looked at Sabin with fresh eyes. As if he was meeting her for the first time with a different first impression. Now he understood her anger and aggression. For the first time, Sabin started to make sense to him.

For a few moments, they ate in silence. Montgomery concentrated on making an impact on the mountain of rice and lobster on his plate. Sabin pushed around a piece of calamari with her chopsticks.

"And now that you've heard my sob story, what's yours? No, wait. Let me guess. You were a model child."

"Compared to you, yeah. I was. But I didn't start out that way."

"Really?" Sabin leaned in closer to Montgomery. "*Do* tell!"

"Well . . . to hear my father recount the story, I didn't want to be born."

"What?"

Eddie cleaned up the space before them where his marvelous feats of showmanship and cooking finesse had taken place.

"Yeah. I was three weeks overdue. The doctor wanted to put my mother in the hospital and try to induce her labor, but she refused. She said I could come in my own time."

Sabin's smile looked delicious on her lips.

"When I was born, she named me Pa'akiki, po'opa'a."

"I like it. But what does it mean?"

Montgomery averted his eyes. "Stubborn."

Other patrons in the restaurant turned from their meals to see what could cause such a gust of laughter.

"It ain't funny," he said, already chuckling.

"Oh, yes, it is! Yes, it *is.*"

"Seriously, though," Montgomery said, reflecting on Sabin's story, "sometimes I don't realize how fortunate I am until I hear about other people's lives. Even though I didn't have my mom that long, I had her. Now my father, on the other hand, I'm not so sure I wouldn't have been better off growing up without him."

"You're only saying that because he was there. If he hadn't been, I think you might feel differently."

"Mmm," he said, reflecting. "Well, my childhood was relatively uneventful. I pretty much did as I was told, until my father got ugly. War does terrible things to people. It wasn't just my dad that was affected by the war. Our whole family was.

"Some vets can leave their war demons on the battlefield. My father is not one of them. At every opportunity, he reminded us just how atrocious it was. Vivid descriptions of death and killing and severed body parts. Just months after he retired, my mother and I felt like we had been there, too. I was twelve at the time. It wasn't until my mother was killed that he stopped all that talk of bloodbaths and combat tactics.

"Even though I had no inclination to go to college, I jumped at the chance to get away from him. I majored in business because I figured that was a generic enough major, and I had no idea what I really wanted to do with my life."

"How did you get into storage?"

"It really started as a furniture moving business. I'd become accustomed to channeling the anger and frustration I felt for my father into weight lifting. One day I realized that when I worked with my body, it was the only time I felt really content."

Sabin's mind strayed a bit to the way he'd worked his body earlier that day, but she kept listening.

"I worked part-time with Tangus Furniture, delivering customer orders. Larry Tangus, the owner, also owned a storage facility. I ended up working there, too, and I liked the opportunity of combining my brain with my brawn.

"Next thing you know, I'm attending entrepreneur workshops, finding out how to write business plans, and learning how to apply for bank loans. I owe a great deal to those classes. I used what I learned and opened Secure Storage."

They looked up and realized that they were the only people at their table. The hostess quietly ran a carpet sweeper under their feet.

Montgomery and Sabin left the restaurant and headed toward the parking lot. She liked the way he strolled into her space. They were so close their arms brushed together. Neither minded.

She matched him, stride for stride, and when he reached over to finger a wisp of her hair, the sensation pulsed across her skin like sweet music. Out of the corner of her eye, she could see him taking her in. His head turned slightly to the right, his eyes traveling. At the very gesture she burned for him.

"What's wrong?" she asked, noticing him slowing.

"Nothing. Keep walking."

Suddenly, she was self-conscious. "Why?"

"Because I think the chef was right. You do move like smoke."

The sound of his words made her feel sweet and tender. There could only be one explanation. She was in love. Sabin wondered what Montgomery would do when she told him.

"It's like you're part of the air," he said. "How do you do that?"

Sabin thought of her training. The principles of *inton-jutsu* taught her to exist as part of the elements, not separate from them. "It's a state of being, I guess. I don't really think about it, though."

Montgomery smiled. "Well, I've been thinking about it." His eyes followed a familiar path from her face to her rear. "I can't stop thinking about it."

They continued through the alley. Darkness had settled around the buildings and between the cracks in the concrete like a heavy blanket. Their steps echoed against brick walls and bounced back to them. Humidity thickened the air around them. The only sound came in the flutter of a bird's wings overhead.

Then, Sabin heard footsteps ahead of them and stopped. She grabbed Montgomery just as a man stepped out from the shadows.

"Don't worry, lady. I won't hurt you. I just want your money."

"That gun in your hand says otherwise," Montgomery said, stepping in front of Sabin.

The man moved closer, cocking his pistol. "Give me your money!"

Montgomery tried to push Sabin backward. Instead, she spun him around and kicked the gunman on the chin. He fell back and the revolver tumbled out of his hand. Montgomery heard the rip of silk as Sabin kicked it away.

"I'll be . . ." the man said, pulling a knife out of his pocket.

"Come on!" Sabin shouted over the adrenaline she heard surging through her veins.

"Sabin?" Montgomery said, pulling at her.

She shrugged him away. "No. This fool needs to be taught a lesson."

The man lunged at her. Sabin deflected his attack by grabbing his wrist and twisting the knife out of his hand. It fell to the ground and she kicked it away, as well. Then she attacked.

"The next time," *foot strike,* "you decide," *open hand,* "you want money," *elbow strike,* "get a job!" *roundhouse kick.*

"Sabin!" Montgomery shouted. This time she didn't resist as he led her away from their would-be-attacker lying disarranged in the alley. "That's enough."

He marched her to his Jaguar. "Get in," he said, unlocking the door.

She got in and rubbed her fingers. Instead of regular practice, she'd been spending time with Montgomery. That small exchange should not have injured her.

He started the car without a word and drove off quickly toward home. Sabin rolled down her window and let the rushing air cool her face. After a few tension-filled miles, Montgomery broke the silence.

"I used to think of you as Cleopatra Jones, but now I'm thinking Laila Ali. What the hell *was* that!"

"That was some idiot trying to rob us." Sabin's heart rate finally returned to normal.

Montgomery took a hard left onto the beltway. "You know what I mean. Was that your martial art?"

"Yes."

"What kind?"

Sabin didn't hesitate. Her feelings for Montgomery made her answer truthfully. "Ninjutsu."

"Ninjutsu?"

"Yes."

"As in ninja?" Montgomery blinked hard. "You're a ninja?"

"Yes."

"As in stars, knives, poison, *assassination?*"

Sabin's voice never faltered. "Yes."

Montgomery shifted away from her. "Damn. All this time I believed that you were really a safety consultant."

"I am," she insisted.

"No, you're not," he said, feeling a coldness that set his teeth on edge. "You don't protect people. You kill them!"

She reached over to touch him. He recoiled. Montgomery pulled on to the shoulder and slammed on the breaks. "Is it you? The one whose been trying to take me out?"

"How can you ask that?"

Montgomery looked her up and down. "If I wasn't a gentleman . . ."

"What?" Sabin shot back. "Speak up!"

"I'd put you out of my damned car."

"No need," Sabin responded, opening the passenger door.

Montgomery leaned back against the leather seat and looked up toward heaven as if searching for an answer there. "Sabin . . ."

She slammed the door. "Now you can go. The big bad assassin is gone," she said, speaking through the open window.

"It's nighttime. Get in the car, Sabin."

"Don't pacify me, Montgomery. Remember, I'm a ninja. If anyone tries anything, I'll just kill them."

"Cool," Montgomery said, and merged his car back onto the expressway.

After ten minutes, Sabin's feet reminded her why she hardly ever wore heels. *How do other women do it?* she wondered, wanting to remove the leather strapped sandals. The next exit loomed three miles ahead of her. As soon as she reached it, she would find a phone and call a cab. Then first thing tomorrow, she would replace the cell phone that was ruined in the accident.

"We always find a way to push away from each other, don't we?"

She heard Montgomery's voice coming from the car rolling beside her, but kept her eyes straight ahead. Maybe then they wouldn't betray her relief that he had turned around and come back for her.

"I just—I don't know what to do with you."

She stopped. "What to *do* with me?"

Montgomery cradled his forehead in his palm. "See what I mean."

She didn't want to laugh, but she did. "You *know* you look pitiful."

"I *feel* pitiful. And I'm sorry. I just can't believe that you're a . . . a . . ."

She crossed her arms. He steered the car in front of her and stepped out. Sabin held her ground, not wanting to give in too much. "I won't change or deny what I am. But if you had given me a chance, you would have heard me say that I don't kill people."

"So ninjutsu is the martial art you learned while in the diversion program."

"Yes."

"That's one hell of a diversion."

"I'm still the same Sabin you had dinner with tonight, that you made love to this morning. I'm the same Sabin that laughs at your corny jokes and survives your cooking. I just happen to have a unique skill—a skill that saved my life when I was younger."

"If you were a kid, I'd put you in the Sankofa program to see if I couldn't temper your aggression."

Sabin's heart sank. Obviously, he couldn't accept her for who she was. She started walking again, noting the rips in her silk dress. The sooner she got home, the better.

Montgomery jogged up behind her and spun her around. "This time you didn't let *me* finish. You're not one of the kids I try to impact. You're a grown woman. A woman I . . ."

Sabin's heart stopped.

"A woman I want in my life," he finished.

Even though those weren't the exact words she wanted to hear, she realized they were good words and they would do for now.

"For someone committed to nonviolence, you sure have a strong temper," she said, turning toward the car.

He played with a strand of her hair. "That's because you provoke me."

He kissed her then. It was long, penetrating, and closed her eyes. Then someone whizzing past them in a car yelled, "Get a room!"

Montgomery smiled into her eyes. "You have the incomparable ability to make me crazy."

Sabin searched his eyes for meaning. "Is that good or bad?"

"Honestly, I don't know."

Silently they walked toward Montgomery's car. Sabin wondered how much longer they would actually be neighbors. Even after all they'd shared, the sooner she left the country, the better.

Sabin rolled the exercise mat out on the floor of the spare bedroom and prepared herself. She hoped closing her eyes and meditating would free her of all the concerns plaguing her mind. It didn't, and they whirled in her head like a tornado. Could she keep Montgomery safe? Could she keep her heart safe from him? Who wanted him dead? Why had she agreed to such a crazy assignment?

She lifted her hands above her head and slowly lowered them, pressing down the air with her palms. She pushed her breaths out through pursed lips and repeated the movement until her energy centered in the middle of her body.

No matter how she worked to clear her mind, Montgomery stayed fixed at the nub of her thoughts. Why did he always smell like hot spiced rum? And why, even after they were apart, did his scent linger on her skin and intoxicate her like a fragrant narcotic? If she pulled on it just a little, she could bring the memory of his smell to her nostrils as surely as if he was standing before her, against her, holding her.

Stop it! she ordered herself. She paused. Stood perfectly still—the stillness of a shadow warrior. She willed her mind to empty, felt her musings seep away like tepid water swirling down a narrow drain. And when her spirit was in perfect balance, she moved. Slowly at first. Then inch by inch she eased her body from one stance to another.

She shifted without a sound while one by one she executed the poses of her *Junan taiso,* body conditioning.

Her goal, always the same, to naturalize her movements and to model elements in the environment.

She allowed only one thought in her mind at a time. *Earth.* Like the planet, she made her movements solid and firm. Twisting from right to left, Sabin hit out in uniform and unbroken movements. *Water.* Fluid and responsive, she used her flexibility to lean into her motions and deliver sharp strikes through the air with her hands. *Fire.* Now her arms, legs, and full torso yielded powerful, more explosive strikes. She bent her knees, swooping down with her left hand, sweeping up into a knife hand with the other. Her kicks barely made a sound as she vigorously released them one after another.

Wind. Her posture melded into an expansive shield and attack weapon. Light on her feet, she directed openhanded rain blows into the air. Her body took up more space while she shifted her weight avoiding an imaginary attacker. *Void.* Her last element was where she came from the best. Spontaneous and improvisational punches and lunges. She allowed her body, mind, and spirit to give her not moves and techniques but an attitude, one that enabled her to explore her emotions through movement.

Left, right, she shifted with increasing speed. In her mind, she deflected flying kicks, war staffs, and iron palms. She jumped, tumbled, rolled, and righted herself. Then with her entire body, she lunged into an attack, bestowing a lightning-quick volley of punishing blows designed to disable any aggressor.

Finally, Sabin returned to the center of the room and stood motionless, guiding her thoughts into perfect order. When her mind calmed and her breathing slowed, she bowed once and then headed toward the shower.

The sun's rays beat down like a mallet against Sabin's back. She tucked in the stray hairs that had come loose from her ponytail and swiped the sweat on her forehead with the back of her hand.

From her metal toolbox, she retrieved a cordless screwdriver and put the final screws in to attach her new windshield to her Big Boy.

She enjoyed working on her Hog. It had been a while since she had the time or the opportunity to customize a motorcycle the way she wanted to. She could envision wheel assemblies that matched the patterns of her ninja stars, slingshot mirrors to broaden her range of visibility, and a digital speedometer so that she would know at a glance exactly how fast she was going. Her mind brimmed with all the enhancements she wanted to make.

After tightening the last screw, Sabin stood and went into her house for some Windex and a cleaning cloth. When she returned to her backyard, Montgomery was there waiting.

"Nice," he said, looking at the windshield and then at her.

She sprayed the windshield with cleaner and wiped it with the cloth. "Thanks." She kept her mind focused on her task and not the man whose skin glowed to golden perfection in the sun.

"So, what's your specialty?" he asked sheepishly.

"You've been doing research."

"Let's just say I got curious."

"My specialty is Shinobi-iri—stealth and entering."

"So you can just break into someone's home or business undetected?"

"Yes."

"Is that how you got into my office the day I was gassed?"

"Yes."

"Hmm."

"Look, Montgomery. If most of what you know about ninjas comes from the movies, then you don't know much at all. Hollywood portrays us as magical, most often evil, and always superhuman. I wouldn't even call those myths. Just gross distortions.

"As a master of ninjutsu, I have a warrior's creed. *Wherever I go, everyone is a little bit safer because I am there. Wherever I am, anyone in need has a friend.*"

Sabin wiped a smudge from the chrome of her bike. "I'm not a killer."

He drew his lips in thoughtfully. "I believe you," he said.

All of the tension fell out of Sabin's body. "So, now what do we do?"

"Now," he said, boldly straddling her Harley, "you teach me to drive."

The jarring sound of a ringing phone vibrated through her body. Groggily, she reached over to the nightstand and picked up the receiver.

"Hello," she said, her voice course from sleep.

"Good morning."

The sultry bass of Montgomery's voice melted her even as it traveled through the telephone wires.

"What time is it?" she asked, turning from the warm spot she'd made in the bed.

"Two A.M."

"Two A.M.?" Sabin bolted upright. "What's the matter?"

"Nothing, baby. Well . . . that's not quite true. I miss you."

Sabin snuggled back down onto the bed and covered herself with a sheet. "Oh, is that all?"

"Is that *all*? I don't think you understand."

"I understand that we've been together all day."

"What's that got to do with the price of tea in China? I'm in need."

A warm smile curled across Sabin's lips. She rolled over on her back and twirled a strand of her hair. "Montgomery Claiborne, is this a booty call?"

"That depends on whether or not you'll come."

"Whether or not I come depends on what you do to me when I get there."

"If that's the case, I promise to do all the things you like."

Sabin's words came out hot and breathy. "I'll be right over."

"I'll be waiting."

She didn't bother to knock or ring the doorbell. Knowing he would unlock the door for her, Sabin walked in and headed for the bedroom. As promised, Montgomery was sitting on the edge of the bed, waiting for her.

Visions of their bodies hot, sweaty, and mingling had driven waves of anticipation up her spine. The sight of his hard naked body made her shudder even more with need.

She stopped in the doorway, surprised by the sounds of Luther Vandross singing to them through Montgomery's speakers.

"That's not blues."

"It's not rock, either. Now, come here."

She stood before him and he unbuttoned her sleep shirt with exquisite slowness while his eyes bore an inferno into hers. When he finished with the last button, he ran his fingers along the edge of the fabric, lightly touching her skin with his thumbs. Then he pulled the shirt apart slightly, then a bit more and placed a soft kiss on her navel.

Sabin held her breath waiting for him to undress her and claim her body where it ached desperately for his touch.

Gradually, inch by excruciating inch, he removed her shirt. His breath came out in one hot and long exhale when it fell to the floor. Montgomery licked his lips and slid his fingers into the top of her matching shorts, dragging them without haste down her thighs, calves, and ankles where she stepped out of them.

As Sabin stood naked before him, his eyes drank her body like a man who had just crossed the desert and found an oasis. "I can't believe how beautiful you are," he said, desire dripping from his voice.

She appraised him appreciatively. "And I can't believe how magnificent *you* are."

Even in the darkness, her skin glowed a perfect golden brown, like warm honey he couldn't wait to taste. *Loving the lioness,* he thought, and pulled her on top of him as he lay back against the bed.

He brushed his lips against hers and then licked her lips with his tongue until they were moist and parted for his entry. With his mouth hungry for hers, he eased his tongue inside until it found its mate and danced in slow motion.

"Ah," she uttered—more plea than moan. He was driving her crazy with his unhurried pleasuring.

He turned her on her back and lifted her legs on to the bed. Then he traced patterns across her skin with his fingers—flowing, lingering patterns. Circles, spirals, twists, curves. He created a galaxy of sensations all over her body, then concentrated more deliberate work on her chest.

His rapt attention made her curious.

"What are you doing?"

"Writing my name on your heart," he answered.

She closed her eyes and prayed, unable to speak. Could he really care for her? Did he have any idea what those words meant to her? For that matter, did she? Before she could ponder further, his mouth fell upon hers—greedy and hot. She extended her arms and pulled him tight to her chest.

He slid his hand along the side of her body, across her hip, and inside her thigh. He rocked her gently back and forth and inserted his fingers into the place where Sabin was already wet and in need.

Montgomery continued his gentle rocking motion and the relaxed tempo of his hand moving in and out of her. Sabin clung tighter when his mouth descended moist and warm on her breast. She moaned as embers of desire flared up in her as if they'd been stoked in a slow oven.

She was close.

"Take your time, baby. Don't rush. I'll be here all night." He left soft kisses on her neck and throat. "Loving you . . . all night."

In the dark night of the room, his eyes flashed at her like amber lightning. The ardor she saw there banked and brought her breathing in harsh and loud gulps.

Still stroking her inside, still suckling a nipple, Montgomery increased his pace, ever so slightly to match the urgent need he saw in her eyes.

"Is this what you like?" he asked, barely above a whisper.

She gasped at the heady sensation building between her legs.

"Is it?"

"Yes," she responded, pulling him closer, arching her back. *Yes, she wanted it.* Her mind, body, and spirit told her it was just right. She moaned deeply as he rocked her with his strong and steady hand.

His fingers slid so easily back and forth. Her womanly juices increased with her need. Montgomery felt his own desire increasing as he watched Sabin's pleasure play itself out across her face. He was mesmerized by the ecstasy he saw there.

"Um," Sabin moaned, nearing the edge. "Ummmm."

"All night," he whispered in response, and the bottom dropped out from under Sabin's world.

She closed her eyes and let herself fall.

"You're so beautiful when you do that."

Montgomery took a condom from his nightstand drawer and put it on. "I want to see it again." And because he couldn't wait any longer, he entered her.

At their joining, Sabin felt as though she'd been dipped in a vat of serene perfection. They stared into each other's eyes and moved in timeless abandon.

How could he be so handsome? she wondered.

How could she be so wonderful? he wanted to know.

They held on to each other, and true to his promise, Montgomery took her in slow uninterrupted time throughout the night.

First on the bed, where he'd brought her to the brink, then carried her to a chair where they began in earnest again.

When an intimate explosion was upon her again,

he returned her to the bed where he turned her over and entered her from the rear.

His lovemaking was Zen-like. Sabin felt weightless and powerless against the man who had become an emissary of all things pleasurable.

As she neared the breaking point yet again, he carried her to his dresser where she wrapped her legs around him tighter than anything he'd ever felt. This time it was Montgomery who came rushing toward the edge. He tried to pull out. She felt so good. He didn't want it to end. And he'd made a promise. But when her hips made that circular gyration that he loved, he gave in.

Pumping strongly in and out of her, he teased a nipple with one hand while sucking generously on the other. She arched and moaned, her hips spinning him into a delirious frenzy.

"Let me see it," he demanded huskily.

Sabin opened her eyes and pulled back so he could watch. For someone who had spent most of her life controlling her emotions, she threw her head back and let go. A second later her eyes closed again and she cried out as a brilliant ribbon of rapture ripped through her.

"Thank you, baby. Thank y—" Montgomery thrust deeply inside her, filled with paralyzing completion as he detonated into her soft warm core.

"What are you doing?"

"Braiding my hair."

"Yes, but"—Montgomery glanced at the clock—"it's five in the morning."

"I know. I couldn't sleep."

After tossing and turning, Sabin had switched on the hall light and cracked the bedroom door so that

just a minimal amount of light entered. Then, she sat
on the floor with a comb and brush and proceeded
to section off her hair.

The mindless activity allowed her to do the one
thing she'd been avoiding; consider how she felt about
Montgomery. After an hour, the same truth surfaced
again and again.

She loved him.

With that realization came another. She would go
to Reeves Claiborne and tell him she no longer
worked for him. He would have to find someone else
to protect his son, or perhaps she would find a re-
placement. But one thing was clear: she refused to put
Montgomery's life in jeopardy. And her feelings for
him meant that she couldn't be completely objective
or detached. In her current state of mind, she could
make careless mistakes, the kind of mistakes that could
get them both killed.

"I think that one is done," he said, shaking her
from her thoughts.

"Oh," she replied, and switched to another section.

He got out of bed and sat on the floor behind her.
"Let me help you."

Sabin turned to stare at him. "What do you know
about doing hair?"

"When my mother died, I had the misfortune of
doing my sister's hair. It wouldn't have been so bad
except, she's tender-headed."

"So am I," Sabin whispered.

With practiced fingers, Montgomery took section after section and carefully braided them. They worked
together until her hair was plaited and hanging down
her back in thick silken cords.

"They're beautiful," he said, playing his fingers
against the braids. "You're beautiful."

She turned to him, and Montgomery thought the

feisty hell spawn had transformed into one of heaven's angels. He leaned forward to kiss her. She drew back.

"What's wrong?" he asked.

"Everything," she said, heart pounding in her ears. "Nothing."

"Sabin . . ."

"I love you."

He blinked and leaned back. "What?"

Here it comes, she thought, unable to stop herself. "I don't sleep around, Montgomery. This . . . what we're doing . . . what we have . . . it means something to me. Something important. And before we go any further, before my heart gets any more invested, I need to know how you feel."

He smiled then. "Hmmm. How do I feel?" He kissed her shoulder and snuggled close. "I feel like I've just been struck by lightning. I feel there are fires burning in me like I've been set off by pyrotechnics. I feel . . . Oh, that's it!"

Montgomery jumped up, and the warm silly feeling that had been taking over Sabin faded.

"Baby, I have to go."

Before Sabin could protest, he was yanking on pants and a shirt.

"Where are you going?" she asked, standing.

He shoved his feet into work boots. "Stay here. I'll be back in an hour. Two at the most."

"Montgomery, wait!" She grabbed her clothes and followed him down the hall.

He removed work gloves, a flashlight, and a toolbox from a shelf in a closet.

"Where are you going?" she asked again.

He rushed to the door. Sabin kept pace behind him, pulling on her sleep shirt.

"You can't go, Sabin. What I have to do might be— *is* dangerous. Now is not the time for you to come charging in on your white horse. When I get back, I'll try to explain everything. Right now I need you to stay here. If I'm not back in two hours, call the police."

"But, Montgom—" His kiss was swift and powerful. Her need to shake some sense into him dissolved into her need to do whatever he asked.

He stepped back, and the passion in his eyes made her tremble.

"I love you, too," he said and walked out the door.

Sabin waited two minutes, then ran to her backyard. As she tossed up the garage door, a bright pain ripped up the side of her body and exploded at the base of her skull.

"Ah," she screamed, and dropped to her knees. She'd had migraines before but nothing as intense as this agony slicing through her head. Despite the pain, she willed every muscle in her body to relax. After several minutes, her suffering abated enough for Sabin to crawl inside her house and collapse on the kitchen floor.

A man knows his limits, and surpasses them.
—Reeves Claiborne

Nineteen

He could still smell the odor of burning wood. In a few days, bulldozers were coming to remove what was left of Secure Storage Building B. A thin chord of remorse snaked through his veins.

"Clyde! Clyde!"

"What are you hollerin' for?"

The old man stumbled up beside him, his familiar coat tattered and hanging askew from his alcohol-ravaged body. He looked like he'd been wide-awake.

"What happened, Clyde?"

Clyde clutched his paper bag. "Somebody came in at around two. Then somebody left at around two-fifteen. Ten minutes later, your man Ted comes runnin' out. Right after that, the fire trucks showed up." Clyde dropped his head. "You were here for everything else."

"Did you get a good look at the person who went in? Man? Woman? Young? Old?"

"Nope. This Wild Irish has me seein' double some-times."

"Thanks, Clyde," he said, and set off toward what was left of the building. Clyde's throat clearing reminded him he'd forgotten something. He went back, slipped a twenty-dollar bill into the man's paper sack, and resumed his walk to the warehouse.

He stopped where the door used to be. Replaced by scorched wood beams, only a charcoal forest of memories remained. He walked right through.

Montgomery took his wallet out and removed a slip of paper that he'd been carrying around for two weeks. The flashlight illuminated the message: RIE DOCS C. BRUMMEND THIRD DRAWER.

C. Brummend, he thought, stepping over the rubble of what used to be a spare office. His boots shuffled and crunched over grimy boards and planks, some still damp from the fire hoses. Each step released a sickening vapor from the combustion, and Montgomery covered his nose and mouth with a gloved hand.

Colonel Brummend, he mused. Ash and soot caked in black rings around the bottom of his pants. He stepped over papers, the backs of chairs, a trash can, severed table legs. The whole sight resembled something apocalyptic and evil.

He prayed he understood what Randy was trying to tell him. "Randy, were you trying to put out the fire?" His words dissipated like mist in the humid night air. Finally, he came upon an area with less damage than the rest of the building. Straining, he lifted away parts of the ceiling and other large debris that covered the area. Hoping vandals had not beaten him, Montgomery cleared a path to a charred storage unit. The fused plastic looked as though it had been cooked in a microwave, leaning to one side, but partially intact. Montgomery pried the door open with the crowbar. He coughed as fumes from the fire rushed out into fresher air. Climbing over the mounds of ruination, he made it back to where eight executive-style desks stacked up like giant building blocks. Carefully, he squeezed himself between the bureaus and the wall and set to work. He hoped he would be finished before Sabin had a chance to call the police.

After searching through each desk and finding nothing, Montgomery's hopes deflated. But something inside him told him he wasn't wrong about his hunch.

"Okay. It wouldn't be obvious," he said to the night air. This time, he searched the desks, looking for hidden latches and secret openings. He was pounding on desk number five when he heard a hollow sound in the third drawer. After pressing, pulling, and tugging at all areas of the drawer to no avail, impatience got the best of him and he smashed the side of the drawer with the crowbar. Wood splintered and shattered revealing a false bottom in the drawer. Montgomery shook away the shards, reached inside, and withdrew a stack of paper two inches thick.

He walked to the door and looked around, refusing to believe that he wasn't being watched. Placing the papers in his duffel bag, he began the hazardous traverse of building remains back to his car.

"Sabin!" he called out, but there was no answer. Montgomery searched his house. She wasn't there. He hitched the duffel bag on his shoulder and went next door. When there was no answer to his knock, he grew concerned. He walked to the back of the house where both the garage door and back door were open. He rushed inside the house. "Sabin!"

Panic rose in his throat when his vision caught sight of her lying on the kitchen floor. Her hands covered her head as if she'd been protecting it from attack. "Sabin!" he called, kneeling by her side.

"I'm all right, Montgomery," she whispered. "I just can't move."

Montgomery placed her gently on her couch and stroked her forehead. "What happened?"

"I was trying to open the garage door and I got this major headache."

"No one attacked you?"

"No. I just feel like I've got a semi trying to get out of my skull and one of its wheels is spinning on a nerve that runs down my spine and into my legs."

"Damn. That's some kinda pain."

"I've been lying on the floor since you left. I've had a lot of time to think about it."

"I'm taking you to the hospital."

"Like hell you are!"

"What were you doing opening the garage anyway? I thought you were waiting for me at my place?"

"I was going to follow you, but my body had other plans." She closed her eyes then. "Just get me some aspirin, and I'll be fine."

"Fine?" he asked, concern quavering his voice. "I'm taking you to the hospital, and since you can't move, you can't stop me."

Her arms and shoulders squirmed a bit, but mostly she was limp in his arms.

"Montgomery!"

He approached the door and stopped. "Remember what I said before I left?"

Her features looked decidedly more pleasant. "Yes," she whispered.

"Did you think I was lying? I *love* you, Sabin. So, if you don't mind, I'm going to do everything in my power to make sure my woman is healthy and safe."

The stubbornness in her jaw relaxed and her protests stopped.

* * *

After nearly two hours of arguing against it, Sabin had finally allowed the doctors to give her Demerol for the pain. Montgomery chuckled at the woozy expression on her face.

"How do you feel now?"

"Like going for a ride on my bike," she said, then snickered into her hand.

He noticed that she was even moving better.

"Babe, can you wiggle your toes?"

"Yep," she said, and slowly her toes moved back and forth. "Why are feet so strange looking?" she asked. "Have you ever wondered that? I mean, look at my feet! That's just strange. Should they look more like hands? Then you could . . ."

"Babe," Montgomery said, taking her hand. "That pain medication is really strong. I think you should be quiet and let it work."

"Are you trying to tell me to shut up? Because if you are you can just forg—"

"Miss Strong, I have your X rays."

The doctor came into the tiny room and shoved the large sheets of film into a light box on the wall.

"I can't tell for sure, but judging from what we see here and the pain you've described, I'd say you have a pinched nerve.

"To be certain, you'll need to see a specialist. Do you have a regular doctor?"

She smiled like a little girl with a new toy. "Nope."

"Well, I could give you a referral if you like."

"That will be fine, Doctor." Montgomery nodded.

"In the meantime, I'll write you a prescription for the pain."

Concern heated Montgomery's face. "What could have caused this?"

"Anything from strenuous exercise to severe trauma.

Have you fallen lately? Lifted something heavy? Or been in an accident?"

Still dopey, Sabin nodded her head. "Mmm-hmm. He tried to kill me. But I love him anyway." She dissolved into a mass of giggles.

The doctor looked concerned.

"We had a traffic accident several weeks ago." A wave of nausea struck Montgomery. *Could he have caused this?*

"Since the accident was so long ago, would she still have problems now?" he asked the doctor.

"Oh, absolutely. Especially if she was never examined or treated for her injuries. And since she doesn't have a regular doctor, that could be the case."

"Oh, God," Montgomery said, sick with guilt.

"She's going to recover, right? She will be able to walk?"

"If it is a pinched nerve and she gets treatment right away, she should recover."

Sabin's slap-happy grin took over her whole face. "I like treatment."

Montgomery took the flashlight out of his bag. "Here, Sabin. Play with this."

She took the tool from him and flicked the switch on and off. "Ooh!" she said.

Montgomery shook his head and turned his attention back to the doctor. "Tell me about the treatment, Doctor."

"Well, I can only speculate. A specialist can tell you more, but it could be massage and PT. It could be chiropractic, it could be heating pads and Motrin, and worst-case scenario, it could also be surgery.

"I'll check her over one more time. I think her motor skills are coming back. She was probably in so much pain that, for lack of a better way to explain it, it overwhelmed her nerves and they started to shut down."

"Sabin? Ah!" Montgomery took back the flashlight. "It's not nice to shine it in people's faces, baby."

She wasn't paying any attention. She just lay back and closed her eyes.

The doctor lifted Sabin's leg slightly. He spoke to her in a loud voice. "Sabin, does this hurt?"

"Naw."

"Can you push against my hand? Good. Hey! You've got some strength there. How about the other side? Okay. That's fine. That's much better."

"Well?" Montgomery's concern was rolling over in his chest.

"I think she's good to go. We'll get her a wheelchair to get her to the car. Can you carry her in to wherever she needs to go?"

"Yes."

The doctor looked over at Sabin blissed out on the examining table. "She may need someone to help her out for a couple of days until the medicine tricks her nerves into thinking that there's nothing wrong."

"No problem."

Montgomery glanced at his ladylove. Ms. Hard as Nails had regressed at least twenty years.

The doctor smiled. "I'll prescribe something that's not so . . . stupefying," he said, stepping out of the room.

Montgomery sat down for the first time since they'd arrived at the hospital. He'd been so afraid that Sabin had been assaulted when he first saw her lying in a heap on her floor. He had to find out all he could about the papers he found and who would want them before anyone else he cared about got hurt.

"I feel better." Sabin sang the words off-key.

"I'm glad, baby." He put his flashlight back in his bag and thought, *No more drugs for you!*

Day one of Sabin's recovery sailed by uneventfully. She spent most of the time sleeping. Instead of making her loopy, the pain medication Montgomery gave her made her groggy. She would come to and he would insist that she eat something. She would take a few bites of some crackers or sip 7UP then flop back against the pillow.

Montgomery enjoyed watching her sleep. The rigid lines set on her face told him that she took her sleeping and healing as seriously as she took everything else. Only the loose cotton shorts and top made her appear soft and gentle.

He was glad when she rolled from one side of the bed to the other, or curled her legs up. Her movements gave him hope that she would be back to normal soon.

As she breathed softly in the bedroom, Montgomery sat in the living room turning page after page of documents gray with copy. The top stack looked like the editor from hell had reviewed them. Someone had crossed out words, blacked out entire sentences and sometimes paragraphs. On a few of the pages, the only words remaining were the *Date, To, and From.* The bottom stack was exactly the opposite. Although the documents were old, forty years by some of the dates, they were otherwise well preserved.

Montgomery had seen similar documents once in a Black Studies class he took in college. They were the paper trail left behind by the government's counter-intelligence programs. If the memos in his hands were part of that, then he had to get rid of them. Stack number two was unaltered and all of the program's dirty work was in plain view. No telling who would want to know about them, or worse, keep them hidden.

He had called Angie and had her look up the records of ownership when the warehouse had caught fire. Colonel Maxwell had been notified that the furniture from the Pentagon was a complete loss and that Secure Storage's insurance would reimburse him for the claim.

Looking at the storage contract, the approximate value of the furniture was only estimated at twenty thousand dollars. The chairs and desks had been old, but now he realized what an underestimate of value that figure had been.

Unwilling to leave Sabin's side, he faxed a copy of one of the memos to his father, then called him for a reaction and perhaps even some advice.

"Put those papers back where you found them!"

"It's too late, Father. I've already seen them."

"But maybe they don't know you've seen them. Maybe you can just pretend all that stuff burned up in the fire."

"Or maybe I can turn these documents over to someone who can do something about all the injustice printed here. Father, there's stuff here about the Black Liberation Movement and the American Indian Movement, which patterned itself after the Panthers."

Disgust sharpened Montgomery's voice. "There are things in here that chronicle the FBI's domestic terrorism against American citizens!"

"So you think by turning it over to the *proper authorities,* they're just going to leave you alone and that will be the end of it?"

"If this corruption is exposed, everyone will know about it. Not just me."

"In a situation like this, there aren't any proper

authorities. Take my advice. Buy yourself a gun, and shoot the first person that smiles at you just a little too much. And don't call me about this again."

Montgomery should have known his father would be no help. He hung up the phone. He had no one to turn to.

Day two of Sabin the Sick was a miraculous demonstration of recovery. Sabin awoke that morning almost back to normal. Montgomery celebrated her improved health by giving her a luxurious bath.

He found some bath salts in a cabinet and the hot water reacted with them to create the aroma of fresh cut flowers. She insisted on walking to the tub, but gave him the pleasure of removing her pajamas. His eyes devoured the beauty of her nakedness. "If you weren't ill, I'd . . ."

"You'd what?" she asked.

"I'd taste every inch of your skin until you screamed for me to stop."

Her eyes sparkled. "I'm feeling better, Montgomery. Really."

"Not that much better."

"But I *want* to scream," she pouted.

He smiled. "You will. Just not now."

He lifted her with ease and lowered her into the water. He had taken off his shirt so that he wouldn't get soaked while he washed Sabin until she was squeaky-clean.

He turned the dimmer switch to make it more cozy. "Would you like some music?"

"Yes. Pop in that Styx tape please."

Montgomery walked over to the small boom box on a shelf above the toilet. He found the tape on the rack and put it in. "Awful!" he said, as lead guitar licks blared out of the speakers. "I thought you might want something a little more mellow."

Sabin lay back against the bath pillow and closed her eyes. "Like the 'My baby left me, my dog died, and my rent is due' blues?"

"Oh, you got jokes!"

She smiled contentedly. "Can I just soak for a while?"

"Sure," he said, reluctant to take his eyes from her. He hadn't realized how accustomed his body had become to having hers. The days until Sabin was well enough to make love again would be long and difficult. He left the bathroom ordering the urgency in his loins to go away.

It didn't. Montgomery paced back and forth in the bedroom with a painful hard-on. He was tempted to take matters into his own hands, but had no idea when Sabin would call him back. So, to shift his thoughts from the woman he loved who was naked and wet in the other room, he focused on a plan to turn over the COINTELPRO documents and remove the threat on his life.

An eternity passed before Sabin called him back. When he walked into the bathroom, his body reacted immediately to her damp skin and the humid temperature in the air. He would never get used to her effect on him.

"How's the water?" he asked, sticking his hand in. "Whoa, that's lukewarm."

He turned on the hot water and took a clean blue washcloth from the towel rack. As the water cascaded from the spigot, he stirred it around. Soon the bath was hot once again.

After turning off the faucet, he dipped the washcloth into the tub and withdrew it, letting the water flow down Sabin's back and chest. He continued in that manner until her skin glistened with moisture. He treated her arms to the same drenching and Sabin moaned her appreciation.

Next, he lathered the cloth with lavender soap gel and with gentle circular motions, proceeded to wash Sabin's body. The foam covered her back and arms. When he moved the cloth to her chest, he paid special attention to her breasts—especially the areas hardening at the press of his fingertips sliding smoothly across them.

Eyes closed, Sabin bit her bottom lip softly as Montgomery lifted her legs one by one and washed them.

"Am I hurting you?"

"No. It just feels so good."

After he finished with her legs, he dipped the washcloth into the water between her knees. She spread herself to accommodate his strokes inside her thighs, higher and higher.

He placed the cloth against her feminine opening and rubbed the area with his thumb. Sabin purred to life and grabbed on to his arm. He brought her heat up slowly, not wanting to aggravate her condition, but knowing that she wanted release. He could have kissed her, or tugged on her breast with his lips and teeth. But he wanted this completion to break softly inside her, relax her, heal her.

With his gentle coaxing, she let go and quivered against his hand. That's when he realized how he'd needed to please her. How he'd felt powerless to do little else. How he had to live for and protect her. How his future now resided in her.

"I love you," he whispered.

She looked up, eyes moist. "Montgomery, I need to tell you something."

"Shh. Just lie back. Let me finish. You've had enough excitement for one day. If you want to thank me, we can do that when you're better."

When Montgomery finished washing Sabin, she was clean and contented. He rubbed lotion into her skin and helped her into fresh pajamas. After giving her another pain pill, he covered her with a sheet and lay next to her on the bed until she fell asleep.

You can't change the past, but you can
correct the future.
—Toda Kai

Twenty

"You what!"

"You heard me. I want out."

"I've already paid you."

"Here's your money back."

Sabin tossed a thick manila envelope on the table.
It slid, clipped Reeves on the hand, then fell into his
lap.

"There's no way for me to find someone else. I had
to move heaven and earth just to locate you."

"Well, maybe I can give you a few leads."

"But you're supposed to be the best."

"I am the best. But usually the person *knows* that
I'm their bodyguard. The arrangement we have is too
complicated. I can't be effective if I have to keep my
distance." She hated lying, but she didn't think *Mr.
Claiborne, I'm in love with your son* would go over very
well.

The incident in the alley finally convinced her. She
went overboard with that guy, all because he posed a
threat to the person she'd come to consider as her

man. Ninja training aside, sometimes the heart casts away all the reason of the mind.

Reeves wheeled himself from the other side of the table and rolled beside her. "Sabin, my son is in trouble. He won't do anything about it." He took the envelope and offered it to her.

"This is a pittance. I'll double it. Whatever you want. But please. You've got to protect Montgomery. He's in more danger than ever!"

Sabin's resolve faltered. "We would have to change our strategy. . . ." She thought out loud.

"Well, telling him that I hired a bodyguard is out of the question."

"Too late for that, Father."

Sabin and Reeves whipped around to see Montgomery standing in the kitchen doorway.

Reeves's expression went stormy. "I thought you said he was in a meeting."

"Father! I'm right here. If you have something to say, talk to me."

Reeves spun his chair around to face his son. "I'd talk to you a lot more if you'd listen sometimes."

"When you say something that makes sense or isn't crazy, I'll listen."

"It makes sense to protect yourself."

"Do you think I'm going to let someone just run up on me?"

Reeves turned to Sabin. "How many lives does my son have?"

Sabin looked down, thinking about her invisibility training, not wanting to enter the argument.

"How many?" Reeves demanded.

"Five," she said, hoping the number would help Montgomery come to his senses.

"Five! What five? I was present each time you saved

me, remember? There was the gas, the cliff, and the mugger."

Sabin swallowed hard. "When we first met, I took out the car that was following you. There was also the night someone broke into your house. It was late. I didn't want to wake you."

Montgomery threw his hands up. "I don't know what's worse—having a woman fight my battles or a father who treats his adult son like an infant."

Now it was Reeves's turn to lower his head.

"No, that's wrong," he said, looking at Sabin. The anger and disappointment in his eyes sliced through her like one of her own swords.

"You perpetrated a vile and deceitful lie, Sabin. You're a fraud and a hack. What you did is repugnant . . . obscene." He turned to Reeves then. "What my father's done . . . is far worse."

The elder Claiborne never lifted his head. He just slowly wheeled himself out of the room.

Then Montgomery's anger exploded like C4. "So, did he pay you for the bed favors, too? Heh, of course he did. Probably thinks I'm not man enough to get a woman."

"Montgomery!"

"No, don't even *speak* my name." His voice broke with anger. "Bodyguard. Humph. What I really needed was someone to protect me from you." He backed away from her. "It always comes down to this, doesn't it? Well, I'll say it loud and clear. That way you can't miss it. Get out of this house, Sabin. Get out now. As a matter of fact, consider your job fait accompli. Feel free to move anytime soon. I'll take care of myself from here on out. And if you're worried about the money, I'll pay you whatever it takes for you to leave me the hell alone."

Sabin's fight left her quietly. She was tired. Tired of

pretending. Tired of trying to keep her feelings tucked in. And tired of taking chances, opening up, being vulnerable, risking her life. She was just plain tired. And to make matters worse, her body ached like someone had just run over her with a tractor.

She left without a word. Before walking out the door, she laid the envelope of money on an end table.

Her ride home was a blur. A jaunt that should have taken less than thirty minutes, took three hours. The Maryland scenery flanked her on both sides. From time to time, she was able to make out dry brown grass, trees thickly huddled like a crowd against the interstate. Anger and sorrow twisted into one thick knot in her chest. Before her tears could fall, they dried on her face. She vaguely registered semis, road construction, and the smell of exhaust. She narrowly acknowledged passing all the other cars, her hair flying behind her, the sobs vibrating in her chest.

When the orange and deep red colors of sunset claimed the horizon, she turned on the CD player. The soul-stirring power of Steve Perry's massive voice urged her on. He sang "Separate Ways" as if he'd been living her life. *God, it hurts. Sing, Steve.* She turned up the music and twisted the throttle.

She wasn't sure what was worse, having grown up without a family, or thinking she'd found one and having it taken from her. Sabin winced as if she'd been struck in the stomach. "He said he'd never hurt me again, and I believed him," she said into the wind. Montgomery had become her connection to the world and the love that was possible in it. Now she felt hurtled away like junk. Claimed by empty anguish, her soul curled into a tight ball as she realized no one would ever want her. The pain made her gasp and tremble with grief.

Her tears blurred her vision, and the uneven road

she traveled reminded her of the broken path her life
had taken. She drove on into the night—away from
Montgomery, away from a tragic childhood, away from
parents she would never know, away from all her mistakes—until her legs ached and sorrow drenched her
face with tears.

Since she'd returned all the money Reeves had
given her, Sabin scheduled several neighborhood
workshops. She offered them free of charge and gave
those who attended a brief overview of how to increase
safety in the neighborhood. Out of those free workshops, she generated six leads. Four of them paid off,
earning Sabin enough money to cushion her moving
expenses.

In the days after the incident with Montgomery, she
busied herself by consulting with new clients, packing,
taking her pain relievers, and keeping a peripheral eye
on the man she loved.

He seemed hell-bent on finding out who was after
him. And even through his investigation, he managed
to find time to devote to young children and in his
own way to safeguard the neighborhood. She admired
his tenacity. She envied the miracles he was able to
achieve in other people's lives. Sabin watched his dedication, and despite their rift, it drew her closer to him.

He lived under her skin now. He'd gotten in.

Before she realized what she was doing, she had
packed nearly all her belongings except her police
scanner, her black ninja suit, and her weapons. She
couldn't bear the thought that Montgomery might be
in trouble and she not be able to protect him from
harm.

Although she'd officially quit, her training and her

heart wouldn't let her leave knowing Montgomery was in danger.

She wondered if he would be able to forgive the way she'd deceived him. If he would ever realize that her love was true. That her body never lied or betrayed him. The more she thought about it, the more her body ached. She was taking two, sometimes three, pills to relieve her pinched nerve. She needed so many things now. She needed a sense of normalcy. She needed Montgomery. And judging from the agony galloping up her spinal column, she needed surgery.

Wincing, she thought maybe there was something to singing the blues after all.

Events in the last three weeks hurtled past Montgomery as if he'd been skydiving. Answering calls from Angie and her boyfriend, Victor. Organizing the quarterly gun buy-back program. Following up on leads in his investigation. Despite all the activities he packed into his life, he thought about Sabin. Why hadn't she moved yet? he wondered. He kept waiting for a FOR SALE sign to go up in the front yard. It never did.

But sometimes, between phone calls to government offices, reviews of his notes, visits to the Mad Dads office, and his sister's futile attempts to reconcile him with his father, the love he still felt for Sabin emerged, as a recurring dream from all the rubble in his heart. It gripped him like a cold vise, relentless and determined to crush his life. "Damn, Sabin. Why'd you have to lie?"

He dialed the number without thinking. The feelings raging inside him threatened to tear him apart. He couldn't take it. When he heard the woman's voice on the other line, he started to believe the hurt in his heart might actually heal.

"Arroya," he said tentatively. "Can you come over? I need you."

Montgomery paced his living room waiting for his friend to arrive. He had to get some of this anguish off his chest or he would suffocate, drown in the regret that the broken promise of Sabin's love left behind.

He pulled on a pair of faded blue jeans and went, bare chest and bare feet, out of his house and on to his front porch. He continued walking back and forth, but at least outside he felt less like a caged animal and more like the frustrated man that he was. Despite himself, he glanced at Sabin's house. A fleeting thought urged him to go over and talk to her. He needed to hear a plausible explanation for her deception. Maybe she could justify it, and his pain would be gone. But what reason could there be? Working for his father meant that she was working against him. And what could be more demeaning than having a father that thought his son needed some woman to protect him? *Who knows what else my father paid for?*

"M?"

Montgomery jerked around. How long had he been staring at Sabin's house?

Arroya stood next to him, a blur of scarlet in a fire engine red dress. Familiar cinnamon-brown eyes appraised him swiftly. Her troubled expression said she understood he was hurting.

They embraced tightly. Chez Noir, he thought, almost smiling. After a few moments, he led her inside.

Kai,
I've lost him. I've lost everything.
S.

* * *

If Sabin needed a final straw, she'd just seen it. At first she was hopeful. Montgomery stared in her direction as if he could see her inside the house. Then she saw them embrace, and her heart turned over and stopped.

In the past, she would simply lash out at someone or something. This time she'd been on the receiving end of enough lashings for at least twelve people. Still, a force drove her to the closet where she grabbed a *ninja ken* knife from where it hung against the door with six others of various sizes and lengths. Assuming a defense stance she sliced the air. Forty-five degrees. Sixty. Straight down. Back and up. Straight across. As if it was her pain she fought away. Her anguish she severed in two. She thrust forward ignoring the sweat falling down the sides of her face, briefly wondering if it was tears. Instead of focusing on her imaginary attacker, she switched her thoughts. She would call Reeves Claiborne and tell him to put the house on the market, and then she would decide on her destination. Maybe she didn't have enough money to leave the country, but she could certainly leave Maryland.

As she advanced and retreated, wielding the knife with the finesse of a fencer, she had another thought: Her body reminded her that wherever she settled, she would require medical attention right away. *As a matter of fact,* she thought slumping onto the floor, *I might need it now.* She crawled fitfully to the kitchen and took her prescription bottle from the table. Sabin swallowed the last pill dry because the pain was too great for her to get a glass of water. Then she laid her head against the cool linoleum and prayed for the medicine's swift effect.

* * *

"Whose side are you on?"

Arroya twisted the silver ring on her middle finger. She always did that when she was real serious, he thought.

"He wouldn't have hired someone if he didn't love you. He just doesn't know how to show his love properly. For some people, affection comes hard."

"Arroya, do you love me?"

"Yes."

"Then say it."

"I love you, Montgomery."

"See how easy that was! The only reason he hired that woman is because he wanted to humiliate me. To step on me again." Montgomery's pacing quickened. "I swear. The man thinks I'm a jellyfish just because I don't believe that war is the answer to every dispute. He's never forgiven me for not joining the service. But who would want to follow in *his* footsteps? From the stories he's told, they're not footsteps anyway. They're blood tracks."

"Lots of fathers want their sons to take the same path they took."

"And lots of fathers want their sons to take the path they create for themselves."

"Why can't you just ignore your father?"

Montgomery slumped onto the couch. "Because it hurts too bad."

Again, he found himself staring in the direction of Sabin's house. The words *conspirator* and *untrue* mingled with the words *lover* and *friend* until they produced one gray smear in his mind.

"You've never looked at me like that and she's not even in the room."

"She betrayed me, Roya."

"I told you I didn't like her. But, no, you wouldn't take my word for it."

Montgomery rolled his eyes and felt his mood changing somewhere deep beneath the somber.

"Maybe next time you'll believe me."

"There won't be a next time. I've learned my lesson."

"Okay, then. Now all we have to do is work on Angela. I'm telling you, M. That woman *and* her boyfriend have got issues."

Montgomery stared out the windows of Trey's small apartment, wrestling with feelings of defeat. He took up the whole room in a tiny peach-colored chair, legs stretched out in front of him, back slumped down.

"Man, how long are you going to mope?"

As long as it takes, he thought. What kind of question was that anyway? His quasirelationship with his father was ruined. The woman he loved had betrayed him. Someone was trying to kill him, and despite all his best efforts, he didn't know who. If anyone deserved to mope, it was him.

"Mr. C., I've never seen you bent out."

"That was before my life went to hell."

"The only reason your life has gone to hell is because you let it. Every curse can be removed."

"Humph. Where'd you get that kind of logic?"

Trey smiled. "Where else? From you."

"Yeah, well," Montgomery said, crossing his arms.

"So . . . is it Sarah or Sabin?"

Montgomery snapped his head around to where Trey was sitting on the carpet. "What?"

"I figure, only a woman can get you down in the dumps *that* far."

Montgomery fingered the edge of his notebook. "Trey, I came over here to stop thinking about my problems, and you're not helping."

"Uh-huh. That's what I thought. It's Sabin."

"It's not Sabin!"

"Well, if it was Sarah, you'd be in some colonel's office and not here with Dr. Love."

Montgomery's laughter surprised him. Sometimes he forgot just how far Trey had come. From a brainiac kid to an entrepreneur. It was hard for him to fathom sometimes, little Trey, all grown up, and calling himself Dr. Love. Why, the thought . . . "What did you say?"

"Aw, you know I got it goin' right on with the ladies."

"I meant the other thing, about the colonel."

"Well, since that virus was specially engineered, I thought you'd go talk to someone about it."

"Like who?"

"Well, the government, of course. They're the only ones capable of pulling off something like what Sarah had."

Montgomery sat up. "I thought maybe it was just some computer hack."

"You probably thought right. The best hacks in the world work for the U.S. government. Somebody sent you a message you weren't supposed to receive, so they sent a tracer program to retrieve it."

"Eradicate it, is more like it."

"You got that right."

"Damn," Montgomery said, stroking his chin. He closed his eyes while his mind made connection after connection. Like a ball in a pinball machine, his thoughts moved in play bouncing from one idea to the next, whizzing through others, banking off more. Levers and gears whirred inside his head. He was almost dizzy with the commotion. And then he had it.

He smiled. It wasn't anything like what you see in the movies, when detectives and investigators get the

great aha! In film and video there was music, dramatic
and deep with promise, then the moment of eureka
when the sleuth thrusts his finger into the air signaling
the end to the mystery.

No, it had taken Montgomery a moment to collect
all the signs, which were now as obvious to him as
neon lights in darkness.

He scribbled a few lines in his notebook. "Trey,
thanks," he said, standing. "Thanks for everything."

"Now that sounds like the Mr. C. I know," the
young man said as Montgomery exited quickly and
headed for his car. He drove to the Westpine part of
the city knowing exactly what he needed to do.

There's always a back door.
—Montgomery Claiborne

Twenty-one

It's here! he thought, tearing through his notes. He turned page after page, running his finger down the center of his handwriting, skimming the words furiously.

"Where are you?"

Government documents, flying planks, computer carnivores, chemical spills, fires, avalanches. It's a wonder he'd lived to tell it at all. And now he was more determined to find out than ever.

Maybe I should have taken better notes, he thought. There were many gaps and spaces in the book—places where the events didn't connect.

If only I hadn't been so busy with work, he mused. It seemed every time he thought he might have been getting somewhere with the investigation, he was interrupted. Mostly by Angie. There was always something she wanted or needed. And for some reason, she had gotten it into her head that she had to conduct some inspections. She'd driven Ted and Randy crazy with her requests. Like Arroya, they didn't like her, either, so they had refused until they got approval from Montgomery. And Montgomery had been too busy trying to keep his ass out of a sling to respond.

Suddenly, he felt a sick twist of his stomach, and words he'd heard on one of the CD's he bought came back like a ghost. *"Emotions will taint your judgment and possibly prevent you from seeing the most obvious piece of evidence simply because feelings often distort what we see."*

It can't be, he thought. Then Arroya's admonishment came back into his consciousness loud and clear. *"That woman and her boyfriend have got issues."*

"It's Angie," he said as a cold shudder reverberated down his spine.

He got up from his desk and paced. No plausible explanation came to mind. Just questions. Why did she really want him dead? Was someone paying her to do it? Did she think she could really get away with it?

When the doorbell sounded, Montgomery's teeth clamped down. His mind blurred with confusion. He opened the door and couldn't believe his eyes. As if he'd conjured her, Angela Miller stood on his porch, eyes wide.

"Thank God you're here, Montgomery! Come on!" she shouted.

"What's wrong?" he asked, caution keeping his distance.

She tugged on his arm. "Building B. It's on fire!"

This is the final showdown, he mused, as they drove in a mad dash to the warehouse. *Now I'll find out, once and for all, what's going on.* He settled back, eyeing Angie suspiciously.

A mile before they got to the warehouse, he searched the sky. If the fire was bad, he would see gray billows of smoke at any moment. So far, bright blue and white were the only colors in the sky.

He prayed that Ted got out in time. Apprehension drove his heart to an erratic pace. If Angie was responsible, he would make her pay for everything she had done. If he had to spend his life's savings on the best lawyer possible, he would see her brought to justice. As they came around the block, he wondered how much Johnnie Cochran's attorney fees were.

As Angie slowed her car, his jaw dropped. They parked and and got out. Secure Storage's remaining facility looked the way it always did. There was no sign of fire.

There was no thin acrid smell of smoke or pungent odor of wood and plastic burning. He strode past the front of the building then marched to the side, to the back, then came around to the front.

"Clyde!" he called to the man lying by the dock. No response. *There goes hoping for answers from the night watchman,* he thought. *Must have passed out.*

"What's going on, Angie?" he asked, unlocking the door to the facility. Something felt wrong, out of place. His mind whirled a million thoughts per minute. Then it hit him. He spun around just in time to see the blur of Victor Willis's arm crash down against the base of his skull. Then everything went black.

Upon hearing the heated discussion outside of Montgomery's house, Sabin donned her ninja suit for what she knew was the last time. After this, if she lived, she would ship all of her belongings to Toda Kai's dojo and never consider the way of the warrior again. She chose her weapons: *fukiya,* a blowgun; *shuko* and *ashiko,* spiked hand and foot bands; *ken,* a short sword; *shuriken,* throwing blades.

Pain danced like a lick of fire inside her. She tried to use her training to push it away from her mind. Too much reliance on medication made that task impossible. Instead she gave in, only to remember as she picked up the empty bottle that she had already taken the last of her pain pills. She stumbled to her motorcycle praying she could get to the warehouse in time, and once there, could fulfill her role as Montgomery's protector one more time.

She parked several blocks away and used the shadows to obscure her approach. Once she reached the warehouse, she used her hand and foot bands to scale the building to the second floor. In her weakened condition, she was careful to set the spikes firmly into the concrete before leveraging them for weight.

Pain streaked like white lightning up her legs and into her brain. She wanted to cry out, needed to cry out. But intuition was the shadow warrior's first ally. And her intuition told her Montgomery was in danger.

At the first window of the upper floor, she eased the blade out of its concealed pocket, pried the window open, and slipped in.

She replaced the blade and crept silently forward. She'd entered the manager's living area. Just as she'd suspected, it was empty. *You can't kill Montgomery with witnesses,* she thought. Smoothly, she took out the blowgun from another pocket and crept toward the stairway inside. When Sabin came to the balcony, her eyes trained on Montgomery bound on the floor and the man standing next to him. It wasn't adrenaline that beat like hard thunder in her chest, but dread that Montgomery's life had depended on her and she had come too late to save him. Quickly, she lifted the weapon to her lips. The pain raging in her body made her hands shake. She concentrated to make her aim sure and expelling the air from her lungs, sent the dart flying.

Her hand wobbled and the dart missed the man's neck by inches.

"Someone's here," he said, looking around. He and Angela pulled guns. He pointed his at Montgomery. Hers was drawn and ready. "Find whoever it is."

Angela did as she was told, heading straight for the stairs. Sabin crouched against the wall behind a small storage bin and waited. As she heard Angela's footsteps approaching, the individual Sabin Strong faded away and was replaced by a being whose spirit and essence became one with the night.

Angela walked directly past the spot where Sabin lay in wait. Sabin leaped behind her, sweeping her leg across her opponent's. Angela toppled to the floor. The gun hit the ground and slid under a small chair. The scrawny woman struggled to get up and Sabin spread her arms wide. The pose shifted her weight and her pain evenly across her body.

Angela lunged. Sabin pivoted in response and instead of tackling her, Angela flew headfirst into the wall. Sabin bent her knees and stretched one knife hand out in front of her, but nothing happened. Angela had knocked herself out cold.

"Baby, what's going on?"

Sabin picked up the gun and made her way to the other side of the balcony.

"Angie!"

Using her bands once again, she crept down the side of the wall adjacent from the man. She needed to hurry, before the lunatic realized his girlfriend was out of commission, but her legs quaked with agony. She wouldn't be able to stand the pain much longer. If she didn't get to Montgomery soon, she would pass out from the pain.

She could see them. If she could just climb down a little bit farther . . .

"Is that you, Sabin? If you want your lover man to die right now, then stay where you are. But I suggest you come out where I can see you!" The man held the gun up to Montgomery's temple. "Now!"

By movements too subtle to register, Sabin peeled herself away from the shadows of the warehouse and finished climbing down the wall. Victor's eyes grew wide. She realized it must look as if she was materializing out of thin air. *Maybe that will shake him up a bit,* she thought.

"I'm not going to allow you to hurt him," she said, pointing the gun at him.

He pulled back the slide, loading a round into the chamber. "I've been watching you, Ms. Strong. I had you checked out, since you always seem to be in the wrong place at the wrong time. I don't care what kind of training you've had. This time, you don't have a choice."

And that's when her body gave up a tremendous fight and let the pain win. She slumped to the floor like a marionette whose strings had just been cut. She tried to pick up the gun, but her arm ignored her command. Sabin closed her eyes in defeat.

When she woke up, she was on the floor tied behind Montgomery.

"So, Monty." Victor spoke in his usual gravelly tones. "I guess this is the end after all."

"I'm telling you for the last time, my name is not Monty!" he shouted, straining against the restraints.

Sabin, tied directly behind him, struggled, as well. "Who is this clown, Montgomery?"

"Angie's boyfriend. He's the one that's been after

me. But I still don't know why." He looked up at the skeletal woman who had come to, staggering toward them rubbing her head. "And I don't understand why you would betray me this way, Angela. I thought we were partners." Then some of the anger disappeared from his eyes. "I thought we were friends."

"I love Victor. I would do anything for him, including help protect his family. We . . ." She lowered her head then. "We just needed you out of the way."

"I don't understand," Montgomery said, losing patience.

"And you never will," Victor broadcast. And then he snatched Angela and crushed her into him, a dangerous smile crawling across his face. "Some people will do anything for love."

Montgomery shifted away from Sabin thinking that *others will do anything for money.* Montgomery's eyes narrowed sharply. "Isn't this the part where you tell us all about why you've done this?"

Victor laughed. "You've been watching too many suspense movies." Then his expression grew warm. "But if you insist." Victor walked over to where a metal letter opener lay on a desk. He looked at it absently and twirled it between his fingers.

"Do you know what it's like to have a father who's a traitor?"

Montgomery thought about that. His father was a tyrant and an ogre, but if there was one thing he was not, it was a traitor.

"My father was a traitor to his own people." Victor rubbed the tip of the letter opener back and forth into the wood of the desk. "Victor Willis, Sr. worked for the FBI. Although you won't find his name on any personnel records. No, sir. My dad was an under-the-table kind of agent. He did mole work for the real agents and in turn they would pay him for all the dirt he could dig up."

Shavings from the desk curled up and fell to the floor where the metal moved back and forth. Victor, lost in memory, didn't notice.

"He actually worked for J. Edgar Hoover. He was one of the guys they paid to get inside information on the Black Panthers or any other group the government deemed subversive. The thing is, my pops wasn't no ordinary snitch." Victor laughed, but his expression remained stoic. "No. My pops . . . was the best.

"He got so good, I guess that for a moment, those miscreants forgot he was black and brought him into the offices where they worked. They got so comfortable around him that they started discussing all their plans openly. Well, my father was a traitor, but he wasn't stupid. It didn't take him long to realize that when they decided that they were finished with him, or whenever another person came along who was better at subversion than he was, there was going to be no pat on the back and a 'See you later.' There was only one way for him to break his service, and that was if he was dead."

The groove in the desk grew more ragged with each twist of opener, exposing raw wood and sharp splinters. "So ol' Victor started collecting *insurance* papers. Whenever he could, he would steal their memos, files, reports—anything he could get his hands on. He figured that if anyone ever threatened him or his family, that information would come in handy."

Victor slammed the tip of the letter opener into the desk. It stuck in the old wood like a missile gone haywire. "Do you know it's been thirty years and the government is *still* looking for those papers. My pops figured, what better place to hide them but right under their noses. It was cool like that for thirty years.

Right there on government property. But then September 11 changed all that.

"I really didn't want to kill you, Mr. Claiborne. I just wanted you out of the way until Angie and I could go through all of the storage units and collect all the documents. If only you hadn't recovered so quickly from the gas, we could have gone through them all.

"But now I'm just pissed, because despite everything," he hissed, grabbing Angela by the neck, "I still don't have the papers!

"So, if you've got them stashed around here somewhere, they're history, just like you and your guard dog." He turned to Sabin.

Montgomery was comforted only slightly by the fact that Victor would not get the documents. They were hidden at his father's house. Even if he died, maybe they would eventually be returned to the proper authorities.

"Come on, Anj. We've wasted enough time." They walked to the exit arm in arm. Victor manipulated the device attached to the door, sliding his fingers over the taped wire on the door frame. "As soon as I close this door, the bomb will arm. If for some reason you two free yourselves, don't even think about opening this door."

A flicker of alarm coursed through Sabin. "Montgomery, I'm sorry."

Victor paused before exiting and pulled a driver's license out of his pocket.

"Just in case you have the documents hidden somewhere else, I'm going to pay your sister, Cherlyn, a visit. I sure hope she's recovered from that *awful attack*." The echo of Victor's maniacal laughter bounced off of the walls.

"I'll kill you, you sick . . . !" The door closed with

a whoosh and Montgomery and Sabin were left alone as the seconds ticked away on the detonator.

"I guess your little rescue attempt didn't work this time," he quipped, throwing the words over his shoulder.

"Little! It's not like I knocked on the door and was politely asked to come in!"

"Yeah, well what happened?" Montgomery stared at the bomb. "Now when it really matters, you come up short."

"I could've said screw you to this whole thing. If I had, I'd be halfway to Ghana."

"What? Your motorcycle can't take you far enough away this time? You gotta fly across the globe now?"

"Go to hell, Montgomery."

"Thanks to you, been there. Done that."

"Forget you."

"It looks like you couldn't."

"What!"

"Never mind. Shut up."

"I know you're not talking to me!"

"Will you be quiet so I can think! That maniac is headed to my father's house. I'm not going to let him harm my family or get his hands on those documents."

It was then that Sabin realized she could no longer feel her legs. "I don't think there's a happy ending to this one, Montgomery."

"In my book, there's always a back door. Now, Ms. Shadow Warrior, do you have a knife or some of those throwing stars?"

"Yes."

"Which?"

"Both. The stars are in my hair. My knife is in a concealed pocket in my jacket sleeve."

"Do you think you can shake loose a star?"

"Not without passing out."

"There's got to be some ninja thing you could do with your head to dislodge one."

Sabin quieted with a sigh, then turned her neck and tilted her head. After shaking her head slightly she gave one smooth twist, and a six-pointed star fell to the ground and rolled beneath a forklift.

Montgomery closed his eyes. The place where Victor brought down his gun throbbed angrily against his neck.

"Sorry," she said.

"Can you try again?"

"Ah!" Sabin screamed as a bolt of pain shot up her left side.

"Are you all right?"

"Hell, no! I'm trapped in a warehouse that's about to explode with a man I can't stand."

Tied back to back and left on the cold concrete floor, Montgomery and Sabin struggled fitfully against the ropes. Sabin gave up after only a few moments—the pain in her limbs being too great. Montgomery on the other hand, continued to twist and thrash angrily against the binding.

"Damn it!" he bellowed in exasperation.

"I'm sorry," Sabin said again.

Still tugging and yanking, Montgomery spoke softly. "Victor's insanity is not your fault."

"I mean about not being able to stop them," she admitted. Of all the things she had ever wanted—a family, a home, someone to love her, peace of mind, parents to love—she never wanted anything as badly as she wanted to get Montgomery safely away from this warehouse. Since she couldn't do that, she could at least tell him how she felt, how her life had come to a standstill without him, and how no matter what he thought and believed, she loved him almost from the moment their lives collided and that she had fallen truly and completely, something she'd promised herself she'd never ever do.

"Montgomery . . ."

The sound of her voice stilled him. He didn't like it. It sounded apologetic and defeated.

"Don't, Sabin."

"But . . ."

"No! I don't want to hear it."

He couldn't bear to listen to anything that might be lies. He needed to hear that his loving her had not been in vain. He needed her to say that she had been true and honest when she had given herself to him. He needed to know that her affection hadn't been bought and paid for. Anything else would crush him. And he would need all his strength to get them out before the bomb went off.

Careening his head toward her arm, Montgomery pushed and insisted until her black jacket covered his head. The movement touched a place inside him where the scent of her had imprinted on his being like DNA.

"Guide me," he said, the heavy cotton cloth muffling his words.

"On the inside of my forearm. A fold of fabric covers the pocket. You won't be able to see it. You'll have to feel it with your face."

As he shifted for more leverage, he became acutely conscious of his body on top of hers. "I'm sorry if I'm heavy."

"It's okay," she said, but he could hear the pain in her voice.

Wasn't it just moments ago when they had been together in his bed laughing and talking all night? Fighting sleep like small children and holding each other like new lovers?

He didn't have time to reminisce about the wonder of her natural fragrance, the silky softness of her flesh, or the sweet taste of her skin.

God, he was drowning.

He continued pressing into her skin and the flesh of her breast. She was damp from perspiration in a sleeveless T-shirt. He nuzzled against her sweat, moving closer into the dark beneath her jacket.

His neck and shoulders rose in time with her breathing, which he could feel hot against the back of his head. With his mind on his task, he burrowed his face into the space between her side and her arm.

"Keep going," she urged, staring at the bomb on the door. It reminded her of a mechanical hive of thin spiders.

She shivered.

When a light above the mass of wires changed from red to green, she jolted with surprise and something else: fear.

"This is not the time to be ticklish" came Montgomery's garbled reaction.

She ignored his remark. "Montgomery, hurry."

"What happened?"

"I'm not sure. I flunked my Kayaku-Jutsu test, but I think that thing just entered some kind of final sequence."

"Damn!" he mumbled.

Rooting urgently, Montgomery paid acute attention to every aspect of his face. Feeling with his chin, cheeks, and lips until he finally sensed the stiff outline of the knife.

"Found it!"

"You'll have to pull the flap out with your teeth. And be careful. It's sharper than any razor you've ever shaved with."

Montgomery tugged until the flap came free. He

couldn't tell which end he'd found and there wasn't enough light to see. *Only one way to find out.*

He winced with great pain as he discovered he'd found the blade end. His mouth filled quickly with blood from the gash on his tongue.

Wrapping his teeth around the handle he ever so slowly pulled it from its hidden pocket. Montgomery's retreat was slothlike as he tried painstaking not to cut Sabin with her own weapon.

When he finally emerged with the knife, Sabin gasped. He'd felt the blood trickling and tried to grip the knife tighter with his mouth to keep it from dripping. By her reaction, he was unsuccessful.

"Oh, God, Montgomery."

Seeing the concern in her eyes shocked him. Since when did she care about his welfare without being paid?

No time to ponder that now, he thought, turning to the thick rope binding them.

Sinking his teeth into the grooves on the knife handle, he held the blade against the rope, then moving his head up and down, began to saw though. Strand by strand he cut until the last fiber sprang apart and freed them.

"Got it!" he exclaimed through clenched teeth. Seconds later he freed himself from the ropes. Then the binding went slack around Sabin's arms and Montgomery lifted the ropes from her chest.

She knew she would be sore from where the bindings cut across her arms and burned her as if she'd been dragged across a carpet. *If* she survived, she would need more patching up than the scarecrow in *The Wizard of Oz* after the flying monkeys got to him.

"You're bleeding!"

"We'll worry about that later . . . if there's a later. Can you stand?"

"No," she answered honestly.

He scooped her into his arms and walked briskly toward the back of the warehouse. He yanked the door. It didn't move. "Welded."

Both Montgomery and Sabin uttered sighs of disbelief.

Montgomery turned and continued down the hallway.

"Where are you going?" Sabin asked, the reality of their demise setting in.

"To the *back door.*"

Sabin had checked out the warehouse on several occasions. She knew there was no back door.

"I'm going to set you down for a moment," he said, and propped her up against the wall.

He pulled away shelving, planks, and other miscellaneous building material from the wall. Sabin saw the outline of a door materialize before them. It was steel and looked older than either one of them.

Montgomery thrust the knife into the lock and twisted the blade.

Sabin's lock-picking training cried out. "Montgomery, that's not the way to—"

A click of the tumblers, a turn of the knob, and he opened the door, picked her up, and ran.

"What is this?" Sabin asked, as Montgomery propelled them down through a dark corridor. She felt the brush of cobwebs. A damp odor engulfed them. Sabin couldn't see or move her own body.

"It's the tunnel that connects the warehouses. We'll come out in Building A. It's still a mess from the fire, but I can maneuver through it."

Sabin hung on as best she could. Montgomery jogged toward a door identical to the one they'd just come though. As before, he used her knife to jimmy the lock then slid the knife into his pants pocket.

The charred remains of the other facility rose like a burned city. Montgomery carefully brought them up out of the tunnel and through the debris. From the corner of his eye, he could see a body in a tattered coat that hung open, gray sweater, and pants. *Clyde*, he thought. This time he didn't need paramedics to tell him a friend was gone.

"Where's your motorcycle?" he asked, anger bottoming out his voice.

"Around the corner, but—"

"Show me," he insisted, and Sabin pointed in the direction of East and Third street.

"You don't know how to drive a motorcycle yet!"

She moaned as he placed her on the back of the vehicle.

Not long ago, she had spent several afternoons trying to teach him how to control her bike.

"I'll learn," he said, jumping on. Despite his feelings, he was determined to get Sabin as far away from this horror as possible.

The explosion came just as he'd started the engine. To Sabin it seemed is if Montgomery's turn of the key caused the loud and thunderous calamity that occurred just s block away. He barely flinched, simply turned the throttle, and placed his feet on the boot rests as the cycle roared forward.

Sabin held him tightly around the waist. Seconds later they were hurtling through the traffic like two passengers tottering atop a heat-seeking rocket.

Sabin felt the steady whir of air whooshing past her. Things had gotten way out of control, and Montgomery was driving much too fast.

"Slow down!" she bellowed.

"What?" he responded, merging on to the express-way.

"I said slow down, Montgomery!"

He ignored her order and maintained a speed of what had to have been eighty miles per hour until traffic came to a slamming halt. At first, they just idled behind a black SUV. Then Montgomery's impatience took over.

"Hold on!" he shouted, gunning the engine.

He maneuvered through the traffic jam until they were beyond the slow spot and back on the semi-open road. Sabin sensed a little of her strength returning and wrapped her arms around his waist just a bit tighter. She settled in for the remainder of the quick ride she knew would take them both right into the center of danger.

He stopped the motorcycle a block away from his father's house. "Stay here," he said, jumping off the bike.

He paused for a moment. Sabin felt the weight of his gaze as their eyes locked. Then impulsively, he kissed her. His lips were hot and quick upon hers. She yielded instantly. A second later, he charged away.

"Montgomery, call the police!" she shouted after him.

"No time!" he answered back and then disappeared around the corner.

Give him time; he's just stubborn.

—Mei Claiborne

Twenty-two

As a teenager, Montgomery sneaked into his father's house when coming home after curfew, but he never imagined himself doing it as adult. *Please,* he thought, *let the hinge on the basement window still be broken.* He pushed hard where the latch held the window in place and heard a snap.

"Thank you," he said under his breath and lifted the window.

Sabin forced her legs to obey. The forest fire of pain burning inside her thighs and calves would not deter her. Drawing her agony-worn body up the sidewalk, she knocked on the door of the first house she saw, to call for help.

He'd gained some weight since the last time he came in this way. He twisted his body, scraping off old white paint as he slid through the window space. When a shot of pain exploded at the base of his skull, he bit his lip to keep from crying out. The place where the gun had come down throbbed incessantly. Montgomery steeled himself against the anguish.

He landed feetfirst in the laundry area. The smell of detergent tickled his nose. Guided by memory and the faint light coming in through the open window, Montgomery headed past the washer and dryer for the stairs.

Walking softly up the steps, he listened for voices. When he reached the top, he heard Victor's gritty rasp cutting through the silence. They were in the living room. His voice sounded menacing even in the darkness of the basement. Think! he ordered himself, looking around for a weapon. All he knew was that the element of surprise was on his side and gave him an advantage. If he could get behind Victor and grab him, maybe even knock him unconscious, he could call the police and his family would be safe.

Montgomery said a silent prayer and twisted the basement doorknob. It was locked.

Slumping against the wall, he cursed the thoughts charging through him mind. This must be how Sabin feels, he reasoned, and took out the small blade stained with his blood.

He worked the sharp point into the lock and wiggled it soundlessly. The pin caught and Montgomery crept from the basement and into the kitchen, his mind feverishly concocting a plan.

He walked softly, letting the voices in the dining room draw him. When he got to the kitchen entryway, his blood turned to ice. He could see Angela tying his father's wrists while his sister and Tilde sat on the couch staring at a gun in Victor's hand.

Forsaking a plan, Montgomery burst from the kitchen. Dark rage set his blood to boil. He threw himself at Victor. His flying tackle caught the man unaware. The force from his collision knocked them both to the ground. The impact dislodged the gun and knife from their hands. Montgomery's rage exploded into left and right fists across Victor's face.

Somewhere in the background, he could hear Angie's shrill shrieks of "Victor! Victor!" but all outside noises soon clouded over with fury that grayed out everything except his maddening need to hurt the man beneath him.

He continued his merciless pummeling. Victor's right hand caught him on the chin. White sparks of pain whizzed through his brain.

Montgomery tumbled backward and tried to steady himself. Another right came at him. This time he ducked, but not far enough. Victor's knuckles struck the side of his temple, staggering him. Then a boot, like a concrete block, rammed into his stomach. He flew back, losing his balance and his wind. Then Victor was upon him—a wild rampage in his eyes. Montgomery gasped for air and lifted his arms to cover his face. Victor's fists sent his head whipping from one side to the other. He heard a crack. Suddenly, the pain in his stomach was nothing compared to the pain in his jaw.

Montgomery twisted hard to the left, rolling into Victor's leg. The man lost his balance and fell to the floor. Montgomery pulled at him. Victor scrambled toward where the revolver was. Despite Montgomery's attempt to hold him back, Victor wriggled until he was inches away from the gun handle. Then Cherlyn leaped from the couch, grabbed the gun, and threw it out the living room window. Tilde jumped into action by grabbing the knife.

Angela, who had been watching the fight with panic-stricken awe, screamed, "You'll pay for that!" and lunged at Cherlyn. Remembering Sabin's self-defense lessons, Cherlyn jumped out of her path. Angela crashed into the dining room table. Shaking off the impact, the woman lurched forward wielding a brass candleholder above her head. She let out a crazed wail and swung the holder wildly. Cherlyn dropped down and kicked Angie in the knee.

Angie doubled over and cried out in pain. Just then Cherlyn clenched her palms and swung them together as one mighty weapon against the side of Angie's face. Angie tumbled backward, dropping the candleholder and then slumped to her knees.

"Had enough?" Cherlyn asked, heart beating a loud staccato in her chest, adrenaline transforming fear into bravado.

Angie looked up slowly. The maniacal grin on her face jolted Cherlyn as if she'd been touched on the back of her neck by an icy hand. *This woman is crazy*, she thought, preparing for her attack. She remembered the message of Sabin's last lessons to her. *"If all else fails, put them to sleep."* And with that, Cherlyn concentrated all of her energy into one jarring right hook and knocked Angela out cold.

Cherlyn rubbed her knuckles and glanced at Montgomery, who was holding his own against Victor. Then she rushed to her father's side, removed the duct tape from his mouth, and proceeded with Tilde's help to untie him.

The other battle royal spilled out of the dining room, turning the living room into a battleground. Montgomery and Victor traded blows like two gladiators in Rome's Coliseum. They crashed into furniture and wedged into corners. Angry grunts mingled with smacks against flesh.

The longer he fought, the angrier Montgomery became. Fury, built up over the months of recent trauma, erupted into a vengeance exacted through strikes, tackles, and strangleholds. Although his body fought with Victor, his mind fought with the past.

Lost lives and lost love. Someone like Victor had killed his mother and thought nothing of it. Someone like Victor had tempted half the kids in the Sankofa program and gotten them into trouble with the law. Because of Victor, his father felt compelled to hire someone to protect him—someone who had done more damage to his heart than any pain he'd ever felt. Because of Victor, his business was no more. Because of Victor, his sister had been accosted, and his close friend was dead. Because of Victor, a man who may have eventually beat his addiction was gone forever.

Montgomery faltered, weary from the constant aching of emotional anguish in his chest. He had moved way past the threshold of human tolerance for pain. *Oh, God, will my heart* ever *heal?* At his pause, Victor grabbed a brass figurine from the living room table and smashed it against Montgomery's skull.

The blow sent Montgomery sailing into the wall where he slid to the floor. Fireworks burst in his brain and his head lolled to one side as his mind went dark.

"Montgomery!" Cherlyn screamed.

"Oh, Jesus," Reeves said.

Cherlyn headed for Victor, but the statue of Saint Augustine in his raised hand stopped her.

"Stay there, or I'll crack his head open," he said, voice scratchy and paper thin.

On the floor, Montgomery wrestled with consciousness. His body felt run over and he could barely move. He struggled to pull the images in front of him into focus. His head exploded into brilliant agony when he tried to turn it, so he held still until his vision cleared. Slowly, he made out the pattern before him. The iron grating of his father's faux heating vent was inches from his outstretched hand.

Using a tactic he never thought he would on another man, Montgomery kicked Victor and lunged for the vent.

While Victor crumbled over and howled, Montgomery yanked the grate off and pulled out the .45. Despite the pain setting fire to all his nerve endings, he got up—keeping the barrel aimed at a spot on Victor's large forehead.

"Good, son," Reeves said. "Now hold him there until the police come. Cher, run across to the Shelbys' and call the police."

"Better call the morgue," Montgomery responded.

"What?" Cherlyn and her father asked in unison.

Montgomery moved closer to where Victor knelt cowering. He had already dropped the statue and held his hands up in defeat.

"I can't, in good conscious, let him live. He's responsible for too much evil."

"Oh, no, son." Reeves wheeled his chair closer.

"Montgomery . . ." Cherlyn's voice quivered.

Montgomery felt strangely calm and clearheaded. He knew that Victor Willis deserved to die as surely as he knew his own name. He placed both hands on the handle of the gun and shoved it into the shuddering man's face.

"I had to protect my own. Don't you understand?" Victor's voice garbled the words into a raspy string of sounds.

"I do now," Montgomery said, placing the gun against Victor's temple. He took a deep breath and prepared himself to dispense the justice he knew the man needed when a familiar voice nearly stopped his heart.

"Montgomery, stop."

* * *

Sabin limped into the Claiborne household, and the raging fury on Montgomery's face turned her blood to water.

"Put the gun down," she insisted.

"What?" he said, keeping his eyes on Victor. "Interesting sentiment coming from a trained assassin."

His words came out as cold as steel and cut her to the bone, but she would not be swayed. "You don't really want to kill that man."

"Man? What man?" He twisted the gun against the side of Victor's face. "This is not a man. This is a menace—a monster. This is a disease that requires eradication." The wound on Montgomery's tongue had reopened in the melee. He wiped away fresh blood on the back of his hand.

The expression on Victor's face deteriorated from acute fear into mortal horror. Reeves and Cherlyn moved closer. Sabin held up hand stopping them.

She supported herself by leaning against a chair. Her body, long past the ability of holding itself up, endured by sheer determination. She hoped the sound of her words wouldn't betray her alarm.

"Montgomery, he *is* a man—a man not worth going to jail for. And most of all, not worth you sacrificing your principles for."

Just then, Lucian Carvell, Gina Vendetti, and Stanford Morrison rushed through the front door, guns drawn. Sabin waved them back. Ignoring her, Lucian moved in.

"Montgomery, I don't know what's going on, but I can handle it from here. Lower your weapon."

"Detective Carvell, you're just in time . . . to witness the permanent and long overdue removal of some trash from this earth." His voice sounded like a missile launching from its silo.

"Well, Father. Isn't this what you always wanted? A

son who would stand up for himself—take matters into his own hands?" He tilted the gun back and forth. "I'd say matters are definitely in my hands now."

The anger in Montgomery's eyes reminded Sabin of a tropical storm—strong, tumultuous, and lethal. Then both he and Lucian cocked their guns at the same time.

All at once, images of Trey, Mad Dads Sankofa celebrations, gun buy-back programs, and bank robbery flashed through Sabin's mind. She couldn't allow this man of peace—and yes, love—to become something ugly and violent. Desperate to gain control over the situation, she stepped in the path of Lucian's revolver. "Montgomery, listen to me. You won't solve anything by shooting that gun."

"Oh, really? Wasn't it you who said sometimes God uses us to carry out his vengeance?"

Sabin felt as if she'd been kicked in the stomach. "Yes," she whispered.

"Speak up!"

"Yes! I said that." She took a deep breath. "And I was wrong."

Seeing a fraction of the wrath diminish in his eyes, she pressed on. "I told you that because I needed to believe it. I needed to be able to justify things I'd done in the past. Terrible things that I'm ashamed of."

He seemed to be listening, so she continued. "Montgomery, you showed me that there's another way. Being with you and the kids you've helped, the lives you've changed, made me believe that justice should be only served by humane means. Not more violence."

Victor's wide eyes darted from Montgomery to Sabin.

"I know your mind is fixated on retribution. But, Montgomery, nothing will right all the wrongs. No

matter what you do here today, it won't even the score.
It won't."

"All right, that's enough," Lucian said, stepping
around Sabin. "I'm giving you until the count of three
to put the gun down. One . . ."

"Son, do what the detective says," Reeves pleaded.

"Please," came Cherlyn's desperate attempt.

"Two . . ."

"Montgomery! You can't do this, and you *know* it!"
Sabin moved close enough to touch him.
"Montgomery . . . please . . . put the gun *down*."

The room fell silent and no one moved. Even with
all of the anger seething inside him, Sabin's words got
through. He realized that he could not allow himself
to become the same type of aberration that he so despised. Then, slowly, Montgomery lowered the gun.

Lucian moved swiftly, handcuffing Victor and taking
Montgomery's weapon almost in one motion. Then
he checked to make sure Cherlyn and her father were
all right, while Morrison and Vendetti were instructed
to put the cuffs on Angie.

A few short seconds later, the world shifted beneath
her and Sabin fell to the ground. The last thing she
remembered was seeing Montgomery's hard glare begin to fade and Cherlyn's voice above her shouting,
"Call an ambulance!"

When it comes to matters of love, the heart
will always forsake the mind.

—Toda Kai

Twenty-three

Montgomery sat in his father's kitchen, nursing a swollen jaw and reviewing the last entries of his notebook.

Montgomery mulled over them in a stupor. Everything he'd read on private investigation was wrong. It was more than trying to put a puzzle together. It was like trying to complete a crossword when you didn't know the language.

It's no use, he thought, closing the notebook. *Some things will just remain a mystery.*

"I'll get it," his father said, wheeling toward the front room. Montgomery had been so caught up in his own thoughts, he hadn't even heard the doorbell.

"Montgomery," his father called from the other room. "There's somebody here to see you."

The younger Claiborne entered the living room wondering who would ask for him at his father's house. The sight of Henry Bijan stopped him cold. "What are you doing here?"

Reeves frowned as the short dark man came in.

"I must speak with you."

Anger charged through Montgomery's veins. "You low-life scavenger! What could you possibly want now?"

"To give you somethin." Henry held out an envelope.

"What's this?" Montgomery asked, taking it.

"Let's just call it . . . compensation."

Montgomery stared at the brown envelope and then up at Henry, who for once was not smiling or laughing, and suddenly minus an accent.

Montgomery opened it and could feel the puzzle coming into focus. "Compensation for what," he asked as a check for one million dollars stared him in the face.

"For helping us find the documents. You do have the documents, don't you?"

Reeves Claiborne recoiled in his chair. "Uh-oh." Slowly, he rolled out of the living room. "Handle your business, son."

"Who are you?" Montgomery demanded.

"Let's sit down, okay?"

Montgomery sat with Henry in the living room, his mind fraught with questions.

"I'm listening."

Henry's smile returned. "All right. I work for . . ."

"Don't tell me . . . *the government.*"

"You could say that. I'm sort of a freelancer. They call me when they need . . . odd jobs. I was contacted when Victor Willis tried to blackmail the government."

"Blackmail?"

"Yes. Mr. Willis had a gambling debt that he thought he could settle by extorting money. My clients, on the other hand, had been searching for the lost documents for years. Imagine how happy they were when they discovered that the documents were going to be delivered on a silver platter for a few thousand dollars."

Montgomery shook his head as the picture came clearer. "But something happened."

"Yes. Before he could get them, they ended up in your storage facility."

"No wonder Angie kept trying to get into the facility. She wanted to search the units." Montgomery glanced at the check again. It was cut against the Triage account. He knew that no amount of money could compensate him for what he'd been through.

"Did you send the virus?"

"Yes."

"Why?"

"Because, Montgomery, there are good sections of our government and then there are the not-so-good. I like to think I work for the good guys. Your partner was doing a lot COINTELPRO research for her boyfriend. No doubt to give him more leverage for the deal he was trying to strike. Victor sent her an encrypted E-mail, telling her the last known whereabouts of the documents. I intercepted that E-mail and destroyed all traces of her research and their correspondence before the bad guys could find out what they were up to."

Montgomery sighed. "And then you set my warehouse on fire."

Henry's expression grew solemn. "I'm sorry about your friend."

"I see." The realization that he was just a pawn in someone else's war sent detonated shock waves of anger throughout Montgomery's body. He rose, crumpling the envelope in his hand. "So, why tell me all this?"

"Because," Henry said, calmly, "I want you to know

that I am one of the good guys. And . . . I need you to give me those papers."

"Those *papers* chronicle some pretty horrific events. The kind of events people need to be made aware of."

Now Henry rose. "And then what? What do you think will happen if people find out that their government is not as pristine as they would like to believe?"

Montgomery thought for a moment.

"Believe me, it wouldn't be a pretty sight. The people who committed those acts are either dead or too old to punish. Exposing those past mistakes will, in the end, cause more harm than good."

He didn't know why, but Montgomery could hear Sabin's words echoing in his mind. *Justice should be only served by humane means. Not more violence.*

"Just a second," he said, heading upstairs.

A few moments later, he returned with a stack of documents. He handed them to Henry and prayed that he was doing the right thing.

He took one last look at the check. A million dollars was a lot of money. "I can't accept this."

"Yes, you can," Henry said, heading for the front door. "And you will."

And with that he was gone.

Montgomery thought it only fitting that he carried his investigation to a close. He returned to the kitchen and jotted down a closing remark in his notebook.

I heard that Victor Willis and Angela Miller mysteriously disappeared after being in Golden Creek Police custody for two days. Then Henry Bijan paid me an interesting visit. For some reason, I trust him, and I don't think that my family nor I will ever be bothered or contacted again.

I wish Angie hadn't gotten involved with that lunatic. But then again, he probably seemed perfectly normal or he intrigued her so much that she overlooked warning signs that he might have had a hidden agenda for seeing her. If that's what happened, I understand how she could have been deceived.

"You're going to wear the ink off of those pages."

Montgomery turned toward the low creak of his father's wheelchair against the linoleum.

"What's it to you?" he asked, ready for a fight, needing an outlet.

"Son," Reeves said, positioning himself across from the younger version of himself.

The pages in his notebook sounded like dry leaves rasping together as Montgomery turned them. He knew his thoughts were tilted in the wrong direction. The past was the past now, and dwelling on recent events, even as awful as they were, would not change what happened. The question now was, how would he move forward? What should he do today to start his life again?

Bruises from his fight with Victor were healing, but the wounds from his failed relationship still ached. Each time his mind had come anywhere near that thought, traces of Sabin drifted into focus and had angered him. So far he had taken his anger out on barbells, his chin bar, and floor mats, determined not to start his new life on a lie. And that's what their relationship had amounted to. A lie. No matter how many people tried to convince him otherwise. One by one, his sister, Ted, even Lucian and Arroya had spoken to him about her. They acted like he had been moping—pining away after their breakup. They had approached him as if he'd needed cheering up and help coming to his senses. But that wasn't the case, *was it?*

Heck, he had gone on and would continue to go on without her. And one day he would wake up and the pain would be over. The ache that had settled like a huge boulder on his heart would vanish. Then his life really and truly would go on. He would . . .

"There you go again." His father's words broke into his thoughts.

"What are you talking about *now*, Father?"

"Hasn't anything anyone has said to you made any difference?"

Montgomery's anger boiled at the pit of his stomach. "No."

Then he watched as a strange expression softened his father's features.

"Maybe the person you need to hear from is me." Reeves steered his chair away from Montgomery and then changed his mind.

"I'm proud of you, son. I always have been."

"Bull."

His father's deep sigh filled the space between them. "I guess I didn't realize I was proud of you until you grabbed that maniac and threatened to blow his head off."

Montgomery's hopes sank like lead in a pool. "So, I was right. The only way you'll approve of me is if I act like an uncivilized thug."

Reeves wheeled closer and placed a hand on his son's arm. The sensation was foreign. They hadn't touched like that since Montgomery was a child.

"You're wrong. What made me proud is that you showed mercy and . . . forgiveness. That's what real men do."

Montgomery saw something else in his father's face. Sincerity.

"Neither one of us has forgiven the other since your mother died. I think it's time we did. Because, son, I almost . . ." Then Reeves broke down into quiet sobs. "I almost lost you," he said tearfully.

Montgomery moved close and embraced his father.

He took deep breaths to keep himself from crying. In each breath came the smell of cedar and English Leather. They were old familiar smells—scents he'd grown up with as a child. He remembered going into his father's chest of clothes, putting them on, and walking around in his shoes. All his life he had been trying to fill his father's shoes, yet knowing he never could. And then, in spite of all his resistance, it happened. A solitary tear fell down his cheek, and Montgomery knew he'd forgiven his father for their difficult past and their strained relationship. And he'd forgiven himself for not making peace sooner.

He decided in that instant that all things had happened for a reason and the only thing that could have struck down the barrier between he and his father was some kind of tragedy—the likes of which they just experienced. And if that's what it took, then so be it. The new life he'd been contemplating would begin with this first step toward healing their rift and building new common ground.

The father and son pulled away, wiping their damp faces. "There's one more thing I have to say, and I hope you listen. There's another broken relationship that needs healing, and I think—"

Montgomery stiffened. "Spare me, Dad. I don't want to hear about that."

"But, son . . ."

"No," he said, holding up his hand. "We just had a Kodak moment here. Please. Don't ruin it."

His father nodded.

Why was everyone taking Sabin's side? he wondered. How could they possibly believe that he could forgive her? How could . . . ?

The knock at the door interrupted his ruminations. Reeves started his wheelchair, but Montgomery stopped him. "I'll get it, Father," he said.

Walking to the door, he wiped his face once more to clear away the wetness. He and his father had a lot of catching up to do, he thought. The sooner they could begin again the better. *A new beginning,* he mused, *will be better for everyone. Maybe then I'll feel some semblance of normalcy.*

Still caught up in his thoughts, Montgomery opened the door. When he saw it was Sabin, he pushed the door closed again, but she caught it before he could close it all the way.

"I'm not here to see *you,*" she said, barging in.

"Just come in, why don't you," he said, stepping aside.

He was ready for it, expected it—hell, he even wanted it. All of the anger, frustration, and blinding rage he'd felt came to a brilliant head. Here she was, the person responsible for the misery he'd been feeling for the past few days. He assumed that if he ever saw her again he would have to restrain himself from shouting at the top of his lungs and telling her exactly what she could do with all of her sweet words, raw temper, and ninja kicks.

As she stood in front of him, hands propped on her hips, his emotions betrayed him. She was as saucy as ever and just a beautiful. He knew she was on heavy medication for her pinched nerve. Cherlyn had kept him informed of her recovery from her recent stint in the emergency room. Despite her ordeal, she looked good. She looked . . . like his.

Remarkably, the enraged person he'd become crept away. The man who was left wanted to grab and hold the woman standing before him.

"Look, I don't have all day!"

"What?" he asked, blinking out of his thoughts.

"I asked if your father was here."

"I'm here," Reeves replied, rolling out of the kitchen.

Sabin glanced at the keys in her hand and then handed them to Reeves.

"What's this?"

"These are the keys to my . . ." *Freedom. Independence. Means of Escape. Contentment. Way of life.* "The motorcycle," she said, feeling a rising emptiness. "When I said I gave you back all the money, I forgot about the cash I used to buy the Harley. I wanted to clear my slate before I left."

Reeves looked up, eyes sad and remorseful. It was one of the few times Montgomery had ever seen that expression on his father's face.

"Sabin," the elder Claiborne began, "you don't have to—"

"Yes, I do," she said, turning toward the door.

Montgomery frowned. *Why hadn't she taken the money?* he wondered.

Reeves rolled up to where Sabin was approaching the doorway. "Don't let her leave!" he shouted to his son.

Then it hit him and he groaned with the realization. The thought of her leaving was a pain more horrible than anything he'd felt in the past few days or even since his mother died.

"Wait!" he said, following her outside.

She turned. All at once he saw a deep sadness on her face. The area around her eyes was slightly puffy. Had she been crying?

"Why didn't you take the money?"

Sabin closed her eyes. She just wanted to leave and be done with this whole ordeal. "Montgomery, it doesn't matter now, I just . . ."

When she opened her eyes, he was standing closer, too close. Her heart jumped to its familiar double-time tempo and she cursed her emotions, her desires, her love.

"Why?" he asked, much softer now.

"Because I couldn't take the money. I couldn't let someone pay me for . . ."

"For what?"

She looked away. Why was he making this so difficult? She had planned a swift departure, but Montgomery was turning it into Truth or Dare.

"For protecting you," she said, looking back.

"Why didn't you tell me the truth?"

"I wanted to, Montgomery. I tried to."

Exasperation cut into his thoughts. "Then why didn't you!"

"Look, I'm not perfect, Montgomery."

"I never *asked* you to be perfect!"

Her body tensed with anxiety. "I made a mistake."

"You made a mockery out of what we had . . . what I believed we had. Every time I look at you, I see a lie."

"What about a woman who loves you? Do you see that? Can you see that?" This time, Sabin stepped closer.

He wondered if she knew she was crying. He wouldn't have thought her capable of it.

"What are those for?"

"W-what?"

"Those tears. Why are you crying?"

She wiped her hand across her face and stared at it. When she looked up, he saw the tears on her fingers had been replaced by fresh ones streaming down her face. "Because I feel you. Like a river flowing through me." Sabin flattened her hand against her chest. "I've never *felt* anyone before. Never had anyone inside me. Never let . . ." Her voice cracked. "I can't get rid of it. No matter what I do. No matter how I try. You just . . . took over my soul. It's like you *live* here now. And . . . there's . . . nothing . . . I can do. I feel you." Her body shook with her sobs. "Montgomery, I f—"

He enfolded her in his arms. God help him. He loved her—so much he thought his heart would explode from it. She clung to him then, and he knew he would hold her forever, and argue with her, and protect her, and love her, and be loved by her . . . for the rest of his life. This woman. This beautiful rogue. She had to want that forever, too.

"I still love you," he said.

Sabin squeezed tighter. "I still love you, too."

After a few bliss-filled seconds, he pulled away.

"So, what do we do now?"

She looked up, tears dancing in her eyes. "We should get married."

"Married!"

Montgomery paced back and forth. "You think she's got a stripper over there?"

Reeves shook his head and blew a loud breath past his lips. "This is supposed to be a party. You're ruining it for all of us."

"I can just see it now, some young guy like that masseuse she had, shakin' his behind in her face!"

"Will you relax?" Lucian said.

"Yeah," Ted added. "You'll make us bachelors think twice about jumping the broom."

Montgomery knew what kind of woman he loved. "There is probably a keg of beer, rum balls, and a Chippendale-like stud over there right now taking it off to 'Who Let the Dogs Out?' "

His father and friends laughed. Montgomery failed to see the humor.

He stopped pacing and headed to his door. "I'm going over there!"

"You'll do no such thing," Reeves insisted.

"Watch me."

Ten seconds later, Montgomery was pounding a fist against Sabin's door. His sister swung open the door, incredulity turning her youthful features into a frown.

"What are you doing here?"

Montgomery pushed past her. "The question is . . . what are *you* doing here?"

"We," Cherlyn responded as a surprised Sabin and Arroya looked on, "are having a movie marathon."

One by one, the three women in Montgomery's life crossed their arms and gave him harsh stares.

"All right!" he relented, throwing up his hands. "I thought there were naked men over here."

"I wish," Arroya said, rolling her eyes.

Cherlyn laughed, but Sabin was not amused.

"What are you watching?" he asked modestly.

"Romantic movies. We each picked our favorite one."

"Yuck!"

"These are great movies, big brother. I mean, *Sleepless in Seattle.*"

"My Best Friend's Wedding," Arroya said, raising an eyebrow.

"The Matrix," Sabin added.

Montgomery smiled at his fiancée and shook his head. "Only you."

Sabin got up and followed Montgomery to the porch. "Are you ever going to trust me?"

He pulled her into his arms, mesmerized by her wondrous beauty and the thought that in less than twenty-four hours, she was going to be his forever. The heat of the day burned inferior to the heat of his passion. "It's other folks that I don't trust, baby."

He gave in to the magnetic allure of her lips. At their touch, his passion for her was immediate and blazed up like the head of a match.

Sabin stepped back, light-headed. Each and every one of Montgomery's kisses wrecked her internal balance and toppled her resolve. At the same time, they made her more sure of herself than she had ever been in her entire life. There was no sense in even trying to play it off. She simply blinked and looked up at him in amazement.

"Me, too," he said, smiling.

He turned and headed back toward his house. Before he stepped off the porch, she swatted his behind playfully.

"I love you, Montgomery Pa'akiki, po'opa'a Claiborne."

"I love you too, Sabin Mess With My Man And I'll Kick Your Butt Strong."

And they lived happily ever after.

—Tilde Parsons

Twenty-four

When Montgomery suggested they have a big wedding, Sabin rolled her eyes and planted one hand on her hip as if to say, "Now, you know better than that." When Sabin suggested that they elope, Montgomery huffed and grumbled until they compromised on a small ceremony in a quaint nondenominational church.

The date was October twenty-fifth, Sabin's birthday. Montgomery could think of no better present to give her than all his love forever.

A group of twenty assorted family and friends gathered and watched with glad hearts as the couple took their matrimonial vows. In the front row, next to her father and Tilde, Cherlyn sat beside Lucian, a Liz Taylor diamond on her ring finger catching the afternoon sun.

They had found each other at last. Now they were becoming the family each of them had so longed for. As Montgomery stood in black tuxedo and Sabin took her place next to him in a white formfitting gown, the two who had been diametrically opposed in so many ways, found agreement in the love they shared and the life they wanted to build together.

Sabin, fully recovered from her surgery, felt as though her legs would melt from under her. But this time, the cause was emotional, not physical.

Montgomery stood at the altar, awash with contentment. It was a feeling he'd nearly forgotten about, but was born once more in him out of Sabin's love. When they were pronounced man and wife, Montgomery couldn't wait. Before the minister could say, "You may now kiss the bride," Montgomery swept Sabin into his arms and poured all the passion in his soul into the kiss he placed on her lips.

The newlyweds locked hands and ran up the aisle while friends and family threw rice to celebrate their union. Once outside, they stepped into a beautiful fall day and Mr. and Mrs. Montgomery Claiborne descended the stairs of the church to where a large motorcycle, complete with a JUST MARRIED sign, waited curbside for their departure.

"I'll drive," Montgomery said, planting one more kiss on his wife's cheek.

"I don't think so," Sabin responded. She pulled up the front fabric of her skirt to reveal the white satin pants she wore beneath. She attached the loose fabric to buttons on the back of the pants and hopped on the Harley. Montgomery waved to the onlookers, shrugged, and got on the bike behind Sabin.

After three loud revs of the engine, Sabin turned toward Montgomery. "Where to?" she asked.

They put on helmets. Montgomery wrapped his arms around her waist. He thought about their first meeting and how far they had come. She had saved him one last time. More importantly, they had saved each other. He thanked God for everything that had happened, even the things he didn't understand, and said, "Let's just see where fate takes us." Sabin smiled and turned the throttle.

Epilogue

Kai,
  I'm so happy, I know you can see my joy from where you are. Finally, I belong to someone. Finally, I'm free.
  S.

Dear Readers:

Whew! What a ride! I hope you held on and felt the rush like I did. This story is about a lot of things, like love and family. It's also about women having the presence of mind to fend for themselves, by being smart, making wise decisions, and yes . . . being strong. Most of us don't realize how much of what and who we are is defined by society. I believe that true freedom comes when we decide for ourselves who we are and what makes us happy and are willing to take a stand to defend what we believe in. Sabin did that. It's my personal mission to do that. May this book help you to do that.

God bless,
Kim Louise

To share your thoughts on this or any of my other novels, please contact me at: MsKimLouise@aol.com, http://www.kimlouise.com, or regular mail (Kim Louise, P.O. Box 31554, Omaha, NE 68131).

BOOK CLUB DISCUSSION QUESTIONS

1. Was Montgomery just an innocent bystander or did the events in his life happen for a reason?
2. Are you familiar with the government's Counter Intelligence Program (COINTELPRO)?
3. Did Reeves Claiborne love his son or was he just trying to humiliate him?
4. What precautions, if any, should women take to be able to defend themselves?
5. What, if anything, did the introductory quotes add to each chapter?
6. Is there always a "back door"?
7. How did Montgomery and Sabin resolve their differences with regard to handgun use . . . Or did they?
8. What was it like to have a secondary character that never said a word?
9. Should Arroya and Montgomery continue to have coffee together every Monday morning?

More Sizzling Romance From
Leslie Esdaile